FELLOWSHIP OF THE FROG

BY
EDGAR WALLACE

WARD, LOCK & CO., LIMITED
LONDON AND MELBOURNE
1926

Printed in Great Britain by Butler & Tanner Ltd., Frome and London

CONTENTS

CHAP.		PAGE
	Foreword: The Frogs	5
I	At Maytree Cottage	9
II	A Talk about Frogs	16
III	The Frog	20
IV	Elk	25
V	Mr. Maitland Goes Home	32
VI	Mr. Maitland Goes Shopping	42
VII	A Call on Mr. Maitland	51
VIII	The Offensive Ray	61
IX	The Man Who Was Wrecked	71
X	On Harley Terrace	76
XI	Mr. Broad Explains	83
XII	The Embellishment of Mr. Maitland	88
XIII	A Raid on Eldor Street	97
XIV	"All Bulls Hear!"	106
XV	The Morning After	110
XVI	Ray Learns the Truth	115
XVII	The Coming of Mills	120
XVIII	The Broadcast	127
XIX	In Elsham Wood	136
XX	Hagn	143
XXI	Mr. Johnson's Visitor	154
XXII	The Inquiry	160

XXIII	A Meeting	167
XXIV	Why Maitland Came	171
XXV	In Regard to Saul Morris	180
XXVI	Promotion for Balder	186
XXVII	Mr. Broad is Interesting	199
XXVIII	Murder	206
XXIX	The Footman	212
XXX	The Tramps	220
XXXI	The Chemical Corporation	231
XXXII	In Gloucester Prison	237
XXXIII	The Frog of the Night	241
XXXIV	The Photo-play	251
XXXV	Getting Through	261
XXXVI	The Power Cable	267
XXXVII	The Get-Away	274
XXXVIII	The Mystery Man	278
XXXIX	The Awakening	282
XL	Frog	288
XLI	In Quarry House	295
XLII	Joshua Broad Explains	301

FOREWORD

THE FROGS

IT was of interest to those who study the psychology of the mass that, until the prosperous but otherwise insignificant James G. Bliss became the object of their attention, the doings and growth of the Frogs were almost unnoticed. There were strong references in some of the country newspapers to the lawless character of the association; one Sunday journal had an amusing article headed

"Tramps' Trade Union Takes Frog for
Symbol of Mystic Order"

and gave a humorous and quite fanciful extract from its rules and ritual. The average man made casual references:

"I say, have you seen this story about the tramps' Union—every member a walking delegate? . . ."

There was a more serious leading article on the growth of trade unionism, in which the Frogs were cited, and although from time to time came accounts of mysterious outrages which had been put to the discredit of the Frogs, the generality of citizens regarded the society, order, or whatever it was, as something benevolent in its intentions and necessarily eccentric in its constitution, and, believing this, were in their turn benevolently tolerant.

In some such manner as the mass may learn with mild interest of a distant outbreak of epidemic disease, which slays its few, and wake one morning to find the sinister malady tapping at their front doors, so did the world become alive and alarmed at the terror-growth which suddenly loomed from the mists.

James G. Bliss was a hardware merchant, and a man well known on exchange, where he augmented the steady profits of the Bliss General Hardware Corporation with occasional windfalls from legitimate speculation. A somewhat pompous and, in argument, aggressive person, he had the advantage which mediocrity, blended with a certain expansive generosity, gives to a man, in that he had no enemies; and since his generosity was run on sane business principles, it could not even be said of him, as is so often said of others, that his worst enemy was himself. He held, and still holds, the bulk of the stock in the B.G.H. Corporation—a fact which should be noted because it was a practice of Mr. Bliss to manipulate from time to time the price of his shares by judicious operations.

It was at a time coincident with the little boom in industrials which brought Bliss Hardware stock at a jump from 12.50 to 23.75, that the strange happening occurred which focussed for the moment all eyes upon the Frogs.

Mr. Bliss has a country place at Long Beach, Hampshire. It is referred to as "The Hut," but is the sort of hut that King Solomon might have built for the Queen of Sheba, had that adventurous man been sufficiently well acquainted with modern plumbing, the newest systems of heating and lighting, and the exigent requirements of up-to-date chauffeurs. In these respects Mr. Bliss was wiser than Solomon.

He had returned to his country home after a strenuous day in the City, and was walking in the garden in the cool of the evening. He was (and is) married, but his wife and two daughters were spending the spring in Paris—a wise course, since the spring is the only season when Paris has the slightest pretensions to being a beautiful city.

He had come from his kennels, and was seen walking across the home park toward a covert which bordered his property. Hearing a scream, his kennel man and a groom ran toward the wood, to discover Bliss lying on the ground unconscious, his face and shoulders covered with blood. He had been struck down by some heavy weapon; there were a slight fracture of the parietal bone and several very ugly scalp wounds.

For three weeks this unfortunate man hovered between life and death, unconscious except at intervals, and unable during his lucid moments to throw any light on, or make any coherent statement concerning, the assault, except to murmur, "Frog . . . frog . . . left arm . . . frog."

It was the first of many similar outrages, seemingly purposeless and wanton, in no case to be connected with robbery, and invariably (except once) committed upon people who occupied fairly unimportant positions in the social hierarchy.

The Frogs advanced instantly to a first-class topic. The disease was found to be widespread, and men who had read, light-heartedly, of minor victimizations, began to bolt their own doors and carry lethal weapons when they went abroad at nights.

And they were wise, for there was a force in being that had been born in fear and had matured in obscurity (to the wonder of its creator) so that it wielded the tyrannical power of governments.

In the centre of many ramifications sat the Frog, drunk with authority, merciless, terrible. One who lived two lives and took full pleasure from both, and all the time nursing the terror that Saul Morris had inspired one foggy night in London, when the grimy streets were filled with armed policemen looking for the man who cleaned the strong-room of the S.S. *Mantania* of three million pounds between the port of Southampton and the port of Cherbourg.

THE

FELLOWSHIP OF THE FROG

CHAPTER I

AT MAYTREE COTTAGE

A DRY radiator coincided with a burst tyre. The second coincidence was the proximity of Maytree Cottage on the Horsham Road. The cottage was larger than most, with a timbered front and a thatched roof. Standing at the gate, Richard Gordon stopped to admire. The house dated back to the days of Elizabeth, but his interest and admiration were not those of the antiquary.

Nor, though he loved flowers, of the horticulturist, though the broad garden was a patchwork of colour and the fragrance of cabbage roses came to delight his senses. Nor was it the air of comfort and cleanliness that pervaded the place, the scrubbed redbrick pathway that led to the door, the spotless curtains behind leaded panes.

It was the girl, in the red-lined basket chair, that arrested his gaze. She sat on a little lawn in the shade of a mulberry tree, with her shapely young limbs stiffly extended, a book in her hand, a large box of chocolates by her side. Her hair, the colour of old gold, an old gold that held life and sheen; a flawless complexion, and, when she turned her head in his direction, a pair of grave, questioning eyes, deeper than grey, yet greyer than blue....

She drew up her feet hurriedly and rose.

"I'm so sorry to disturb you,"—Dick, hat in hand, smiled his apology—"but I want water for my poor little Lizzie. She's developed a prodigious thirst."

She frowned for a second, and then laughed.

"Lizzie—you mean a car? If you'll come to the back of the cottage I'll show you where the well is."

He followed, wondering who she was. The tiny hint of patronage in her tone he understood. It was the tone of matured girlhood addressing a boy of her own age. Dick, who was thirty and looked eighteen, with his smooth, boyish face, had been greeted in that "little boy" tone before, and was inwardly amused.

"Here is the bucket and that is the well," she pointed. "I would send a maid to help you, only we haven't a maid, and never had a maid, and I don't think ever shall have a maid!"

"Then some maid has missed a very good job," said Dick, "for this garden is delightful."

She neither agreed nor dissented. Perhaps she regretted the familiarity she had shown. She conveyed to him an impression of aloofness, as she watched the process of filling the buckets, and when he carried them to the car on the road outside, she followed.

"I thought it was a—a—what did you call it—Lizzie?"

"She is Lizzie to me," said Dick stoutly as he filled the radiator of the big Rolls, "and she will never be anything else. There are people who think she should be called 'Diana,' but those high-flown names never had any attraction for me. She is Liz—and will always be Liz."

She walked round the machine, examining it curiously.

"Aren't you afraid to be driving a big car like that?" she asked. "I should be scared to death. It is so tremendous and . . . and unmanageable."

Dick paused with a bucket in hand.

"Fear," he boasted, "is a word which I have expunged from the bright lexicon of my youth."

For a second puzzled, she began to laugh softly.

"Did you come by way of Welford?" she asked.

He nodded.

"I wonder if you saw my father on the road?"

"I saw nobody on the road except a sour-looking gentleman of middle age who was breaking the Sabbath by carrying a large brown box on his back."

"Where did you pass him?" she asked, interested.

"Two miles away—less than that." And then, a doubt intruding: "I hope that I wasn't describing your parent?"

"It sounds rather like him," she said without annoyance. "Daddy is a naturalist photographer. He takes moving pictures of birds and things—he is an amateur, of course."

"Of course," agreed Dick.

He brought the buckets back to where he had found them and lingered. Searching for an excuse, he found it in the garden. How far he might have exploited this subject is a matter for conjecture. Interruption came in the shape of a young man who emerged from the front door of the cottage. He was tall and athletic, good-looking. . . . Dick put his age at twenty.

"Hello, Ella! Father back?" he began, and then saw the visitor.

"This is my brother," said the girl, and Dick Gordon nodded. He was conscious that this free-and-easy method of getting acquainted was due largely, if not entirely, to his youthful appearance. To be treated as an inconsiderable boy had its advantages. And so it appeared.

"I was telling him that boys ought not to be allowed to drive big cars," she said. "You remember the awful smash there was at the Shoreham cross-roads?"

Ray Bennett chuckled.

"This is all part of a conspiracy to keep me from getting a motor-bicycle. Father thinks I'll kill somebody, and Ella thinks I'll kill myself."

Perhaps there was something in Dick Gordon's quick smile that warned the girl that she had been premature in her appraisement of his age, for suddenly, almost abruptly, she nodded an emphatic dismissal and turned away. Dick was at the gate when a further respite arrived. It was the man he had passed on the road. Tall, loose-framed, grey and gaunt of face, he regarded the stranger with suspicion in his deep-set eyes.

"Good morning," he said curtly. "Car broken down?"

"No, thank you. I ran out of water, and Miss—er——"

"Bennett," said the man. "She gave you the water, eh? Well, good morning."

He stood aside to let Gordon pass, but Dick opened the gate and waited till the owner of Maytree Cottage had entered.

"My name is Gordon," he said. Out of the corner of his eye he saw Ella had turned back and stood with her brother within earshot. "I am greatly obliged to you for your kindness."

The old man, with a nod, went on carrying his heavy burden into the house, and Dick in desperation turned to the girl.

"You are wrong when you think this is a difficult car to drive — won't you experiment? Or perhaps your brother?"

The girl hesitated, but not so young Bennett.

"I'd like to try," he said eagerly. "I've never handled a big machine."

That he could handle one if the opportunity came, he showed. They watched the car gliding round the corner, the girl with a little frown gathering between her eyes, Dick Gordon oblivious to everything except that he had snatched a few minutes' closer association with the girl. He was behaving absurdly, he told himself. He, a public official, an experienced lawyer, was carrying on like an irresponsible, love-smitten youth of nineteen. The girl's words emphasized his folly.

"I wish you hadn't let Ray drive," she said. "It doesn't help a boy who is always wanting something better, to put him in charge of a beautiful car . . . perhaps you don't understand me. Ray is very ambitious and dreams in millions. A thing like this unsettles him."

The older man came out at that moment, a black pipe between his teeth, and, seeing the two at the gate, a cloud passed over his face.

"Let him drive your car, have you?" he said grimly. "I wish you hadn't — it was very kind of you, Mr. Gordon, but in Ray's case a mistaken kindness."

"I'm very sorry," said the penitent Dick. "Here he comes!"

The big car spun toward them and halted before the gate.

"She's a beauty!"

Ray Bennett jumped out and looked at the machine with admiration and regret.

"My word, if she were mine!"

"She isn't," snapped the old man, and then, as though regretting his petulance: "Some day perhaps you'll own a fleet, Ray—are you going to London, Mr. Gordon?"

Dick nodded.

"Maybe you wouldn't care to stop and eat a very frugal meal with us?" asked the elder Bennett, to his surprise and joy. "And you'll be able to tell this foolish son of mine that owning a big car isn't all joy-riding."

Dick's first impression was of the girl's astonishment. Apparently he was unusually honoured, and this was confirmed after John Bennett had left them.

"You're the first boy that has ever been asked to dinner," she said when they were alone. "Isn't he, Ray?"

Ray smiled.

"Dad doesn't go in for the social life, and that's a fact," he said. "I asked him to have Philo Johnson down for a week-end, and he killed the idea before it was born. And the old philosopher is a good fellow and the boss's confidential secretary. You've heard of Maitlands Consolidated, I suppose?"

Dick nodded. The marble palace on the Strand Embankment in which the fabulously rich Mr. Maitland operated, was one of the show buildings of London.

"I'm in his office—exchange clerk," said the young man, "and Philo could do a whole lot for me if dad would pull out an invitation. As it is, I seem doomed to be a clerk for the rest of my life."

The white hand of the girl touched his lips.

"You'll be rich some day, Ray dear, and it is foolish to blame daddy."

The young man growled something under the hand, and then laughed a little bitterly.

"Dad has tried every get-rich-quick scheme that the mind and ingenuity of man——"

"And why?"

The voice was harsh, tremulous with anger. None of them had noticed the reappearance of John Bennett.

"You're doing work you don't like. My God! What of me? I've been trying for twenty years to get out. I've tried every silly scheme—that's true. But it was for you——"

He stopped abruptly at the sight of Gordon's embarrassment.

"I invited you to dinner, and I'm pulling out the family skeleton," he said with rough good-humour.

He took Dick's arm and led him down the garden path between the serried ranks of rose bushes.

"I don't know why I asked you to stay, young man," he said. "An impulse, I suppose . . . maybe a bad conscience. I don't give these young people all the company they ought to have at home, and I'm not much of a companion for them. It's too bad that you should be the witness of the first family jar we've had for years."

His voice and manner were those of an educated man. Dick wondered what occupation he followed, and why it should be so particularly obnoxious that he should be seeking some escape.

The girl was quiet throughout the meal. She sat at Dick's left hand and she spoke very seldom. Stealing an occasional glance at her, he thought she looked preoccupied and troubled, and blamed his presence as the cause.

Apparently no servant was kept at the cottage. She did the waiting herself, and she had replaced the plates when the old man asked:

"I shouldn't think you were as young as you look, Mr. Gordon—what do you do for a living?"

"I'm quite old," smiled Dick. "Thirty-one."

"Thirty-one?" gasped Ella, going red. "And I've been talking to you as though you were a child!"

"Think of me as a child at heart," he said gravely. "As to my occupation—I'm a persecutor of thieves and murderers and bad characters generally. My name is Richard Gordon——"

The knife fell with a clatter from John Bennett's hand and his face went white.

"Gordon—Richard Gordon?" he said hollowly.

For a second their eyes met, the clear blue and the faded blue.

"Yes—I am the Assistant Director of Prosecutions," said Gordon quietly. "And I have an idea that you and I have met before."

The pale eyes did not waver. John Bennett's face was a mask.

"Not professionally, I hope," he said, and there was a challenge in his voice.

Dick laughed again as at the absurdity of the question.

"Not professionally," he said with mock gravity.

On his way back to London that night his memory worked overtime, but he failed to place John Bennett of Horsham.

CHAPTER II

A TALK ABOUT FROGS

MAITLANDS Consolidated had grown from one small office to its present palatial proportions in a comparatively short space of time. Maitland was a man advanced in years, patriarchal in appearance, sparing of speech. He had arrived in London unheralded, and had arrived, in the less accurate sense of the word, before London was aware of his existence.

Dick Gordon saw the speculator for the first time as he was waiting in the marble-walled vestibule. A man of middle height, bearded to his waist; his eyes almost hidden under heavy white brows; stout and laborious of gait, he came slowly through the outer office, where a score of clerks sat working under their green-shaded lamps, and, looking neither to the right nor left, walked into the elevator and was lost to view.

"That is the old man: have you seen him before?" asked Ray Bennett, who had come out to meet the caller a second before. "He's a venerable old cuss, but as tight as a soundproof door. You couldn't pry money from him, not if you used dynamite! He pays Philo a salary that the average secretary wouldn't look at, and if Philo wasn't such an easygoing devil, he'd have left years ago."

Dick Gordon was feeling a little uncomfortable. His presence at Maitlands was freakish, his excuse for calling as feeble as any weak brain could conceive. If he had spoken the truth to the flattered young man on whom he called in business hours, he would have said: "I have idiotically fallen in love with your sister. I am not especially interested in you, but I regard you as a line that will lead me to another meeting, therefore I have made my being in the neighbourhood an excuse for calling. And because of this insane love I have for your sister, I am willing to meet even Philo, who will surely bore me." Instead he said:

"You are a friend of Philo—why do you call him that?"

"Because he's a philosophical old horse—his other name is Philip," said the other with a twinkle in his eye. "Everybody is a friend of Philo's—he's the kind of man that makes friendship easy."

The elevator door opened at that moment and a man came out. Instinctively Dick Gordon knew that this bald and middle-aged man with the good-humoured face was the subject of their discussion. His round, fat face creased in a smile as he recognized Ray, and after he had handed a bundle of documents to one of the clerks, he came over to where they were standing.

"Meet Mr. Gordon," said Ray. "This is my friend Johnson."

Philo grasped the extended hand warmly.

"Warm" was a word which had a special significance in relation to Mr. Johnson. He seemed to radiate a warming and quickening influence. Even Dick Gordon, who was not too ready to respond, came under the immediate influence of his geniality.

"You're Mr. Gordon of the Public Prosecution Department—Ray was telling me," he said. "I should like you to come one day and prosecute old man Maitland! He is certainly the most prosecutable gentleman I've met for years!"

The jest tickled Mr. Johnson. He was, thought Dick, inclined to laugh at himself.

"I've got to get back: he's in a tantrum this morning. Anyone would think the Frogs were after him."

Philo Johnson, with a cheery nod, hurried back to the lift. Was it imagination on Dick's part? He could have sworn the face of Ray Bennett was a deeper shade of red, and that there was a look of anxiety in his eyes.

"It's very good of you to keep your promise and call . . . yes, I'll be glad to lunch with you, Gordon. And my sister will also, I'm sure. She is often in town."

His adieux were hurried and somewhat confused. Dick Gordon went out into the street puzzled. Of one thing he was certain: that behind the young man's distress lay that joking reference to the Frogs.

When he returned to his office, still sore with himself that he had acted rather like a moon-calf or a farm hand making his awkward advances to the village belle, he found a troubled-looking chief of police waiting for him, and at the sight of him Dick's eyes narrowed.

"Well?" he asked. "What of Genter?"

The police chief made a grimace like one who was swallowing an unpleasant potion.

"They slipped me," he said. "The Frog arrived in a car—I wasn't prepared for that. Genter got in, and they were gone before I realized what had happened. Not that I'm worried. Genter has a gun, and he's a pretty tough fellow in a rough house."

Dick Gordon stared at and through the man, and then:

"I think you should have been prepared for the car," he said. "If Genter's message was well founded, and he is on the track of the Frog, you should have expected a car. Sit down, Wellingdale."

The grey-haired man obeyed.

"I'm not excusing myself," he growled. "The Frogs have got me rattled. I treated them as a joke once."

"Maybe we'd be wiser if we treated them as a joke now," suggested Dick, biting off the end of a cigar. "They may be nothing but a foolish secret society. Even tramps are entitled to their lodges and pass-words, grips and signs."

Wellingdale shook his head.

"You can't get away from the record of the past seven years," he said. "It isn't the fact that every other bad road-criminal we pull in has the frog tattooed on his wrist. That might be sheer imitation—and, in any case, all crooks of low mentality have tattoo marks. But in that seven years we've had a series of very unpleasant crimes. First there was the attack upon the *chargé d'affaires* of the United States Embassy—bludgeoned to sleep in Hyde Park. Then there was the case of the President of the Northern Trading Company—clubbed as he was stepping out of his car in Park Lane. Then the big fire which destroyed the Mersey Rubber Stores, where four million pounds' worth of raw rubber went up in smoke. Obviously the work of a dozen fire bugs, for the stores consist of six big warehouses and each was fired simultaneously and in two places. And the Frogs were in it. We caught two of the men for the Rubber job; they were both 'Frogs' and bore the totem of the tribe—they were both ex-convicts, and one of them admitted that he had had instructions to carry out the job, but took back his words next day. I never saw a man more scared than he was. And I can't blame him. If half that is said about the Frog is true, his admission cost him something. There it is, Mr. Gordon. I can give you a dozen cases. Genter has been two years on their track. He has been tramping the country, sleeping under hedges, hogging in with all sorts of tramps, stealing rides with them and thieving with them; and when he wrote me and said he had got into touch with the organization and expected to be initiated, I thought we were near to getting them. I've had Genter shadowed since he struck town. I'm sick about this morning."

Dick Gordon opened a drawer of his desk, took out a leather folder and turned the leaves of its contents. They consisted of pages of photographs of men's wrists. He studied them carefully, as though he were looking at them for the first time, though, in truth, he had examined these records of captured men almost every day for years. Then he closed the portfolio thoughtfully and put it away in the drawer. For a few minutes he sat, drumming his fingers on the edge of the writing-table, a frown on his youthful face.

"The frog is always on the left wrist, always a little lob-sided, and there is always one small blob tattooed underneath," he said. "Does that strike you as being remarkable?"

The Superintendent, who was not a brilliant man, saw nothing remarkable in the fact.

CHAPTER III

THE FROG

IT was growing dark when the two tramps, skirting the village of Morby, came again to the post road. The circumvention of Morby had been a painful and tiring business, for the rain which had been falling all day had transformed the ploughed fields into glutinous brown seas that made walking a test of patience.

One was tall, unshaven, shabby, his faded brown coat was buttoned to his chin, his sagged and battered hat rested on the back of his head. His companion seemed short by comparison, though he was a well-made, broad-shouldered man, above the average height.

They spoke no word as they plodded along the muddy road. Twice the shorter man stopped and peered backward in the gathering darkness, as though searching for a pursuer, and once he clutched the big man's arm and drew him to hiding behind the bushes that fringed the road. This was when a car tore past with a roar and a splattering of liquid mud.

After a while they turned off the road, and crossing a field, came to the edge of a wild waste of land traversed by an ancient cart track.

"We're nearly there," growled the smaller man, and the other grunted. But for all his seeming indifference, his keen eyes were taking in every detail of the scene. Solitary building on the horizon . . . looked like a barn. Essex County (he guessed this from the indicator number on the car that had passed); waste land probably led to a disused clay pit . . . or was it quarry? There was an old notice-board fixed to a groggy post near the gate through which the cart track passed. It was too dark to read the faded lettering, but he saw the word "lime." Limestone? It would be easy to locate.

The only danger was if the Frogs were present in force. Under cover of his overcoat, he felt for the Browning and slipped it into his overcoat pocket.

If the Frogs were in strength, there might be a tough fight. Help there was none. He never expected there would be. Carlo had picked him up on the outskirts of the city in his disreputable car, and had driven him through the rain, tacking and turning, following secondary roads, avoiding towns and hamlets, so that, had he been sitting by the driver's side, he might have grown confused. But he was not. He was sitting in the darkness of the little van, and saw nothing. Wellingdale, with the shadows who had been watching him, had not been prepared for the car. A tramp with a motor-car was a monstrosity. Even Genter himself was taken aback when the car drew up to the pavement where he was waiting, and the voice of Carlo hissed, "Jump in!"

They crossed the crest of a weed-grown ridge. Below, Genter saw a stretch of ground littered with rusting trollies, twisted Decourville rails, and pitted with deep, rain-filled holes. Beyond, on the sharp line of the quarry's edge, was a small wooden hut, and towards this Carlo led the way.

"Not nervous, are you?" he asked, and there was a sneer in his voice.

"Not very," said the other coolly. "I suppose the fellows are in that shack?"

Carlo laughed softly.

"There are no others," he said, "only the Frog himself. He comes up the quarry face—there's a flight of steps that come up under the hut. Good idea, eh? The hut hangs over the edge, and you can't even see the steps, not if you hang over. I tried once. They'd never catch him, not if they brought forty million cops."

"Suppose they surrounded the quarry?" suggested Genter, but the man scoffed.

"Wouldn't he know it was being surrounded before he came in? He knows everything, does the Frog."

He looked down at the other's hand.

"It won't hurt," he said, "and it's worth it if it does! You'll never be without a friend again, Harry. If you get into trouble, there's always the best lawyer to defend you. And you're the kind of chap we're looking for—there is plenty of trash. Poor fools that want to get in for the sake of the pickings. But you'll get big work, and if you do a special job for him, there's hundreds and hundreds of money for you! If you're hungry or ill, the Frogs will find you out and help you. That's pretty good, ain't it?"

Genter said nothing. They were within a dozen yards of the hut now, a strong structure built of stout timber bulks, with one door and a shuttered window.

Motioning Genter to remain where he was, the man called Carlo went forward and tapped on the door. Genter heard a voice, and then he saw the man step to the window, and the shutter open an inch. There followed a long conversation in an undertone, and then Carlo came back.

"He says he has a job for you that will bring in a thousand—you're lucky! Do you know Rochmore?"

Genter nodded. He knew that aristocratic suburb.

"There's a man there that has got to be coshed. He comes home from his club every night by the eleven-five. Walks to his house. It is up a dark road, and a fellow could get him with a club without trouble. Just one smack and he's finished. It's not killing, you understand."

"Why does he want me to do it?" asked the tall tramp curiously.

The explanation was logical.

"All new fellows have to do something to show their pluck and straightness. What do you say?"

Genter had not hesitated.

"I'll do it," he said.

Carlo returned to the window, and presently he called his companion.

"Stand here and put your left arm through the window," he ordered.

Genter pulled back the cuff of his soddened coat and thrust his bare arm through the opening. His hand was caught in a firm grip, and immediately he felt something soft and wet pressed against his wrist. A rubber stamp, he noted mentally, and braced himself for the pain which would follow. It came, the rapid pricking of a thousand needles, and he winced. Then the grip on his hand relaxed and he withdrew it, to look wonderingly on the blurred design of ink and blood that the tattooer had left.

"Don't wipe it," said a muffled voice from the darkness of the hut. "Now you may come in."

The shutter closed and was bolted. Then came the snick of a lock turning and the door opened. Genter went into the pitch-black darkness of the hut and heard the door locked by the unseen occupant.

"Your number is K 971," said the hollow voice. "When you see that in the personal column of *The Times*, you report here, wherever you are. Take that...."

Genter put out his hand and an envelope was placed in his outstretched palm. It was as though the mysterious Frog could see, even in that blackness.

"There is journey money and a map of the district. If you spend the journey money, or if you fail to come when you are wanted, you will be killed. Is that clear?"

"Yes."

"You will find other money—that you can use for your expenses. Now listen. At Rochmore, 17 Park Avenue, lives Hallwell Jones, the banker——"

He must have sensed the start of surprise which the recruit gave.

"You know him?"

"Yes—worked for him years ago," said Genter.

Stealthily, he drew his Browning from his pocket and thumbed down the safety catch.

"Between now and Friday he has to be clubbed. You need not kill him. If you do, it doesn't matter. I expect his head's too hard ——"

Genter located the man now, and, growing accustomed to the darkness, guessed rather than saw the bulk of him. Suddenly his hand shot out and grasped the arm of the Frog.

"I've got a gun and I'll shoot," he said between his teeth. "I want you, Frog! I am Inspector Genter from police headquarters, and if you resist I'll kill you!"

For a second there was a deathly silence. Then Genter felt his pistol wrist seized in a vice-like grip. He struck out with his other hand, but the man stooped and the blow fell in the air, and then with a wrench the pistol was forced out of the big man's hand and he closed with his prisoner. So doing, his face touched the Frog's. Was it a mask he was wearing? . . . The cold mica goggles came against his cheek. That accounted for the muffled voice. . . .

Powerful as he was, he could not break away from the arms which encircled him, and they struggled backward and forward in the darkness.

Suddenly the Frog lifted his foot, and Genter, anticipating the kick, swerved round. There was a crash of broken glass, and then something came to the detective—a faint but pungent odour. He tried to breathe, but found himself strangling, and his arms fell feebly by his side.

The Frog held him for a minute, and then let the limp figure fall with a thud to the ground. In the morning a London police patrol found the body of Inspector Genter lying in the garden of an empty house, and rang for an ambulance. But a man who has been gassed by the concentrated fumes of hydrocyanic acid dies very quickly, and Genter had been dead ten seconds after the Frog smashed the thin glass cylinder which he kept in the hut for such emergencies as these.

CHAPTER IV

ELK

THERE was no detective in the world who looked less like a police officer, and a clever police officer, than Elk. He was tall and thin, and a slight stoop accentuated his weediness. His clothes seemed ill-fitting, and hung upon rather than fitted him. His dark, cadaverous face was set permanently in an expression of the deepest gloom, and few had ever seen him smile. His superiors found him generally a depressing influence, for his outlook on life was prejudiced and apparently embittered by his failure to secure promotion. Faulty education stood in his way here. Ten times he had come up for examination, and ten times he had failed, invariably in the same subject—history.

Dick, who knew him better than his immediate chiefs, guessed that these failures did not worry Mr. Elk as much as people thought. Indeed, he often detected a glum pride in his inability to remember historical dates, and once, in a moment of astonishing confidence, Elk had confessed that promotion would be an embarrassment to a man of his limited educational attainments. For Elk's everyday English was one of his weaknesses.

"There's no rest for the wicked, Mr. Gordon," he sighed as he sat down. "I thought I'd get a holiday after my trip to the U.S.A."

"I want to know all about Lola Bassano—who are her friends, why she has suddenly attached herself to Raymond Bennett, a clerk in the employ of Maitlands Consolidated. Particularly why she picked him up at the corner of St. James's Square and drove him to Horsham last night. I saw them by accident as I was coming out of my club, and followed. They sat in her coupé for the greater part of two hours within a hundred yards of Bennett's house, and they were talking. I know, because I stood in the rain behind the car, listening. If he had been making love to her I should have understood—a little. But they were talking, and talking money. I heard certain sums mentioned. At four o'clock he got out of the car and went into his house, and Lola drove off."

Elk, puffing, sadly shook his head.

"Lola wouldn't talk about anything but money anyway," he said. "She's like Queen What's-her-name who died in 1077, or maybe it was 1573. She married King Henry, or it may have been Charles, because she wanted a gold snuff-box he had. I'm not sure whether it was a gold snuff-box or a silver bed. Anyway, she got it an' was be'eaded in . . . I don't remember the date."

"Thank you for the parallel," smiled Dick. "But Lola is not after snuff-boxes of gold or silver. Young Bennett hasn't twopence of his own. There is something particularly interesting to me about this acquaintance."

Elk smoked thoughtfully, watching the smoke rings rise to the ceiling.

"Bennett's got a sister," he said, to the other's amazement. "Pretty, as far as looks go. Old man Bennett's a crook of some kind. Doesn't do any regular work, but goes away for days at a time and comes back looking ill."

"You know them?"

Elk nodded.

"Old man Bennett attracted me. Somebody reported his movements as suspicious—the local police. They've got nothing to do except guard chickens, and naturally they look on anybody who doesn't keep chickens as bein' a suspicious character. I kept old Bennett under observation, but I never got to the bottom of his movements. He has run lots of queer stunts. He wrote a play once and put it on. It went dead on the fourth night. Then he took to playing the races on a system. That nearly broke him. Then he started a correspondence school at Horsham—'How to write good English'—and he lost money. Now he's taking pictures."

"How long has he been trying those methods of getting a living?"

"Years. I traced a typewriting agency to him seventeen years ago. They haven't all been failures. He made money out of some. But I'd give my head to know what his regular game is. Once a month regular, sometimes twice, sometimes more often, he disappears and you can't find him or trail him. I've sounded every crook in town, but they're as much puzzled as I am. Lew Brady—that's the big sporting fellow who worked with Lola—he's interested too. He hates Bennett. Years ago he tackled the old man and tried to bully him into telling him what his lay was, and Bennett handled him rough."

"The old man?" asked Dick incredulously.

"The old man. He's as strong as an ox. Don't forget it. I'll see Lola. She's not a bad girl—up to a point. Personally, vamps never appeal to me. Genter's dead, they tell me? The Frog's in that too?"

"There's no doubt about it," said Dick, rising. "And here, Elk, is one of the men who killed him."

He walked to the window and looked out, Elk behind him. The man who had stood on the sidewalk had disappeared.

"Where?" asked Elk.

"He's gone now. I— —"

At that moment the window shattered inward, and splinters of glass stung his face. Another second, and Elk was dragged violently to cover.

"From the roof of Onslow Gardens," said Richard Gordon calmly. "I wondered where the devils would shoot from—that's twice they've tried to get me since daylight."

A spent cartridge on the flat roof of 94, Onslow Gardens, and the print of feet, were all the evidence that the assassin left behind. No. 94 was empty except for a caretaker, who admitted that he was in the habit of going out every morning to buy provisions for the day. Admission had been gained by the front door; there was a tradesman who saw a man let himself into the house, carrying what looked to be a fishing-rod under his arm, but which undoubtedly was a rifle in a cloth case.

"Very simple," said Dick; "and, of course, from the Frog's point of view, effective. The shooter had half-a-dozen ways of escape, including the fire-escape."

Elk was silent and glum. Dick Gordon as silent, but cheerful, until the two men were back in his office.

"It was my inquiry at the garage that annoyed them," he said, "and I'll give them this credit, that they are rapid! I was returning to my house when the first attempt was made. The most ingenious effort to run me down with a light car—the darned thing even mounted the pavement after me."

"Number?"

"XL.19741," said Dick, "but fake. There is no such number on the register. The driver was gone before I could stop him."

Elk scratched his chin, surveying the youthful Public Prosecutor with a dubious eye.

"Almost sounds interesting to me," he said. "Of course I've heard of the Frogs, but I didn't give much attention. Nowadays secret societies are so common that every time a man shakes hands with me, he looks sort of disappointed if I don't pull my ear or flap my feet. And gang work on a large scale I've always looked upon as something you only hear about in exciting novels by my old friend Shylock——"

"Sherlock—and he didn't write them," murmured Dick.

Again Elk fingered his cheek.

"I don't believe in it, anyway," he said after thought. "It's not natural that tramps should do anything systematic. It's too much like work. I'll bet there's nothing in it, only a lot of wild coincidences stickin' together. I'll bet that the Frogs are just a silly society without any plan or reason. And I'll bet that Lola knows all about 'em," he added inconsistently.

Elk walked back to "The Yard" by the most circuitous route. With his furled and ancient umbrella hanging on his arm, he had the appearance of an out-of-work clerk. His steel-rimmed spectacles, clipped at a groggy angle, assisted the illusion. Winter and summer he wore a soiled fawn top-coat, which was invariably unbuttoned, and he had worn the same yellowish-brown suit for as long as anybody could remember. The rain came down, not in any great quantities, but incessantly. His hard derby hat glistened with moisture, but he did not put up his umbrella. Nobody had ever seen that article opened.

He walked to Trafalgar Square and then stopped, stood in thought for some time, and retraced his steps. Opposite the Public Prosecutor's office stood a tall street-seller with a little tray of matches, key-rings, pencils and the odds and ends that such men sell. His wares, for the moment, were covered by a shining oil-cloth. Elk had not noticed him before, and wondered why the man had taken up so unfavourable a stand, for the end of Onslow Gardens, the windiest and least comfortable position in Whitehall, is not a place where the hurrying pedestrian would stop to buy, even on a fine day. The hawker was dressed in a shabby raincoat that reached to his heels; a soft felt hat was pulled down over his eyes, but Elk saw the hawk-like face and stopped.

"Busy?"

"Naw."

Elk was immediately interested. This man was American, and was trying to disguise his voice so that it appeared Cockney—the most impossible task that any American had ever undertaken, for the whine and intonation of the Cockney are inimitable.

"You're American—what state?"

"Georgia," was the reply, and this time the hawker made no attempt at disguise. "Came over on a cattle-boat during the war."

Elk held out his hand.

"Let me see that licence of yours, brother," he said.

Without hesitation the man produced the written police permit to sell on the streets. It was made out in the name of "Joshua Broad," and was in order.

"You're not from Georgia," said Elk, "but that doesn't matter. You're from Hampshire or Massachusetts."

"Connecticut, to be exact," said the man coolly, "but I've lived in Georgia. Want a key-ring?"

There was a gleam of amusement in his eyes—the merest flash.

"No. Never had a key. Never had anything worth locking up," said Elk, fingering the articles on the tray. "Not a good pitch, this."

"No," said the other; "too near to Scotland Yard, Mr. Elk."

Elk cast a swift glance at the man.

"Know me, do you?"

"Most people do, don't they?" asked the other innocently.

Elk took the pedlar in from the soles of his stout shoes to his soddened hat, and, with a nod, went on. The hawker looked after the detective until he was out of sight, and then, fixing a cover over his tray, strapped it tight and walked in the direction Elk had taken.

Coming out of Maitlands to lunch, Ray Bennett saw a shabby and saturnine man standing on the edge of the pavement, but gave him no more than a passing glance. He, at any rate, did not know Elk and was quite unconscious of the fact that he was being followed to the little chop-house where Philo Johnson and he took their modest luncheon.

In any circumstances Ray would not have observed the shadow, but to-day, in his condition of mind, he had no thought for anybody but himself, or any offence but the bearded and ancient Maitland's outrageous behaviour.

"The old devil!" he said as he walked by Johnson's side. "To make a ten per cent cut in salaries and to start on me! And this morning the papers say that he has given five thousand to the Northern Hospitals!"

"He's a charitable cuss, and as to the cut, it was either that or standing you off," said Johnson cheerfully. "What's the use of kicking? Trade has been bad, and the stock market is as dead as Ptolemy. The old man wanted to put you off—said that you were superfluous anyway. If you'd only look on the bright side of things, Ray——"

"Bright!" snorted the young man, his face going pink with anger. "I'm getting a boy's salary, and I want money mighty badly, Philo."

Philo sighed, and for once his good-humoured face was clouded. Then it relaxed into a broad grin.

"If I thought the same way as you, I'd go mad or turn into a first-class crook. I only earn about fifty per cent more than you, and yet the old man allows me to handle hundreds of thousands. It's too bad."

Nevertheless, the "badness" of the parsimonious Maitland did not interfere with his appetite.

"The art of being happy," he said as he pushed back his plate and lit a cigarette, "is to want nothing. Then you're always getting more than you need. How is your sister?"

"She's all right," said Ray indifferently. "Ella's the same mind as you. It's easy to be a philosopher over other people's worries. Who's that disreputable bird?" he added, as a man seated himself at a table opposite to them.

Philo fixed his glasses—he was a little near-sighted.

"That's Elk—a Scotland Yard man," he said, and grinned at the new-comer, a recognition which, to Ray's annoyance—and his annoyance was tinged with uneasiness—brought the seedy man to their table.

"This is my friend, Mr. Bennett—Inspector Elk, Ray."

"Sergeant," suggested Elk dourly. "Fate has always been against me in the matter of promotion. Can't remember dates."

So far from making a secret of his failure, Mr. Elk was never tired of discussing the cause.

"Though why a man is a better thief-taker for knowin' when George Washington was born and when Napoleon Bonaparte died, is a mystery to me. Dine here every day, Mr. Bennett?"

Ray nodded.

"Know your father, I think—John Bennett of Horsham, isn't it? Thought so."

In desperation Ray got up with an excuse and left them alone.

"Nice boy, that," said Elk.

CHAPTER V

MR. MAITLAND GOES HOME

THEY were nearing the imposing home of Maitlands Consolidated, when Mr. Johnson suddenly broke off in the middle of an interesting exposition of his philosophy and quickened his pace. On the pavement ahead of them he saw Ray Bennett, and by his side the slim figure of a girl. Their backs were toward the two men, but Elk guessed rightly when he decided that the girl was Ella Bennett. He had seen her twice before, and he had a wonderful memory for backs.

Turning as the stout man came up to her, hat in hand, she greeted him with a quick and friendly smile.

"This is an unexpected pleasure, Miss Bennett."

There was a pink tinge to Johnson's homely face ("Sweet on her," thought Elk, interested), and his handshake was warm and something more than cordial.

"I didn't intend coming to town, but father has gone off on one of his mysterious excursions," she said with a little laugh, "this time to the West. And, curiously enough, I am absolutely sure I saw him on a 'bus just now, though his train left two hours ago."

She glanced at Elk hovering in the background, and the sight of his glum countenance seemed to arouse some unpleasant memory, for the brightness went out of her face.

"My friend, Mr. Elk," said Johnson a little awkwardly, and Elk nodded.

"Glad to meet you, Miss Bennett," he said, and noted Ray's annoyance with inward satisfaction which, in a more cheerful man, would have been mirth.

She bowed slightly and then said something in a low tone to her brother. Elk saw the boy frown.

"I shan't be very late," he said, loudly enough for the detective to hear.

She put out her hand to Johnson, Elk she favoured with a distant inclination of her head, and was gone, leaving the three men looking after her. Two, for when Mr. Elk looked around, the boy had disappeared into the building.

"You know Miss Bennett?"

"Slightly," said Elk grudgingly. "I know almost everybody slightly. Good people and bad people. The gooder they are, the slighter I know 'em. Queer devil."

"Who?" asked the startled Johnson. "You mean her father? I wish he wasn't so chilly with me."

Elk's lips twitched.

"I guess you do," he said drily. "So long."

He strolled aimlessly away as Johnson walked up the steps into Maitlands, but he did not go far. Crossing the road, he retraced his steps and took up his station in the doorway.

At four o'clock a taxicab drew up before the imposing door of Maitlands Consolidated, and a few minutes later the old man shuffled out, looking neither to the right nor to the left. Elk regarded him with more than ordinary interest. He knew the financier by sight, and had paid two or three visits to the office in connection with certain petty thefts committed by cleaners. In this way he had become acquainted with Philo Johnson, for old Maitland had delegated the interview to his subordinate.

Elk judged the old man to be in the region of seventy, and wondered for the first time where he lived, and in what state. Had he relations? It was a curious fact that he knew nothing whatever about the financier, the least paragraphed of any of the big City forces.

The detective had no business with the head of this flourishing firm. His task was to discover the association between Lola Bassano and this impecunious clerk. He knew inside him that Dick Gordon's interest in the young man was not altogether disinterested, and suspected rightly that the pretty sister of Ray Bennett lay behind it.

But the itch for knowledge about Maitland, suddenly aroused by the realization that the old man's home life was an unknown quantity, was too strong to be resisted. As the taxicab moved off, Elk beckoned another.

"Follow that cab," he said, and the driver nodded his agreement without question, for there was no taximan on the streets who did not know this melancholy policeman.

The first of the cabs drove rapidly in the direction of North London, and halted at a busy junction of streets in Finsbury Park. This is a part of the town which great financiers do not as a rule choose for their habitations. It is a working-class district, full of small houses, usually occupied by two or more families; and when the cab stopped and the old man nimbly descended, Elk's mouth opened in an 'O' of surprise.

Maitland did not pay the cabman, but hurried round the corner into the busy thoroughfare, with Elk at his heels. He walked a hundred yards, and then boarded a street car. Elk sprinted, and swung himself on board as the car was moving. The old man found a seat, took a battered newspaper from his pocket, and began reading.

The car ran down Seven Sisters Road into Tottenham, and here Mr. Maitland descended. He turned into a side street of apparently interminable length, crossed the road, and came into a narrow and even meaner street than that which he had traversed; and then, to Elk's amazement, pushed open the iron gate of a dark and dirty little house, opened the door and went in, closing it behind him.

The detective looked up and down the street. It was crowded with poor children. Elk looked at the house again, scarcely believing his eyes. The windows were unclean, the soiled curtains visible were ragged, and the tiny forecourt bore an appearance of neglect. And this was the home of Ezra Maitland, a master of millions, the man who gave £5,000 to the London hospitals! It was incredible.

He made up his mind, and, walking to the door, knocked. For some time there was no reply, and then he heard the shuffle of slippered feet in the passage, and an old woman with a yellow face opened the door.

"Excuse me," said Elk; "I think the gentleman who just came in dropped this." He produced a handkerchief from his pocket, and she glared at it for a moment, and then, reaching out her hand, took it from him and slammed the door in his face.

"And that's the last of my good handkerchief," thought Elk bitterly.

He had caught one glimpse of the interior. A grimy-looking passage with a strip of faded carpet, and a flight of uncovered stairs. He proceeded to make a few local inquiries.

"Maitland or Mainland, I don't know which," said a tradesman who kept a general store at the corner. "The old gentleman goes out every morning at nine, and comes home just about this hour. I don't know who or what he is. I can tell you this, though; he doesn't eat much! He buys all his goods here. What those two people live on, an ordinary healthy child would eat at one meal!"

Elk went back to the west, a little mystified. The miser was a common figure of fiction, and not uncommonly met with in real life. But old Maitland must be a super-miser, he thought, and decided to give the matter a little further attention. For the moment, he was concentrating his efforts upon Miss Lola Bassano, that interesting lady.

In one of the fashionable thoroughfares leading from Cavendish Square is a block of flats, occupied by wealthy tenants. Its rents are remarkably high, even for that exclusive quarter, and even Elk, who was not easily surprised, was a little staggered when he learnt that Lola Bassano occupied a suite in this expensive building.

It was to Caverley House that he made his way after returning to Maitland's office, to find the premises closed. There was no indicator on the wall, but the lift-man, who regarded Elk with some suspicion, as he was entitled to do, announced that Miss Bassano lived on the third floor.

"How long has she been here?" asked Elk.

"That's no business of yours," said the lift-man; "and I think what you want, my friend, is the tradesmen's entrance."

"I've often wondered," ruminated Elk, "what people like you do their thinking with."

"Now look here — — !" began the lift-man indignantly.

"Look here," retorted Elk, and at the sight of his badge the man grew more polite and more informative.

"She's been here two months," he said. "And, to tell you the truth, Mr. Elk, I've often wondered how she got a suite in Caverley House. They tell me she used to run a gambling joint on Jermyn Street. You haven't come to raid her, have you?" he asked anxiously. "That'd get Caverley House a pretty bad name."

"I've come to make a friendly call," said Elk carefully.

"That's the door." The man stepped out of the lift and pointed to one of the two sober mahogany doors on the landing. "This other flat belongs to an American millionaire."

"Is there such a thing?" asked Elk.

He was about to say something more when the lift-man walked to the door and peered at one of its polished panels.

"That's queer," he said. "What do you make of this?"

Elk joined him, and at a glance saw and understood.

On the panel had been stamped a small white frog—an exact replica of those he had seen that morning on the photographs that Dick Gordon had shown him. A squatting frog, slightly askew.

He touched it. The ink was still wet and showed on his finger. And then the strangest thing of all happened. The door opened suddenly, and a man of middle age appeared in the doorway. In his hand was a long-barrelled Browning, and it covered the detective's heart.

"Put up your hands!" he said sharply. Then he stopped and stared at the detective.

Elk returned the gaze, speechless; for the elegantly dressed man who stood there was the hawk-faced pedlar he had seen in Whitehall!

The American was the first to recover. Not a muscle of his face moved, but Elk saw again that light of amusement in his eyes as he stepped back and opened the door still wider.

"Come right in, Mr. Elk," he said, and, to the amazed lift-man; "It's all right, Worth. I was practising a little joke on Mr. Elk."

He closed the door behind him, and with a gesture beckoned the detective into a prettily furnished drawing-room. Elk went in, leaving the matter of the frog on the door for discussion later.

"We're quite alone, Mr. Elk, so you needn't lower your voice when you talk of my indiscretions. Will you smoke a cigar?"

Elk stretched out his fingers mechanically and selected a big Cabana.

"Unless I'm greatly mistaken, I saw you this morning," he began.

"You weren't mistaken at all," interrupted the other coolly. "You saw me on Whitehall. I was peddling key-rings. My name is Joshua Broad. You haven't anything on me for trading in a false name."

The detective lit his cigar before he spoke.

"This apartment must cost you a whole lot to keep up," he said slowly, "and I don't blame you for trying to earn something on the side. But it seems to me that peddling key-rings is a very poor proposition for a first-class business man."

Joshua Broad nodded.

"I haven't made a million out of that business," he said, "but it amuses me, Mr. Elk. I am something of a philosopher."

He lit a cigar and settled himself comfortably in a deep, chintz-covered arm-chair, his legs crossed, the picture of contentment.

"As an American, I am interested in social problems, and I have found that the best way to understand the very poor of any country is to get right down amongst them."

His tone was easy, apologetic, but quite self-possessed.

"I think I forestalled any question on your part as to whether I had a licence in my own name, by telling you that I had."

Elk settled his glasses more firmly on his nose, and his eyes strayed to Mr. Broad's pocket, whither the pistol had returned.

"This is a pretty free country," he said in his deliberate way, "and a man can peddle key-rings, even if he's a member of the House of Lords. But one thing he mustn't do, Mr. Broad, is to stick fire-arms under the noses of respectable policemen."

Broad chuckled.

"I'm afraid I was a little rattled," he said. "But the truth is, I've been waiting for the greater part of an hour, expecting somebody to come to my door, and when I heard your stealthy footsteps"—he shrugged—"it was a fool mistake for a grown man to make," he said, "and I guess I'm feeling as badly about it as you would have me feel."

The unwavering eyes of Mr. Elk did not leave his face.

"I won't insult your intelligence by asking you if you were expecting a friend," he said. "But I should like to know the name of the other guest."

"So should I," said the other, "and so would a whole lot of people."

He reached out his hand to flick the ash from his cigar, looking at Elk thoughtfully the while.

"I was expecting a man who has every reason to be very much afraid of me," he said. "His name is—well, it doesn't matter, and I've only met him once in my life, and then I didn't see his face."

"And you beat him up?" suggested Elk.

The other man laughed.

"I didn't even beat him up. In fact, I behaved most generously to him," he said quietly. "I was not with him more than five minutes, in a darkened room, the only light being a lantern which was on the table. And I guess that's about all I can tell you, Inspector."

"Sergeant," murmured Elk. "It's curious the number of people who think I'm an Inspector."

There was an awkward pause. Elk could think of no other questions he wanted to ask, and his host displayed as little inclination to advance any further statement.

"Neighbour friends of yours?" asked Elk, and jerked his head toward the passage.

"Who—Bassano and her friend? No. Are you after them?" he asked quickly.

Elk shook his head.

"Making a friendly call," he said. "Just that. I've just come back from your country, Mr. Broad. A good country, but too full of distances."

He ruminated, looking down at the carpet for a long time, and presently he said:

"I'd like to meet that friend of yours, Mr. Broad—American?"

Broad shook his head. Not a word was spoken as they went up the passage to the front door, and it almost seemed as if Elk was going without saying good-bye, for he walked out absent-mindedly, and only turned as though the question of any farewell had occurred to him.

"Shall be glad to meet you again, Mr. Broad," he said. "Perhaps I shall see you in Whitehall——"

And then his eyes strayed to the grotesque white frog on the door. Broad said nothing. He put his finger on the imprint and it smudged under his touch.

"Recently stamped," he drawled. "Well, now, what do you think of that, Mr. Elk?"

Elk was examining the mat before the door. There was a little spot of white, and he stooped and smeared his finger over it.

"Yes, quite recent. It must have been done just before I came in," he said. And there his interest in the Frog seemed to evaporate. "I'll be going along now," he said with a nod.

In the exquisitely appointed drawing-room of Suite No. 6, Lola Bassano sat cuddled up in a deep, over-cushioned chair, her feet tucked under her, a thin cigarette between her lips, a scowl upon her pretty face. From time to time she glanced at the man who stood by the window, hands in pockets, staring down into the square. He was tall, heavily built, heavily jowled, unprepossessing. All the help that tailor and valet gave to him could not disguise his origin. He was pugilist, run to fat. For a time, a very short time, Lew Brady had been welter-weight champion of Europe, a terrific fighter with just that yellow thread in his composition which makes all the difference between greatness and mediocrity in the ring. A harder man had discovered his weakness, and the glory of Lew Brady faded with remarkable rapidity. He had one advantage over his fellows which saved him from utter extinction. A philanthropist had found him in the gutter as a child, and had given him an education. He had gone to a good school and associated with boys who spoke good English. The benefit of that association he had never lost, and his voice was so curiously cultured that people who for the first time heard this brute-man speak, listened open-mouthed.

"What time do you expect that rat of yours?" he asked.

Lola lifted her silk-clad shoulders, took out her cigarette to yawn, and settled herself more cosily.

"I don't know. He leaves his office at five."

The man turned from the window and began to pace the room slowly.

"Why Frog worries about him I don't know," he grumbled. "Lola, I'm surely getting tired of old man Frog."

Lola smiled and blew out a ring of smoke.

"Perhaps you're tired of getting money for nothing, Brady," she said. "Personally speaking, that kind of weariness never comes to me. There is one thing sure; Frog wouldn't bother with young Bennett if there wasn't something in it."

He pulled out a watch and glanced at its jewelled face.

"Five o'clock. I suppose that fellow doesn't know you're married to me?"

"Don't be a fool," said Lola wearily. "Am I likely to boast about it?"

He grinned and resumed his pacings. Presently he heard the faint tinkle of the bell and glanced at the girl. She got up, shook the cushions and nodded.

"Open the door," she said, and the man went out of the room obediently.

Ray Bennett crossed the room with quick strides and caught the girl's hand in both of his.

"I'm late. Old Johnson kept me running round after the clerks had gone. Moses, this is a fine room, Lola! I hadn't any idea you lived in such style."

"You know Lew Brady?"

Ray nodded smilingly. He was a picture of happiness, and the presence of Lew Brady made no difference to him. He had met Lola at a supper club, and knew that she and Brady had some business association. Moreover, Ray prided himself upon that confusion of standards which is called "broad-mindedness." He visualized a new social condition which was superior to the bondage which old-fashioned rules of conduct imposed upon men and women in their relationship one to the other. He was young, clean-minded, saw things as he would have them be. Breadth of mind not infrequently accompanies limitation of knowledge.

"Now for your wonderful scheme," he said as, at a gesture from her, he settled himself by the girl's side. "Does Brady know?"

"It is Lew's idea," she said lightly. "He is always looking out for opportunities—not for himself but for other people."

"It's a weakness of mine," said Lew apologetically. "And anyway, I don't know if you'll like the scheme. I'd have taken it on myself, but I'm too busy. Did Lola tell you anything about it?"

Ray nodded.

"I can't believe it," he said. "I always thought such things belonged to magazine stories! Lola says that the Government of Japan wants a secret agent in London. Somebody they can disown, if necessary. But what is the work?"

"There you've got me," said Lew, shaking his head. "So far as I can discover, you've nothing to do but live! Perhaps they'll want you to keep track of what is going on in the political world. The thing I don't like about it is that you'll have to live a double life. Nobody must know that you're a clerk at Maitlands. You can call yourself by any name you like, and you'll have to make your domestic arrangements as best you know."

"That will be easy," interrupted the boy. "My father says I ought to have a room in town—he thinks the journey to and from Horsham every day is too expensive. I fixed that with him on Sunday. I shall have to go down to the cottage some week-ends—but what am I to do, and to whom do I report?"

Lola laughed softly.

"Poor boy," she mocked. "The prospect of owning a beautiful flat and seeing me every day is worrying him."

CHAPTER VI

MR. MAITLAND GOES SHOPPING

ELDOR STREET, Tottenham, was one of thousands of drab and ugly thoroughfares that make up the central suburbs of London. Imagine two rows of houses set on either side of a straight street, lighted at economic intervals by yellow lamps. Each house has a protuberance, called a bay window; each house is separated from the road by iron railings pierced by an iron gate. There is a tiny forecourt in which the hardiest of shrubs battle desperately for existence; there is one recessed door, and on the floor above two windows exactly alike.

Elk found himself in Eldor Street at nine o'clock that night. The rain was pelting down, and the street in consequence was a desert. Most of the houses were dark, for Eldor Street lives in its kitchens, which are back of the houses. In the front window of No. 47 one crack of light showed past the edge of the lowered blind, and, creeping up to the window, he heard, at long intervals, the mumble of conversation.

It was difficult to believe that he was standing at the door of Ezra Maitland's home. That morning the newspapers had given prominence to the newest speculation of Maitlands Consolidated —a deal involving something over a million. And the mastermind of the concern lived in this squalor!

Whilst he was standing there, the light was extinguished and there came to him the sound of feet in the uncarpeted passage. He had time to reach the obscurity of the other side of the street, when the door opened and two people came out: Maitland and the old woman he had seen. By the light of a street-lamp he saw that Maitland wore an overcoat buttoned to his chin. The old woman had on a long ulster, and in her hand she carried a string bag. They were going marketing! It was Saturday night, and the main street, through which Elk had passed, had been thronged with late shoppers—Tottenham leaves its buying to the last, when food can be had at bargain prices.

Waiting until they were out of sight, Elk walked down the street to the end and turned to the left. He followed a wall covered with posters until he reached a narrow opening. This was the passage between the gardens—a dark, unlighted alleyway, three feet wide and running between tar-coated wooden fences. He counted the gates on his left with the help of his flash-lamp, and after a while stopped before one of them and pushed gently. The gate was locked—it was not bolted. There was a keyhole that had the appearance of use. Elk grunted his satisfaction, and, taking from his pocket a wallet, extracted a small wooden handle, into which he fitted a steel hook, chosen with care from a dozen others. This he inserted into the lock and turned. Evidently the lock was more complicated than he had expected. He tried another hook of a different shape, and yet another. At the fourth trial the lock turned and he pushed open the door gently.

The back of the house was in darkness, the yard singularly free from the obstructions which he had anticipated. He crossed to the door leading into the house. To his surprise it was unfastened, and he replaced his tools in his pocket. He found himself in a small scullery. Passing through a door into the bare passage, he came to the room in which he had seen the light. It was meanly and shabbily furnished. The arm-chair near the fireplace had broken springs, there was an untidy bed in one corner, and in the centre of the room a table covered with a patched cloth. On this were two or three books and a few sheets of paper covered with the awkward writing of a child. Elk read curiously.

"Look at the dog," it ran. "The man goes up to the dog and the dog barks at the man."

There was more in similar strain. The books were children's primers of an elementary kind. Looking round, he saw a cheap gramophone and on the sideboard half a dozen scratched and chipped records.

The child must be in the house. Turning on the gas, he lit it, after slipping a bolt in the front door to guard against surprise. In the more brilliant light, the poverty of the room staggered him. The carpet was worn and full of holes; there was not one article of furniture which had not been repaired at some time or other. On the dingy sideboard was a child's abacus—a frame holding wires on which beads were strung, and by means of which the young are taught to count. A paper on the mantelpiece attracted him. It was a copy of the million pound contract which Maitland had signed that morning. His neat signature, with the characteristic flourish beneath, was at the foot.

Elk replaced the paper and began a search of the apartment. In a cupboard by the side of the fireplace he found an iron money-box, which he judged was half-full of coins. In addition, there were nearly a hundred letters addressed to E. Maitland, 47 Eldor Street, Tottenham. Elk, glancing through them, recognized their unimportance. Every one was either a tradesman's circular or those political pamphlets with which candidates flood their constituencies. And they were all unopened. Mr. Maitland evidently knew what they were also, and had not troubled to examine their contents. Probably the hoarding instincts of age had made him keep them. There was nothing else in the room of interest. He was certain that this was where the old man slept—where was the child?

Turning out the light, he went upstairs. One door was locked, and here his instruments were of no avail, for the lock was a patent one and was recently fixed. Possibly the child was there, he thought. The second room, obviously the old woman's, was as meanly furnished as the parlour.

Coming back to the landing, his foot was poised to reach the first stair when he heard a faint "click." It came from below, and was the sound of a door closing. Elk waited, listening. The sound was not repeated, and he descended softly. At first he thought that the old man had returned, and was trying his key on the bolted door, but when he crept to the door to listen, he heard no sound, and slipping back the bolt, he went to the second of the rooms on the ground floor and put his light on the door.

Elk was a man of keen observation; very little escaped him, and he was perfectly certain that this door had been ajar when he had passed it on entering the house. It was closed now and fastened from the inside, the key being in the lock.

Was it the child, frightened by his presence? Elk was wise enough a man not to investigate too closely. He made the best of his way back to the garden passage and into the street. Here he waited, taking up a position which enabled him to see the length of Eldor Street and the passage opening in the wall. Presently he saw Maitland returning. The old man was carrying the string bag, which now bulged. Elk saw the green of a cabbage as they passed under the light. He watched them until the darkness swallowed them up, and heard the sound of their closing door. Five minutes later, a dark figure came from the passage behind the houses. It was a man, and Elk, alert and watchful, swung off in pursuit.

The stranger plunged into a labyrinth of little streets with the detective at his heels. He was walking quickly, but not too quickly for Elk, who was something of a pedestrian. Into the glare of the main road the stranger turned, Elk a dozen paces behind him. He could not see his face, nor did he until his quarry stopped by the side of a waiting car, opened the door and jumped in. Then it was that Elk came abreast and raised his hand in cheery salutation.

For a second the man in the closed limousine was taken aback, and then he opened the door.

"Come right in out of the rain, Elk," he said, and Elk obeyed.

"Been doing your Sunday shopping?" he asked innocently.

The man's hawk-like face relaxed into a smile.

"I never eat on Sundays," he said.

It was Joshua Broad, that rich American who peddled key-rings in Whitehall, lived in the most expensive flats in London, and found time to be intensely interested in Ezra Maitland.

He turned abruptly as Elk seated himself.

"Say, Elk, did you see the child?"

Elk shook his head.

"No," he said, and heard the chuckle of his companion as the car moved toward the civilized west.

"Yes, I saw that baby," said Mr. Broad, puffing gently at the cigar he had lit; "and, believe me, Elk, I've stopped loving children. Yes, sir. The education of the young means less than nothing to me for evermore."

"Where was she?"

"It's a 'he,'" replied Broad calmly, "and I hope I'll be excused answering your question. I had been in the house an hour when you arrived—I was in the back room, which is empty, by the way. You scared me. I heard you come in and thought it was old St.

Nicholas of the Whiskers. Especially when I saw the light go on. I'd had it on when you opened the scullery door—I left that unfastened, by the way. Didn't want to stop my bolt hole. Well, what do you think?"

"About Maitland?"

"Eccentric, eh? You don't know how eccentric!"

As the car stopped before the door of Caverley House, Elk broke a long silence.

"What are you, Mr. Broad?"

"I'll give you ten guesses," said the other cheerfully as they got out.

"Secret Service man," suggested Elk promptly.

"Wrong—you mean U.S.? No, you're wrong. I'm a private detective who makes a hobby of studying the criminal classes—will you come up and have a drink?"

"I will come up, but I won't drink," said Elk virtuously, "not if you offer gin and orange. That visit to the United States has spoilt my digestion."

Broad was fitting a key in the lock of his flat, when a strange cold sensation ran down the spine of the detective, and he laid his hand on the American's arm.

"Don't open that door," he said huskily.

Broad looked round in surprise. The yard man's face was tense and drawn.

"Why not?"

"I don't know . . . just a feeling, that's all. I'm Scot by birth . . . we've got a word 'fey,' which means something supernatural. And it says inside me, 'don't open that door.'"

Broad put down his hand.

"Are you being fey or funny?" he asked.

"If I look funny," said Elk, "I'm entitled to sue my face for libel. There's something at the other side of that door that isn't good. I'll take an oath on it! Give me that!"

He took the key from the unwilling hand of Joshua Broad, thrust it in the lock and turned it. Then, with a quick push, he threw open the door, pushing Broad to the cover of the wall.

Nothing happened for a second, and then:

"Run!" cried Elk, and leapt for the stairs.

The American saw the first large billow of greenish-yellowy mist that rolled from the open door, and followed.

The hall-porter was closing his office for the night when Elk appeared, hatless and breathless.

"Can you 'phone the flats?—good! Get on at once to every one on and below the third floor, and tell them on no account to open their doors. Tell 'em to close all cracks with paper, to stop up their letter-boxes, and open all windows. Don't argue—do it! The building is full of poison gas!"

He himself 'phoned the fire station, and in a few seconds the jangle of bells sounded in the street outside, and men in gas-masks were clattering up the stairs.

Fortunately, every tenant except Broad and his neighbour was out of town for the week-end.

"And Miss Bassano doesn't come in till early morning," said the porter.

It was daylight before the building was cleared by the aid of high-pressure air-hoses and chemical precipitants. Except that his silver was tarnished black, and every window glass and mirror covered with a yellow deposit, little harm had been done. A musty odour pervaded the flat in spite of the open windows, but later came the morning breeze to dispel the last trace of this malodorous souvenir of the attempt.

Together the two men made a search of the rooms to discover the manner in which the gas was introduced.

"Through that open fireplace," Elk pointed. "The gas is heavier than air, and could be poured down the chimney as easily as pouring water."

A search of the flat roof satisfied him that his theory was right. They found ten large glass cylinders and a long rope, to which a wicker cradle was attached. Moreover, one of the chimney-pots (easily reached from the roof) was scratched and discoloured.

"The operator came into the building when the porter was busy—working the lift probably. He made his way to the roof, carrying the rope and the basket. Somebody in the street fixed the cylinders in the basket, which the man hauled to the roof one by one. It was dead easy, but ingenious. They must have made a pretty careful survey beforehand, or they wouldn't have known which chimney led to your room."

They returned to the flat, and for once Joshua Broad was serious.

"Fortunately, my servant is on a holiday," he said, "or he would have been in heaven!"

"I hope so," responded Elk piously.

The sun was tipping the roofs of the houses when he finally left, a sleepy and a baffled man. He heard the sound of boisterous voices before he reached the vestibule. A big car stood at the entrance of the flats, and, seated at the wheel, was a young man in evening dress. By him sat Lew Brady, and on the pavement was a girl in evening finery.

"A jolly evening, eh, Lola! When I get going, I'm a mover, eh?"

Ray Bennett's voice was thick and unsteady. He had been drinking—was within measurable distance of being drunk.

With a yell he recognized the detective as he came into the street.

"Why, it's old Elk—the Elk of Elks! Greetings, most noble copper! Lola, meet Elky of Elksburg, the Sherlock of Fact, the Sleuth——"

"Shut up!" hissed the savage-voiced Lew Brady in his ear, but Ray was in too exalted a mood to be silenced.

"Where's the priceless Gordon?—say, Elk, watch Gordon! Look after poor old Gordon—my sister's very much attached to Gordon."

"Fine car, Mr. Bennett," said Elk, regarding the machine thoughtfully. "Present from your father?"

The mention of his father's name seemed to sober the young man.

"No, it isn't," he snapped, "it belongs to a friend. 'Night, Lola." He pumped at the starter, missed picking up, and stamped again. "S'long, Elk!"

With a jerk the car started, and Elk watched it out of sight.

"That young fellow is certainly in danger of knocking his nut against the moon," he said. "Had a good time, Lola?"

"Yes—why?"

She fixed her suspicious eyes upon him expectantly.

"Didn't forget to turn off the gas when you went out, did you? If I was Shylock Holmes, maybe I'd tell from the stain on your glove that you didn't."

"What do you mean about gas? I never use the cooker."

"Somebody does, and he nearly cooked me and a friend of mine—nearly cooked us good!"

He saw her frown. Since she was a woman he expected her to be an actress, but somehow he was ready to believe in her sincerity.

"There's been a gas attack on Caverley House," he explained, "and not cooking gas either. I guess you'll smell it as you go up."

"What kind of gas—poison?"

Elk nodded.

"But who put it there—emptied it, or whatever is done with gas?"

Elk looked at her with that wounded expression which so justly irritated his victims.

"If I knew, Lola, would I be standing here discussing the matter? Maybe my old friend Shylock Holmes would, but I wouldn't. I don't know. It was upset in Mr. Broad's flat."

"That is the American who lives opposite to us—to me," she said. "I've only seen him once. He seems a nice man."

"Somebody didn't think so," said Elk. "I say, Lola, what's that boy doing—young Bennett?"

"Why do you ask me? He is making a lot of money just now, and I suppose he is running a little wild. They all do."

"I didn't," said Elk; "but if I'd made money and started something, I'd have chosen a better pacemaker than a dud fighting man."

The angry colour rose to her pretty face, and the glance she shot at him was as venomous as the gas he had fought all night.

"And I think I'd have put through a few enquiries to central office about my female acquaintances," Elk went on remorselessly. "I can understand why you're glued to the game, because money naturally attracts you. But what gets me is where the money comes from."

"That won't be the only thing that will get you," she said between her teeth as she flounced into the half-opened door of Caverley House.

Elk stood where she had left him, his melancholy face expressionless. For five minutes he stood so, and then walked slowly in the direction of his modest bachelor home.

He lived over a lock-up shop, a cigar store, and he was the sole occupant of the building. As he crossed Gray's Inn Road, he glanced idly up at the windows of his rooms and noted that they were closed. He noticed something more. Every pane of glass was misty with some yellow, opalescent substance.

Elk looked up and down the silent street, and at a short distance away saw where road repairers had been at work. The night watchman dozed before his fire, and did not hear Elk's approach or remark his unusual action. The detective found in a heap of gravel, three rounded pebbles, and these he took back with him. Standing in the centre of the road, he threw one of the pebbles unerringly.

There was a crash of glass as the window splintered. Elk waited, and presently he saw a yellow wraith of poison-vapour curl out and downward through the broken pane.

"This is getting monotonous," said Elk wearily, and walked to the nearest fire alarm.

CHAPTER VII

A CALL ON MR. MAITLAND

OUTWARDLY, John Bennett accepted his son's new life as a very natural development which might be expected in a young man. Inwardly he was uneasy, fearful. Ray was his only son; the pride of his life, though this he never showed. None knew better than John Bennett the snares that await the feet of independent youth in a great city. Worst of all, for his peace of mind, he knew Ray.

Ella did not discuss the matter with her father, but she guessed his trouble and made up her mind as to what action she would take.

The Sunday before, Ray had complained bitterly about the new cut to his salary. He had been desperate and had talked wildly of throwing up his work and finding a new place. And that possibility filled Ella with dismay. The Bennetts lived frugally on a very limited income. Apparently her father had few resources, though he always gave her the impression that from one of these he received a fairly comfortable income.

The cottage was Bennett's own property, and the cost of living was ridiculously cheap. A woman from the village came in every morning to do heavy work, and once a week to assist with the wash. That was the only luxury which her father's meagre allowance provided for. So that she faced the prospect of an out-of-work Ray with alarm and decided upon her line of action.

One morning Johnson, crossing the marble floor of Maitland's main office, saw a delicious figure come through the swing doors, and almost ran to meet it.

"My dear Miss Bennett, this is a wonderful surprise—Ray is out, but if you'll wait— —"

"I'm glad he is out," she said, relieved. "I want to see Mr. Maitland. Is it possible?"

The cheery face of the philosopher clouded.

"I'm afraid that will be difficult," he said. "The old man never sees people—even the biggest men in the City. He hates women and strangers, and although I've been with him all these years, I'm not so sure that he has got used to me! What is it about?"

She hesitated.

"It's about Ray's salary," and then, as he shook his head, she went on urgently: "It is so important, Mr. Johnson. Ray has extravagant tastes, and if they cut his salary it means—well, you know Ray so well!"

He nodded.

"I don't know whether I can do anything," he said dubiously. "I'll go up and ask Mr. Maitland, but I'm afraid that it is a million to one chance against his seeing you."

When he came back, the jovial face of Mr. Johnson was one broad smile.

"Come up before he changes his mind," he said, and led her to the lift. "You'll have to do all the talking, Miss Bennett—he's an eccentric old cuss and as hard as flint."

He showed her into a small and comfortably furnished room, and waved his hand to a writing-table littered with papers.

"My little den," he explained.

From the "den" a large rosewood door opened upon Mr. Maitland's office.

Johnson knocked softly, and, with a heart that beat a little faster, Ella was ushered into the presence of the strange old man who at that moment was dominating the money market.

The room was large, and the luxury of the fittings took her breath away. The walls were of rosewood inlaid with exquisite silver inlay. Light came from concealed lamps in the cornice as well as from the long stained-glass windows. Each article of furniture in the room was worth a fortune, and she guessed that the carpet, into which her feet sank, equalled in costliness the whole contents of an average house.

Behind a vast ormolu writing-table sat the great Maitland, bolt upright, watching her from under his shaggy white brows. A few stray hairs of his spotless beard rested on the desk, and as he raised his hand to sweep them into place, she saw he wore fingerless woollen gloves. His head was completely bald . . . she looked at his big ears, standing away from his head, fascinated. Patriarchal, yet repulsive. There was something gross, obscene, about him that hurt her. It was not the untidiness of his dress, it was not his years. Age brings refinement, that beauty of decay that the purists call caducity. This old man had grown old coarsely.

His scrutiny lacked the assurance she expected. It almost seemed that he was nervous, ill at ease. His gaze shifted from the girl to his secretary, and then to the rich colouring of the windows, and then furtively back to Ella again.

"This is Miss Bennett, sir. You remember that Bennett is our exchange clerk, and a very smart fellow indeed. Miss Bennett wants you to reconsider your decision about that salary cut."

"You see, Mr. Maitland," Ella broke in, "we're not particularly well off, and the reduction makes a whole lot of difference to us."

Mr. Maitland wagged his bald head impatiently.

"I don't care whether you're well off or not well off," he said loudly. "When I reduces salaries I reduces 'um, see?"

She stared at him in amazement. The voice was harsh and common. The language and tone were of the gutter. In that sentence he confirmed all her first impressions.

"If he don't like it he can go, and if you don't like it"—he fixed his dull eyes on the uncomfortable-looking Johnson—"you can go too. There's lots of fellers I can get—pick 'um up on the streets! Millions of 'um! That's all." Johnson tiptoed from the presence and closed the door behind her.

"He's a horror!" she gasped. "How can you endure contact with him, Mr. Johnson?"

The stout man smiled quietly.

"'Millions of 'um,'" he repeated, "and he's right. With a million and a half unemployed on the streets, I can't throw up a good job——"

"I'm sorry," she said, impulsively putting her hand on his arm. "I didn't know he was like that," she went on more mildly. "He's —terrible!"

"He's a self-made man, and perhaps he would have been well advised to have got an artisan to do the job," smiled Johnson, "but he's not really bad. I wonder why he saw you?"

"Doesn't he see people?"

He shook his head.

"Not unless it is absolutely necessary, and that only happens about twice a year. I don't think there is anybody in this building that he's ever spoken to—not even the managers."

He took her down to the general office. Ray had not come back.

"The truth is," confessed Johnson when she asked him, "that Ray hasn't been to the office this morning. He sent word to say that he wasn't feeling any too good, and I fixed it so that he has a day off."

"He's not ill?" she asked in alarm, but Johnson reassured her.

"No. I got on the telephone to him—he has a telephone at his new flat."

"I thought he had an ordinary apartment!" she said, aghast, the housewife in her perturbed. "A flat—where is it?"

"In Knightsbridge," replied Johnson quietly. "Yes, it sounds expensive, but I believe he has a bargain. A man who was going abroad sub-let it to him for a song. I suppose he wrote to you from the lodgings in Bloomsbury where he intended going. May I be candid, Miss Bennett?"

"If it is about Ray, I wish you would," she answered quickly.

"Ray is rather worrying me," said Johnson. "Naturally I want to do all that I can for him, for I am fond of him. At present my job is covering up his rather frequent absences from the office—you need not mention this fact to him—but it is rather a strain, for the old man has an uncanny instinct for a shirker. He is living in better style than he ought to be able to afford, and I've seen him dressed to kill with some of the swellest people in town—at least, they looked swell."

The girl felt herself go cold, and the vague unrest in her mind became instantly a panic.

"There isn't . . . anything wrong at the office?" she asked anxiously.

"No. I took the liberty of going through his books. They're square. His cash account is right to a centimo. Crudely stated, he isn't stealing—at least, not from us. There's another thing. He calls himself Raymond Lester at Knightsbridge. I found this out by accident, and asked him why he had taken another name. His explanation was fairly plausible. He didn't want Mr. Bennett to hear that he was cutting a shine. He has some profitable outside work, but he won't tell me what it is."

Ella was glad to get away, glad to reach the seclusion which the wide spaces of the park afforded. She must think and decide upon the course she would take. Ray was not the kind of boy to accept the draconic attitude, either in her or in John Bennett. His father must not know—she must appeal to Ray. Perhaps it was true that he had found a remunerative sideline. Lots of young men ran spare time work with profit to themselves—only Ray was not a worker.

She sat down on a park chair to wrestle with the problem, and so intent was she upon its solution that she did not realize that somebody had stopped before her.

"This is a miracle!" said a laughing voice, and she looked up into the blue eyes of Dick Gordon. "And now you can tell me what is the difficulty?" he asked as he pulled another chair toward her and sat down.

"Difficulty . . . who . . . who said I was in difficulties?" she countered.

"Your face is the traitor," he smiled. "Forgive this attire. I have been to make an official call at the United States Embassy."

She noticed for the first time that he wore the punctilious costume of officialdom, the well-fitting tail-coat, the polished top-hat and regulation cravat. She observed first of all that he looked very well in them, and that he seemed even younger.

"I have an idea it is your brother," he said. "I saw him a few minutes ago—there he is now."

She followed the direction of his eyes, and half rose from her chair in her astonishment. Riding on the tan track which ran parallel to the park road, were a man and a girl. The man was Ray. He was smartly dressed, and from the toes of his polished riding-boots to the crown of his grey hat, was all that was creditable to expensive tailoring. The girl at his side was young, pretty, petite.

The riders passed without Ray noticing the interested spectators. He was in his gayest mood, and the sound of his laughter came back to the dumbfounded girl.

"But . . . I don't understand—do you know the lady, Mr. Gordon?"

"Very well by repute," said Dick drily. "Her name is Lola Bassano."

"Is she—a lady?"

Dick's eyes twinkled.

"Elk says she's not, but Elk is prejudiced. She has money and education and breed. Whether or not these three assets are sufficient to constitute a lady, I don't know. Elk says not, but, as I say, Elk is considerably prejudiced."

She sat silent, her mind in a whirl.

"I have an idea that you want help . . . about your brother," said Dick quietly. "He is frightening you, isn't he?"

She nodded.

"I thought so. He is puzzling *me*. I know all about him, his salary and prospects and his queer masquerade under an *alias*. I'm not troubling about that, because boys love those kinds of mysteries. Unfortunately, they are expensive mysteries, and I want to know how he can afford to keep up this suddenly acquired position."

He mentioned a sum and she gasped.

"It costs all that," said Dick. "Elk, who has a passion for exact detail, and who knows to a penny what the riding suit costs, supplied me with particulars."

She interrupted him with such a gesture of despair that he felt a brute.

"What can I do . . . what can I do?" she asked. "Everybody wants to help—you, Mr. Johnson, and, I'm sure, Mr. Elk. But he is impossible—Ray, I mean. It will be fighting a feather bed. It may seem absurd to you, so much fuss over Ray's foolish escapade, but it means, oh, so much to us, father and me!"

Dick said nothing. It was too delicate a matter for an outsider to intrude upon. But the real delicacy of the situation was comprised in the boy's riding companion. As though guessing his thoughts, she asked suddenly:

"Is she a nice girl—Miss Bassano? I mean, is she one whom Ray should know?"

"She is very charming," he answered after a pause, and she noted the evasion and carried the subject no farther. Presently she turned the talk to her call on Ezra Maitland, and he heard her description without expressing surprise.

"He's a rough diamond," he said. "Elk knows something about him which he refuses to tell. Elk enjoys mystifying his chiefs even more than detecting criminals. But I've heard about Maitland from other sources."

"Why does he wear gloves in the office?" she asked unexpectedly.

"Gloves—I didn't know that," he said, surprised. "Why shouldn't he?"

She shook her head.

"I don't know . . . it was a silly idea, but I thought—it has only occurred to me since . . ."

He waited.

"When he put up his hand to smooth his beard, I'm almost sure I saw a tattoo mark on his left wrist—just the edge of it showing above the end of the glove—the head and eyes of a frog."

Dick Gordon listened, thunderstruck.

"Are you sure it wasn't your imagination, Miss Bennett?" he asked. "I am afraid the Frog is getting on all our nerves."

"It may have been," she nodded; "but I was within a few feet of him, and a patch of light, reflected from his blotter, caught the wrist for a second."

"Did you speak to Johnson about it?"

She shook her head.

"I thought afterwards that even he, with all his long years of service, might not have observed the tattoo mark. I remember now that Ray told me Mr. Maitland always wore gloves, summer or winter."

Dick was puzzled. It was unlikely that this man, the head of a great financial corporation, should be associated with a gang of tramps. And yet— —

"When is your brother going to Horsham?" he asked.

"On Sunday," said the girl. "He has promised father to come to lunch."

"I suppose," said the cunning young man, "that it isn't possible to ask me to be a fourth?"

"You will be a fifth," she smiled. "Mr. Johnson is coming down too. Poor Mr. Johnson is scared of father, and I think the fear is mutual. Father resembles Maitland in that respect, that he does not like strangers. I'll invite you anyway," she said, and the prospect of the Sunday meeting cheered her.

Elk came to see him that night, just as he was going out to a theatre, and Dick related the girl's suspicion. To his surprise, Elk took the startling theory very coolly.

"It's possible," he said, "but it's more likely that the tattoo mark isn't a frog at all. Old Maitland was a seaman as a boy—at least, that is what the only biography of him in existence says. It's a half-column that appeared in a London newspaper about twelve years ago, when he bought up Lord Meister's place on the Embankment and began to enlarge his offices. I'll tell you this, Mr. Gordon, that I'm quite prepared to believe anything of old Maitland."

"Why?" asked Dick in astonishment. He knew nothing of the discoveries which the detective had made.

"Because I just should," said Elk. "Men who make millions are not ordinary. If they were ordinary they wouldn't be millionaires. I'll inquire about that tattoo mark."

Dick's attention was diverted from the Frogs that week by an unusual circumstance. On the Tuesday he was sent for by the Foreign Minister's secretary, and, to his surprise, he was received personally by the august head of that department. The reason for this signal honour was disclosed.

"Captain Gordon," said the Minister, "I am expecting from France the draft commercial treaty that is to be signed as between ourselves and the French and Italian Governments. It is very important that this document should be well guarded because—

and I tell you this in confidence—it deals with a revision of tariff rates. I won't compromise you by telling you in what manner the revisions are applied, but it is essential that the King's Messenger who is bringing the treaty should be well guarded, and I wish to supplement the ordinary police protection by sending you to Dover to meet him. It is a little outside your duties, but your Intelligence work during the war must be my excuse for saddling you with this responsibility. Three members of the French and Italian secret police will accompany him to Dover, when you and your men will take on the guard duty, and remain until you personally see the document deposited in my own safe."

Like many other important duties, this proved to be wholly unexciting. The Messenger was picked up on the quay at Dover, shepherded into a Pullman coupé which had been reserved for him, and the passage-way outside the coupé was patrolled by two men from Scotland Yard. At Victoria a car, driven by a chauffeur-policeman and guarded by armed men, picked up the Messenger and Dick, and drove them to Calden Gardens. In his library the Foreign Secretary examined the seals carefully, and then, in the presence of Dick and the Detective-Inspector who had commanded the escort, placed the envelope in the safe.

"I don't suppose for one moment," said the Foreign Minister with a smile, after all the visitors but Dick had departed, "that our friends the Frogs are greatly interested. Yet, curiously enough, I had them in my mind, and this was responsible for the extraordinary precautions we have taken. There is, I suppose, no further clue in the Genter murder?"

"None, sir—so far as I know. Domestic crime isn't really in my department. And any kind of crime does not come to the Public Prosecutor until the case against an accused person is ready to be presented."

"It is a pity," said Lord Farmley. "I could wish that the matter of the Frogs was not entirely in the hands of Scotland Yard. It is so out of the ordinary, and such a menace to society, that I should feel more happy if some extra department were controlling the investigations."

Dick Gordon might have said that he was itching to assume that control, but he refrained. His lordship fingered his shaven chin thoughtfully. He was an austere man of sixty, delicately featured, as delicately wrinkled, the product of that subtle school of diplomacy which is at once urbane and ruthless, which slays with a bow, and is never quite so dangerous as when it is most polite.

"I will speak to the Prime Minister," he said. "Will you dine with me, Captain Gordon?"

Early in the next afternoon, Dick Gordon was summoned to Downing Street, and was informed that a special department had been created to deal exclusively with this social menace.

"You have *carte blanche*, Captain Gordon. I may be criticized for giving you this appointment, but I am perfectly satisfied that I have the right man," said the Prime Minister; "and you may employ any officer from Scotland Yard you wish."

"I'll take Sergeant Elk," said Dick promptly, and the Prime Minister looked dubious.

"That is not a very high rank," he demurred.

"He is a man with thirty years' service," said Dick; "and I believe that only his failure in the educational test has stopped his further promotion. Let me have him, sir, and give him the temporary rank of Inspector."

The older man laughed.

"Have it your own way," he said.

Sergeant Elk, lounging in to report progress that afternoon, was greeted by a new title. For a while he was dazed, and then a slow smile dawned on his homely face.

"I'll bet I'm the only inspector in England who doesn't know where Queen Elizabeth is buried!" he said, not without pride.

CHAPTER VIII

THE OFFENSIVE RAY

IT was perfectly absurd, Dick told himself a dozen times during the days which followed, that a grown man of his experience should punctiliously and solemnly strike from the calendar, one by one, the days which separated him from Sunday. A schoolboy might so behave, but it would have to be a very callow schoolboy. And a schoolboy might sit at his desk and dream away the time that might have been devoted to official correspondence.

A pretty face . . . ? Dick had admired many. A graciousness of carriage, an inspiring refinement of manner . . . ? He gave up the attempt to analyse the attraction which Ella Bennett held. All that he knew was, that he was waiting impatiently for Sunday.

When Dick opened the garden gate, he saw the plump figure of philosophical Johnson ensconced cosily in a garden chair. The secretary rose with a beaming smile and held out his hand. Dick liked the man. He stood for that patient class which, struggling under the stifling handicap of its own mediocrity, has its superlative virtue in loyalty and unremitting application to the task it finds at hand.

"Ray told me you were coming, Mr. Gordon—he is with Miss Bennett in the orchard, and from a casual view of him just now, he is hearing a few home truths. What do you make of it?"

"Has he given up coming to the office?" asked Dick, as he stripped his dust-coat.

"I am afraid he is out for good." Johnson's face was sad. "I had to tell him to go. The old man found out that he'd been staying away, and by some uncanny and underground system of intelligence he has learnt that Ray was going the pace. He had an accountant in to see the books, but thank heaven they were O.K.! I was very nearly fired myself."

This was an opportunity not to be missed.

"Do you know where Maitland lives—in what state? Has he a town house?"

Johnson smiled.

"Oh yes, he has a town house all right," he said sarcastically. "I only discovered where it was a year ago, and I've never told a single soul until now. And even now I won't give details. But old Maitland is living in some place that is nearly a slum—living meanly and horribly like an unemployed labourer! And he is worth millions! He has a cheap house in one of the suburbs, a place I wouldn't use to stable a cow! He and his sister live there; she looks after the place and does the housekeeping. I guess she has a soft job. I've never known Maitland to spend a penny on himself. I'm sure that he is wearing the suit he wore when I first came to him. He has a penny glass of milk and a penny roll for lunch, and tries to swindle me into paying for that, some days!"

"Tell me, Mr. Johnson, why does the old man wear gloves in the office?"

Johnson shook his head.

"I don't know. I used to think it was to hide the scar on the back of his hand, but he's not the kind of man to wear gloves for that. He is tattooed with crowns and anchors and dolphins all up his arms. . . ."

"And frogs?" asked Dick quietly, and the question seemed to surprise the other.

"No, I've never seen a frog. There's a bunch of snakes on one wrist—I've seen that. Why, old man Maitland wouldn't be a Frog, would he?" he asked, and Dick smiled at the anxiety in his tone.

"I wondered," he said.

Johnson's usually cheerful countenance was glum.

"I reckon he is mean enough to be a Frog or 'most anything," he said, and at that minute Ray and his sister came into view. On Ray's forehead sat a thundercloud, which deepened at the sight of Dick Gordon. The girl was flushed and obviously on the verge of tears.

"Hallo, Gordon!" the boy began without preliminary. "I fancy you're the fellow that has been carrying yarns to my sister. You set Elk to spy on me—I know, because I found Elk in the act ——"

"Ray, you're not to speak like that to Mr. Gordon," interrupted the girl hotly. "He has never told me anything to your discredit. All I know I have seen. You seem to forget that Mr. Gordon is father's guest."

"Everybody is fussing over me," Ray grumbled. "Even old Johnson!" He grinned sheepishly at the bald man, but Johnson did not return the smile.

"Somebody has got to worry about you, boy," he said.

The strained situation was only relieved when John Bennett, camera on back, came up the red path to greet his visitors.

"Why, Mr. Johnson, I owe you many apologies for putting you off, but I'm glad to see you here at last. How is Ray doing at the office?"

Johnson shot a helpless and pathetic glance at Dick.

"Er—fine, Mr. Bennett," he blurted.

So John Bennett was not to be told that his son had launched forth on a new career? The fact that he was fathering this deception made Dick Gordon a little uncomfortable. Apparently it reduced Mr. Johnson to despair, for when a somewhat tense luncheon had ended and they were alone again in the garden, that worthy man unburdened himself of his trouble.

"I feel that I'm playing it low on old Bennett," he said. "Ray should have told him."

Dick could only agree. He was in no mood to discuss Ray at the moment. The boy's annoyance and self-assurance irritated him, and it did not help matters to recognize the sudden and frank hostility which the brother of Ella Bennett was showing toward him. That was disconcerting, and emphasized his anomalous position in relation to the Bennetts. He was discovering what many young men in love have to discover: that the glamour which surrounds their dears does not extend to the relations and friends of their dears. He made yet another discovery. The plump Mr. Johnson was in love with the girl. He was nervous and incoherent in her presence; miserable when she went away. More miserable still when Dick boldly took her arm and led her into the rose-garden behind the house.

"I don't know why that fellow comes here," said Ray savagely as the two disappeared. "He isn't a man of our class, and he loathes me."

"I don't know that he loathes you, Ray," said Johnson, waking from the unhappy daydream into which he seemed to have fallen. "He's an extremely nice man——"

"Fiddlesticks!" said the other scornfully. "He's a snob! Anyway, he's a policemen, and I hate cops! If you imagine the he doesn't look good on you and me, you're wrong. I'm as good as he is, and I bet I'll make more money before I'm finished!"

"Money isn't everything," said Johnson tritely. "What work are you doing, Ray?"

It required a great effort on his part to bring his mind back to his friend's affairs.

"I can't tell you. It's very confidential," said Ray mysteriously. "I couldn't even tell Ella, though she's been jawing at me for hours. There are some jobs that a man can't speak about without betraying secrets that aren't his to tell. This is one of them."

Mr. Johnson said nothing. He was thinking of Ella and wondering how long it would be before her good-looking companion brought her back.

Good-looking and young. Mr. Johnson was not good-looking, and only just on the right side of fifty. And he was bald. But, worst of all, in her presence he was tongue-tied. He was rather amazed with himself.

In the seclusion of the rose-garden another member of the Bennett family was relating her fears to a more sympathetic audience.

"I feel that father guesses," she said. "He was out most of last night. I was awake when he came in, and he looked terrible. He said he had been walking about half the night, and by the mud on his boots I think he must have been."

Dick did not agree.

"Knowing very little about Mr. Bennett, I should hardly think he is the kind of man to suffer in silence where your brother is concerned," he said. "I could better imagine a most unholy row. Why has your brother become so unpleasant to me?"

She shook her head.

"I don't know. Ray has changed suddenly. This morning when he kissed me, his breath smelt of whisky—he never used to drink. This new life is ruining him—why should he take a false name if . . . if the work he is doing is quite straight?"

She had ceased addressing him as "Mr. Gordon." The compromise of calling him by no name at all was very pleasant to Dick Gordon, because he recognized that it *was* a compromise. The day was hot and the sky cloudless. Ella had made arrangements to serve tea on the lawn, and she found two eager helpers in Dick and Johnson, galvanized to radiant activity by the opportunity of assisting. The boy's attitude remained antagonistic, and after a few futile attempts to overcome this, Dick gave it up.

Even the presence of his father, who had kept aloof from the party all afternoon, brought no change for the better.

"The worst of being a policeman is that you're always on duty," he said during the meal. "I suppose you're storing every scrap of talk in your mind, in case you have to use it."

Dick folded a thin slice of bread and butter very deliberately before he replied.

"I have certainly a good memory," he said. "It helps me to forget. It also helps me keep silent in circumstances which are very difficult and trying."

Suddenly Ray spun round in his chair.

"I told you he was on duty!" he cried triumphantly. "Look! There's the chief of the spy corps! The faithful Elk!"

Dick looked in astonishment. He had left Elk on the point of going north to follow up a new Frog clue that had come to light. And there he was, his hands resting on the gate, his chin on his chest, gazing mournfully over his glasses at the group.

"Can I come in, Mr. Bennett?"

John Bennett, alert and watchful, beckoned.

"Happened to be round about here, so I thought I'd call. Good afternoon, miss—good afternoon, Mr. Johnson."

"Give Sergeant Elk your chair," growled John Bennett, and his son rose with a scowl.

"Inspector," said Elk. "No, I'd rather stand, mister. Stand and grow good, eh? Yes, I'm Inspector. I don't realize it myself sometimes, especially when the men salute me—forget to salute 'em back. Now, in America I believe patrol men salute sergeants. That's as it should be."

His sad eyes moved from one to the other.

"I suppose your promotion has made a lot of crooks very scared, Elk?" sneered Ray.

"Why, yes. I believe it has. Especially the amatchoors," said Elk. "The crooks that are only fly-nuts. The fancy crooks, who think they know it all, and will go on thinking so till one day somebody says, 'Get your hat—the chief wants you!' Otherwise," confessed Elk modestly, "the news has created no sensation, and London is just as full as ever of tale-pitchers who'll let you distribute their money amongst the poor if you'll only loan 'em a hundred to prove your confidence. And," Elk continued after a moment's cogitation, "there's nearly as many dud prize-fighters living on blackmail an' robbery, an' almost as many beautiful young ladies running faro parlours and dance emporiums."

Ray's face went a dull red, and if looks could blast, Inspector Elk's friends would have been speaking of him in hushed tones.

Only then did he turn his attention to Dick Gordon.

"I was wondering, Captain, if I could have a day off next week—I've a little family trouble."

Dick, who did not even know that his friend had a family was startled.

"I'm sorry to hear that, Elk," he said sympathetically.

Elk sighed.

"It's hard on me," he said, "but I feel I ought to tell you, if you'll excuse me, Miss Bennett?"

Dick rose and followed the detective to the gate, and then Elk spoke in a low tone.

"Lord Farmley's house was burgled at one o'clock this morning, and the Frogs have got away with the draft treaty!"

Watching the two furtively, the girl saw nothing in Dick Gordon's demeanour to indicate that he had received any news which was of consequence to himself. He came slowly back to the table.

"I am afraid I must go," he said. "Elk's trouble is sufficiently important to take me back to town."

He saw the regret in Ella's eyes and was satisfied. The leave-taking was short, for it was very necessary that he should get back to town as quickly as his car could carry him.

On the journey Elk told all that he knew. Lord Farmley had spent the week-end in his town house. He was working on two new clauses which had been inserted on the private representation of the American ambassador, who, as usual, held a watching brief in the matter, but managed (also as usual) to secure the amendment of a clause dealing with transshipments that, had it remained unamended, would have proved detrimental to his country. All this Dick learnt later. He was unaware at the time that the embassy knew of the treaty's existence.

Lord Farmley had replaced the document in the safe, which was a "Cham" of the latest make, and built into the wall of his study, locked and double-locked the steel doors, switched on the burglar alarm, and went to bed.

He had no occasion to go to the safe until after lunch. To all appearances, the safe-doors had not been touched. After lunch, intending to work again on the treaty, he put his key in the lock, to discover that, when it turned, the wards met no resistance. He pulled at the handle. It came away in his hand. The safe was open in the sense that it was not locked, and the treaty, together with his notes and amendments, had gone.

"How did they get in?" asked Dick as the car whizzed furiously along the country road.

"Pantry window—butlers' pantries were invented by a burglar-architect," said Elk. "It's a real job—the finest bit of work I've seen in twenty years, and there are only two men in the world who could have done it. No finger-prints, no ugly holes blown into the safe, everything neat and beautifully done. It's a pleasure to see."

"I hope Lord Farmley has got as much satisfaction out of the workmanship as you have," said Dick grimly, and Elk sniffed.

"He wasn't laughing," he said, "at least, not when I came away."

His lordship was not laughing when Elk returned.

"This is terrible, Gordon—terrible! We're holding a Cabinet on the matter this evening; the Prime Minister has returned to town. This means political ruin for me."

"You think the Frogs are responsible?"

Lord Farmley's answer was to pull open the door of the safe. On the inside panel was a white imprint, an exact replica of that which Elk had seen on the door of Mr. Broad's flat. It was almost impossible for the non-expert to discover how the safe had been opened. It was Elk who showed the fine work that had extracted the handle and had enabled the thieves to shatter the lock by some powerful explosive which nobody in the house had heard.

"They used a silencer," said Elk. "It's just as easy to prevent gases escaping too quickly from a lock as it is from a gun barrel. I tell you, there are only two men who could have done this."

"Who are they?"

"Young Harry Lyme is one—he's been dead for years. And Saul Morris is the other—and Saul's dead too."

"As the work is obviously not that of two dead men, you would be well advised to think of a third," said his lordship, pardonably annoyed.

Elk shook his head slowly.

"There must be a third, and he's the cleverest of the lot," he said, speaking his thoughts aloud. "I know the lot—Wal Cormon, George the Rat, Billy Harp, Ike Velleco, Pheeny Moore—and I'll take an oath that it wasn't any of them. This is master work, my lord. It's the work of a great artist such as we seldom meet nowadays. And I fancy I know who he is."

Lord Farmley, who had listened as patiently as he could to this rhapsody, stalked from the library soon after, leaving the men alone.

"Captain," said Elk, walking after the peer and closing the door, "do you happen to know where old Bennett was last night?"

Elk's tone was careless, but Dick Gordon felt the underlying significance of the question, and for a moment, realizing all that lay behind the question, all that it meant to the girl, who was dearer to him than he had guessed, his breath came more quickly.

"He was out most of the night," he said. "Miss Bennett told me that he went away on Friday and did not return until this morning at daybreak. Why?"

Elk took a paper from his pocket, unfolded it slowly and adjusted his glasses.

"I've had a man keeping tag of Bennett's absences from home," he said slowly. "It was easy, because the woman who goes every morning to clean his house has a wonderful memory. He has been away fifteen times this past year, and every time he has gone there's been a first-class burglary committed somewhere!"

Dick drew a long breath.

"What are you suggesting?" he asked.

"I'm suggesting," replied Elk deliberately, "that if Bennett can't account for his movements on Saturday night, I'm going to pull him in. Saul Morris I've never met, nor young Wal Cormon either—they were before I did big work. But if my idea is right, Saul Morris isn't as dead as he ought to be. I'm going down to see Brother Bennett, and I think perhaps I'll be doing a bit of resurrecting!"

CHAPTER IX

THE MAN WHO WAS WRECKED

JOHN BENNETT was working in his garden in the early morning when Elk called, and the inspector came straight to the point.

"There was a burglary committed at the residence of Lord Farmley on Saturday night and Sunday morning. Probably between midnight and three o'clock. The safe was blown and important documents stolen. I'm asking you to account for your movements on Saturday night and Sunday morning."

Bennett looked the detective straight in the eyes.

"I was on the London road—I walked from town. At two o'clock I was speaking with a policeman in Dorking. At midnight I was in Kingbridge, and again I spoke to a policeman. Both these men know me because I frequently walk to Dorking and Kingbridge. The man at Dorking is an amateur photographer like myself."

Elk considered.

"I've a car here; suppose you come along and see these policemen?" he suggested, and to his surprise Bennett agreed at once.

At Dorking they discovered their man; he was just going off duty.

"Yes, Inspector, I remember Mr. Bennett speaking to me. We were discussing animal photography."

"You're sure of the time?"

"Absolutely. At two o'clock the patrol sergeant visits me, and he came up whilst we were talking."

The patrol sergeant, wakened from his morning sleep, confirmed this statement. The result of the Kingbridge inquiries produced the same results.

Elk ordered the driver of his car to return to Horsham.

"I'm not going to apologize to you, Bennett," he said, "and you know enough about my work to appreciate my position."

"I'm not complaining," said Bennett gruffly. "Duty is duty. But I'm entitled to know why you suspect me of all men in the world."

Elk tapped the window of the car and it stopped.

"Walk along the road: I can talk better," he said.

They got out and went some distance without speaking.

"Bennett, you're under suspicion for two reasons. You're a mystery man in the sense that nobody knows how you get a living. You haven't an income of your own. You haven't an occupation, and at odd intervals you disappear from home and nobody knows where you go. If you were a younger man I'd suspect a double life in the usual sense. But you're not that kind. That is suspicious circumstance Number One. Here is Number Two. Every time you disappear there's a big burglary somewhere. And I've an idea it's a Frog steal. I'll give you my theory. These Frogs are mostly dirt. There isn't enough brain in the whole outfit to fill an average nut—I'm talking about the mass of 'em. There are clever men higher up, I grant. But they don't include the regular fellows who make a living from crime. These boys haven't any time for such nonsense. They plan a job and pull it off, or they get pinched. If they make a getaway, they divide up the stuff and sit around in cafés with girls till all the stuff is gone, and then they go out for some more. But the Frogs are willing to pay good men who are outside the organization for extra work."

"And you suggest that I may be one of the 'good men'?" said Bennett.

"That's just what I am suggesting. This Frog job at Lord Farmley's was done by an expert—it looks like Saul Morris."

His keen eyes were focused upon Bennett's face, but not by so much as a flicker of an eyelash did he betray his thoughts.

"I remember Saul Morris," said Bennett slowly. "I've never seen him, but I've heard of his work. Was he—anything like me?"

Elk pursed his lips, his chin went nearer to his chest, and his gaze became more and more intensified.

"If you know anything about Saul Morris," he said slowly, "you also know that he was never in the hands of the police, that nobody except his own gang ever saw him, so as to be able to recognize him again."

Another silence.

"I wasn't aware of that," said Bennett.

On the way back to the car, Bennett spoke again.

"I bear no malice. My movements are suspicious, but there is a good reason. As to the burglaries—I know nothing about them. I should say that in any case, whether I knew or not. I ask you not to mention this matter to my daughter, because—well, you don't want me to tell you why."

Ella was standing at the garden gate when the car came up, and at the sight of Elk the smile left her face. Elk knew instinctively that the thought of her brother, and the possibility of his being in trouble, were the causes of her apprehension.

"Mr. Elk came down to ask me a few questions about the attack on Mr. Gordon," said her father briefly.

Whatever else he was, thought Elk, he was a poor and unconvincing liar. That the girl was not convinced, he was sure. When they were alone she asked:

"Is anything wrong, Mr. Elk?"

"Nothing, miss. Just come down to refresh my memory—which was never a good one, especially in the matter of dates. The only date I really remember is the landing of William the Conqueror—1140 or thereabouts. Brother gone back to town?"

"He went last night," she said, and then, almost defiantly: "He is in a good position now, Mr. Elk."

"So they tell me," said Elk. "I wish he wasn't working in the same shop as the bunch who are with him. I'm not letting him out of my sight. Miss Bennett," he said in a kinder tone. "Perhaps I'll be able to slip in the right word one of these days. He wouldn't listen now if I said 'get!'—he's naturally in the condition of mind when he's making up press cuttings about himself. And in a way he's right. If you don't know it all at twenty-one you never will. What's that word that begins with a 'z'?—'zenith,' that's it. He's at the zenith of his sure-and-certainness. From now on he'll start unloading his cargo of dreams an' take in ballast. But he'll hate to hear the derricks at work."

"You talk like a sailor," she smiled in spite of her trouble.

"I was that once," said Elk, "the same as old man Maitland—though I've never sailed with him—I guess he left the sea years before I was born. Like him?"

"Mr. Maitland? No!" she shivered. "I think he is a terrible man."

Elk did not disagree.

To Dick Gordon that morning he confessed his error.

"I don't know why I jumped at Bennett," he said. "I'm getting young! I see the evening newspapers have got the burglary."

"But they do not know what was stolen," said Dick in a low voice. "That must be kept secret."

They were in the inner bureau, which Dick occupied temporarily. Two men were at work in his larger office replacing a panel which had been shattered by the bullet which had been fired at him on the morning Elk came into the case, and it was symptomatic of the effect that the Frogs had had upon headquarters that both men had almost mechanically scrutinized the left arms of the workmen. The sight of the damaged panel switched Elk's thoughts to a matter which he had intended raising before—the identity of the tramp Carlo. In spite of the precautions Gordon had taken, and although the man was under observation, Carlo had vanished, and the combined efforts of headquarters and the country offices had failed to locate him. It was a sore point with Gordon, as Elk had reason to know.

For Carlo was the reputable "Number Seven," the most important man in the organization after the Frog himself.

"I'd like to see this Carlo," he said thoughtfully. "There's not much use in putting another man out on the road to follow up Genter's work. That system doesn't work twice. I wonder how much Lola knows?"

"Of the Frogs? They wouldn't trust a woman," said Dick. "She may work for them, but, as you said, it is likely they bring in outsiders for special jobs and pay them well."

Elk did not carry the matter any further, and spent the rest of the day in making fruitless inquiries. Returning to his room at headquarters that night, he sat for a long time hunched up in his chair, his hands thrust into his trousers pockets, staring down at the blotting-pad. Then he pressed a bell, and his clerk, Balder, came.

"Go to Records, get me all that is known about every safe-breaker known in this country. You needn't worry about the German and French, but there's a Swede or two who are mighty clever with the lamp, and of course there are the Americans."

They came after a long interval—a considerable pile of papers, photographs and finger-prints.

"You can go, Balder—the night man can take them back." He settled himself down to an enjoyable night's reading.

He was nearing the end of the pile when he came to the portrait of a young man with a drooping moustache and a bush of curly hair. It was one of those sharp positives that unromantic police officials take, and showed whatever imperfections of skin there were. Beneath the photograph was the name, carefully printed: "Henry John Lyme, R.V."

"R.V." was the prison code. Every year from 1874 to 1899 was indicated by a capital letter in the alphabet. Thereafter ran the small letters. The "R" meant that Henry J. Lyme had been sentenced to penal servitude in 1891. The "V" that he had suffered a further term of convict imprisonment in 1895.

Elk read the short and terrible record. Born in Guernsey in 1873, the man had been six times convicted before he was twenty (the minor convictions are not designated by letters in the code). In the space at the foot of the blank in which particulars were given of his crime, were the words:

"Dangerous; carries firearms." In another hand, and in the red ink which is used to close a criminal career, was written: "Died at sea. *Channel Queen*. Black Rock. Feb. 1, 1898."

Elk remembered the wreck of the Guernsey mail packet on the Black Rocks.

He turned back the page to read particulars of the dead man's crimes, and the comments of those who from time to time had been brought into official contact with him. In these scraps of description was the real biography. "Works alone," was one comment, and another; "No women clue—women never seen with him." A third scrawl was difficult to decipher, but when Elk mastered the evil writing, he half rose from the chair in his excitement. It was:

"Add to body marks in general D.C.P. 14 frog tattooed left wrist. New. J. J. M."

The date against which this was written was the date of the man's last conviction. Elk turned up the printed blank "D.C.P.14" and found it to be a form headed "Description of Convicted Person." The number was the classification. There was no mention of tattooed frogs: somebody had been careless. Word by word he read the description:

"Henry John Lyme, *a*. Young Harry, *a*. Thomas Martin, *a*. Boy Peace, *a*. Boy Harry (there were five lines of aliases). Burglar (dangerous; carries firearms). Height 5 ft. 6 in. Chest 38. Complexion fresh, eyes grey, teeth good, mouth regular, dimple in chin. Nose straight. Hair brown, wavy, worn long. Face round. Moustache drooping; wears side-whiskers. Feet and hands normal. Little toe left foot amputated first joint owing to accident, H.M. Prison, Portland. Speaks well, writes good hand. Hobbies none. Smokes cigarettes. Poses as public official, tax collector, sanitary inspector, gas or water man. Speaks French and Italian fluently. Never drinks; plays cards but no gambler. Favourite hiding place, Rome or Milan. No conviction abroad. No relations. Excellent organizer. Immediately after crime, look for him at good hotel in Midlands or working to Hull for the Dutch or Scandinavian boats. Has been known to visit Guernsey. . . ."

Here followed the Bertillon measurements and body marks—this was in the days before the introduction of the finger-print system. But there was no mention of the Frog on the left wrist. Elk dropped his pen in the ink and wrote in the missing data. Underneath he added:

"This man may still be alive," and signed his initials.

CHAPTER X

ON HARLEY TERRACE

SO writing, the telephone buzzed, and in his unflurried way he finished his entry and blotted it before he took up the instrument.

"Captain Gordon wishes you to take the first taxi you can find and come to his house—the matter is very urgent," said a voice. "I am speaking from Harley Terrace."

"All right." Elk found his hat and umbrella, stopped long enough to return the records to their home, and went out into the dark courtyard.

There are two entrances to Scotland Yard: one that opens into Whitehall and was by far the best route for him, since Whitehall is filled with cabs; the other on to the Thames Embankment, which, in addition to offering the longest way round, would bring him to a thoroughfare where, at this hour of the night, taxis would be few and far between. So engrossed was Elk with his thoughts that he was on the Embankment before he realized where he was going. He turned toward the Houses of Parliament into Bridge Street, found an ancient cab and gave the address. The driver was elderly and probably a little fuddled, for, instead of stopping at No. 273, he overshot the mark by a dozen houses, and only stopped at all on the vitriolic representations of his fare.

"What's the matter with you, Noah?—this ain't Mount Ararat!" snapped Elk as he descended. "You're boozed, you poor fish."

"Wish I was," murmured the driver, holding out his hand for the fare.

Elk would have argued the matter but for the urgency of the summons. Whilst he was waiting for the driver to unbutton his many coats to find change, he glanced back along the street. A car was standing near the door of Dick Gordon's house, its headlights dimmed to the least possible degree. That in itself was not remarkable. The two men who waited on the pavement were.

They stood with their backs to the railings, one (as he guessed) on either side of the door. To him came the soft purring of the motor-car's engine. He took a step back and brought the opposite pavement into his range of vision. There were two other men, also lounging idly, and they were exactly opposite 273.

Elk looked round. The cab had stopped before a doctor's house, and the detective did not take a long time to make up his mind.

"Wait till I come out."

"Don't be long," pleaded the aged driver. "The bars will be shut in a quarter of an hour."

"Wait, Batchus," said Elk, who had a nodding acquaintance with ancient mythology, but only a hazy idea of pronunciation. Bacchus growled, but waited.

Fortunately, the doctor was at home, and to him Elk revealed his identity. In a few seconds he was connected with Mary Lane Police Station.

"Elk, Central Office, speaking," he said rapidly, and gave his code number. "Send every man you can put your hand on, to close Harley Terrace north and south of 273. Stop all cars from the moment you get my signal—two long two short flashes. How soon can your men be in place?"

"In five minutes, Mr. Elk. The night reliefs are parading, and I have a couple of motor-trucks here—just pinched the drivers for being drunk."

He replaced the receiver and went into the hall.

"Anything wrong?" asked the startled doctor as Elk slid back the jacket of his automatic and pushed the safety catch into place.

"I hope so, sir," said Elk truthfully. "If I've turned out the division because a few innocent fellows are leaning against the railings of Harley Terrace, I'm going to get myself into trouble."

He waited five minutes, then opened the door and went out. The men were still in their positions, and as he stood there two motor-trucks drove into the thoroughfare from either end, turned broadside in the middle of the road and stopped.

Elk's pocket lamp flashed to left and right, and he jumped for the pavement.

And now he saw that his suspicions were justified. The men on the opposite pavement came across the road at the double, and leapt to the running-board of the car with the dim lights as it moved. Simultaneously the two who had been guarding the entrance of 273 sprang into the machine. But the fugitives were too late. The car swerved to avoid the blocking motor-truck, but even as it turned, the truck ran backwards. There was a crash, a sound of splintering glass, and by the time Elk arrived, the five occupants of the car were in the hands of the uniformed policemen who swarmed at the end of the street.

The prisoners accepted their capture without resistance. One (the chauffeur) who tried to throw away a revolver unobtrusively, was detected in the act and handcuffed, but the remainder gave no trouble.

At the police-station Elk had a view of his prisoners. Four very fine specimens of the genus tramp, wearing their new ready-to-wear suits awkwardly. The fifth, who gave a Russian name, and was obviously the driver, a little man with small, sharp eyes that glanced uneasily from face to face.

Two of the prisoners carried loaded revolvers; in the car they found four walking-sticks heavily weighted.

"Take off your coats and roll up your sleeves," commanded the inspector.

"You needn't trouble, Elk." It was the little chauffeur speaking. "All us boys are good Frogs."

"There ain't any good Frogs," said Elk. "There's only bad Frogs and worse Frogs and the worst Frog of all. But we won't argue. Let these men into their cells, sergeant, and keep them separate. I'll take Litnov to headquarters."

The chauffeur looked uneasily from Elk to the station sergeant.

"What's the great idea?" he asked. "You're not allowed to use the third degree in England."

"The law has been altered," said Elk ominously, and re-snapped the handcuffs on the man's wrists.

The law had not been altered, but this the little Russian did not know. Throughout the journey to headquarters he communed with himself, and when he was pushed into Elk's bare-looking room, he was prepared to talk. . . .

Dick was waiting for the detective when he came back to Harley Terrace, and heard the story.

"I never dreamt that it was a plant until I spotted the lads waiting for me," said Elk. "Of course you didn't telephone; they caught me napping there. Thorough! The Frogs are all that! They expected me to leave headquarters by the Whitehall entrance, and had a taxi waiting to pick me up, but in case they missed me that way, they told off a party to meet me in Harley Terrace. Thorough!"

"Who gave them their orders?"

Elk shrugged.

"Mr. Nobody. Litnov had his by post. It was signed 'Seven,' and gave him the rendezvous, and that was all. He says he has never seen a Frog since he was initiated. Where he was sworn in he doesn't remember. The car belongs to Frogs, and he receives so much a week for looking after it. Ordinarily he is employed by Heron's Club—drives a truck for them. He tells me that there are twenty other cars cached in London somewhere, just standing in their garages, and each has its own driver, who goes once a week to give it a clean up."

"Heron's Club—that is the dance club which Lola and Lew Brady are interested in!" said Dick thoughtfully, and Elk considered.

"I never thought of that. Of course, it doesn't mean that the management of Heron's know anything about Litnov's evening work. I'll look up that club."

He was saved the trouble, for the next morning, when he reached the office, he found a man waiting to see him.

"I'm Mr. Hagn, the manager of the Heron's Club," he introduced himself. "I understand one of my men has been in trouble."

Hagn was a tall, good-looking Swede who spoke without any trace of a foreign accent.

"How have you heard that, Mr. Hagn?" asked Elk suspiciously. "The man has been under lock and key since last night, and he hasn't held any communication with anybody."

Mr. Hagn smiled.

"You can't arrest people and take them to a police-station without somebody knowing all about it," he said with truth. "One of my waiters saw Litnov being taken to Mary Lane handcuffed, and as Litnov hasn't reported for duty this morning, there was only one conclusion to be drawn. What is the trouble, Mr. Elk?"

Elk shook his head.

"I can't give you any information on the matter," he said.

"Can I see him?"

"You can't even see him," said Elk. "He has slept well, and sends his love to all kind friends."

Mr. Hagn seemed distressed.

"Is it possible to discover where he put the key of the coal cellar?" he urged. "This is rather important to me. This man usually keeps it."

The detective hesitated.

"I can find out," he said, and, leaving Mr. Hagn under the watchful eyes of his secretary, he crossed the yard to the cells where the Russian was held.

Litnov rose from his plank bed as the cell door opened.

"Friend of yours called," said Elk. "Wants to know where you put the key of the coal cellar."

It was only the merest flicker of light and understanding that came to the little man's eyes, but Elk saw it.

"Tell him I believe I left it with the Wandsworth man," he said.

"Um!" said Elk, and went back to the waiting Hagn.

"He said he left it in the Pentonville Road," said Elk untruthfully, but Mr. Hagn seemed satisfied.

Returning to the cells, Elk saw the gaoler.

"Has this man asked you where he was to be taken from here?"

"Yes, sir," said the officer. "I told him he was going to Wandsworth Prison—we usually tell prisoners where they are going on remand, in case they wish to let their relatives know."

Elk had guessed right. The inquiry about the key was prearranged. A telephone message to Mary Lane, where the remainder of the gang were held, produced the curious information that a woman, reputedly the wife of one of the men, had called that morning, and, on being refused an interview, begged for news about the missing key of the coal cellar, and had been told that it was in the possession of "the Brixton man."

"The men are to be remitted to Wormwood Scrubbs Prison, and they are not to be told where they are going," ordered Elk.

That afternoon a horse-driven prison-van drew out of Cannon Row and rumbled along Whitehall. At the juncture of St. Martin's Lane and Shaftesbury Avenue, a carelessly-driven motor lorry smashed into its side, slicing off the near wheel. Instantly there came from nowhere a crowd of remarkable appearance. It seemed as if all the tramps in the world had been lying in wait to crowd about the crippled van. The door was wrenched open, and the gaoler on duty hauled forth. Before he could be handled, the van disgorged twenty Central Office men, and from the side streets came a score of mounted policemen, clubs in hand. The riot lasted less then three minutes. Some of the wild-looking men succeeded in making their escape, but the majority, chained in twos, went, meekly enough, between their mounted escorts.

Dick Gordon, who was also something of an organizer, watched the fight from the top of an omnibus, which, laden with policemen, had shadowed the van. He joined Elk after the excitement had subsided.

"Have you arrested anybody of importance?" he asked.

"It's too early to say," said Elk. "They look like ordinary tadpoles to me. I guess Litnov is in Wandsworth by now—I sent him in a closed police car before the van left."

Arrived at Scotland Yard, he paraded the Frogs in two open ranks, watched, at a distance, by the curious crowd which packed both entrances. One by one he examined their wrists, and in every case the tattoo mark was present.

He finished his scrutiny at last, and his captives were herded into an inner yard under an armed guard.

"One man wants to speak to you, sir."

The last file had disappeared when the officer in charge reported, and Elk exchanged a glance with his chief.

"See him," said Dick. "We can't afford to miss any information."

A policeman brought the Frog to them—a tall man with a week's growth of beard, poorly dressed and grimy. His battered hat was pulled down over his eyes, his powerful wrists visible beneath the sleeves of a jacket that was made for a smaller man.

"Well, Frog?" said Elk, glowering at him. "What's your croak?"

"Croak is a good word," said the man, and at the sound of his voice Elk stared. "You don't think that old police car of yours is going to reach Wandsworth, do you?"

"Who are you?" asked Elk, peering forward.

"They want Litnov badly," said the Frog. "They want to settle with him, and if the poor fish thinks it's brotherly love that makes old man Frog go to all this trouble, he's reserved a big jar for himself."

"Broad! What . . . !"

The American licked his finger and wiped away the frog from his wrist.

"I'll explain after, Mr. Elk, but take a friend's advice and call up Wandsworth."

Elk's telephone was buzzing furiously when he reached his office.

It was Wandsworth station calling.

"Your police car was held up on the Common, two of your men were wounded, and the prisoner was shot dead," was the report.

"Thank you!" said Elk bitterly.

CHAPTER XI

MR. BROAD EXPLAINS

DETAINED under police supervision, Mr. Broad did not seem in any way surprised or disconcerted. Dick Gordon and his assistant reached Wandsworth Common ten minutes after the news came through, and found the wreckage of the police car surrounded by a large crowd, kept at a distance by police.

The dead prisoner had been taken into the prison, together with one of the attackers, who had been captured by a party of warders, returning to the gaol after their luncheon hour.

A brief examination of Litnov told them no more than they knew. He had been shot through the heart, and death, must have been instantaneous.

The prisoner, brought from a cell, was a man of thirty and better educated than the average run of Frogs. No weapon had been found upon him and he protested his innocence of any complicity in the plot. According to his story, he was an out-of-work clerk who had been strolling across the Common when the ambush occurred. He had seen the fight, seen the second motor-car which carried the attackers away, and had been arrested whilst running in pursuit of the murderers.

His captors told a different story. The warder responsible for his arrest said that the man was on the point of boarding the car when the officer had thrown his truncheon at him and brought him down. The car was moving at the time, and the remainder of the party had not dared to stop and pick up their comrade. Most damning evidence of all was the tattoo mark on his wrist.

"Frog, you're a dead man," said Elk in his most sepulchral voice. "Where did you live when you were alive?"

The captive confessed that his home was in North London.

"North Londoners don't come to Wandsworth to walk on the Common," said Elk.

He had a conference with the chief warder, and, taking the prisoner into the courtyard, Elk spoke his mind.

"What happens to you if you spill the beans, Frog?" he asked.

The man showed his teeth in an unpleasant smile.

"The beans aren't grown that I can spill," he said.

Elk looked around. The courtyard was a small, stone-paved quadrangle, surrounded by high, discoloured walls. Against one of these was a little shed with grey sliding doors.

"Come here," said Elk.

He took the key that the chief warder had given him, unlocked the doors and slid them back. They were looking into a bare, clean apartment with whitewashed walls. Across the ceiling ran two stout oak beams, and between them three stubby steel bars.

The prisoner frowned as Elk walked to a long steel lever near one of the walls.

"Watch, Frog!" he said.

He pulled at the lever, and the centre of the floor divided and fell with a crash, revealing a deep, brick-lined pit.

"See that trap . . . see that 'T' mark in chalk? That's where a man puts his feet when the hangman straps his legs. The rope hangs from that beam, Frog!"

The man's face was livid as he shrank back.

"You . . . can't . . . hang—me," he breathed. "I've done nothing!"

"You've killed a man," said Elk as he pulled the doors to and locked them. "You're the only fellow we've got, and you'll have to suffer for the lot. Are them beans growin'?"

The prisoner raised his shaking hand to his lips.

"I'll tell you all I know," he said huskily.

Elk led him back to his cell.

An hour later, Dick was speeding back to his headquarters with considerable information. His first act was to send for Joshua Broad, and the eagle-faced "tramp" came cheerfully.

"Now, Mr. Broad, I'll have your story," said Dick, and motioned the other to be seated.

Joshua seated himself slowly.

"There's nothing much to tell," he said. "For a week I've been getting acquainted with the Frogs. I guessed that it was unlikely that the bulk of them would be unknown to one another, and I just froze on to the first I found. Met him in a Deptford lodging-house. Then I heard there was a hurry-up call for a big job to-day and joined. The Frogs knew that the real attack might be somewhere else, and on the way to Scotland Yard I heard that a party had been told off to watch for Litnov at Wandsworth."

"Did you see any of the big men?"

Broad shook his head.

"They looked all alike, but undoubtedly there were two or three section leaders in charge. There was never any question of rescuing. They were out to kill. They knew that Litnov had told all that he knew, and he was doomed—they got him, I suppose?"

"Yes—they got him!" said Dick, and then: "What is your interest in the Frogs?"

"Purely adventitious," replied the other lazily. "I'm a rich man with a whole lot of time on my hands, and I have a big interest in criminology. A few years ago I heard about the Frogs, and they seized on my imagination. Since then I've been trailing them."

His gaze did not waver under Dick Gordon's scrutiny.

"Now will you tell me," said Dick quietly, "how you became a rich man? In the latter days of the war you arrived in this country on a cattle-boat—with about twenty dollars in your pocket. You told Elk you had arrived by that method, and you spoke the truth. I've been almost as much interested in you as you have been in the Frogs," he said with a half-smile, "and I have been putting through a few inquiries. You came to England 1917 and deserted your ship. In May, 1917, you negotiated for the hire of an old tumbledown shack near Eastleigh, Hampshire. There you lived, patching up this crazy cottage and living, so far as I can discover, on the few dollars you brought from the ship. Then suddenly you disappeared, and were next seen in Paris on Christmas Eve of that year. You were conspicuous in rescuing a family that had been buried in a house bombed in an air raid, and your name was taken by the police with the idea of giving you some reward. The French police report is that you were 'very poorly dressed'—they thought you might be a deserter from the American Army. Yet in February you were staying at the Hôtel de

Paris in Monte Carlo, with plenty of money and an extensive wardrobe!"

Joshua Broad sat through the recital unmoved, except for the ghost of a smile which showed at the corner of his unshaven mouth.

"Surely, Captain, Monte Carlo is the place where a man *would* have money?"

"If he brought it there," said Dick, and went on: "I'm not suggesting that you are a bad character, or that your money came in any other way than honestly. I merely state the facts that your sudden rise from poverty to riches was, to say the least, remarkable."

"It surely was," agreed the other; "and, judging by appearances, my change from riches to poverty is as sudden."

Dick looked at the dirty-looking tramp who sat on the other side of the table and laughed silently.

"You mean, if it is possible for you to masquerade now, it was possible then, and that, even though you were apparently broke in 1917, you might very well have been a rich man?"

"Exactly," said Mr. Joshua Broad.

Gordon was serious again.

"I would prefer that you remained your more presentable self," he said. "I hate telling an American that I may have to deport him, because that sounds as if it is a punishment to return to the United States. But I may find myself with no other alternative."

Joshua Broad rose.

"That, Captain Gordon, is too broad for a hint and too kindly for a threat—henceforth, Joshua Broad is a respectable member of society. Maybe I'll take the Prince of Caux's house and entertain bims and be a modern Harun al Raschid. I've got to meet them somehow."

At the mention of that show house that had cost a king's ransom to build and a queen's dowry to furnish, Dick smiled.

"It isn't necessary you should advertise your respectability that way," he said. But Broad was not smiling.

"The only thing I ask is that you do not advise the police to withdraw my permits," he said.

Dick's eyebrows rose.

"Permits?"

"I carry two guns, and the time is coming when two won't be enough," said Mr. Broad. "And it is coming soon."

CHAPTER XII

THE EMBELLISHMENT OF MR. MAITLAND

THERE was a concert that night at the Queen's Hall, and the spacious auditorium was crowded to hear the summer recital of a great violinist. Dick Gordon, in the midst of an evening's work, remembered that he had reserved a seat. He felt fagged, baffled, inclined to hopelessness. A note from Lord Farmley had come to him, urging instant action to recover the lost commercial treaty. It was such a letter as a man, himself worried, would write without realizing that in so doing he was passing on his panic to those who it was very necessary should not be stampeded into precipitate action. It was a human letter, but not statesmanlike. Dick decided upon the concert.

He had finished dressing when he remembered that it was more than likely that the omniscient Frogs would know of his reservation. He must take the risk, if risk there was. He 'phoned to the garage where his own machine was housed and hired a closed car, and in ten minutes was one of two thousand people who were listening, entranced, to the master. In the interval he strolled out to the lobby to smoke, and almost the first person he saw was a Central Office man who avoided his eye. Another detective stood by the stairway leading to the bar, a third was smoking on the steps of the hall outside. But the sensation of the evening was not this evidence of Elk's foresight. The warning bell had sounded, and Dick was in the act of throwing away his cigarette, when a magnificent limousine drew up before the building, a smart footman alighted to open the door, and there stepped heavily to the pavement—Mr. Ezra Maitland!

Dick heard a gasp behind him, and turned his head to see Elk in the one and only dress suit he had ever possessed.

"Mother of Moses!" he said in an awed voice.

And there was reason for his astonishment. Not only was Mr. Maitland's equipage worthy of a reigning monarch, with its silver fittings, lacquered body and expensively uniformed servants, but the old man was wearing a dress suit of the latest fashion. His beard had been shortened a few inches, and across the spotless white waistcoat was stretched a heavy gold chain. On his hand many rings blazed and flashed in the light of the street standard. There was a camellia in his perfect lapel, and on his head the glossiest of silk hats. Leaning on a stick of ebony and ivory, he strutted across the pavement.

"Silk socks . . . patent leather shoes. My God! Look at his *rings*," hissed Elk.

His profanity was almost excusable. The vision of splendour passed through the doors into the hall.

"He's gone gay!" said Elk hollowly, and followed like a man in a dream.

From where he was placed, Dick had a good view of the millionaire. He sat throughout the second part of the programme with closed eyes, and so slow was he to start applauding after each item, that Dick was certain that he had been asleep and the clapping had awakened him.

Once he detected the old man stifling a yawn in the very midst of the second movement of Elgar's violin concerto, which held the audience spellbound by its delicate beauty. With his big hands, now enshrined in white kid gloves, crossed on his stomach, the head of Mr. Maitland nodded and jerked.

When at last the concert was over, he looked round fearfully, as though to make absolutely certain that it *was* over, then rose and made his way out of the hall, his silk hat held clumsily in his hand.

A manager came in haste to meet him.

"I hope, Mr. Maitland, you enjoyed yourself?" Dick heard him say.

"Very pooty—very pooty," replied Maitland hoarsely. "That fiddler ought to play a few toons, though—nothing like a hornpipe on a fiddle."

The manager looked after him open-mouthed, then hurried out to help the old man into his car.

"Gay—he's gay!" said Elk, as bewildered as the manager. "Jumping snakes! Who was that?"

He addressed the unnecessary question to the manager, who had returned from his duty.

"That is Maitland, the millionaire, Mr. Elk," said the other. "First time we've had him here, but now that he's come to live in town— —"

"Where is he living?" asked Elk.

"He has taken the Prince of Caux's house in Berkeley Square," said the manager.

Elk blinked at him.

"Say that again?"

"He has taken the Prince of Caux's house," said the manager. "And what is more, has bought it—the agent told me this afternoon."

Elk was incapable of comment, and the manager continued his surprising narrative.

"I don't think he knows much about music, but he has booked seats for every big musical event next season—his secretary came in this afternoon. He seemed a bit dazed."

Poor Johnson! thought Dick.

"He wanted me to fix dancing lessons for the old boy— —"

Elk clapped his hand to his mouth—he had an insane desire to scream.

"And as a matter of fact, I fixed them. He's a bit old, but Socrates or somebody learnt Greek at eighty, and maybe Mr. Maitland's regretting the wasted years of his life. I admit it is a bit late to start night clubs— —"

Elk laid a chiding hand upon the managerial shoulder.

"You certainly deceived me, brother," he said. "And here was I, drinking it all in, and you with a face as serious as the dial of a poorhouse clock! You've put it all over Elk, and I'm man enough to admit you fooled me."

"I don't think our friend is trying to fool you," said Dick quietly. "You really mean what you say—old Maitland has started dancing and night clubs?"

"Certainly!" said the other. "He hasn't started dancing, but that is where he has gone to-night—to the Heron's. I heard him tell the chauffeur."

It was incredible, but a little amusing—most amusing of all to see Elk's face.

The detective was frankly dumbfounded by the news.

"Heron's is my idea of a good finish to a happy evening," said Elk at last, drawing a long breath. He beckoned one of his escort. "How many man do you want to cover Heron's Club?" he asked.

"Six," was the prompt reply. "Ten to raid it, and twenty for a rough house."

"Get thirty!" said Elk emphatically.

Heron's from the exterior was an unpretentious building. But once under the curtained doors, and the character of its exterior was forgotten. A luxurious lounge, softly lit and heavily carpeted, led to the large saloon, which was at once restaurant and dance-hall.

Dick stood in the doorway awaiting the arrival of the manager, and admired the richness and subtle suggestion of cosiness which the room conveyed. The tables were set about an oblong square of polished flooring; from a gallery at the far end came the strain of a coloured orchestra; and on the floor itself a dozen couples swayed and glided in rhythm to the staccato melody.

"Gilded vice," said Elk disparagingly. "A regular haunt of sin and self-indulgence. I wonder what they charge for the food—there's Mathusalem."

"Mathusalem" was sitting, a conspicuous figure, at the most prominent table in the room. His polished head glistened in the light from the crystal candelabras, and in the shadow that it cast, his patriarchal beard so melted into the white of his snowy shirt front that for a moment Dick did not recognize him.

Before him was set a large glass mug filled with beer.

"He's human anyway," said Elk.

Hagn came at that moment, smiling, affable, willing to oblige.

"This is an unexpected pleasure, Captain," he said. "You want me to pass you in? Gentlemen, there is no necessity! Every police officer of rank is an honorary member of the club."

He bustled in, threading his way between the tables, and found them a vacant sofa in one of the alcoves. There were revellers whose faces showed alarm at the arrival of the new guests—one at least stole forth and did not come back.

"We have many notable people here to-night," said Hagn, rubbing his hands. "There are Lord and Lady Belfin" . . . he mentioned others; "and that gentleman with the beard is the great Maitland . . . his secretary is here somewhere. Poor gentleman, I fear he is not happy. But I invited him myself—it is sometimes desirable that we should elect the . . . what shall I say? . . . higher servants of important people?"

"Johnson?" asked Dick in surprise. "Where?"

Presently he saw that plump and philosophical man. He sat in a remote corner, looking awkward and miserable in his old-fashioned dress clothes. Before him was a glass which, Dick guessed, contained an orange squash.

A solemn, frightened figure he made, sitting on the edge of his chair, his big red hands resting on the table. Dick Gordon laughed softly and whispered to Elk:

"Go and get him!"

Elk, who was never self-conscious, walked through the dancers and reached Mr. Johnson, who looked up startled and shook hands with the vigour of one rescued from a desert island.

"It was good of you to ask me to come over," said Johnson, as he greeted Dick. "This is new to me, and I'm feeling about as much at home as a chicken in a pie."

"Your first visit?"

"And my last," said Johnson emphatically. "This isn't the kind of life that I care for. It interferes with my reading, and it—well, it's sad."

His eyes were fixed on a noisy little party in the opposite alcove. Gordon had seen them almost as soon as he had sat down. Ray, in his most hectic mood, Lola Bassano, beautifully and daringly gowned, and the heavy-looking ex-pugilist, Lew Brady.

Presently, with a sigh, Johnson's eyes roved toward the old man and remained fixed on him, fascinated.

"Isn't it a miracle?" he asked in a hushed voice. "He changes his habits in a day! Bought the house in Berkeley Square, called in an army of tailors, sent me rushing round to fix theatre seats, bought jewellery . . ."

He shook his head.

"I can't understand it," he confessed, "because it has made no difference to him in the office. He's the same old hog. He wanted me to become his resident secretary, but I struck at that. I must have some sort of life worth living. What scares me is that he may fire me if I don't agree. He's been very unpleasant this week. I wonder if Ray has seen him?"

Ray Bennett had not seen his late employer. He was too completely engrossed in the joy of being with Lola, too inspired and stimulated from more material sources, to take an interest in anything but himself and the immediate object of his affections.

"You are making a fool of yourself, Ray. Everybody is looking at you," warned Lola.

He glanced round, and for the first time began to notice who was in the room. Presently his eyes fell upon the shining pate of Mr. Maitland, and his jaw dropped. He could not believe the evidence of his vision, and, rising, walked unsteadily across the floor, shouldering the other guests, stumbling against chairs and tables, until he stood by the table of his late employer.

"Gosh!" he gasped. "It *is* you!"

The old man raised his eyes slowly from the cloth which he had been contemplating steadily for ten minutes, and his steely eyes met the gaze steadily.

"You hoary old sinner!" breathed Ray.

"Go away," snarled Mr. Maitland.

"'Go away,' is it? I'm going to talk to you and give you a few words of advice and warning, Moses!"

Ray sat down suddenly in a chair, and faced his glaring victim with drunken solemnity. His words of warning remained unuttered. Somebody gripped his arm and jerked him to his feet, and he looked into the dark face of Lew Brady.

"Here, what— —" he began. But Brady led him and pushed him back to his own table.

"You fool!" he hissed. "Why do you want to advertise yourself in this way? You're a hell of a Secret Service man!"

"I don't want any of that stuff from you," said Ray roughly as he jerked his arm free.

"Sit down, Ray," said Lola in a low voice. "Half Scotland Yard is in the club, watching you."

He followed the direction of her eyes and saw Dick Gordon regarding him gravely, and the sight and knowledge of that surveillance maddened him. Leaping to his feet, he crossed the room to where they sat.

"Looking for me?" he asked loudly. "Want me for anything?"

Dick shook his head.

"You damned police spy!" stormed the youth, white with unreasoning passion. "Bringing your bloodhounds after me! What are you doing with this gang, Johnson? Are you turned policeman too?"

"My dear Ray," murmured Johnson.

"My dear Ray!" sneered the other. "You're jealous, you poor worm—jealous because I've got away from the bloodsucker's clutches! As to you"—he waved a threatening finger in Dick's face—"you leave me alone—see? You've got a whole lot of work to do without carrying tales to my sister."

"I think you had better go back to your friends," said Dick coolly. "Or, better still, go home and sleep."

All this had occurred between the dances, and now the band struck up, but if the attention of the crowded clubroom was in no wise relaxed, there was this change, that Ray's high voice now did not rise above the efforts of the trap drummer.

Dick looked round for the watchful Hagn. He knew that the manager, or one of the officials of the club, would interfere instantly. It was not Hagn, but a head waiter, who came up and pushed the young man back.

So intent was everybody on that little scene that followed, in the spectacle of that flushed youth struggling against the steady pressure which the head waiter and his fellows asserted, that nobody saw the man who for a while stood in the doorway surveying the scene, before pushing aside the attendants he strode into the centre of the room.

Ray, looking round, was almost sobered by the sight of his father.

The rugged, grey-haired man, in his worn, tweed suit, made a striking contrast to that gaily-dressed throng. He stood, his hands behind him, his face white and set, surveying his son, and the boy's eyes dropped before him.

"I want you, Ray," he said simply.

The floor was deserted; the music ceased, as though the leader of the orchestra had been signalled that something was wrong.

"Come back with me to Horsham, boy."

"I'm not going," said Ray sullenly.

"He is not with you, Mr. Gordon?"

Dick shook his head, and at this intervention the fury of Ray Bennett flamed again.

"With him!" he said scornfully. "Would I be with a sneaking policeman?"

"Go with your father, Ray." It was Johnson's urgent advice, and his hand lay for a second on the boy's shoulder.

Ray shook him off.

"I'll stay here," he said, and his voice was loud and defiant. "I'm not a baby, that I can't be trusted out alone. You've no right to come here, making me look a fool." He glowered at his father. "You've kept me down all these years, denied me money that I ought to have had—and who are you that you should pretend to be shocked because I'm in a decent club, wearing decent clothes? I'm straight: can you say the same? If I wasn't straight, could you blame me? You're not going to put any of that kind father stuff over——"

"Come away." John Bennett's voice was hoarse.

"I'm staying here," said Ray violently. "And in future you can leave me alone. The break had to come some time, and it might as well come now."

They stood facing one another, father and son, and in the tired eyes of John Bennett was a look of infinite sadness.

"You're a silly boy, Ray. Perhaps I haven't done all I could ——"

"Perhaps!" sneered the other. "Why, you know it! You get out!"

And then, as he turned his head, he saw the suppressed smiles on the face of the audience, and the hurt to his vanity drove him mad.

"Come," said John gently, and laid his hand on the boy's arm.

With a roar of fury Ray broke loose . . . in a second the thing was done. The blow that struck John Bennett staggered him, but he did not fall.

And then, through the guests who thronged about the two, came Ella. She realized instantly what had happened. Elk had slipped from his seat and was standing behind the boy, ready to pin him if he raised his hand again. But Ray Bennett stood, frozen with horror, speechless, incapable of movement.

"Father!" The white-faced girl whispered the word.

The head of John Bennett dropped, and he suffered himself to be led away.

Dick Gordon wanted to follow and comfort, but he saw Johnson going after them and went back to his table. Again the music started, and they took Ray Bennett back to his table, where he sat, head on hand, till Lola signalled a waiter to bring more wine.

"There are times," said Elk, "when the prodigal son and the fatted calf look so like one another that you can't tell 'em apart."

Dick said nothing, but his heart bled for the mystery man of Horsham. For he had seen in John Bennett's face the agony of the damned.

CHAPTER XIII

A RAID ON ELDOR STREET

JOHNSON did not come back, and in many respects the two men were glad. Elk had been on the point of telling the secretary to clear, and he hoped that Mr. Maitland would follow his example. As if reading his thoughts, the old man rose soon after the room had quietened down. He had sat through the scene which had followed Ray's meeting with his father, and had apparently displayed not the slightest interest in the proceedings. It was as though his mind were so far away that he could not bring himself to a realization of actualities.

"He's going, and he hasn't paid his bill," whispered Elk.

In spite of his remissness, the aged millionaire was escorted to the door by the three chief waiters, his top-coat, silk hat and walking-stick were brought to him, and he was out of Dick Gordon's sight before the bowing servants had straightened themselves.

Elk looked at his watch: it wanted five minutes of one. Hagn had not returned—a circumstance which irritated the detective and was a source of uneasiness to Dick Gordon. The merriment again worked up to its highest point, when the two men rose from the table and strolled toward the door. A waiter came after them hurriedly.

"Monsieur has not paid his bill."

"We will pay that later," said Dick, and at that moment the hands of the clock pointed to the hour.

Precisely five minutes later the club was in the hands of the police. By 1.15 it was empty, save for the thirty raiding detectives and the staff.

"Where is Hagn?" Dick asked the chief waiter.

"He has gone home, monsieur," said the man sullenly. "He always goes home early."

"That's a lie," said Elk. "Show me to his room."

Hagn's office was in the basement, a part of the old mission hall that had remained untouched. They were shown to a large, windowless cubicle, comfortably furnished, which was Hagn's private bureau, but the man had disappeared. Whilst his subordinates were searching for the books and examining, sheet by sheet, the documents in the clerk's office, Elk made an examination of the room. In one corner was a small safe, upon which he put the police seal; and lying on a sofa in some disorder was a suit of clothes, evidently discarded in a hurry. Elk looked at them, carried them under the ceiling light, and examined them. It was the suit Hagn had been wearing when he had shown them to their seats.

"Bring in that head waiter," said Elk.

The head waiter either wouldn't or couldn't give information.

"Mr. Hagn always changes his clothes before he goes home," he said.

"Why did he go before the club was closed?"

The man shrugged his shoulders.

"I don't know anything about his private affairs," he said, and Elk dismissed him.

Against the wall was a dressing-table and a mirror, and on each side of the mirror stood a small table-lamp, which differed from other table-lamps in that it was not shaded. Elk turned the switch, and in the glaring light scrutinized the table. Presently he found two wisps of hair, and held them against the sleeve of his black coat. In the drawer he found a small bottle of spirit gum, and examined the brush. Then he picked up a little wastepaper basket and turned its contents upon the table. He found a few torn bills, business letters, a tradesman's advertisement, three charred cigarette ends, and some odd scraps of paper. One of these was covered with gum and stuck together.

"I reckon he wiped the brush on this," said Elk, and with some difficulty pulled the folded slip apart.

It was typewritten, and consisted of three lines:

"Urgent.   See Seven at E.S.2.   No raid.   Get M.'s statement. Urgent. F.1."

Dick took the paper from his subordinate's hand and read it.

"He's wrong about the no raid," he said. "E. S., of course, is Eldor Street, and two is either the number two or two o'clock."

"Who's 'M.'?" asked Elk, frowning.

"Obviously Mills—the man we caught at Wandsworth. He made a written statement, didn't he?"

"He has signed one," said Elk thoughtfully.

He turned the papers over, and after a while found what he was looking for—a small envelope. It was addressed in typewritten characters to "G. V. Hagn," and bore on the back the stamp of the District Messenger service.

The staff were still held by the police, and Elk sent for the doorkeeper.

"What time was this delivered?" he asked.

The man was an ex-soldier, the only one of the prisoners who seemed to feel his position.

"It came at about nine o'clock, sir," he said readily, and produced the letter-book in confirmation. "It was brought by a District Messenger boy," he explained unnecessarily.

"Does Mr. Hagn get many notes by District Messenger?"

"Very few, sir," said the doorkeeper, and added an anxious inquiry as to his own fate.

"You can go," said Elk. "Under escort," he added, "to your own home. You're not to communicate with anybody, or tell any of the servants here that I have made inquiries about this letter. Do you understand?"

"Yes, sir."

To make assurance doubly sure, Elk had called up exchange and placed a ban upon all 'phone communications. It was now a quarter to two, and, leaving half-a-dozen detectives in charge of the club, he got the remainder on to the car that had brought them, and, accompanied by Dick, went full speed for Tottenham.

Within a hundred yards of Eldor Street the car stopped and unloaded. The first essential was that whoever was meeting No. 7 in Eldor Street should not be warned of their approach. It was more than possible that Frog scouts would be watching at each end of the street.

"I don't know why they should," said Elk, when Dick put this possibility forward.

"I can give you one very excellent reason," said Dick quietly. "It is this: that the Frogs know all about your previous visit to Maitland's slum residence."

"What makes you think that?" asked Elk in surprise, but Dick did not enlighten him.

Sending the men round by circuitous routes, he went forward with Elk, and at the very corner of Eldor Street, Elk found that his chief's surmise was well founded. Under a lamp-post Elk saw the dim figure of a man standing, and instantly began an animated and raucous conversation concerning a mythical Mr. Brown. Realizing that this was intended for the watcher, Gordon joined in. The man under the lamp-post hesitated just a little too long. As they came abreast of him, Elk turned.

"Have you got a match?" he asked.

"No," growled the other, and the next instant was on the ground, with Elk's knee on his chest and the detective's bony hand around his throat.

"Shout, Frog, and I'll throttle you," hissed the detective ferociously.

There was no scuffle, no sound. The thing was done so quickly that, if there were other watchers in the street, they could not have known what had happened, or have received any warning from their comrade's fate. The man was in the hands of the following detective, gagged and handcuffed, and on his way to the police car, before he knew exactly what tornado had struck him.

"Do you mind if I sing?" said Elk as they turned into the street on the opposite side to that where Mr. Maitland's late residence was situated.

Without waiting permission Elk broke into song. His voice was thin and flat. As a singer, he was a miserable failure, and Dick Gordon had never in his life listened with so much patience to sounds more hideous. But there would be watchers at each end of the street, he thought, and soon saw that Elk's precautions were necessary.

Again it was in the shadow of a street-lamp that the sentinel stood—a tall, thickset man, more conscientious in the discharge of his duties than his friend, for Dick saw something glittering in his mouth, and knew that it was a whistle.

"Give me the woild for a wishing well," wailed Elk, staggering slightly, "Say that my dre-em will come true . . ."

And as he sang he made appropriate gestures. His outflung hand caught the whistle and knocked it from the man's mouth, and in a second the two sprang at him and flung him face downward on the pavement. Elk pulled his prisoner's cap over his mouth; something black and shiny flashed before the sentry's eyes, and a cold, circular instrument was thrust against the back of his ear.

"If you make a sound, you're a dead Frog," said Elk; and that portion of his party which had made the circuit coming up at that moment, he handed his prisoner over and replaced his fountain-pen in his pocket.

"Everything now depends upon whether the gentleman who is patrolling the passage between the gardens has witnessed this disgusting fracas," said Elk, dusting himself. "If he was standing at the entrance to the passage he has seen it, and there's going to be trouble."

Apparently the patrol was in the alleyway itself and had heard no sound. Creeping to the entrance, Elk listened and presently heard the soft pad of footsteps. He signalled to Dick to remain where he was, and slipped into the passage, walking softly, but not so softly that the man on guard at the back gate of Mr. Maitland's house did not hear him.

"Who's that?" he demanded in a gruff voice.

"It's me," whispered Elk. "Don't make so much noise."

"You're not supposed to be here," said the other in a tone of authority. "I told you to stay under the lamp-post— —"

Elk's eyes had grown accustomed to the darkness, and now he saw his man.

"There are two queer-looking people in the street: I wanted you to see them," he whispered.

All turned now upon the discipline which the Frogs maintained.

"Who are they?" asked the unknown in a low voice.

"A man and a woman," whispered Elk.

"I don't suppose they're anybody important," grumbled the other.

In his youth Elk had played football; and, measuring the distance as best he could, he dropped suddenly and tackled low. The man struck the earth with a jerk which knocked all the breath out of his body and made him incapable of any other sound than the involuntary gasp which followed his knock-out. In a second Elk was on him, his bony knee on the man's throat.

"Pray, Frog," he whispered in the man's ear, "but don't shout!"

The stricken man was incapable of shouting, and was still breathless when willing hands threw him into the patrol wagon.

"We'll have to go the back way, boys," said Elk in a whisper.

This time his task was facilitated by the fact that the garden gate was not locked. The door into the scullery was, however, but there was a window, the catch of which Elk forced noiselessly. He had pulled off his boots and was in his stockinged feet, and he sidled along the darkened passage. Apparently none of the dilapidated furniture had been removed from the house, for he felt the small table that had stood in the hall on his last visit. Gently turning the handle of Maitland's room, he pushed.

The door was open, the room in darkness and empty. Elk came back to the scullery.

"There's nobody here on the ground floor," he said. "We'll try upstairs."

He was half-way up when he heard the murmur of voices and stopped. Raising his eyes to the level of the floor, he saw a crack of light under the doorway of the front room—the apartment which had been occupied by Maitland's housekeeper. He listened, but could distinguish no consecutive words. Then, with a bound, he took the remaining stairs in three strides, flew along the landing, and flung himself upon the door. It was locked. At the sound of his footsteps the light inside went out. Twice he threw himself with all his weight at the frail door, and at the third attempt it crashed in.

"Hands up, everybody!" he shouted.

The room was in darkness, and there was a complete silence. Crouching down in the doorway, he flung the gleam of his electric torch into the room. It was empty!

His officers came crowding in at his heels, the lamp on the table was relit—the glass chimney was hot—and a search was made of the room. It was too small to require a great deal of investigation. There was a bed, under which it was possible to hide, but they drew blank in this respect. At one end of the room near the bed was a wardrobe, which was filled with old dresses suspended from hangers.

"Throw out those clothes," ordered Elk. "There must be a door there into the next house."

A glance at the window showed him that it was impossible for the inmates of the room to have escaped that way. Presently the clothes were heaped on the floor, and the detectives were attacking the wooden back of the wardrobe, which did, in fact, prove to be a door leading into the next house. Whilst they were so engaged, Dick made a scrutiny of the table, which was littered with papers. He saw something and called Elk.

"What is this, Elk?"

The detective took the four closely-typed sheets of paper from his hand.

"Mills' confession," he said in amazement. "There are only two copies, one of which I have, and the other is in the possession of your department, Captain Gordon."

At this moment the wardrobe backing was smashed in, and the detectives were pouring through to the next house.

And then it was that they made the interesting discovery that, to all intents and purposes, communication was continuous between a block of ten houses that ran to the end of the street. And they were not untenanted. Three typical Frogs occupied the first room into which they burst. They found others on the lower floor; and it soon became clear that the whole of the houses comprising the end block had been turned into a sleeping-place for the recruits of Frogdom. Since any one of these might have been No. 7, they were placed under arrest.

All the communicating doors were now opened. Except in the case of Maitland's house, no attempt had been made to camouflage the entrances, which in the other houses consisted of oblong apertures, roughly cut through the brick party walls.

"We may have got him, but I doubt it," said Elk, coming back, breathless and grimy, to where Dick was examining the remainder of the documents which he had found. "I haven't seen any man who looks like owning brains."

"Nobody has escaped from the block?"

Elk shook his head.

"My men are in the passage and the street. In addition, the uniformed police are here. Didn't you hear the whistle?"

Elk's assistant reported at that moment.

"A man has been found in one of the back yards, sir," he said. "I've taken the liberty of relieving the constable of his prisoner. Would you like to see him?"

"Bring him up," said Elk, and a few minutes later a handcuffed man was pushed into the room.

He was above medium height; his hair was fair and long, his yellow beard was trimmed to a point.

For a moment Dick looked at him wonderingly, and then:

"Carlo, I think?" he said.

"Hagn, I'm sure!" said Elk. "Get those whiskers off, you Frog, and we'll talk numbers, beginning with seven!"

Hagn! Even now Dick could not believe his eyes. The wig was so perfectly made, the beard so cunningly fixed, that he could not believe it was the manager of Heron's Club. But when he heard the voice, he knew that Elk was right.

"Number Seven, eh?" drawled Hagn. "I guess Number Seven will get through your cordon without being challenged, Mr. Elk. He's friendly with the police. What do you want me for?"

"I want you for the part you played in the murder of Chief Inspector Genter on the night of the fourteenth of May," said Elk.

Hagn's lips curled.

"Why don't you take Broad?—he was there. Perhaps he'll come as witness for me."

"When I see him— —" began Elk.

"Look out of the window," interrupted Hagn. "He's there!"

Dick walked to the window and, throwing up the sash, leant out. A crowd of locals in shawls and overcoats were watching the transference of the prisoners. Dick caught the sheen of a silk hat and the unmistakable voice of Broad hailed him.

"Good morning, Captain Gordon—Frog stock kind of slumped, hasn't it? By the way, did you see the baby?"

CHAPTER XIV

"ALL BULLS HEAR!"

ELK went out on the street to see the American. Mr. Broad was in faultless evening dress, and the gleaming headlamps of his car illuminated the mean street.

"You've certainly a nose for trouble," said Elk with respect; "and whilst you're telling me how you came to know about this raid, which hadn't been decided on until half-an-hour ago, I'll do some quiet wondering."

"I didn't know there was a raid," confessed Joshua Broad, "but when I saw twenty Central Office men dash out of Heron's Club and drive furiously away, I am entitled to guess that their haste doesn't indicate their anxiety to get to bed before the clock strikes two. I usually call at Heron's Club in the early hours. In many ways its members are less desirable acquaintances than the general run of Frogs, but they amuse me. And they are mildly instructive. That is my explanation—I saw you leave in a hurry and I followed you. And I repeat my question. Did you see the dear little baby who is learning to spell R-A-T, Rat?"

"No," said Elk shortly. He had a feeling that the suave and self-possessed American was laughing at him. "Come in and see the chief."

Broad followed the inspector to the bedroom, where Dick was assembling the papers which in his hurried departure No. 7 had left behind. The capture was the most important that had been made since the campaign against the Frogs was seriously undertaken.

In addition to the copy of the secret report on Mills, there was a bundle of notes, many of them cryptic and unintelligible to the reader. Some, however, were in plain English. They were typewritten, and obviously they corresponded to the General Orders of an army. They were, in fact, the Frog's own instructions, issued under the name of his chief of staff, for each bore the signature "Seven."

One ran:

"Raymond Bennett must go faster. L. to tell him that he is a Frog. Whatever is done with him must be carried out with somebody unknown as Frog."

Another slip:

"Gordon has an engagement to dine American Embassy Thursday. Settle. Elk has fixed new alarm under fourth tread of stairs. Elk goes to Wandsworth 4.15 to-morrow for interview with Mills."

There were other notes dealing with people of whom Dick had never heard. He was reading again the reference to himself, and smiling over the laconic instruction "settle," when the American came in.

"Sit down, Mr. Broad—by the sad look on Elk's face I guess you have explained your presence satisfactorily?"

Broad nodded smilingly.

"And Mr. Elk takes quite a lot of convincing," he said. His eyes fell upon the papers on the table. "Would it be indiscreet to ask if that is Frog stuff?" he asked.

"Very," said Dick, "In fact, any reference to the Frogs would be the height of indiscretion, unless you're prepared to add to the sum of our knowledge."

"I can tell you, without committing myself, that Frog Seven has made a getaway," said the American calmly.

"How do you know?"

"I heard the Frogs jubilating as they passed down the street in custody," said Broad. "Frog Seven's disguise was perfect—he wore the uniform of a policeman."

Elk swore softly but savagely.

"That was it!" he said. "He was the 'policeman' who was spiriting Hagn away under the pretence of arresting him! And if one of my men had not taken his prisoner from him they would both have escaped. Wait!"

He went in search of the detective who had brought in Hagn.

"I don't know the constable," said that officer. "This is a strange division to me. He was a tallish man with a heavy black moustache. If it was a disguise, it was perfect, sir."

Elk returned to report and question. But again Mr. Broad's explanation was a simple one.

"I tell you that the Frogs were openly enjoying the joke. I heard one say that the 'rozzer' got away—and another refer to the escaped man as a 'flattie'—both, I believe, are cant terms for policemen?"

Elk nodded.

"What is your interest in the Frogs, Broad?" he asked bluntly. "Forget for the minute that you're a parlour-criminologist and imagine that you're writin' the true story of your life."

Broad considered for a while, examining the cigar he had been smoking.

"The Frogs mean nothing to me—the Frog everything." The American puffed a ring of smoke into the air and watched it dissolve.

"I'm mighty curious to know what game he is playing with Ray Bennett," he said. "That is certainly the most intriguing feature of Frog strategy."

He rose and took up his hat.

"I envy you your search of this fine old mansion," he said, and, with a twinkle in his eye: "Don't forget the kindergarten, Mr. Elk."

When he had gone, Elk made a close scrutiny of the house. He found two children's books, both well-thumbed, and an elementary copybook, in which a childish hand had followed, shakily, the excellent copperplate examples. The *abacus* was gone, however. In the cupboard where he had seen the unopened circulars, he made a discovery. It was a complete outfit, as far as he could judge, for a boy of six or seven. Every article was new—not one had been worn. Elk carried his find to where Dick was still puzzling over some of the more obscure notes which "No. 7" had left in his flight.

"What do you make of these?" he asked.

The Prosecutor turned over the articles one by one, then leant back in his chair and stared into vacancy.

"All new," he said absently, and then a slow smile dawned on his face.

Elk, who saw nothing funny in the little bundle, wondered what was amusing him.

"I think these clothes supply a very valuable clue; does this?" He passed a paper across the table, and Elk read:

"All bulls hear on Wednesday 3.1.A. L.V.M.B. Important."

"There are twenty-five copies of that simple but moving message," said Dick; "and as there are no envelopes for any of the instructions, I can only suppose that they are despatched by Hagn either from the club or his home. This is how far I have got in figuring the organization of the Frogs. Frog Number One works through 'Seven,' who may or may not be aware of his chief's identity. Hagn—whose number is thirteen, by the way, and mighty unlucky it will be for him—is the executive chief of Number Seven's bureau, and actually communicates with the section chiefs. He may or may not know 'Seven'—probably he does. Seven takes orders from the Frog, but may act without consultation if emergencies arise. There is here," he tapped the paper, "an apology for employing Mills, which bears this out."

"No handwriting?"

"None—nor finger-prints."

Elk took up one of the slips on which the messages were written, and held it to the light.

"Watermark Three Lion Bond," he read. "Typewriter new, written by somebody who was taught and has a weak little finger of the left hand—the 'q' and 'a' are faint. That shows he's a touch typist—uses the same finger every time. Self-taught typists seldom use their little fingers. Especially the little finger of the left hand. I once caught a bank thief through knowing this." He read the message again.

"'All bulls hear on Wednesday . . .' Bulls are the big men, the bull frogs, eh? Where do they hear? '3.1.A.'? That certainly leaves me guessing, Captain. Why, what do you think?"

Dick was regarding him oddly.

"It doesn't get me guessing," he said slowly. "At 3.1 a.m. on Wednesday morning, I shall be listening in for the code signal L.V.M.B.—we are going to hear that great Frog talk!"

"Will he talk about the durned treaty?" growled Elk.

CHAPTER XV

THE MORNING AFTER

RAY BENNETT woke with a groan. His temples were splitting, his tongue was parched and dry. When he tried to lift his aching head from the pillow he groaned again, but with an effort of will succeeded in dragging himself from the bed and staggering to the window. He pushed open a leaded casement and looked out upon the green of Hyde Park, and all the time his temples throbbed painfully.

Pouring a glass of water from a carafe, he drank greedily, and, sitting down on the edge of the bed, his head between his hands, he tried to think. Only dimly did he recall the events of the night before, but he was conscious that something dreadful had happened. Slowly his mind started to sort out his experiences, and with a sinking heart he remembered he had struck his father! He shuddered at the recollection, and then began a frantic mental search for justification. The vanity of youth does not readily reject excuses for its own excesses, and Ray was no exception. By the time he had had his bath and was in the first stages of dressing, he had come to the conclusion that he had been very badly treated. It was unpardonable in him to strike his father—he must write to him expressing his sorrow and urging his condition as a reason for the act. It would not be a crawling letter (he told himself) but something dignified and a little distant. After all, these quarrels occurred in every family. Parents were temporarily estranged from their children, and were eventually reconciled. Some day he would go to his father a rich man....

He pursed his lips uneasily. A rich man? He was well off now. He had an expensive flat. Every week crisp new banknotes came by registered post. He had the loan of a car—how long would this state of affairs continue?

He was no fool. Not perhaps as clever as he thought he was, but no fool. Why should the Japanese or any other Government pay him for information they could get from any handbook available to all and purchasable for a few shillings at most booksellers?

He dismissed the thought—he had the gift of putting out of his mind those matters which troubled him. Opening the door which led into his dining-room, he stood stock-still, paralysed with astonishment.

Ella was sitting at the open window, her elbow on the ledge, her chin in her hand. She looked pale, and there were heavy shadows under her eyes.

"Why, Ella, what on earth are you doing here?" he asked. "How did you get in?"

"The porter opened the door with his pass-key when I told him I was your sister," she said listlessly. "I came early this morning. Oh, Ray—aren't you . . . aren't you ashamed?"

He scowled.

"Why should I be?" he asked loudly. "Father ought to have known better than tackle me when I was lit up! Of course, it was an awful thing to do, but I wasn't responsible for my actions at the time. What did he say?" he asked uncomfortably.

"Nothing—he said nothing. I wish he had. Won't you go to Horsham and see him, Ray?"

"No—let it blow over for a day or two," he said hastily. He most assuredly had no anxiety to meet his father. "If . . . if he forgives me he'll only want me to come back and chuck this life. He had no right to make me look little before all those people. I suppose you've been to see your friend Gordon?" he sneered.

"No," she said simply, "I have been nowhere but here. I came up by the workmen's train. Would it be a dreadful sacrifice, Ray, to give up this?"

He made an impatient gesture.

"It isn't—this, my dear Ella, if by 'this' you mean the flat. It is my work that you and father want me to give up. I have to live up to my position."

"What is your work?" she asked.

"You wouldn't understand," he said loftily, and her lips twitched.

"It would have to be very extraordinary if I could not understand it," she said. "Is it Secret Service work?"

Ray went red.

"I suppose Gordon has been talking to you," he complained bitterly. "If that fellow sticks his nose into my affairs he is going to have it pulled!"

"Why shouldn't he?" she asked.

This was a new tone in her, and one that made him stare at her. Ella had always been the indulgent, approving, excusing sister. The buffer who stood between him and his father's reproof.

"Why shouldn't he?" she repeated. "Mr. Gordon should know something of Secret Service work—he himself is an officer of the law. You are either working lawfully, in which case it doesn't matter what he knows, or unlawfully, and the fact that he knows should make a difference to you."

He looked at her searchingly.

"Why are you so interested in Gordon—are you in love with him?" he asked.

Her steady eyes did not waver, and only the faintest tinge of pink came to the skin that sleeplessness had paled.

"That is the kind of question that a gentleman does not ask in such a tone," she said quietly, "not even of his sister. Ray, you are coming back to daddy, aren't you—to-day?"

He shook his head.

"No. I'm not. I'm going to write to him. I admit I did wrong. I shall tell him so in my letter. I can't do more than that."

There came a discreet knock on the door.

"Come in," growled Ray. It was his servant, a man who came by the day.

"Will you see Miss Bassano and Mr. Brady, sir?" he asked in a hoarse whisper, and glanced significantly at Ella.

"Of course he'll see me," said a voice outside. "Why all this formality—oh, I see."

Lola Bassano's eyes fell upon the girl seated by the window.

"This is my sister—Ella, this is Miss Bassano and Mr. Brady."

Ella looked at the petite figure in the doorway, and, looking, could only admire. It was the first time they had met face to face, and she thought Lola was lovely.

"Glad to meet you, Miss Bennett. I suppose you've come up to roast this brother of yours for his disgraceful conduct last night. Boy, you were certainly mad! It *was* your father, Miss Bennett?"

Ella nodded, and heard with gratitude the sympathetic click of Lew Brady's lips.

"If I'd been near you, Ray, I'd have beaten you. Too bad, Miss Bennett."

A strange coldness came suddenly to the girl—and a second before she had glowed to their sympathy. It was the suspicion of their insincerity that chilled her. Their kindness was just a little too glib and too ready. Brady's just a little too overpowering.

"Do you like your brother's flat?" asked Lola, sitting down and stretching her silk-covered legs to a patch of sunlight.

"It is very—handsome," said Ella. "He will find Horsham rather dull when he comes back."

"Will he go back?" Lola flashed a smile at the youth as she asked the question.

"Not much I won't," said Ray energetically. "I've been trying to make Ella understand that my business is too important to leave."

Lola nodded, and now the antagonism which Ella in her charity was holding back came with a rush.

"What is the business?" she asked.

He went on to give her a vague and cautious exposition of his work, and she listened without comment.

"So if you think that I'm doing anything crooked, or have friends that aren't as straight as you and father are, get the idea out of your head. I'm not afraid of Gordon or Elk or any of that lot. Don't think I am. Nor is Brady, nor Miss Bassano. Gordon is one of those cheap detectives who has got his ideas out of books."

"That's perfectly true, Miss Bennett," said Lew virtuously. "Gordon is just a bit too clever. He's got the idea that everybody but himself is crook. Why, he sent Elk down to cross-examine your own father! Believe me, I'm not scared of Gordon, or any — —"

Tap . . . tap . . . tappity . . . tap.

The taps were on the door, slow, deliberate, unmistakable. The effect on Lew Brady was remarkable. His big body seemed to shrink, his puffed face grew suddenly hollow.

Tap . . . tap . . . tappity . . . tap.

The hand that went up to Brady's mouth was trembling. Ella looked from the man to Lola, and she saw, to her amazement, that Lola had grown pale under her rouge. Brady stumbled to the door, and the sound of his heavy breathing sounded loud in the silence.

"Come in," he muttered, and flung the door wide open.

It was Dick Gordon who entered.

He looked from one to the other, laughter in his eyes.

"The old Frog tap seems to frighten some of you," he said pleasantly.

CHAPTER XVI

RAY LEARNS THE TRUTH

LOLA was the quickest to recover.

"What do you mean . . . Frog tap? Got that Frog stuff roaming loose in your head, haven't you?"

"It is a new accomplishment," said Dick with mock gravity. "A thirty-third degree Frog taught me. It's the signal the old Grand Master Frog gives when he enters the presence of his inferiors."

"Your thirty-third degree Frog is probably lying," said Lola, her colour returning. "Anyway, Mills— —"

"I never mentioned Mills," said Dick.

"I know it was he. His arrest was in the newspapers."

"It hasn't even appeared in the newspapers," said Dick, "unless it was splashed in *The Frog Gazette*—probably on the personality page."

He inclined his head toward the girl. Ray, for the moment, he would have ignored if the young man had not taken a step toward him.

"Do you want anything, Gordon?" he asked.

"I want a private talk with you, Bennett," said Dick.

"There's nothing you can't say before my friends," said Ray, his ready temper rising.

"The only person I recognize by that title is your sister," replied Gordon.

"Let us go, Lew," said Lola with a shrug, but Ray Bennett stopped them.

"Wait a minute! Is this my house, or isn't it?" he demanded furiously. "You can clear out, Gordon! I've had just about as much of your interference as I want. You push your way in here, you're offensive to my friends—you practically tell them to get out—I like your nerve! There's the door—you can go."

"I'll go if you feel that way," said Dick, "but I want to warn you— —"

"Pshaw! I'm sick of your warnings."

"I want to warn you that the Frog has decided that you've got to earn your money! That is all."

There was a dead silence, which Ella broke.

"The Frog?" she repeated, open-eyed. "But . . . but, Mr. Gordon, Ray isn't . . . with the Frogs?"

"Perhaps it will be news to him—but he is," said Dick. "These two people are faithful servants of the reptile," he pointed. "Lola is financed by him—her husband is financed by him——"

"You're a liar!" screamed Ray. "Lola isn't married! You're a sneaking liar—get out before I throw you out! You poor Frog-chaser—you think everything that's green lives in a pond! Get out and stay out!"

It was Ella's appealing glance that made Dick Gordon walk to the door. Turning, his cold gaze rested on Lew Brady.

"There is a big question-mark against your name in the Frog-book, Brady. You watch out!"

Lew shrank under the blow, for blow it was. Had he dared, he would have followed Gordon into the corridor and sought further information. But here his moral courage failed him, and he stood, a pathetic figure, looking wistfully at the door that the visitor had closed behind him.

"For God's sake let us get some air in the room!" snarled Ray, thrusting open the windows. "That fellow is a pestilence! Married! Trying to get me to believe that!"

Ella had taken up her handbag from the sideboard where she had placed it.

"Going, Ella?"

She nodded.

"Tell father . . . I'll write anyway. Talk to him, Ella, and show him where he was wrong."

She held out her hand.

"Good-bye, Ray," she said. "Perhaps one day you will come back to us. Please God this madness will end soon. Oh, Ray, it isn't true about the Frogs, is it? You aren't with those people?"

His laugh reassured her for the moment.

"Of course I'm not—it's about as true as the yarn that Lola is married! Gordon was trying to make a sensation; that's the worst of these third-rate detectives, they live on sensation."

She nodded to Lola as he escorted her to the lift. Lew Brady watched her with hungry eyes.

"What did he mean, Lola?" asked Brady as the door closed behind the two. "That fellow knows something! There's a mark against my name in the Frog-book! That sounds bad to me. Lola, I'm finished with these Frogs! They're getting on my nerves."

"You're a fool," she said calmly. "Gordon has got just the effect he wanted—he has scared you!"

"Scared?" he answered savagely. "Nothing scares me. You're not scared because you've no imagination. I'm . . . not scared, but worried, because I'm beginning to see that the Frogs are bigger than I dreamt. They killed that Scotsman Maclean the other day, and they're not going to think twice about settling with me. I've talked to these Frogs, Lola—they'd do anything from murder upwards. They look on the Frog as a god—he's a religion with them! A question-mark against my name! I believe it too—I've talked flip about 'em, and they won't forgive that——"

"Hush!" she warned him in a low voice as the door handle turned and Ray came back.

"Phew!" he said. "Thank God she's gone! What a morning! Frogs—Frogs—Frogs! The poor fool!"

Lola opened a small jewelled case and took out a cigarette and lit it, extinguishing the match with a snick of her fingers. Then she turned her beautiful eyes upon Ray.

"What is the matter with the Frogs anyway?" she asked coolly. "They pay well and they ask for little."

Ray gaped at her.

"You're not working for them, are you?" he asked astonished. "Why, they're just low tramps who murder people!"

She shook her head.

"Not all of them," she corrected. "They are only the body—the big Frogs are different. I am one and Lew is one."

"What the devil are you talking about?" demanded Lew, half in fear, half in wrath.

"He ought to know—and he has got to know sooner or later," said Lola, unperturbed. "He's too sensible a boy to imagine that the Japanese or any other embassy is paying his overhead charges. He's a Frog."

Ray collapsed into a chair, incapable of speech.

"A Frog?" he repeated mechanically. "What . . . what do you mean?"

Lola laughed.

"I don't see that it is any worse being a Frog than an agent of another country, selling your own country's secrets," she said. "Don't be silly, Ray! You ought to be pleased and honoured. They chose you from thousands because they wanted the right kind of intelligence . . ."

And so she flattered and soothed him, until his plastic mind, wax in her hands, took another shape.

"I suppose it is all right," he said at last. "Of course, I wouldn't do anything really bad, and I don't approve of all this clubbing, but, as you say, the Frog can't be responsible for all that his people do. But on one thing I'm firm, Lola! I'll have no tattooing!"

She laughed and extended her white arm.

"Am I marked?" she asked. "Is Lew marked? No; the big people aren't marked at all. Boy, you've a great future."

Ray took her hand and fondled it.

"Lola . . . about that story that Gordon told . . . your being married: it isn't true?"

She laughed again and patted the hand on hers.

"Gordon is jealous," she said. "I can't tell you why—now. But he has good reasons." Suddenly her mood grew gay, and she slipped away. "Listen, I'm going to 'phone for a table for lunch, and you will join us, and we'll drink to the great little Frog who feeds us!"

The telephone was on the sideboard, and as she lifted the receiver she saw the square black metal box clamped to its base.

"Something new in 'phones, Ray?" she asked.

"They fixed it yesterday. It's a resistance. The man told me that somebody who was talking into a 'phone during a thunderstorm had a bad shock, so they're fitting these things as an experiment. It makes the instrument heavier, and it's ugly, but — —"

Slowly she put the receiver down and stooped to look at the attachment.

"It's a detectaphone," she said quietly. "And all the time we've been talking somebody has been making a note of our conversation."

She walked to the fireplace, took up a poker and brought it down with a crash on the little box. . . .

Inspector Elk, with a pair of receivers clamped to his head, sat in a tiny office on the Thames Embankment, and put down his pencil with a sigh. Then he took up his telephone and called Headquarters Exchange.

"You can switch off that detectaphone to Knightsbridge 93718," he said. "I don't think we shall want it any more."

"Did I put you through in time, sir?" asked the operator's voice. "They had only just started talking when I called you."

"Plenty of time, Angus," said Elk, "plenty of time."

He gathered up his notes and went to his desk and placed them tidily by the side of his blotting-pad.

Strolling to the window, he looked out upon the sunlit river, and there was peace and comfort in his heart, for overnight the prisoner Mills had decided to tell all he knew about the Frogs on the promise of a free pardon and a passage to Canada. And Mills knew more than he had, as yet, told.

"I can give you a line to Number 7 that will put him into your hands," his note had run.

Number Seven! Elk caught a long breath. No. 7 was the hub on which the wheel turned.

He rubbed his hands cheerfully, for it seemed that the mystery of the Frog was at last to be solved. Perhaps "the line" would lead to the missing treaty—and at the thought of the lost document Elk's face clouded. Two ministers, a great state department and innumerable under-secretaries spent their time in writing frantic notes of inquiry to headquarters concerning Lord Farmley's loss.

"They want miracles," said Elk, and wondered if the day would produce one.

119

He went to his overcoat pocket to find a cigar, and his hand touched a thick roll of papers. He pulled them out and threw them upon the desk, and as he did so the first words on the first sheet caught his eye.

"*By the King's Most Excellent Majesty in Council——*"

Elk tried to yell, but his voice failed him, and then he snatched up the paper from the desk and turned the leaves with trembling hands.

It was the lost treaty!

Elk held the precious document in his hand, and his mind went back quickly over the night's adventures. When had he taken off his top-coat? When had he last put his hand in his pocket? He had taken off the coat at Heron's Club, and he could not remember having used the pockets since. It was a light coat that he either carried or wore, summer or winter. He had brought it to the office that morning on his arm.

At the club! Probably when he had parted with the garment to the cloak-room attendant. Then the Frog must have been there. One of the waiters probably—an admirable disguise for the chief of the gang. Elk sat down to think.

To question anybody in the building would be futile. Nobody had touched the coat but himself.

"Dear me!" said Elk, as he hung up the coat again.

At the touch of his bell, Balder came.

"Balder, do you remember seeing me pass your room?"

"Yes, sir."

"I had my coat on my arm, didn't I?"

"I never looked," said Balder with satisfaction.

He invariably gave Elk the impression that he derived a great deal of satisfaction out of not being able to help.

"It's queer," said Elk.

"Anything wrong, sir?"

"No, not exactly. You understand what has to be done with Mills? He is to see nobody. Immediately he arrives he is to be put into the waiting-room—alone. There is to be no conversation of any kind, and, if he speaks, he is not to be answered."

In the privacy of his office he inspected his find again. Everything was there—the treaty and Lord Farmley's notes. Elk called up his lordship and told the good news. Later came a small deputation from the Foreign Office to collect the precious document, and to offer, in the name of the Ministry, their thanks for his services in recovering the lost papers. All of which Elk accepted graciously. He would have been cursed with as great heartiness if he had failed, and would have been equally innocent of responsibility.

He had arranged for Mills to be brought to Headquarters at noon. There remained an hour to be filled, and he spent that hour unprofitably in a rough interrogation of Hagn, who, stripped of his beard, occupied a special cell segregated from the ordinary places of confinement in Cannon Row Station—which is virtually Scotland Yard itself.

Hagn refused to make any statement—even when formally charged with the murder of Inspector Genter. He did, however, make a comment on the charge when Elk saw him this morning.

"You have no proof, Elk," he said, "and you know that I am innocent."

"You were the last man seen in Genter's company," said Elk sternly. "It is established that you brought his body back to town. In addition to which, Mills has spilt everything."

"I'm aware what Mills has said," remarked the other.

"You're not so aware either," suggested Elk. "And now I'll tell you something: we've had Number Seven under lock and key since morning—now laugh!"

To his amazement the man's face relaxed in a broad grin.

"Bluff!" he said. "And cheap bluff. It might deceive a poor little thief, but it doesn't get past with me. If you'd caught 'Seven,' you wouldn't be talking fresh to me. Go and find him, Elk," he mocked, "and when you've got him, hold him tight. Don't let him get away—as Mills will."

Elk returned from the interview feeling that it had not gone as well as it might—but as he was leaving the station he beckoned the chief inspector.

"I'm planting a pigeon on Hagn this afternoon. Put 'um together and leave 'um alone," he said.

The inspector nodded understandingly.

CHAPTER XVII

THE COMING OF MILLS

ON the morning that Elk waited for the arrival of the informer, elaborate precautions were being made to transfer the man to headquarters. All night the prison had been surrounded by a cordon of armed guards, whilst patrols had remained on duty in the yard where he was confined.

The captured Frog was a well-educated man who had fallen on evil times and had been recruited when "on the road" through the agency of two tramping members of the fraternity. From the first statement he made, it appeared that he had acted as section leader, his duty being to pass on instructions and "calls" to the rank and file, to report casualties and to assist in the attacks which were made from time to time upon those people who had earned the Frog's enmity. Apparently only section leaders and trustees were given this type of work.

They brought him from his cell at eleven o'clock, and the man, despite his assurance, was nervous and apprehensive. Moreover, he had a cold and was coughing. This may have been a symptom of nerves also.

At eleven-fifteen the gates of the prison were opened, and three motor-cyclists came out abreast. A closed car followed, the curtains drawn. On either side of the car rode other armed men on motor-cycles, and a second car, containing Central Office men, followed.

The cortège reached Scotland Yard without mishap; the gates at both ends were closed, and the prisoner was rushed into the building.

Balder, Elk's clerk, and a detective-sergeant, took charge of the man, who was now white and shaking, and he was put into a small room adjoining Elk's office, a room the windows of which were heavily barred (it had been used for the safe holding of spies during the war). Two men were put on duty outside the door, and the discontented Balder reported.

"We've put that fellow in the waiting-room, Mr. Elk."

"Did he say anything?" asked Dick, who had arrived for the interrogation.

"No, sir—except to ask if the window could be shut. I shut it."

"Bring the prisoner," said Elk.

They waited a while, heard the clash of keys, and then an excited buzz of talk. Then Balder rushed in.

"He's ill . . . fainted or something," he gasped, and Elk sprang past him, along the corridor into the guard-room.

Mills half sat, half lay, against the wall. His eyes were closed, his face was ashen.

Dick bent over the prisoner and laid him flat on the ground. Then he stooped and smelt.

"Cyanide of potassium," he said. "The man is dead."

That morning Mills had been stripped to the skin and every article of clothing searched thoroughly and well. As an additional precaution his pockets had been sewn up. To the two detectives who accompanied him in the car he had spoken hopefully of his forthcoming departure to Canada. None but police officers had touched him, and he had had no communication with any outsider.

The first thing that Dick Gordon noticed was the window, which Balder said he had shut. It was open some six inches at the bottom.

"Yes, sir, I'm sure I shut it," said the clerk emphatically. "Sergeant Jeller saw me."

The sergeant was also under that impression. Dick lifted the window higher and looked out. Four horizontal bars traversed the brickwork, but, by craning his head, he saw that, a foot away from the window and attached to the wall, was a long steel ladder running from the roof (as he guessed) to the ground. The room was on the third floor, and beneath was a patch of shrub-filled gardens. Beyond that, high railings.

"What are those gardens?" he asked, pointing to the space on the other side of the railings.

"They belong to Onslow Gardens," said Elk.

"Onslow Gardens?" said Dick thoughtfully. "Wasn't it from Onslow Gardens that the Frogs tried to shoot me?"

Elk shook his head helplessly.

"What do you suggest. Captain Gordon?"

"I don't know what to suggest," admitted Dick. "It doesn't seem an intelligent theory that somebody climbed the ladder and handed poison to Mills—less acceptable, that he would be willing to take the dose. There is the fact. Balder swears that the window was shut, and now the window is open. You can trust Balder?"

Elk nodded.

The divisional surgeon came soon after, and, as Dick had expected, pronounced life extinct, and supported the view that cyanide was the cause.

"Cyanide has a peculiar odour," he said. "I don't think there's any doubt at all that the man was killed, either by poison administered from outside, or by poison taken voluntarily by himself."

After the body had been removed. Elk accompanied Dick Gordon to his Whitehall office.

"I have never been frightened in my life," said Elk, "but these Frogs are now on top of me! Here is a man killed practically under our eyes! He was guarded, he was never let out of our sight, except for the few minutes he was in that room, and yet the Frog can reach him—it's frightening, Captain Gordon."

Dick unlocked the door of his office and ushered Elk into the cosy interior.

"I know of no better cure for shaken nerves than a *Cabana Cesare*," he said cheerfully. "And without desiring to indulge in a boastful gesture, I can only tell you, Elk, that they don't frighten me, any more than they frighten you. Frog is human, and has very human fears. Where is friend Broad?"

"The American?"

Dick nodded, and Elk, without a second's hesitation, pulled the telephone toward him and gave a number.

After a little delay, Broad's voice answered him.

"That you, Mr. Broad? What are you doing now?" asked Elk, in that caressing tone he adopted for telephone conversation.

"Is that Elk? I'm just going out."

"Thought I saw you in Whitehall about five minutes ago," said Elk.

"Then you must have seen my double," replied the other, "for I haven't been out of my bath ten minutes. Do you want me?"

"No, no," cooed Elk. "Just wanted to know you were all right."

"Why, is anything wrong?" came the sharp question.

"Everything's fine," said Elk untruthfully. "Perhaps you'll call round and see me at my office one of these days—good-bye!"

He pushed the telephone back, and raising his eyes to the ceiling, made a quick calculation.

"From Whitehall to Cavendish Square takes four minutes in a good car," he said. "So his being in the flat means nothing."

He pulled the telephone toward him again, and this time called Headquarters.

"I want a man to shadow Mr. Joshua Broad, of Caverley House; not to leave him until eight o'clock to-night; to report to me."

When he had finished, he sat back in his chair and lit the long cigar that Dick had pressed upon him.

"To-day is Tuesday," he ruminated, "to-morrow's Wednesday. Where do you propose to listen in, Captain Gordon?"

"At the Admiralty," said Dick. "I have arranged with the First Lord to be in the instrument room at a quarter to three."

He bought the early editions of the evening newspapers, and was relieved to find that no reference had been made to the murder—as murder he believed it to be. Once, in the course of the day, looking out from his window on to Whitehall, he saw Elk walking along on the other side of the road, his umbrella hanging on his arm, his ancient derby hat at the back of his head, an untidy and unimposing figure. Then, an hour later, he saw him again, coming from the opposite direction. He wondered what particular business the detective was engaged in. He learnt, quite by accident, that Elk had made two visits to the Admiralty that day, but he did not discover the reason until they met later in the evening.

"Don't know much about wireless," said Elk, "though I'm not one of those people who believe that, if God had intended us to use wireless, telegraph poles would have been born without wires. But it seems to me that I remember reading something about 'directional.' If you want to know where a wireless message is coming from, you listen in at two or three different points——"

"Of course! What a fool I am!" said Dick, annoyed with himself. "It never occurred to me that we might pick up the broadcasting station."

"I get these ideas," explained Elk modestly. "The Admiralty have sent messages to Milford Haven, Harwich, Portsmouth and Plymouth, telling ships to listen in and give us the direction. The evening papers haven't got that story."

"You mean about Mills? No, thank heaven! It is certain to come out at the inquest, but I've arranged for that to be postponed for a week or two; and somehow I feel that within the next few weeks things will happen."

"To us," said Elk ominously. "I dare not eat a grilled sausage since that fellow was killed! And I'm partial to sausages."

CHAPTER XVIII

THE BROADCAST

HIS jaundiced clerk was, as usual, in a complaining mood. "Records have been making a fuss and have been blaming me," he said bitterly. "Records give themselves more airs than the whole darned office."

The war between Balder and "Records"—which was a short title for that section of Headquarters which kept exact data of criminals' pasts,—was of long standing. "Records" was aloof, detached, sublimely superior to everything except tabulated facts. It was no respecter of persons; would as soon snap at a Chief Commissioner who broke its inflexible rules, as it would at the latest joined constable.

"What's the trouble?" asked Elk.

"You remember you had a lot of stuff out the other day about a man called—I can't remember his name now."

"Lyme?" suggested Elk.

"That's the fellow. Well, it appears that one of the portraits is missing. The morning after you were looking at them, I went to Records and got the documents again for you, thinking you wanted to see them in the morning. When you didn't turn up, I returned them, and now they say the portrait and measurements are short."

"Do you mean to say they're lost?"

"If they're lost," said the morose Balder, "then Records have lost 'em! I suppose they think I'm a Frog or somethin'. They're always accusing me of mislaying their finger-print cards."

"I've promised you a chance to make a big noise, Balder, and now I'm going to give it to you. You've been passed over for promotion, son, because the men upstairs think you were one of the leaders of the last strike. I know that 'passed over' feeling—it turns you sour. Will you take a big chance?"

Balder nodded, holding his breath.

"Hagn's in the special cell," said Elk. "Change into your civilian kit, roughen yourself up a bit, and I'll put you in with him. If you're scared I'll let you carry a gun and fix it so that you won't be searched. Get Hagn to talk. Tell him that you were pulled in over the Dundee murder. He won't know you. Get that story, Balder, and I'll have the stripes on your arm in a week."

Balder nodded. The querulous character of his voice had changed when he spoke again.

"It's a chance," he said; "and thank you, Mr. Elk, for giving it to me."

An hour later, a detective brought a grimy-looking prisoner into Cannon Row and pushed him into the steel pen, and the only man who recognized the prisoner was the chief inspector who had waited for the arrival of the pigeon.

It was that high official himself who conducted Balder to the separate cell and pushed him in.

"Good night, Frog!" he said.

Balder's reply was unprintable.

After seeing his subordinate safely caged, Elk went back to his room, locked the door, cut off his telephone and lay down to snatch a few hours' sleep. It was a practice of his, when he was engaged in any work which kept him up at night, to take these intermediate siestas, and he had trained himself to sleep as and when the opportunity presented itself. It was unusual in him, however, to avail himself of the office sofa, a piece of furniture to which he was not entitled, and which, as his superiors had often pointed out, occupied space which might better be employed.

For once, however, he could not sleep. His mind ranged from Balder to Dick Gordon, from Lola Bassano to the dead man Mills. His own position had been seriously jeopardized, but that worried him not at all. He was a bachelor, had a snug sum invested. His mind went to the puzzling Maitland. His association with the Frogs had been proved almost up to the hilt. And Maitland was in a position to benefit by these many inexplicable attacks which had been made upon seemingly inoffensive people.

The old man lived a double life. By day the business martinet, before whom his staff trembled, the cutter of salaries, the shrewd manipulator of properties; by night the associate of thieves and worse than thieves. Who was the child? That was another snag.

"Nothing but snags!" growled Elk, his hands under his head, looking resentfully at the ceiling. "Nothing but snags."

Finding he could not sleep, he got up and went across to Cannon Row. The gaoler told him that the new prisoner had been talking a lot to Hagn, and Elk grinned. He only hoped that the "new prisoner" would not be tempted to discuss his grievances against the police administration.

At a quarter to three he joined Dick Gordon in the instrument room at the Admiralty. An operator had been placed at their disposal; and after the preliminary instructions they took their place at the table where he manipulated his keys. Dick listened, fascinated, hearing the calls of far-off ships and the chatter of transmitting stations. Once he heard a faint squeak of sound, so faint that he wasn't sure that he had not been mistaken.

"Cape Race," said the operator. "You'll hear Chicago in a minute. He usually gets talkative round about now."

As the hands of the clock approached three, the operator began varying his wave lengths, reaching out into the ether for the message which was coming. Exactly at one minute after three he said suddenly:

"There is your L.V.M.B."

Dick listened to the staccato sounds, and then:

"*All Frogs listen. Mills is dead. Number Seven finished him this morning. Number Seven receives a bonus of a hundred pounds.*"

The voice was clear and singularly sweet. It was a woman's.

"*Twenty-third district will arrange to receive Number Seven's instructions at the usual place.*"

Dick's heart was beating thunderously. He recognized the speaker, knew the soft cadences, the gentle intonations.

There could be no doubt at all: it was Ella Bennett's voice! Dick felt a sudden sensation of sickness, but, looking across the table and seeing Elk's eyes fixed upon him, he made an effort to control his emotions.

"There doesn't seem to be any more coming through," said the operator after a few minutes' wait.

Dick took off the headpiece and rose.

"We must wait for the direction signals to come through," he said as steadily as he could.

Presently they began to arrive, and were worked out by a naval officer on a large scale map.

"The broadcasting station is in London," he said. "All the lines meet somewhere in the West End, I should imagine; possibly in the very heart of town. Did you find any difficulty in picking up the Frog call?" he asked the operator.

"Yes, sir," said the man. "I think they were sending from very close at hand."

"In what part of town would you say it would be?" asked Elk.

The officer indicated a pencil mark that he had ruled across the page.

"It is somewhere on this mark," he said, and Elk, peering over, saw that the line passed through Cavendish Square and Cavendish Place and that, whilst the Portsmouth line missed Cavendish Place only by a block, the Harwich line crossed the Plymouth line a little to the south of the square.

"Caverley House, obviously," said Dick.

He wanted to get out in the open, he wanted to talk, to discuss this monstrous thing with Elk. Had the detective also recognized the voice, he wondered? Any doubt he had on that point was set at rest. He had hardly reached Whitehall before Elk said:

"Sounded very like a friend of ours, Captain Gordon?"

Dick made no reply.

"Very like," said Elk as if he were speaking half to himself. "In fact, I'll take any number of oaths that I know the young lady who was talking for old man Frog."

"Why should she do it?" groaned Dick. "Why, for the love of heaven, should she do it?"

"I remember years ago hearing her," said Elk reminiscently.

Dick Gordon stopped, and, turning, glared at the other.

"You remember . . . what do you mean?" he demanded.

"She was on the stage at the time—quite a kid," continued Elk. "They called her 'The Child Mimic.' There's another thing I've noticed, Captain: if you take a magnifying glass and look at your skin, you see its defects, don't you? That wireless telephone acts as a sort of magnifying glass to the voice. She always had a little lisp that I jumped at straight away. You may not have noticed it, but I've got pretty sharp ears. She can't pronounce her 'S's' properly, there's a sort of faint 'th' sound in 'um. You heard that?"

Dick had heard, and nodded.

"I never knew that she was ever on the stage," he said more calmly. "You are sure, Elk?"

"Sure. In some things I'm . . . what's the word?—infall-i-able. I'm a bit shaky on dates, such as when Henry the First an' all that bunch got born—I never was struck on birthdays anyway—but I know voices an' noses. Never forget 'um."

They were turning into the dark entrance of Scotland Yard when Dick said in a tone of despair:

"It was her voice, of course. I had no idea she had been on the stage—is her father in this business?"

"She hasn't a father so far as I know," was the staggering reply, and again Gordon halted.

"Are you mad?" he asked. "Ella Bennett has a father——"

"I'm not talking about Ella Bennett," said the calm Elk. "I'm talking about Lola Bassano."

There was a silence.

"Was it her voice?" asked Gordon a little breathlessly.

"Sure it was Lola. It was a pretty good imitation of Miss Bennett, but any mimic will tell you that these soft voices are easy. It's the pace of a voice that makes it . . ."

"You villain!" said Dick Gordon, as a weight rolled from his heart. "You knew I meant Ella Bennett when I was talking, and you strung me along!"

"Blame me," said Elk. "What's the time?"

It was half-past three. He gathered his reserves, and ten minutes later the police cars dropped a party at the closed door of Caverley House. The bell brought the night porter, who recognized Elk.

"More gas trouble?" he asked.

"Want to see the house plan," said Elk, and listened as the porter detailed the names, occupations and peculiarities of the tenants.

"Who owns this block?" asked the detective.

"This is one of Maitland's properties — Maitlands Consolidated. He's got the Prince of Caux's house in Berkeley Square and——"

"Don't worry about giving me his family history. What time did Miss Bassano come in?"

"She's been in all the evening — since eleven."

"Anybody with her?"

The man hesitated.

"Mr. Maitland came in with her, but he went soon after."

"Nobody else?"

"Nobody except Mr. Maitland."

"Give me your master-key."

The porter demurred.

"I'll lose my job," he pleaded. "Can't you knock?"

"Knocking is my speciality — I don't pass a day without knocking somebody," replied Elk, "but I want that key."

He did not doubt that Lola would have bolted her door, and his surmise proved sound. He had both to knock and ring before the light showed behind the transom, and Lola in a kimono and boudoir cap appeared.

"What is the meaning of this, Mr. Elk?" she demanded. She did not even attempt to appear surprised.

"A friendly call — can I come in?"

She opened the door wider, and Elk went in, followed by Gordon and two detectives. Dick she ignored.

"I'm seeing the Commissioner to-morrow," she said, "and if he doesn't give me satisfaction I'll get on to the newspapers. This persecution is disgraceful. To break into a single girl's flat in the middle of the night, when she is alone and unprotected——"

"If there is any time when a single girl should be alone and unprotected, it is in the middle of the night," said Elk primly. "I'm just going to have a look at your little home, Lola. We've got information that you've been burgled, Lola. Perhaps at this very minute there's a sinister man hidden under your bed. The idea of leaving you alone, so to speak, at the mercy of unlawful characters, is repugnant to our feelin's. Try the dining-room, Williams; I'll search the parlour — *and* the bedroom."

"You'll keep out of my room if you've any sense of decency," said the girl.

"I haven't," admitted Elk, "no false sense, anyway. Besides, Lola, I'm a family man. One of ten. And when there's anything I shouldn't see, just say 'Shut your eyes' and I'll shut 'um."

To all appearances there was nothing that looked in the slightest degree suspicious. A bathroom led from the bedroom, and the bathroom window was open. Flashing his lamp along the wall outside, Elk saw a small glass spool attached to the wall.

"Looks to me like an insulator," he said.

Returning to the bedroom, he began to search for the instrument. There was a tall mahogany wardrobe against one of the walls. Opening the door, he saw row upon row of dresses and thrust in his hand.

It was the shallowest wardrobe he had ever seen, and the backing was warm to the touch.

"Hot cupboard, Lola?" he asked.

She did not reply, but stood watching him, a scowl on her pretty face, her arms folded.

Elk closed the door and his sensitive fingers searched the surface for a spring. It took him a long time to discover it, but at last he found a slip of wood that yielded to the pressure of his hand.

There was a "click" and the front of the wardrobe began to fall.

"A wardrobe bed, eh? Grand little things for a flat."

But it was no sleeping-place that was revealed (and he would have been disappointed if it had been) as he eased down the "bed." Set on a frame were row upon row of valve lamps, transformers—all the apparatus requisite for broadcasting.

Elk looked, and, looking, admired.

"You've got a licence, I suppose?" asked Elk. He supposed nothing of the kind, for licences to transmit are jealously issued in England. He was surprised when she went to a bureau and produced the document. Elk read and nodded.

"You've got *some* pull," he said with respect. "Now I'll see your Frog licence."

"Don't get funny, Elk," she said tartly. "I'd like to know whether you're in the habit of waking people to ask for their permits."

"You've been using this to-night to broadcast the Frogs," Elk nodded accusingly; "and perhaps you'll explain to Captain Gordon why?"

She turned to Dick for the first time.

"I've not used the instrument for weeks," she said. "But the sister of a friend of mine—perhaps you know her—asked if she might use it. She left here an hour ago."

"You mean Miss Bennett, of course," said Gordon, and she raised her eyebrows in simulated astonishment.

"Why, how did you guess that?"

"I guessed it," said Elk, "the moment I heard you giving one of your famous imitations. I guessed she was around, teaching you how to talk like her. Lola, you're cooked! Miss Bennett was standing right alongside me when you started talking Frog-language. She was right at my very side, and she said 'Now, Mr. Elk, isn't she the artfullest thing!' You're cooked, Lola, and you can't do better than sit right down and tell us the truth. I'll make it right for you. We caught 'Seven' last night and he's told us everything. Frog will be in irons to-day, and I came here to give you the last final chance of getting out of all your trouble."

"Isn't that wonderful of you?" she mocked him. "So you've caught 'Seven' and you're catching the Frog! Put a pinch of salt on his tail!"

"Yes," said the imperturbable Elk, untruthfully, "we caught Seven and Hagn's split. But I like you, Lol—always did. There's something about you that reminds me of a girl I used to be crazy about—I never married her; it was a tragedy."

"Not for her," said Lola. "Now I'll tell *you* something, Elk! You haven't caught anybody and you won't. You've put a flat-footed stool pigeon named Balder into the same cell as Hagn, with the idea of getting information, and you're going to have a jar."

In other circumstances Dick Gordon would have been amused by the effect of this revelation upon Elk. The jaw of the unhappy detective dropped as he glared helplessly over his glasses at the girl, smiling her triumph. Then the smile vanished.

"Hagn wouldn't talk, because Frog could reach him, as he reached Mills and Litnov. As he will reach you when he decides you're worth while. And now you can take me if you want. I'm a Frog—I never pretend I'm not. You heard all the tale that I told Ray Bennett—heard it over the detectaphone you planted. Take me and charge me!"

Elk knew that there was no charge upon which he could hold her. And she knew that he knew.

"Do you think you'll get away with it, Bassano?"

It was Gordon who spoke, and she turned her wrathful eyes upon him.

"I've got a Miss to my name, Gordon," she rapped at him.

"Sooner or later you'll have a number," said Dick calmly. "You and your crowd are having the time of your young lives—perhaps because I'm incompetent, or because I'm unfortunate. But some day we shall get you, either I or my successor. You can't fight the law and win because the law is everlasting and constant."

"A search of my flat I don't mind—but a sermon I will not have," she said contemptuously. "And now, if you men have finished, I should like to get a little beauty sleep."

"That is the one thing you don't require," said the gallant Elk, and she laughed.

"You're not a bad man, Elk," she said. "You're a bad detective, but you've a heart of gold."

"If I had, I shouldn't trust myself alone with you," was Elk's parting shot.

CHAPTER XIX

IN ELSHAM WOOD

DICK GORDON, in the sudden lightening of his heart which had come to him when he realized that his horrible fears were without foundation, was inclined to regard the night as having been well spent. This was not Elk's view. He was genuinely grave as they drove back to headquarters.

"I'm frightened of these Frogs, and I admit it," he confessed. "There's a bad leakage somewhere—how should she know that I put Balder in with Hagn? That has staggered me. Nobody but two men, in addition to ourselves, is in the secret; and if the Frogs are capable of getting that kind of news, it is any odds on Hagn knowing that he is being drawn. They frighten me, I tell you, Captain Gordon. If they only knew a little, and hadn't got that quite right, I should be worried. But they know everything!"

Dick nodded.

"The whole trouble, Elk, is that the Frogs are not an illegal association. It may be necessary to ask the Prime Minister to proclaim the society."

"Perhaps he's a Frog too," said Elk gloomily. "Don't laugh, Captain Gordon! There are big people behind these Frogs. I'm beginning to suspect everybody."

"Start by suspecting me," said Gordon good-humouredly.

"I have," was the frank reply. "Then it occurred to me that possibly I walk in my sleep—I used to as a boy. Likely I lead a double life, and I am a detective by day and a Frog by night—you never know. It is clear that there is a genius at the back of the Frogs," he went on, with unconscious immodesty.

"Lola Bassano?" suggested Dick.

"I've thought of her, but she's no organizer. She had a company on the road when she was nineteen, and it died the death from bad organization. I suppose you think that that doesn't mean she couldn't run the Frogs—but it does. You want exactly the same type of intelligence to control the Frogs as you want to control a bank. Maitland is the man. I narrowed the circle down to him after I had a talk with Johnson. Johnson says he's never seen the old man's pass-book, and although he is his private secretary, knows nothing whatever of his business transactions except that he buys property and sells it. The money old Maitland makes on the side never appears in the books, and Johnson was a very surprised man when I suggested that Maitland transacted any business at all outside the general routine of the company. And it's not a company at all—not an incorporated company. It's a one man show. Would you like to make sure, Captain Gordon?"

"Sure of what?" asked Dick, startled.

"That Miss Bennett isn't in this at all."

"You don't think for one moment she is?" asked Dick, aghast at the thought.

"I'm prepared to believe anything," said Elk. "We've got a clear road; we could be at Horsham in an hour, and it is our business to make sure. In my mind I'm perfectly satisfied that it was not Miss Bennett's voice. But when we come down to writing out reports for the people upstairs to read" ('the people upstairs' was Elk's invariable symbol for his superiors) "we are going to look silly if we say that we heard Miss Bennett's voice and didn't trouble to find out where Miss Bennett was."

"That is true," said Dick thoughtfully, and, leaning out to the driver, Elk gave new directions.

The grey of dawn was in the sky as the car ran through the deserted streets of Horsham and began the steady climb toward Maytree Cottage, which lay on the slope of the Shoreham Road.

The cottage showed no signs of life. The blinds were drawn; there was no light of any kind. Dick hesitated, with his hand on the gate.

"I don't like waking these people," he confessed. "Old Bennett will probably think that I've brought some bad news about his son."

"I have no conscience," said Elk, and walked up the brick path.

But John Bennett required no waking. Elk was hailed from one of the windows above, and, looking up, saw the mystery man leaning with his elbows on the window-sill.

"What's the trouble, Elk?" he asked in a low voice, as though he did not wish to awaken his daughter.

"No trouble at all," said Elk cheerfully. "We picked up a wireless telephone message in the night, and I'm under the impression that it was your daughter's voice I heard."

John Bennett frowned, and Dick saw that he doubted the truth of this explanation.

"It is perfectly true, Mr. Bennett," he said. "I heard the voice too. We were listening in for a rather important message, and we heard Miss Bennett in circumstances which make it necessary for us to assure ourselves that it was not she who was speaking."

The cloud passed from John Bennett's face.

"That's a queer sort of story, Captain Gordon, but I believe you. I'll come down and let you in."

Wearing an old dressing-gown, he opened the door and ushered them into the darkened sitting-room.

"I'll call Ella, and perhaps she'll be able to satisfy you that she was in bed at ten o'clock last night."

He went out of the room, after drawing the curtains to let in the light, and Dick waited with a certain amount of pleasurable anticipation. He had been only too glad of the excuse to come to Horsham, if the truth be told. This girl had so gripped his heart that the days between their meetings seemed like eternity. They heard the feet of Bennett on the stairs, and presently the old man came in, and distress was written largely on his face.

"I can't understand it," he said. "Ella is not in her room! The bed has been slept in, but she has evidently dressed and gone out."

Elk scratched his chin, avoiding Dick's eyes.

"A lot of young people like getting up early," he said. "When I was a young man, nothing gave me greater pleasure than to see the sun rise—before I went to bed. Is she in the habit of taking a morning stroll?"

John Bennett shook his head.

"I've never known her to do that before. It's curious I did not hear her, because I slept very badly last night. Will you excuse me, gentlemen?"

He went upstairs and came down in a few minutes, dressed. Together they passed out into the garden. It was now quite light, though the sun had not yet tipped the horizon. John Bennett made a brief but fruitless search of the ground behind the cottage, and came back to them with a confession of failure. He was no more troubled than Dick Gordon. It was impossible that it could have been she, that Elk was mistaken. Yet Lola had been emphatic. Against that, the hall-porter at Caverley House had been equally certain that the only visitor to Lola's flat that night was the aged Mr. Maitland; and so far as he knew, or Elk had been able to discover, there was no other entrance into the building.

"I see you have a car here. You came down by road. Did you pass anybody?"

Dick shook his head.

"Do you mind if we take the car in the opposite direction toward Shoreham?"

"I was going to suggest that," said Gordon. "Isn't it rather dangerous for her, walking at this hour? The roads are thronged with tramps."

The older man made no reply. He sat with the driver, his eyes fixed anxiously upon the road ahead. The car went ten miles at express speed, then turned, and began a search of the side roads. Nearing the cottage again, Dick pointed.

"What is that wood?" he asked pointing to a dense wood to which a narrow road led.

"That is Elsham Wood; she wouldn't go there," he hesitated.

"Let us try it," said Dick, and the bonnet of the car was turned on to a narrow road. In a few minutes they were running through a glade of high trees, the entwining tops of which made the road a place of gloom.

"There are car tracks here," said Dick suddenly, but John Bennett shook his head.

"People come here for picnics," he said, but Dick was not satisfied.

These marks were new, and presently he saw them turn off the road to a 'ride' between the trees. He caught no glimpse of a car, however. The direction of the tracks supported the old man's theory. The road ended a mile farther along, and beyond that was a waste of bracken and tree stumps, for the wood had been extensively thinned during the war.

With some difficulty the car was turned and headed back again. They came through the glade into the open, and then Dick uttered a cry.

John Bennett had already seen the girl. She was walking quickly in the centre of the road, and stepped on to the grassy border without looking round as the car came abreast of her. Then, looking up, she saw her father, and went pale.

He was in the road in a moment.

"My dear," he said reproachfully, "where have you been at this hour?"

She looked frightened, Dick thought. The eyes of Elk narrowed as he surveyed her.

"I couldn't sleep, so I dressed and went out, father," she said, and nodded to Dick. "You're a surprising person, Captain Gordon. Why are you here at this hour?"

"I came to interview you," said Dick, forcing a smile.

"Me!" She was genuinely astonished. "Why me?"

"Captain Gordon heard your voice on a wireless telephone in the middle of the night, and wanted to know all about it," said her father.

If he was relieved, he was also troubled. Looking at him, Elk suddenly saw the relief intensified, and with his quick intuition guessed the cause before John Bennett put the question.

"Was it Ray?" he asked eagerly. "Did he come down?"

She shook her head.

"No, father," she said quietly. "And as to the wireless telephone, I have never spoken into a wireless telephone, and I don't think I've ever seen one," she said.

"Of course you haven't," said Dick. "Only we were rather worried when we heard your voice, but Mr. Elk's explanation, that it was somebody speaking whose voice was very much like yours, is obviously correct."

"Tell me this, Miss Bennett," said Elk quietly. "Were you in town last night?"

She did not reply.

"My daughter went to bed at ten," said John Bennett roughly. "What is the sense of asking her whether she was in London last night?"

"Were you in town in the early hours of this morning, Miss Bennett?" persisted Elk, and to Dick's amazement she nodded.

"Were you at Caverley House?"

"No," she answered instantly.

"But, Ella, what were you doing in town?" asked John Bennett. "Did you go to see that wretched brother of yours?"

Again the hesitation, and then:

"No."

"Did you go by yourself?"

"No," said Ella, and her lip trembled. "I wish you wouldn't ask me any further questions. I'm not a free agent in the matter. Daddy, you've always trusted me: you'll trust me now, won't you?"

He took her hand and held it in both of his.

"I'll trust you always, girlie," he said; "and these gentlemen must do the same."

Her challenging eyes met Dick's, and he nodded.

"I am one who will share that trust," he said, and something in her look rewarded him.

Elk rubbed his chin fiercely.

"Being naturally of a trusting nature, I should no more think of doubting your word, Miss Bennett, than I should of believing myself." He looked at his watch. "I think we'll go along and fetch poor old Balder from the house of sin," he said.

"You'll stop and have some breakfast?"

Dick looked pleadingly at Elk, and the detective, with an air of resignation, agreed.

"Anyway, Balder won't mind an hour more or less," he said.

Whilst Ella was preparing the breakfast, Dick and Elk paced the road outside.

"Well, what do you think of it, Captain?"

"I don't understand, but I have every confidence that Miss Bennett has not lied," said Dick.

"Faith is a wonderful thing," murmured Elk, and Dick turned on him sharply.

"What do you mean?"

"I mean what I say. I have got faith in Miss Bennett," he said soothingly; "and, after all, she's only another little bit of the jigsaw puzzle that will fall into place when we fix the piece that's shaped like a Frog. And John Bennett's another," he said after a moment's thought.

From where they stood they could see, looking toward Shoreham, the opening of the narrow Elsham Wood road.

"The thing that puzzles me," Elk was saying, "is why she should go into that wood in the middle of the night——" He stopped, lowering his head. There came to them the soft purr of a motor-car. "Where is that?" he asked.

The question was answered instantly. Slowly there came into view from the wood road the bonnet of a car, followed immediately by the remainder of a large limousine, which turned toward them, gathering speed as it came. A moment later it flashed past them, and they saw the solitary occupant.

"Well, I'm damned!" said Elk, who very infrequently indulged in profanity, but Dick felt that on this occasion at least he was justified. For the man in the limousine was the bearded Ezra Maitland; and he knew that it was to see Maitland that the girl had gone to Elsham Wood.

CHAPTER XX

HAGN

A MINUTE later Ella came to the door to call them.

"Was that a car went past?" she asked, and they detected a note of anxiety in her tone.

"Yes," said Elk, "it was a big car. Didn't see who was in it, but it was a big car."

Dick heard her sigh of relief.

"Will you come in, please?" she said. "Breakfast is waiting for you."

They left half an hour later, and each man was so busy with his own thoughts that Dick did not speak until they were passing the villas where the body of Genter had been found. It was near Horsham that Genter was killed, he remembered with a little shudder. Outside of Horsham he himself had seen the dead man's feet extended beyond the back of a motor-van. Hagn should die for that; whether he was Frog or not, he was party to that murder. As if reading his thoughts, Elk turned to him and said:

"Do you think your evidence is strong enough to hang Hagn?"

"I was wondering," said Dick. "There is no supporting evidence, unfortunately, but the car which you have under lock and key, and the fact that the garage keeper may be able to identify him."

"With his beard?" asked Elk significantly. "There is going to be some difficulty in securing a conviction against this Frog, believe me, Captain Gordon. And unless old Balder induces him to make a statement, we shall have all the difficulty in the world in convincing a jury. Personally," he added, "if I was condemned to spend a night with Balder, I should tell the truth, if it was only to get rid of him. He's a pretty clever fellow, is Balder. People don't realize that—he has the makings of a first-class detective, if we could only get him to take a happier view of life."

He directed the driver to go straight to the door of Cannon Row.

Dick's mind was on another matter.

"What did she want with Maitland?" he asked.

Elk shook his head.

"I don't know," he confessed. "Of course, she might have been persuading him to take back her brother, but old Maitland isn't the kind of adventurer who'd get up in the middle of the night to discuss giving Ray Bennett his job back. If he was a younger man, yes. But he's not young. He's darned old. And he's a wicked old man, who doesn't care two cents whether Ray Bennett is working at his desk for so much per, or whether he's breaking stones on Dartmoor. I tell you, that's one of the minor mysteries which will be cleared up when we get the Frog piece in its place."

The car stopped at the entrance of Cannon Row police-station, and the men jumped down. The desk sergeant stood up as they came in, and eyed them wonderingly.

"I'm going to take Balder out, sergeant."

"Balder?" said the man in surprise. "I didn't know Balder was in."

"I put him in with Hagn."

A light dawned upon the station official.

"That's queer. I didn't know it was Balder," he said. "I wasn't on duty when he came in, but the other sergeant told me that a man had been put in with Hagn. Here is the gaoler."

That official came in at that moment, and was as astonished as the sergeant to learn the identity of the second prisoner.

"I had no idea it was Balder, sir," he said. "That accounts for the long talk they had—they were talking up till one o'clock."

"Are they still talking?" asked Elk.

"No, sir, they're sleeping now. I had a look at them a little time ago—you remember you gave me orders to leave them alone and not to go near them."

Dick Gordon and his subordinate followed the gaoler down a long passage faced with glazed brick, the wall of which was studded at intervals by narrow black doors. Reaching the end of the corridor, they turned at right angles. The second passage had only one door, and that was at the end. Snapping back the lock, the gaoler threw open the door, and Elk went in.

Elk went to the first of the figures and pulled aside the blanket which covered the face. Then, with an oath, he drew the blanket clear.

It was Balder, and he was lying on his back, covered from head to foot with a blanket. A silk scarf was twisted round his mouth; his wrists were not only handcuffed but strapped, as were his legs.

Elk dashed at the second figure, but as he touched the blanket, it sank under his hands. A folded coat, to give resemblance to a human figure, a pair of battered shoes, placed artificially at the end of the blanket—these were all. Hagn had disappeared!

When they got the man into Elk's office, and had given him brandy, and Elk, by sheer bullying, had reduced him to coherence, Balder told his story.

"I think it was round about two o'clock when it happened," he said. "I'd been talking all the evening to this Hagn, though it was very clear to me, with my experience, that he spotted me the moment I came in, as a police officer, and was kidding me along all the evening. Still, I persevered, Mr. Elk. I'm the sort of man that never says die. That's the peculiar thing about me——"

"The peculiar thing about you," said Elk wearily, "is your passionate admiration of Balder. Get on!"

"Anyway, I did try," said Balder in an injured voice; "and I thought I'd got over his suspicion, because he began talking about Frogs, and telling me that there was going to be a wireless call to all the heads to-night—that is, last night. He told me that Number Seven would never be captured, because he was too clever. He asked me how Mills had been killed, but I'm perfectly sure, the way he put the question, that he knew. We didn't talk very much after one, and at a quarter-past one I lay down, and I must have gone to sleep almost at once. The first thing I knew was that they were putting a gag in my mouth. I tried to struggle, but they held me——"

"They?" said Elk. "How many were there?"

"There may have been two or three—I'm not certain," said Balder. "If it had been only two, I think I could have managed, for I am naturally strong. There must have been more. I only saw two besides Hagn."

"Was the cell door open?"

"Yes, sir, it was ajar," said Balder after he had considered a moment.

"What did they look like?"

"They were wearing long black overcoats, but they made no attempt to hide their faces. I should know them anywhere. They were young men—at least, one was. What happened after that I don't know. They put a strap round my legs, pulled the blanket over me, and that's all I saw or heard until the cell door closed. I have been lying there all night, sir, thinking of my wife and children . . ."

Elk cut him short, and, leaving the man in charge of another police clerk, he went across to make a more careful examination of the cell. The two passages were shaped like a capital L, the special cell being at the end of the shorter branch. At the elbow was a barred door leading into the courtyard, where men waiting trial were loaded into the prison-van and distributed to various places of detention. The warder sat at the top of the L, in a small glass-panelled cubby-hole, where the cell indicators were. Each cell was equipped with a bell-push in case of illness, and the signals showed in this tiny office. From where he sat, the warder commanded, not only a view of the passage, but a side view of the door. Questioned, he admitted that he had been twice into the charge-room for a few minutes at a time; once when a man arrested for drunkenness had demanded to see a doctor, and another time, about half-past two in the morning, to take over a burglar who had been captured in the course of the night.

"And, of course, it was during that time that the men got away," said Elk.

The door into the courtyard was locked but not bolted. It could be opened from either side. The cell door could also open from both sides. In this respect it differed from every other cell in the station; but the explanation was that it was frequently used for important prisoners, whom it was necessary to subject to lengthy interrogations; and the lock had been chosen to give the police officers who were inside an opportunity of leaving the cell when they desired, without calling for the gaoler. The lock had not been picked, neither had the lock of the yard door.

Elk sent immediately for the policemen who were on duty at either entrance of Scotland Yard. The officer who was on guard at the Embankment entrance had seen nobody. The man at the Whitehall opening remembered seeing an inspector of police pass out at half-past two. He was perfectly sure the officer was an inspector, because he wore the hanging sword-belt, and the policeman had seen the star on his shoulder and had saluted him —a salute which the officer had returned.

"This may or may not be one of them," said Elk. "If it is, what happened to the other two?"

But here evidence failed. The men had disappeared as though they had dissipated into air.

"We're going to get a roasting for this, Captain Gordon," said Elk; "and if we escape without being scorched, we're lucky. Fortunately, nobody but ourselves knows that Hagn has been arrested; and when I say 'ourselves,' I wish I meant it! You had better go home and go to bed; I had some sleep in the night. If you'll wait while I send this bleating clerk of mine home to his well-advertised wife and family, I'll walk home with you."

Dick was waiting on the edge of Whitehall when Elk joined him.

"There will be a departmental inquiry, of course. We can't help that," he said. "The only thing that worries me is that I've got poor old Balder into bad odour, and I was trying to put him right. I don't know what the experience of the Boy Scouts is," he went off at a tangent, "but my own is that the worst service you can render to any man is to try to do him a good turn."

It was now nearly ten o'clock, and Dick was feeling faint with hunger and lack of sleep, for he had eaten nothing at Horsham. Once or twice, as they walked toward Harley Terrace, Elk looked back over his shoulder.

"Expecting anybody?" asked Dick, suddenly alive to the possibility of danger.

"No-o, not exactly," said Elk. "But I've got a hunch that we're being followed."

"I saw a man just now who I thought was following us," said Dick, "a man in a fawn raincoat."

"Oh, him?" said Elk, indifferent alike to the rules of grammar and the presence of his shadow. "That is one of my men. There's another on the other side of the road. I'm not thinking of them, my mind for the moment being fixed on Frogs. Do you mind if we cross the road?" he asked hurriedly, and, without waiting for a reply, caught Gordon's arm and led him across the broad thoroughfare. "I always object to walking on the same side of a street as the traffic runs. I like to meet traffic; it's not good to be overtaken. I thought so!"

A small Ford van, painted with the name of a laundry, which had been crawling along behind them, suddenly spurted and went ahead at top speed. Elk followed the car with his eyes until it reached the Trafalgar Square end of Whitehall. Instead of branching left toward Pall Mall or right to the Strand, the van swung round in a half-circle and came back to meet them. Elk half turned and made a signal.

"This is where we follow the example of the chicken," said Elk, and made another hurried crossing.

When they reached the pavement he looked round. The detectives who were following him had understood his signal, and one had leaped on the running-board of the van, which was pulled up to the pavement. There was a few minutes' talk between the driver and the officer, and then they all drove off together.

"Pinched," said Elk laconically. "He'll take him to the station on some charge or other and hold him. I guessed he'd see what I was after—my man, I mean. The easiest way to shadow is to shadow in a trade truck," said Elk. "A trade van can do anything it likes; it can loiter by the pavement, it can turn round and go back, it can go fast or slow, and nobody takes the slightest notice. If that had been a limousine, it would have attracted the attention of every policeman by drawling along by the pavement, so as to overtake us just at the right minute. Probably it wasn't any more than a shadow, but to me," he said with a quiver of his shoulder, "it felt rather like sudden death!"

Whether Elk's cheerfulness was assumed or natural, he succeeded in impressing his companion.

"Let's take a cab," said Dick, and such was his doubt that he waited for three empty taxis to pass before he hailed the fourth.

"Come in," said Dick when the cab dropped them at Harley Terrace. "I've got a spare room if you want to sleep."

Elk shook his head to the latter suggestion, but accompanied Gordon into the house. The man who opened the door had evidently something to say.

"There's a gentleman waiting to see you, sir. He's been here for half an hour."

"What is his name?"

"Mr. Johnson, sir."

"Johnson?" said Dick in surprise, and hurried to the dining-room, into which the visitor had been ushered.

It was, indeed, "the philosopher," though Mr. Johnson lacked for the moment evidence of that equilibrium which is the chiefest of his possessions. The stout man was worried; his face was unusually long; and when Dick went into the room, he was sitting uncomfortably on the edge of a chair, as he had seen him sitting at Heron's Club, his gloomy eyes fixed upon the carpet.

"I hope you'll forgive me for coming to see you, Captain Gordon," he said. "I've really no right to bring my troubles to you."

"I hope your troubles aren't as pressing as mine," smiled Dick as he shook hands. "You know Mr. Elk?"

"Mr. Elk is an old friend," said Johnson, almost cheerful for a second.

"Well, what is your kick?—sit down, won't you?" said Dick. "I'm going to have a real breakfast. Will you join me?"

"With pleasure, sir. I've eaten nothing this morning. I usually have a little lunch about eleven, but I can't say that I feel very hungry. The fact is, Captain Gordon, I'm fired."

Dick raised his eyebrows.

"What—has Maitland fired you?"

Johnson nodded.

"And to think that I've served the old devil all these years faithfully, on a clerk's salary! I've never given him any cause for complaint, I've handled hundreds of thousands—yes, and millions! And although it's not for me to blow my own trumpet, I've never once been a penny out in my accounts. Of course, if I had been, he would have found it out in less than no time, for he is the greatest mathematician I've ever met. And as sharp as a needle! He can write twice as fast as any other man I've known," he added with reluctant admiration.

"It's rather curious that a man of his uncouth appearance and speech should have those attainments," said Dick.

"It's a wonder to me," confessed Johnson. "In fact, it has been a standing wonder to me ever since I've known him. You'd think he was a dustman or a tramp, to hear him talk, yet he's a very well-read man, of extraordinary educational qualities."

"Can he remember dates?" asked Elk.

"He can even remember dates," replied Johnson seriously. "A queer old man, and in many ways an unpleasant old man. I'm not saying this because he's fired me; I've always had the same view. He's without a single spark of kindness; I think the only human thing about him is his love for this little boy."

"What little boy?" asked Elk, immediately interested.

"I've never seen him," said Johnson. "The child has never been brought to the office. I don't know who he is or whose he is; I've an idea he's a grandchild of Maitland's."

There was a pause.

"I see," said Dick softly, and well he did see, for in that second began his understanding of the Frog and the secret of the Frog.

"Why were you fired?" he asked.

Johnson shrugged his shoulders.

"Over a stupid thing; in fact, it's hardly worth talking about. It appears the old man saw me at Heron's Club the other night, and ever since then he's been going carefully into my petty cash account, probably under the impression that I was living a fast life! Beyond the usual grousing, there was nothing in his manner to suggest that he intended getting rid of me; but this morning, when I came, I found that he had already arrived, which was an unusual circumstance. He doesn't as a rule get to the office until about an hour after we start work. 'Johnson,' he said, 'I understand that you know a Miss Ella Bennett.' I replied that I was fortunate enough to know the lady. 'And I understand,' he went on, 'that you've been down there to lunch on one or two occasions.' 'That is perfectly true, Mr. Maitland,' I replied. 'Very well, Johnson,' said Maitland, 'you're fired.'"

"And that was all?" asked Dick in amazement.

"That was all," said Johnson in a hushed voice. "Can you understand it?"

Dick could have said yes, but he did not. Elk, more curious, and passionately anxious to extend his knowledge of the mysterious Maitland, had something to ask.

"Johnson, you've been right close to this man Maitland for years. Have you noticed anything about him that's particularly suspicious?"

"Like what, Mr. Elk?"

"Has he had any visitors for whom you couldn't account? Have you known him, for example, to do anything which would suggest to you that he had something to do with the Frogs?"

"The Frogs?" Johnson opened his eyes wide, and his voice emphasized his incredulity. "Bless you, no! I shouldn't imagine he knows anything about these people. You mean the tramps who have committed so many crimes? No, Mr. Elk, I've never heard or seen or read anything which gave me that impression."

"You've seen the records of most of his transactions; are there any that he has made which would lead you to believe that he had benefited, say, by the death of Mr. Maclean in Dundee, or by the attack which was made upon the woollen merchant at Derby? For example, do you know whether he has been engaged in the buying or selling of French brandies or perfumes?"

Johnson shook his head.

"No, sir, he deals only in real estate. He has properties in this country and in the South of France and in America. He has done a little business in exchanges; in fact, we did a very large exchange business until the mark broke."

"What are you going to do now, Mr. Johnson?" asked Dick.

The other made a gesture of helplessness.

"What can I do, sir?" he asked. "I am nearly fifty; I've spent most of my working life in one job, and it is very unlikely that I can get another. Fortunately for me, I've not only saved money, but I have had one or two lucky investments, and for those I must be grateful to the old man. I don't think he was particularly pleased when he found that I'd followed his advice, but that's beside the question. I do owe him that. I've just about enough money to keep me for the rest of my life if I go quietly and do not engage in any extraordinary speculations. Why I came to see you was to ask you, Captain Gordon, if you had any kind of opening. I should like a little spare time work, and I'd be most happy to work with you."

Dick was rather embarrassed, because the opportunities for employing Mr. Johnson were few and far between. Nevertheless, he was anxious to help the man.

"Let me give the matter a day or two's thought," he said. "What is Maitland doing for a secretary?"

"I don't know. That is my chief worry. I saw a letter lying on his desk, addressed to Miss Ella Bennett, and I have got an idea that he intends offering her the job."

Dick could hardly believe his ears.

"What makes you think that?"

"I don't know, sir, only once or twice the old man has inquired whether Ray has a sister. He took quite an interest in her for two or three days, and then let the matter drop. It is as astonishing as anything he has ever done."

Elk for some reason felt immensely sorry for the man. He was so obviously and patently unfitted for the rough and tumble of competition. And the opportunities which awaited a man of fifty worn to one groove were practically non-existent.

"I don't know that I can help you either, Mr. Johnson," he said. "As far as Miss Bennett is concerned, I imagine that there is no possibility of her accepting any such offer, supposing Maitland made it. I'll have your address in case I want to communicate with you."

"431, Fitzroy Square," replied Johnson, and produced a somewhat soiled card with an apology. "I haven't much use for cards," he said.

He walked to the door and hesitated with his hand on its edge.

"I'm—I'm very fond of Miss Bennett," he said, "and I'd like her to know that Maitland isn't as bad as he looks. I've got to be fair to him!"

"Poor devil!" said Elk, watching the man through the window as he walked dejectedly along Harley Terrace. "It's tough on him. You nearly told him about seeing Maitland this morning! I saw that, and was ready to jump in. It's the young lady's secret."

"I wish to heaven it wasn't," said Dick sincerely, and remembered that he had asked Johnson to stay to breakfast.

CHAPTER XXI

MR. JOHNSON'S VISITOR

THERE is a certain murky likeness between the houses in Fitzroy Square, London, and Gramercy Park, New York. Fitzroy Square belongs to the Georgian days, when Soho was a fashionable suburb, and St. Martins-in-the-Fields was really in the fields, and was not tucked away between a Vaudeville house and a picture gallery.

No. 431 had been subdivided by its owner into three self-contained flats, Johnson's being situated on the ground floor. There was a fourth basement flat, which was occupied by a man and his wife who acted for the owners, and, incidentally, were responsible, in the case of Johnson, for keeping his apartments clean and supplying him with the very few meals that he had on the premises.

It was nearly ten o'clock when philosopher Johnson arrived home that evening, and he was a very tired man. He had spent the greater part of the day in making a series of calls upon financial and real estate houses. To his inevitable inquiries he received an inevitable answer. There were no vacancies, and certainly no openings for a stoutish man of fifty, who looked, to the discerning eyes of the merchants concerned or their managing clerks, past his best years of work. Patient Mr. Johnson accepted each rebuff and moved on to another field, only to find his experience repeated.

He let himself in with a latchkey, walked wearily into a little sitting-room, and dropped with a sigh to the Chesterfield, for he was not given to violent exercise.

The room in which he sat was prettily, but not expensively furnished. A large green carpet covered the floor; the walls were hidden by book-shelves; and there was about the place a certain cosiness which money cannot buy. Rising after some little time, he walked to his book-shelf, took down a volume and spent the next two hours in reading. It was nearly midnight when he turned out the light and went to bed.

His bedroom was at the farther end of the short corridor, and in five minutes he was undressed and asleep.

Mr. Johnson was usually a light but consistent sleeper, but tonight he had not been asleep an hour before he was awake again. And wider awake than he had been at any portion of the day. Softly he got out of bed, put on his slippers and pulled a dressing-gown round him; then, taking something from a drawer in his bureau, he opened the door and crept softly along the carpeted passage toward his sitting-room.

He had heard no sound; it was sheer premonition of a pressing danger which had wakened him. His hand was on the door-knob, and he had turned it, when he heard a faint click. It was the sound of a light being turned off, and the sound came from the sitting-room.

With a quick jerk he threw open the door and reached out his hand for the switch; and then, from the blackness of the room, came a warning voice.

"Touch that light and you die! I've got you covered. Put your gun on the floor at your feet—quick!"

Johnson stooped and laid down the revolver he had taken from his bureau.

"Now step inside, and step lively," said the voice.

"Who are you?" asked Johnson steadily.

He strained his eyes to pierce the darkness, and saw the figure now. It was standing by his desk, and the shine of something in its hand warned him that the threat was no idle one.

"Never met me?" There was a chuckle of laughter in the voice of the Unknown. "I'll bet you haven't! Friend—meet the Frog!"

"The Frog?" Johnson repeated the words mechanically.

"One name's as good as another. That will do for mine," said the stranger. "Throw over the key of your desk."

There was a silence.

"I haven't my key here," said Johnson. "It is in the bedroom."

"Stay where you are," warned the voice.

Johnson had kicked off his slippers softly, and was feeling with his feet for the pistol he had laid so obediently on the floor in the first shock of surprise. Presently he found it and drew it toward him with his bare toes.

"What do you want?" he asked, temporizing.

"I want to see your office papers—all the papers you've brought from Maitlands."

"There is nothing here of any value," said Johnson.

The revolver was now at his feet and a little ahead of him. He kept his toes upon the butt, ready to drop just as soon as he could locate with any certainty the position of the burglar. But now, though his eyes were growing accustomed to the darkness, he could no longer see the owner of the voice.

"Come nearer," said the stranger, "and hold out your hands."

Johnson made as though to obey, but dropped suddenly to his knees. The explosion deafened him. He heard a cry, saw, in the flash of his pistol, a dark figure, and then something struck him.

He came to consciousness ten minutes later, to find the room empty. Staggering to his feet, he put on the light and walked unsteadily back to his bedroom, to examine the extent of his injuries. He felt the bump on his head gingerly, and grinned. Somebody was knocking at the outer door, a peremptory, authoritative knocking. With a wet towel to his injured head he went out into the passage and opened the front door. He found two policemen at the step and a small crowd gathered on the pavement.

"Has there been shooting here?"

"Yes, constable," said Johnson, "I did a little shooting, but I don't think I hit anything."

"Have you been hurt, sir? Was it burglars?"

"I can't tell you. Come in," said Johnson, and led the way back to the disordered library.

The blind was flapping in the draught, for the window, which looked out upon a side street, was open.

"Have you missed anything?"

"No, I don't think so," said Johnson. "I think it was rather more important than an ordinary burglary. I am going to call Inspector Elk of Scotland Yard, and I think you had better leave the room as it is until he arrives."

Elk was in his office, laboriously preparing a report on the escape of Hagn, when the call came through. He listened attentively, and then:

"I'll come down, Johnson. Tell the constable to leave things — ask him to speak to me."

By the time Elk had arrived, the philosopher was dressed.

"He gave you a pretty hefty one," said Elk, examining the contusion with a professional eye.

"I wasn't prepared for it. I expected him to shoot, and he must have struck at me as I fired."

"You say it was the Frog himself?" said the sceptical Elk. "I doubt it. The Frog has never undertaken a job on his own, so far as I can remember."

"It was either the Frog or one of his trusted emissaries," said Johnson with a good-humoured smile. "Look at this."

On the centre of his pink blotting-pad was stamped the inevitable Frog. It appeared also on the panel of the door.

"That is supposed to be a warning, isn't it?" said Johnson. "Well, I hadn't time to get acquainted with the warning before I got mine!"

"There are worse things than a clubbing," said Elk cheerfully. "You've missed nothing?"

Johnson shook his head.

"No, nothing."

Elk's inspection of the room was short but thorough. It was near the open window, blown by the breeze into the folds of the curtain, that he found the parcel-room ticket. It was a green slip acknowledging the reception of a handbag, and it was issued at the terminus of the Great Northern Railway.

"Is this yours?" he asked.

Johnson took the slip from him, examined it and shook his head.

"No," he said, "I've never seen it before."

"Anybody else in your flat likely to have left a bag at King's Cross station?"

Again Johnson shook his head and smiled.

"There is nobody else in this flat," he said, "except myself."

Elk took the paper under the light and scrutinized the date-stamp. The luggage had been deposited a fortnight before, and, as is usual in such tickets, the name of the depositor was not given.

"It may have blown in from the garden," he said. "There is a stiff breeze to-night, but I should not imagine that anybody who had got an important piece of luggage would leave the ticket to fly around. I'll investigate this," he said, and put the ticket carefully away in his pocket-book. "You didn't see the man?"

"I caught a glimpse of him as I fired, and I am under the impression that he was masked."

"Did you recognize his voice?"

"No," said Johnson, shaking his head.

Elk examined the window. The catch had been cleverly forced—"cleverly" because it was a new type of patent fastening familiar to him, and which he did not remember ever having seen forced from the outside before. Instinctively his mind went back to the burglary at Lord Farmley's, to that beautifully cut handle and blown lock; and though, by no stretch of imagination, could the two jobs be compared, yet there was a similarity in finish and workmanship which immediately struck him.

What made this burglary all the more remarkable was that, for the first time, there had appeared somebody who claimed to be the Frog himself. Never before had the Frog given tangible proof of his existence. He understood the organization well enough to know that none of the Frog's willing slaves would have dared to use his name. And why did he consider that Johnson was worthy of his personal attention?

"No," said Johnson in answer to his question, "there are no documents here of the slightest value. I used to bring home a great deal of work from Maitlands; in fact, I have often worked into the middle of the night. That is why my dismissal is such a scandalous piece of ingratitude."

"You have never had any private papers of Maitland's here, which perhaps you might have forgotten to return?" asked Elk thoughtfully, and Johnson's ready smile and twinkling eyes supplied an answer.

"That's rather a graceful way of putting the matter," he said. "No, I have none of Maitland's documents here. If you care, you can see the contents of all my cupboards, drawers and boxes, but I can assure you that I'm a very methodical man; I know practically every paper in my possession."

Walking home, Elk reviewed the matter of this surprising appearance. If the truth be told, he was very glad to have some additional problem to keep his mind off the very unpleasant interview which was promised for the morning. Captain Dick Gordon would assume all responsibility, and probably the Commissioners would exonerate Elk from any blame; but to the detective, the "people upstairs" were almost as formidable as the Frog himself.

CHAPTER XXII

THE INQUIRY

HE intended making an early call at King's Cross to examine the contents of the bag, but awoke the next morning, his mind filled with the coming inquiry to the exclusion of all other matters; and although he entered Johnson's burglary in his report book very carefully, and locked away the cloak-room ticket in his safe, he was much too absorbed and worried to make immediate inquiries.

Dick arrived for the inquiry, and his assistant gave him a brief sketch of the burglary in Fitzroy Square.

"Let me see that ticket," he asked.

Elk, unlocking the safe, produced the green slip.

"The ticket has been attached to something," said Dick, carrying the slip to the window. "There is the mark of a paper-fastener, and the mark is recent. This may produce a little information," he said as he handed it back.

"It's very unlikely," said Elk despondently as he locked the door of the safe. "Those people upstairs are going to give us hell."

"Don't worry," said Dick. "I tell you, our friends above are so tickled to death at recovering the Treaty that they're not going to worry much about Hagn."

It was a remarkable prophecy, remarkably fulfilled. Elk was gratified and surprised when he was called into the presence of the great—every Commissioner and Chief Constable sat round the green board of judgment—to discover that the attitude of his superiors was rather one of benevolent interest than of disapproval.

"With an organization of this character we are prepared for very unexpected developments," said the Chief Commissioner. "In ordinary circumstances, the escape of Hagn would be a matter calling for severe measures against those responsible. But I really cannot apportion the blame in this particular case. Balder seems to have behaved with perfect propriety; I quite approve of your having put him into the cell with Hagn; and I do not see what I can do with the gaoler. The truth is, that the Frogs are immensely powerful—more powerful than the agents of an enemy Government, because they are working with inside knowledge, and in addition, of course, they are our own people. You think it is possible, Captain Gordon, to round up the Frogs?—I know it will be a tremendous business. Is it worth while?"

Dick shook his head.

"No, sir," he replied. "They are too numerous, and the really dangerous men are going to be difficult to identify. It has come to our knowledge that the chiefs of this organization—at least, some of them—are not so marked."

Not all the members of the Board of Inquiry were as pleasant as the Chief Commissioner.

"It comes to this," said a white-haired Chief Constable, "that in the space of a week we have had two prisoners killed under the eyes of the police, and one who has practically walked out of the cell in which he was guarded by a police officer, without being arrested or any clue being furnished as to the method the Frogs employed." He shook his head. "That's bad, Captain Gordon."

"Perhaps you would like to take charge of the inquiry, sir," said Dick. "This is not the ordinary petty larceny type of crime, and I seem to remember having dealt with a case of yours whilst I was in the Prosecutor's Department, presenting less complicated features, in which you were no more successful than I and my officers have been in dealing with the Frogs. You must allow me the greatest latitude and exercise patience beyond the ordinary. I know the Frog," he said simply.

For some time they did not realize what he had said.

"You know him?" asked the Chief Commissioner incredulously.

Dick nodded.

"If I were to tell you who it was," he said, "you would probably laugh at me. And obviously, whilst it is quite possible for me to secure an arrest this morning, it is not as easy a matter to produce overwhelming evidence that will convict. You must give me rope if I am to succeed."

"But how did you discover him, Captain Gordon?" asked the Chief, and Elk, who had listened, dumbfounded, to this claim of his superior, waited breathlessly for the reply.

"It was clear to me," said Dick, speaking slowly and deliberately, "when I learnt from Mr. Johnson, who was Maitland's secretary, that somewhere concealed in the old man's house was a mysterious child." He smiled as he looked at the blank faces of the Board. "That doesn't sound very convincing, I'm afraid," he said, "but nevertheless, you will learn in due course why, when I discovered this, I was perfectly satisfied that I could take the Frog whenever I wished. It is not necessary to say that, knowing as I do, or as I am convinced I do, the identity of this individual, events from now on will take a more interesting and a more satisfactory course. I do not profess to be able to explain how Hagn came to make his escape. I have a suspicion—it is no more than a suspicion—but even that event is soluble if my other theory is right, as I am sure it is."

Until the meeting was over and the two men were again in Elk's office, the detective spoke no word. Then, closing the door carefully, he said:

"If that was a bluff of yours, Captain Gordon, it was the finest bluff I have ever heard, and I've an idea it wasn't a bluff."

"It was no bluff," said Dick quietly. "I tell you I am satisfied that I know the Frog."

"Who is it?"

Dick shook his head.

"This isn't the time to tell you. I don't think any useful purpose would be served if I made my views known—even to you. Now what about your cloak-room ticket?"

Dick did not accompany him to King's Cross, for he had some work to do in his office, and Elk went alone to the cloak-room. Producing the ticket, he paid the extra fees for the additional period of storage, and received from the attendant a locked brown leather bag.

"Now, son," said Elk, having revealed his identity, "perhaps you will tell me if you remember who brought this bag?"

The attendant grinned.

"I haven't that kind of memory," he said.

"I sympathize with you," said Elk, "but possibly if you concentrated your mind, you might be able to recall something. Faces aren't dates."

The attendant turned over the leaves of his book to make sure.

"Yes, I was on duty that day."

"What time was it handed in?"

He examined the counterfoils.

"About eleven o'clock in the morning," he said. He shook his head. "I can't remember who brought it. We get so much luggage entered at that time in the morning that it's almost impossible for me to recall any particular person. I know one thing, that there wasn't anything peculiar about him, or I should have remembered."

"You mean that the person who handed this in was very ordinary. Was he an American?"

Again the attendant thought.

"No, I don't think he was an American, sir," he said. "I should have remembered that. I don't think we have had an American here for weeks."

Elk took the bag to the office of the station police inspector, and with the aid of his key unlocked and pulled it wide open. Its contents were unusual. A suit of clothes, a shirt, collar and tie, a brand-new shaving outfit, a small bottle of Annatto, a colouring material used by dairymen, a passport made out in the name of "John Henry Smith," but with the photograph missing, a Browning pistol, fully loaded, an envelope containing 5,000 francs and five one-hundred-dollar bills; these comprised the contents.

Elk surveyed the articles as they were spread on the inspector's table.

"What do you make of that?"

The railwayman shook his head.

"It's a fairly complete outfit," he said.

"You mean a get-away outfit? That's what I think," said Elk; "and I'd like to bet that one of these bags is stored at every railway terminus in London!"

The clothing bore no marks, the Browning was of Belgian manufacture, whilst the passport might, or might not, have been forged, though the blank on which it was written was obviously genuine. (A later inquiry put through to the Foreign Office revealed the fact that it had not been officially issued.)

Elk packed away the outfit into the bag.

"I shall take these to the Yard. Perhaps they'll be called for—but more likely they won't."

Elk came out of the Inspector's office on to the broad platform, wondering what it would be best to do. Should he leave the bag in the cloak-room and set a man to watch? . . . That would be a little futile, for nobody could call unless he had the ticket, and it would mean employing a good officer for nothing. He decided in the end to take the bag to the Yard and hand it over for a more thorough inspection.

One of the Northern expresses had just pulled into the station, two hours late, due to a breakdown on the line. Elk stood looking idly at the stream of passengers passing out through the barrier, and, so watching, he saw a familiar face. His mind being occupied with this, the familiarity did not force itself upon his attention until the man he had recognized had passed out of view. It was John Bennett—a furtive, hurrying figure, with his battered suitcase in his hand, a dark felt hat pulled over his eyes.

Elk strolled across to the barrier where a station official was standing.

"Where does this train come from?"

"Aberdeen, sir."

"Last stop?" asked Elk.

"Last stop Doncaster," said the official.

Whilst he was speaking, Elk saw Bennett returning. Apparently he had forgotten something, for there was a frown of annoyance on his face. He pushed his way through the stream of people that were coming from the barriers, and Elk wondered what was the cause of his return. He had not long to wait before he learnt.

When Bennett appeared again, he was carrying a heavy brown box, fastened with a strap, and Elk recognized the motion picture camera with which this strange man pursued his paying hobby.

"Queer bird!" said Elk to himself and, calling a cab, carried his find back to headquarters.

He put the bag in his safe, and sent for two of his best men.

"I want the cloak-rooms of every London terminus inspected for bags of this kind," he said, showing the bag. "It has probably been left for weeks. Push the usual inquiries as to the party who made the deposit, select all likely bags, and, to make sure, have them opened on the spot. If they contained a complete shaving kit, a gun, a passport and money, they are to be brought to Scotland Yard and held for me."

Gordon, whom he afterwards saw, agreed with his explanation for the presence of this interesting find.

"At any hour of the day or night he's ready to jump for safety," said Elk admiringly; "and at any terminus we shall find money, a change of kit and the necessary passport to carry him abroad, Annatto to stain his face and hands—I expect he carries his own photograph. And by the way, I saw John Bennett."

"At the station?" asked Dick.

Elk nodded.

"He was returning from the north, from one of five towns—Aberdeen, Arbroath, Edinburgh, York or Doncaster. He didn't see me, and I didn't push myself forward. Captain, what do you think of this man Bennett?"

Dick did not reply.

"Is he your Frog?" challenged Elk, and Dick Gordon chuckled.

"You're not going to get my Frog by a process of elimination. Elk, and you can save yourself a whole lot of trouble if you cut out the idea that cross-examining me will produce good results."

"I never thought anything so silly," said Elk. "But John Bennett gets me guessing. If he were the Frog, he couldn't have been in Johnson's sitting-room last night."

"Not unless he motored to Doncaster to catch an alibi train," said Dick, and then: "I wonder if the Doncaster police are going to call in headquarters, or whether they'll rely upon their own intelligence department."

"About what?" asked Elk surprised.

"Mabberley Hall, which is just outside Doncaster, was burgled last night," said Dick, "and Lady FitzHerman's diamond tiara was stolen—rather supports your theory, doesn't it, Elk?"

Elk said nothing, but he wished most fervently that he had some excuse or other for searching John Bennett's bag.

CHAPTER XXIII

A MEETING

HERON'S CLUB had been temporarily closed by order of the police, but now was allowed to open its doors again. Ray invariably lunched at Heron's unless he was taking the meal with Lola, who preferred a brighter atmosphere than the club offered at midday.

Only a few tables were occupied when he arrived. The stigma of the police raid lay upon Heron's, and its more cautious clients had not yet begun to drift back. It was fairly well known that something had happened to Hagn, the manager, for the man had not appeared since the night of the raid. There were unconfirmed rumours of his arrest. Ray had not troubled to call for letters as he passed through the hall, for very little correspondence came to him at the club. He was therefore surprised when the waiter, having taken his order, returned, accompanied by the clerk carrying in his hand two letters, one heavily sealed and weighty, the other smaller.

He opened the big envelope first, and was putting in his fingers to extract the contents when he realized that the envelope contained nothing but money. He did not care to draw out the contents, even before the limited public. Peeping, he was gratified to observe the number and denomination of the bills. There was no message, but the other letter was addressed in the same handwriting. He tore this open. It was innocent of address or date, and the typewritten message ran:

"On Friday morning you will assume a dress which will be sent to you, and you will make your way towards Nottingham by road. You will take the name of Jim Carter, and papers of identification in that name will be found in the pockets of the clothes which will reach you by special messenger to-morrow. From now onward you are not to appear in public, you are not to shave, receive visitors or pay visits. Your business at Nottingham will be communicated to you. Remember that you are to travel by road, sleeping in such lodging-houses, casual wards or Salvation Army shelters as tramps usually patronize. At Barnet, on the Great North Road, near the ninth milestone, you will meet another whom you know, and will accompany him for the remainder of the journey. At Nottingham you will receive further orders. It is very likely that you will not be required, and certainly, the work you will be asked to do will not compromise you in any way. Remember your name is Carter. Remember you are not to shave. Remember also the ninth milestone on Friday morning. When these facts are impressed upon you, take this letter, the envelope, and the envelope containing the money, to the club fireplace, and burn them. I shall see you."

The letter was signed "Frog."

So the hour had come when the Frogs had need of him. He had dreaded the day, and yet in a way had looked forward to it as one who wished to know the worst.

He faithfully carried out the instructions, and, under the curious eyes of the guests, carried the letter and the envelopes to the empty brick fireplace, lit a match and burnt them, putting his foot upon the ashes.

His pulse beat a little quicker, the thump of his heart was a little more pronounced, as he went back to his untouched lunch. So the Frog would see him—was here! He looked round the sparsely filled tables, and presently he met the gaze of a man whose eyes had been fixed upon him ever since he had sat down. The face was familiar, and yet unfamiliar. He beckoned the waiter.

"Don't look immediately," he said in a low voice, "but tell me who is that gentleman sitting in the second alcove."

The waiter looked carelessly round.

"That is Mr. Joshua Broad, sir," he said.

Almost as the waiter spoke, Joshua Broad rose from his seat, walked across the room to where Ray was sitting.

"Good morning, Mr. Bennett. I don't think we have met before, though we are fellow-members of Heron's and I've seen you a lot of times here. My name is Broad."

"Won't you sit down?" Ray had some difficulty in controlling his voice. "Glad to meet you, Mr. Broad. Have you finished your lunch? If not, perhaps you'll take it with me."

"No," he said, "I've finished lunch. I eat very little. But if it doesn't annoy you, I'll smoke a cigarette."

Ray offered his case.

"I'm a neighbour of a friend of yours," said Broad, choosing a cigarette, "Miss Lola Bassano. She has an apartment facing mine in Caverley House—I guess that's where I've seen you most often."

Now Ray remembered. This was the strange American who lived opposite to Lola, and about whose business he had so often heard Lola and Lew Brady speculate.

"And I think we have a mutual friend in—Captain Gordon," suggested the other, his keen eyes fixed upon the boy.

"Captain Gordon is not a friend of mine," said Ray quickly. "I'm not particularly keen on police folk as friends."

"They can be mighty interesting," said Broad, "but I can quite understand your feeling in the matter. Have you known Brady long?"

"Lew? No, I can't say that I have. He's a very nice fellow," said Ray unenthusiastically. "He's not exactly the kind of friend I'd have chosen, but it happens that he is a particularly close friend of a friend of mine."

"Of Miss Bassano," said Broad. "You used to be at Maitlands?"

"I was there once," said Ray indifferently, and from his tone one might have imagined that he had merely been a visitor attracted by morbid curiosity to that establishment.

"Queer cuss, old Maitland."

"I know very little of him," said Ray.

"A very queer fellow. He's got a smart secretary, though."

"You mean Johnson?" Ray smiled. "Poor old philosopher, he's lost his job!"

"You don't say? When did this happen?" Mr. Broad's voice was urgent, eager.

"The other day—I don't know when. I met Johnson this morning and he told me. I don't know how the old boy will get on without Philo."

"I was wondering the same thing," said Broad softly. "You surprise me. I wonder he has the nerve, though I don't think he's lacking in that quality."

"The nerve?" said the puzzled Ray. "I don't think it requires much nerve to fire a secretary."

A fleeting smile played on the hard face of the American.

"By that I meant that it requires nerve for a man of Maitland's character to dismiss a man who must share a fair number of his secrets. Not that I should imagine there would be any great confidence between these two. What is Johnson doing?"

"He's looking for a job, I think," said Ray. He was getting a little irritated by the persistence of the stranger's questions. He had a feeling that he was being "pumped." Possibly Mr. Broad sensed this suspicion, for he dropped his flow of interrogations and switched to the police raid, a prolific source of discussion amongst the members of Heron's.

Ray looked after him as he walked out a little later and was puzzled. Why was he so keen on knowing all these things? Was he testing him? He was glad to be alone to consider this extraordinary commission which had come to him. The adventure of it, the disguise of it, all were particularly appealing to a romantic young man; and Ray Bennett lacked nothing in the matter of romance. There was a certain delightful suggestion of danger, a hint almost as thrilling of lawlessness, in these instructions. What might be the end of the adventure, he did not trouble to consider. It was well for his peace of mind that he was no seer; for, if he had been, he would have flown that very moment, seeking for some desolate place, some hole in the ground where he could lie and shiver and hide.

CHAPTER XXIV

WHY MAITLAND CAME

ELLA BENNETT was cooking the dinner when her father came in, depositing his heavy camera on the floor of the sitting-room, but carrying, as was usual, his grip to the bedroom. She heard the closing of the cupboard door and the turning of the lock, but had long ceased to wonder why he invariably kept his bag locked in that cupboard. He was looking very tired and old; there were deeper lines under his eyes, and the pallor of his cheeks was even more pronounced.

"Did you have a good time, father?" she asked. It was the invariable question, and invariably John Bennett made no other reply than a nod.

"I nearly lost my camera this morning—forgot it," he said. "It was quite a success—taking the camera away with me—but I must get used to remembering that I have it. I found a stretch of country full of wild fowl, and got some really good pictures. Round about Horsham my opportunities are limited, and I think I shall take the machine with me wherever I go."

He seated himself in the old chair by the fireplace and was filling his pipe slowly.

"I saw Elk on the platform at King's Cross," he said. "I suppose he was looking for somebody."

"What time did you leave where you were?" she asked.

"Last night," he replied briefly, but did not volunteer any further information about his movements.

She was in and out of the kitchen, laying the table, and she did not speak to him on the matter which was near her heart, until he had drawn up his chair, and then:

"I had a letter from Ray this morning, father," she said. It was the first time she had mentioned the boy's name since that night of horrible memories at Heron's Club.

"Yes?" he answered, without looking up from his plate.

"He wanted to know if you had his letter."

"Yes, I had his letter," said John Bennett, "but I didn't answer it. If Ray wants to see me, he knows where I am. Did you hear from anybody else?" he asked, with surprising calm.

She had been dreading what might follow the mention of Ray's name.

"I heard from Mr. Johnson. He has left Maitlands."

Bennett finished his glass of water and set it down before he replied.

"He had a good job, too. I'm sorry. I suppose he couldn't get on with the old man."

Should she tell him? she wondered again. She had been debating the advisability of taking her father into her confidence ever since— —

"Father, I've met Mr. Maitland," she said.

"I know. You saw him at his office; you told me."

"I've met him since. You remember the morning I was out, when Captain Gordon came—the morning I went to the wood? I went to see Mr. Maitland."

He put down his knife and fork and stared at her incredulously.

"But why on earth did you see him at that hour of the morning? Had you made arrangements to meet him?"

She shook her head.

"I hadn't any idea that I was going to see him," she said, "but that night I was wakened by somebody throwing a stone at the window. I thought it was Ray, who had come back late. That was his habit; I never told you, but sometimes he was very late indeed, and he used to wake me that way. It was just dawn, and when I looked out, to my astonishment, I saw Mr. Maitland. He asked me to come down in that queerly abrupt way of his, and, thinking it had something to do with Ray, I dressed and went out into the garden, not daring to wake you. We walked up the road to where his car was. It was the queerest interview you could imagine, because he said—nothing."

"Nothing?"

"Well, he asked me if I'd be his friend. If it had been anybody else but Mr. Maitland, I should have been frightened. But he was so pathetic, so very old, so appealing. He kept saying 'I'll tell you something, miss,' but every time he spoke he looked round with a frightened air. 'Let's go where we can't be seen,' he said, and begged me to step into the car. Of course I refused, until I discovered that the chauffeur was a woman—a very old woman, his sister. It was a most extraordinary experience. I think she must be nearly seventy, but during the war she learnt to drive a motor-car, and apparently she was wearing one of the chauffeur's coats, and a more ludicrous sight you could not imagine, once you realized that she was a woman.

"I let him drive me down to the wood, and then: 'Is it about Ray?' I asked. But it wasn't about Ray at all that he wanted to speak. He was so incoherent, so strange, that I really did get nervous. And then, when he had begun to compose himself and had even made a few connected remarks, you came along in Mr. Elk's car. He was terrified and was shaking from head to foot! He begged me to go away, and almost went on his knees to implore me not to say that I had seen him."

"Phew!" John Bennett pushed back his chair. "And you learnt nothing?"

She shook her head.

"He came again last night," she said, "but this time I did not go out, and he refused to come in. He struck me as a man who was expecting to be trapped."

"Did he give you any idea of what he wanted to say?"

"No, but it was something which was vitally important to him, I think. I couldn't understand half that he said. He spoke in loud whispers, and I've told you how harsh his voice is."

Bennett relit his pipe, and sat for a while with downcast eyes, revolving the matter in his mind.

"The next time he comes you'd better let me see him," he said.

"I don't think so, daddy," she answered quietly. "If he has anything very important to say, I think I ought to know what it is. I have a feeling that he is asking for help."

John Bennett looked up.

"A millionaire asking for help? Ella, that sounds queer to me."

"And it *is* queer," she insisted. "He didn't seem half so terrible as he appeared when I first saw him. There was something tragic about him, something very sad. He will come to-night, and I've promised to see him. May I?"

Her father considered.

"Yes, you may see him, provided you do not go outside this garden. I promise that I will not appear, but I shall be on hand. Do you think it is about Ray—that Ray has committed some act of folly that he wants to tell you about?" he asked with a note of anxiety.

"I don't think so, daddy. Maitland was quite indifferent to Ray or what becomes of him. I've been wondering whether I ought to tell somebody."

"Captain Gordon or Mr. Elk," suggested her father dryly, and the girl flushed. "You like that young man, Ella? No, I'm not referring to Elk, who is anything but young; I mean Dick Gordon."

"Yes," she said after a pause, "I like him very much."

"I hope you aren't going to like him too much, darling," said John Bennett, and their eyes met.

"Why not, daddy?" It almost hurt her to ask.

"Because"—he seemed at a loss as to how he should proceed —"because it's not desirable. He occupies a different position from ourselves, but that isn't the only reason. I don't want you to have a heartache, and I say this, knowing that, if that heartache comes, I shall be the cause."

He saw her face change, and then:

"What do you wish me to do?" she asked.

He rose slowly, and, walking to her, put his arm about her shoulder.

"Do whatever you like, Ella," he said gently. "There is a curse upon me, and you must suffer for my sin. Perhaps he will never know—but I am tired of expecting miracles."

"Father, what do you mean?" she asked anxiously.

"I don't know what I mean," he said as he patted her shoulder. "Things may work out as they do in stories. Perhaps . . ." He ruminated for a while. "Those pictures I took yesterday may be the making of me, Ella. But I've thought that of so many things. Always there seems to be a great possibility opening out, and always I have been disappointed. But I'm getting the knack of this picture taking. The apparatus is working splendidly, and the man who buys them—he has a shop in Wardour Street—told me that the quality of the films is improving with every new 'shot.' I took a mother duck on the nest, just as the youngsters were hatching out. I'm not quite sure how the picture will develop, because I had to be at some distance from the nest. As it was, I nearly scared the poor lady when I fixed the camera."

Very wisely she did not pursue a subject which was painful to her.

That afternoon she saw a strange man standing in the roadway opposite the gate, looking toward the house. He was a gentleman, well dressed, and he was smoking a long cigar. She thought, by his shell glasses, that he might be an American, and when he spoke to her, his New England accent left no doubt. He came toward the gate, hat in hand.

"Am I right in thinking that I'm speaking to Miss Bennett?" he asked, and when she nodded: "My name is Broad. I was just taking a look round, and I seemed to remember that you lived somewhere in the neighbourhood. In fact, I think your brother told me to-day."

"Are you a friend of Ray?" she asked.

"Why, no," said Broad with a smile. "I can't say that I'm a friend of Mr. Bennett; I'm what you might call a club acquaintance."

He made no attempt to approach her any closer, and apparently he did not expect to be invited into the house on the strength of his acquaintance with Ray Bennett. Presently, with a commonplace remark about the weather (he had caught the English habit perfectly) he moved off, and from the gate she saw him walking up towards the wood road. That long *cul-de-sac* was a favourite parking place of motorists who came to the neighbourhood, and she was not surprised when, a few minutes later, she saw the car come out. Mr. Broad raised his hat as he passed, and waved a little greeting to some person who was invisible to her. Her curiosity whetted, she opened the gate and walked on to the road. A little way down, a man was sitting on a tree trunk, reading a newspaper and smoking a large-bowled pipe. An hour later, when she came out, he was still there, but this time he was standing; a tall, soldier-like-looking man, who turned his head away when she looked in his direction. A detective, she thought, in dismay.

Her instinct was not at fault: of that she was sure. For some reason or other, Maytree Cottage was under observation. At first she was frightened, then indignant. She had half a mind to go into the village and telephone to Elk, to demand an explanation. Somehow it never occurred to her to be angry with Dick, though he was solely responsible for placing the men who were guarding her day and night.

She went to bed early, setting her alarm for three o'clock. She woke before the bell roused her, and, dressing quickly, went down to make some coffee. As she passed her father's door, he called her.

"I'm up, if you want me, Ella."

"Thank you, daddy," she said gratefully. She was glad to know that he was around. It gave her a feeling of confidence which she had never before possessed in the presence of this old man.

The first light was showing in the sky when she saw the silhouette of Mr. Maitland against the dawn, and heard the soft click of the latch as he opened the garden gate. She had not heard the car nor seen it. This time Maitland had alighted some distance short of the house.

He was, as usual, nervous and for the time being speechless. A heavy overcoat, which had seen its best days, was buttoned up to his neck, and a big cap covered his hairless head.

"That you, miss?" he asked in a husky whisper.

"Yes, Mr. Maitland."

"You coming along for a little walk? . . . Got something to tell you. . . . Very important, miss."

"We will walk in the garden," she said, lowering her voice.

He demurred.

"Suppose anybody sees us, eh? That'd be a fine lookout for me! Just a little way up the road, miss," he pleaded. "Nobody will hear us."

"We can go on to the lawn. There are some chairs there."

"Is everybody asleep? All your servant gels?"

"We have no servant girls," she smiled.

He shook his head.

"I don't blame you. I hate 'um. Got six fellows in uniform at my house. They frighten me stiff!"

She led him across the lawn, carrying a cushion, and, settling him in a chair, waited. The beginnings of these interviews had always seemed as promising, but after a while Mr. Maitland had a trick of rambling off at a tangent into depths which she could not plumb.

"You're a nice gel," said Maitland huskily. "I thought so the first time I saw you . . . you wouldn't do a poor old man any 'arm, would you, miss?"

"Why, of course not, Mr. Maitland."

"I know you wouldn't. I told Matilda you wouldn't. She says you're all right. . . . Ever been in the workhouse, miss?"

"In the poorhouse?" she said, smiling in spite of herself. "Why, no, I've never been in a poorhouse."

He looked round fearfully from side to side, peering under his white eyebrows at a clump of bushes which might conceal an eavesdropper.

"Ever been in quod?"

She did not recognize the word.

"I have," he went on. "Quod's prison, miss. Naturally you wouldn't understand them words."

Again he looked round.

"Suppose you was me. . . . It all comes to that question—suppose you was me!"

"I'm afraid I don't understand, Mr. Maitland."

She watched his frightened scrutiny of the grounds, and then he bent over toward her.

"Them fellows will get me," he said slowly and impressively. "They'll get me, *and* Matilda. And I've left all my money to a certain person. That's the joke. That's the whole joke of it, miss." He chuckled wheezily. "And then they'll get him."

He slapped his knee, convulsed with silent laughter, and the girl honestly thought he was mad and edged away from him.

"But I've got a great idea—got it when I saw you. It's one of the greatest ideas I've ever had, miss. Are you a typewriter?"

"A typist?" she smiled. "No, I can type, but I'm not a very good typist."

His voice sank until it was almost unintelligible.

"You come up to my office one day, and we'll have a great joke. Wouldn't think I was a joker, would you? Eighty-seven I am, miss. You come up to my office and I'll make you laugh!"

Suddenly he became more serious.

"They'll get me—I know it. I haven't told Matilda, because she'd start screaming. But *I* know. *And* the baby!"

This seemed to afford the saturnine old man the greatest possible enjoyment. He rocked from side to side with mirth, until a fit of coughing attacked him.

"That's all, miss. You come up to my office. Old Johnson isn't there. You come up and see me. Never had a letter from me, have you?" he suddenly asked, as he rose.

"No, Mr. Maitland," she said in surprise.

"There was one wrote," said he. "Maybe I didn't post it. Maybe I thought better. I dunno."

He started and drew back as a figure appeared before the house.

"Who's that?" he asked, and she felt a hand on her arm that trembled.

"That is my father, Mr. Maitland," she said. "I expect he got a little nervous about my being out."

"Your father, eh?" He was more relieved than resentful. "Mr. John Bennett, his name is, by all accounts. Don't tell him I've been in the workhouse," he urged, "or in quod. And I have been in quod, miss. Met all the big men, every one of 'um. And met a few of 'um out, too. I bet I'm the only man in this country that's ever seen Saul Morris, the grandest feller in the business. Only met him once, but I shall never forget him."

John Bennett saw them pacing toward him, and stood undecided as to whether he should join them or whether Ella would be embarrassed by such a move. Maitland decided the matter by hobbling over to him.

"Morning, mister," he said. "Just having a talk to your gel. Rather early in the morning, eh? Hope you don't mind, Mr. Bennett."

"I don't mind," said John Bennett. "Won't you come inside, Mr. Maitland?"

"No, no, no," said the other fearfully. "I've got to get on. Matilda will be waiting for me. Don't forget, miss: come up to my office and have that joke!"

He did not offer to shake hands, nor did he take off his hat. In fact, his manners were deplorable. A curt nod to the girl, and then:

"Well, so long, mister——" he began, and at that moment John Bennett moved out from the shadow of the house.

"Good-bye, Mr. Maitland," he said.

Maitland did not speak. His eyes were open wide with terror, his face blanched to the colour of death.

"You . . . you!" he croaked. "Oh, my God!"

He seemed to totter, and the girl sprang to catch him, but he recovered himself, and, turning, ran down the path with an agility which was surprising in one of his age, tore open the gate and flew along the road. They heard his dry sobs coming back to them.

"Father," whispered the girl in fear, "did he know you? Did he recognize you?"

"I wonder," said John Bennett of Horsham.

CHAPTER XXV

IN REGARD TO SAUL MORRIS

DICK GORDON 'phoned across to headquarters, and Elk reported immediately.

"I've discovered six good get-away bags, and each one is equipped as completely and exactly as the one we found at King's Cross."

"No clue as to the gentleman who deposited them?"

"No, sir, not so much as a clue. We've tested them all for finger-prints, and we've got a few results; but as they have been handled by half a dozen attendants, I don't think we shall get much out of it. Still, we can but try."

"Elk, I would give a few years of my life to get to the inside of this Frog mystery. I'm having Lola shadowed, though I shouldn't think she'd be in that lot. I know of nobody who looks less like a tramp than Lola Bassano! Lew has disappeared, and when I sent a man round this morning to discover what had happened to that young man about town, Mr. Raymond Bennett, he was not visible. He refused to see the caller on the plea that he was ill, and is staying in his room all day. Elk, who's the Frog?"

Elk paced up and down the apartment, his hands in his pockets, his steel-rimmed spectacles sliding lower and lower down his long nose.

"There are only two possibilities," he said. "One is Harry Lyme—an ex-convict who was supposed to have been drowned in the *Channel Queen* some years ago. I put him amongst them, because all the records we have of him show that he was a brilliant organizer, a super-crook, and one of the two men capable of opening Lord Farmley's safe and slipping that patent catch on Johnson's window. And believe me, Captain Gordon, it was an artist who burgled Johnson!"

"The other man?" said Dick.

"He's also comfortably dead," said Elk grimly. "Saul Morris, the cleverest of all. He's got Lyme skinned to death—an expression I picked up in my recent travels, Captain. And Morris is American; and although I'm as patriotic as any man in this country, I hand it to the Americans when it comes to smashing safes. I've examined two thousand records of known criminals, and I've fined it down to these two fellows—and they're both dead! They say that dead men leave no trails, and if Frog is Morris or Lyme, they're about right. Lyme's dead—drowned. Morris was killed in a railway accident in the United States. The question is, which of the ghosts we can charge."

Dick Gordon pulled open the drawer of his desk and took out an envelope that bore the inscription of the Western Union. He threw it across the table.

"What's this. Captain Gordon?"

"It's an answer to a question. You mentioned Saul Morris before, and I have been making inquiries in New York. Here's the reply."

The cablegram was from the Chief of Police, New York City.

"Answering your inquiry. Saul Morris is alive, and is believed to be in England at this moment. No charges pending against him here, but generally supposed to be the man who cleared out strong room of ss. *Mantania*, February 17, 1898, Southampton, England, and got away with 55,000,000 francs. Acknowledge."

Elk read and re-read the cablegram, then he folded it carefully, put it back in its envelope and passed it across the table.

"Saul Morris is in England," he said mechanically. "That seems to explain a whole lot."

The search which detectives had conducted at the railway termini had produced nine bags, all of which contained identical outfits. In every case there was a spare suit, a clean shirt, two collars, one tie, a Browning pistol with cartridges, a forged passport without photograph, the Annatio and money. Only in one respect did the grips differ. At Paddington the police had recovered one which was a little larger than its fellows, all of which were of the same pattern and size. This held the same outfit as the remainder, with the exception that, in addition, there was a thick pad of cheque forms, every cheque representing a different branch of a different bank. There were cheques upon the Credit Lyonnais, upon the Ninth National Bank of New York, upon the

Burrowstown Trust, upon the Bank of Spain, the Banks of Italy and Roumania, in addition to about fifty branches of the five principal banks of England. Occupied as he had been, Elk had not had time to make a very close inspection, but in the morning he determined to deal seriously with the cheques. He was satisfied that inquiries made at the banks and branches would reveal different depositors; but the numbers might enable him to bring the ownership home to one man or one group of men.

As the bags were brought in, they had been examined superficially and placed in Elk's safe, and to accommodate them, the ordinary contents of the safe had been taken out and placed in other repositories. Each bag had been numbered and labelled with the name of the station from whence it was taken, the name of the officer who had brought it in, and particulars of its contents. These facts are important, as having a bearing upon what subsequently happened.

Elk arrived at his office soon after ten o'clock, having enjoyed the first full night's sleep he had had for weeks. He had, as his assistants, Balder and a detective-sergeant named Fayre, a promising young man, in whom Elk placed considerable trust. Dick Gordon arrived almost simultaneously with the detective chief, and they went into the building together.

"There isn't the ghost of a chance that we shall be rewarded for the trouble we've taken to trace these cheques," said Elk, "and I am inclined to place more hope upon the possibility of the handbags yielding a few items which were not apparent at first examination. All these bags are lined, and there is a possibility that they have false bottoms. I am going to cut them up thoroughly, and if there's anything left after I'm through, the Frogs are welcome to their secret."

In the office, Balder and the detective-sergeant were waiting, and Elk searched for his key. The production of the key of the safe was invariably something of a ritual where Elk was concerned. He gave Dick Gordon the impression that he was preparing to disrobe, for the key reposed in some mysterious region which involved the loosening of coat, waistcoat, and the diving into a pocket where no pocket should be. Presently the ceremony was through, Elk solemnly inserted the key and swung back the door.

The safe was so packed with bags that they began to slide toward him, when the restraining pressure of the door was removed. One by one he handed them out, and Fayre put them on the table.

"We'll take that Paddington one first," said Elk, pointing to the largest of the bags. "And get me that other knife, Balder."

The two men walked out into the passage, leaving Fayre alone.

"Can you see the end of this, Captain Gordon?" asked Elk.

"The end of the Frogs? Why, yes, I think I can. I could almost say I was sure."

They had reached the door of the clerk's office and found Balder holding a murderous looking weapon in his hand.

"Here it is— —" he began, and the next instant Dick was flung violently to the floor, with Elk on top of him.

There was the shrill shriek of smashed glass, a pressure of wind, and, through all this violence, the deafening thunder of an explosion.

Elk was first to his feet and flew back to his room. The door hung on its hinges; every pane of glass was gone, and the sashes with them. From his room poured a dense volume of smoke, into which he plunged. He had hardly taken a step before he tripped on the prostrate figure of Fayre, and, stooping, he half-lifted and half-dragged him into the corridor. One glance was sufficient to show that, if the man was not dead, there seemed little hope of his recovery. The fire-bells were ringing throughout the building. A swift rush of feet on the stairs, and the fire squad came pelting down the corridor, dragging their hose behind them.

What fire there was, was soon extinguished, but Elk's office was a wreck. Even the door of the safe had been blown from its hinges. There was not a single article of furniture left, and a big hole gaped in the floor.

"Save those bags," said Elk and went back to look after the injured man, and not until he had seen his assistant placed in the ambulance did he return to a contemplation of the ruin which the bomb had made.

"Oh, yes, it was a bomb, sir," said Elk.

A group of senior officers stood in the corridor, looking at the havoc.

"And something particularly heavy in the shape of bombs. The wonder is that Captain Gordon and I were not there. I told Fayre to open the bag, but I thought he'd wait until we returned with the knife—we intended examining the lining. Fayre must have opened the bag and the bomb exploded."

"But weren't the bags examined before?" asked the Commissioner wrathfully.

Elk nodded.

"They were examined by me yesterday—every one. The Paddington bag was turned inside out, every article it contained was placed on my table, and catalogued. I myself returned them. There was no bomb."

"But how could they be got at?" asked the other.

Elk shook his head.

"I don't know, sir. The only other person who has a key to this safe is the Assistant Commissioner of my department, Colonel McClintock, who is on his holidays. We might all have been killed."

"What was the explosive?"

"Dynamite," said Elk promptly. "It blew down." He pointed to the hole in the floor. "Nitro-glycerine blows up and sideways," he sniffed. "There's no doubt about it being dynamite."

In his search of the office he found a twisted coil of thin steel, later the blackened and crumpled face of a cheap alarm dock.

"Both time and contact," he said. "Those Frogs are taking no chances."

He shifted such of his belongings as he could discover into Balder's office.

There was little chance that this outrage would be kept from the newspapers. The explosion had blown out the window and a portion of the brickwork and had attracted a crowd on the Embankment outside. Indeed, when Elk left headquarters, he was confronted by newspaper bills telling of the event.

His first call was at the near-by hospital, to where the unfortunate Fayre had been taken, and the news he received was encouraging. The doctors thought that, with any kind of luck, they would not only save the man's life, but also save him from any serious mutilation.

"He may lose a finger or two, and he's had a most amazing escape," said the house surgeon. "I can't understand why he wasn't blown to pieces."

"What I can't understand," said Elk emphatically, "is why *I* wasn't blown to pieces."

The surgeon nodded.

"These high explosives play curious tricks," said the surgeon. "I understand that the force of the explosion blew off the door of the safe, and yet this paper, which must also have been within range, is scarcely singed."

He took a square of paper out of his pocket; the edges were blackened; one corner had been burnt off.

"I found this in his clothing. It must have been driven there when the bomb detonated," said the surgeon.

Elk smoothed out the paper and read:

"*With the compliments of Number Seven.*"

Carefully he folded the paper.

"I'll take this," he said, and put it tenderly away in the interior of his spectacle case. "Do you believe in hunches, doctor?"

"Do you mean premonitions?" smiled the surgeon. "To an extent I do."

Elk nodded.

"I have a hunch that I'm going to meet Number Seven—very shortly," he said.

CHAPTER XXVI

PROMOTION FOR BALDER

A WEEK had passed, and the explosion at headquarters was ancient history. The injured detective was making fair progress toward recovery, and in some respects the situation was stagnant.

Elk apparently accepted failure as an inevitability, and seemed, even to his greatest admirer, to be hypnotized into a fatalistic acceptance of the situation. His attitude was a little deceptive. On the sixth day following the explosion, headquarters made a raid upon the cloak-rooms, and again, as Elk had expected, produced from every single terminus parcels office, a brand-new bag with exactly the same equipment as the others had had, except that the Paddington find differed from none of its fellows.

The bags were opened by an Inspector of Explosives, after very careful preliminary tests; but they contained nothing more deadly than the Belgian pistols and the self-same passports, this time made out in the name of "Clarence Fielding."

"These fellows are certainly thorough," said Elk with reluctant admiration, surveying his haul.

"Are you keeping the bags in your office?" asked Dick, but Elk shook his melancholy head.

"I think not," said he.

He had had the bags immediately emptied, their contents sent to the Research Department; the bags themselves were now stripped of leather and steel frames, for they had been scientifically sliced, inch by inch.

"My own opinion," said Balder oracularly, "is that there's somebody at police headquarters who is working against us. I've been considering it for a long time, and after consulting my wife ——"

"You haven't consulted your children, too, have you?" asked Elk unpleasantly. "The less you talk about headquarters' affairs in your domestic circle, the better will be your chance of promotion."

Mr. Balder sniffed.

"There's no fear of that, anyway," he said sourly. "I've got myself in their bad books. And I did think there was a chance for me—it all comes of your putting me in with Hagn."

"You're an ungrateful devil," said Elk.

"Who's this Number Seven, sir?" asked Balder. "Thinking the matter over, and having discussed it with my wife, I've come to the conclusion that he's one of the most important Frogs, and if we could only get him, we'd be a long way towards catching the big fellow."

Elk put down his pen—he was writing his report at the time—and favoured his subordinate with a patient and weary smile.

"You ought to have gone into politics," he said, and waved his subordinate from the room with the end of his penholder.

He had finished his report and was reading it over with a critical eye, when the service 'phone announced a visitor.

"Send him up," said Elk when he had heard the name. He rang his bell for Balder. "This report goes to Captain Gordon to initial," he said, and as he put down the envelope, Joshua Broad stood in the doorway.

"Good morning, Mr. Elk." He nodded to Balder, although he had never met him. "Good morning," he said.

"Good morning," said Elk. "Come right in and sit down, Mr. Broad. To what do I owe the pleasure of this call?—excuse my politeness, but in the early morning I'm that way. All right, Balder, you can go."

Broad offered his cigar-case to the detective. "I've come on a curious errand," he said.

"Nobody ever comes to headquarters on any other," replied Elk.

"It concerns a neighbour of mine."

"Lola Bassano?"

"Her husband," said the other, "Lew Brady."

Elk pushed up his spectacles.

"You don't tell me that she's properly married to Lew Brady?" he asked in surprise.

"I don't think there's any doubt about that," said Broad, "though I'm perfectly certain that her young friend Bennett is not aware of the fact. Brady has been staying at Caverley House for a week, and during that time he has not gone out of doors. What is more, the boy hasn't called; I don't think there's a quarrel—I have a notion there's something much deeper than that. I saw Brady by accident as I was coming out of my door. Bassano's door also happened to be open: the maid was taking in the milk: and I caught a glimpse of him. He has the finest crop of whiskers I've seen on a retired pugilist and their ambitions do not as a rule run to hair! That made me pretty curious," he said, carefully knocking the ash of his cigar into a tray that was on the table, "and I wondered if there was any connection between this sudden defiance of the barber and Ray Bennett's actions. I made a call on him—I met him the other day at the club and had, as an excuse, the fact that I have also managed to meet Miss Ella Bennett. His servant—he has a man in by the day to brush his clothes and tidy up the place—told me that he was not well and was not visible."

Mr. Broad blew out a ring of smoke and watched it thoughtfully.

"If you want a servant to be faithful, he must live on the premises," he said. "These occasional men aren't with you long enough to get trustworthy. It cost me, at the present rate of exchange, two dollars and thirty-five cents to discover that Mr. Ray Bennett is also in the hair-restoring business. If there were an election on, these two fellows might be political cranks who had vowed a vow that they wouldn't touch their razors until their party was returned to power. And if Lew Brady were a real sportsman, I should guess that they were doing this for a bet. As it is, I'm rather intrigued."

Elk rolled his cigar from one corner of his mouth to the other.

"I'm not well acquainted with the Statute Book," he said, "but I'm under the impression there is no law preventing people from cultivating undergrowth. The—what's the word?—psych——"

"Psychology," suggested Mr. Broad.

"That's it. The psychology of whiskers has never quite reached me. You're American, aren't you, Mr. Broad?"

"I have the distinction," said the other with that half-smile that came so readily to his eyes.

"Ah!" said Elk absently, as he stared through the window. "Ever heard of a man called Saul Morris?"

He brought his eyes back to the other's face. Mr. Joshua Broad was frowning in an effort of thought.

"I seem to remember the name. He was a criminal of sorts, wasn't he—an American criminal, if I remember rightly? Yes, I've heard of him. I seem to remember that he was killed a few years ago."

Elk scratched his chin irritably.

"I'd like to meet somebody who was at his funeral," he said, "somebody I could believe on oath."

"You're not suggesting that Lew Brady——"

"No. I'm not suggesting anything about Lew Brady, except that he's a very poor boxer. I'll look into this distressing whisker competition, Mr. Broad, and thank you for telling me."

He wasn't especially interested in the eccentric toilet of Ray Bennett. At five o'clock Balder came to him and asked if he might go home.

"I promised my wife——" he began.

"Keep it," said Elk.

After his subordinate's departure there came an official letter to Inspector Elk, and, reading its contents, Mr. Elk beamed. It was a letter from the Superintendent who controlled the official careers of police officers at headquarters.

"Sir," it ran, "I am directed by the Chief Commissioner of Police to inform you that the promotion of Police-Constable J. J. Balder to the rank of Acting-Sergeant has been approved. The appointment will date as from the 1st May."

Elk folded up the paper and was genuinely pleased. He rang the bell for Balder before he remembered that he had sent his assistant home. Elk's evening was free, and in the kindness of his heart he decided upon conveying the news personally.

"I'd like to see this wife of his," said Elk, addressing nobody, "and the children!"

Elk turned up the official pass register, and found that Balder lived at 93, Leaford Road, Uxbridge. The names of his wife and children were not entered, to Elk's disappointment. He would like to have addressed the latter personally, but no new entry had been made on the sheet since Balder's enlistment.

His police car took him to Leaford Road; 93 was a respectable little house—such a house as Elk always imagined his assistant would live in. His knock was answered by an elderly woman who was dressed for going out, and Elk was surprised to see that she wore the uniform of a nurse.

"Yes, Mr. Balder lives here," she said, apparently surprised to see the visitor. "That is to say, he has two rooms here, though he very seldom stays here the night. He usually comes here to change, and then I think he goes on to his friends."

"Does his wife live here?"

"His wife?" said the woman in surprise. "I didn't know that he was married."

Elk had brought Balder's official record with him, to procure some dates which it was necessary he should certify for pension purposes. In the space against Balder's address, he noticed for the first time that there were two addresses given, and that Leaford Road had been crossed out with ink so pale that he only noticed it now that he saw the paper in daylight. The second address was one in Stepney.

"I seem to have made a mistake," he said. "His address here is Orchard Street, Stepney." But the nurse smiled.

"He was with me many years ago," she said, "then he went to Stepney, but during the war he came here, because the air raids were rather bad in the East End of London. I am under the impression he has still a room in Stepney."

"Oh?" said Elk thoughtfully.

He was at the gate when the nurse called him back.

"I don't think he goes to Stepney, though I don't know whether I ought to talk about his business to a stranger; but if you want him particularly, I should imagine you would find him at Slough. I'm a monthly nurse," she said, "and I've seen his car twice going into Seven Gables on the Slough Road. I think he must have a friend there."

"Whose car?" asked the startled Elk.

"It may be his or his friend's car," said the nurse. "Is he a friend of yours?"

"He is in a way," said Elk cautiously.

She stood for a moment thinking.

"Will you come in, please?"

He followed her into the clean and tidy little parlour.

"I don't know why I told you, or why I've been talking so freely to you," she said, "but the truth is, I've given Mr. Balder notice. He makes so many complaints, and he's so difficult to please, that I can't satisfy him. It isn't as though he paid me a lot of money—he doesn't. I make very little profit out of his rooms, and I've a chance of letting them at a better rent. And then he's so particular about his letters. I've had a letter-box put on the door, but even that is not big enough to hold them some days. What his other business is, I don't know. The letters that come here are for the Didcot Chemical Works. You probably think that I am a very difficult woman to please, because, after all, he's out all day and seldom sleeps here at night."

Elk drew a long breath.

"I think you're nearly the finest woman I've ever met," he said. "Are you going out now?"

She nodded.

"I've an all night case, and I shan't be back till eleven tomorrow. You were very fortunate in finding anybody at home."

"I think you said 'his car'; what sort of a car is it?" asked Elk.

"It's a black machine—I don't know the make; I think it is an American make. And he must have something to do with the ownership because once I found a lot of tyre catalogues in his bedroom, and some of the tyres he had marked with a pencil, so I suppose he's responsible to an extent."

One last question Elk asked.

"Does he come back here at night after you've gone?"

"Very rarely, I imagine," replied the woman. "He has his own key, and as I'm very often out at night I'm not sure whether he returns or not."

Elk stood with one foot on the running-board of his car.

"Perhaps I can drop you somewhere, madam?" he said, and the elderly woman gratefully accepted.

Elk went back to headquarters, opened a drawer of his desk and took out a few implements of his profession, and, after filing a number of urgent instructions, returned to the waiting car, driving to Harley Terrace. Dick Gordon had an engagement that night to join a theatre party with the members of the American Embassy, and he was in one of the boxes at the Hilarity Theatre when Elk opened the door quietly, tapped him on the shoulder, and brought him out into the corridor, without the remainder of the party being aware that their guest had retired.

"Anything wrong, Elk?" asked Gordon.

"Balder's got his promotion," said Elk solemnly, and Dick stared at him. "He's an Acting-Sergeant," Elk went on, "and I don't know a better rank for Balder. When this news comes to him and his wife and children, there'll be some happy hearts, believe me."

Elk never drank: this was the first thought that came to Dick Gordon's mind; but there was a possibility that the anxieties and worries of the past few weeks might have got on top of him.

"I'm very glad for Balder," he said gently, "and I'm glad for you too, Elk, because I know you tried hard to get this miserable devil a step in the right direction."

"Go on with what you were thinking," said Elk.

"I don't know that I was thinking anything," laughed Dick.

"You were thinking that I must be suffering from sunstroke, or I shouldn't take you out of your comfortable theatre to announce Balder's promotion. Now will you get your coat, Captain Gordon, and come along with me? I want to break the news to Balder."

Mystified, but asking no further questions, Gordon went to the cloak-room, got his coat, and joined the detective in the vestibule.

"We're going to Slough—to the Seven Gables," he added. "It's a fine house. I haven't seen it, but I know it's a fine house, with a carriage drive and grand furniture, electric light, telephone and a modern bathroom. That's deduction. I'll tell you something else—also deduction. There are trip wires on the lawn, burglar alarms in the windows, about a hundred servants——"

"What the devil are you talking about?" asked Dick, and Elk chuckled hysterically.

They were running through Uxbridge when a long-bodied motor-car whizzed past them at full speed. It was crowded with men who were jammed into the seats or sat upon one another's knees.

"That's a merry little party," said Dick.

"Very," replied Elk laconically.

A few seconds later, a second car flashed past, going much faster than they.

"That looks to me like one of your police cars," said Dick.

This, too, was crowded.

"It certainly looks like one of my police cars," agreed Elk. "In America they've got a better stunt. As you probably know, they've a fine patrol wagon system. I'd like to introduce it into this country; it's very handy."

As the car slowed to pass through the narrow, crooked street of Colnebrook, a third of the big machines squeezed past, and this time there was no mistaking its character. The man who sat with the driver, Dick knew as a detective inspector. He winked at Elk as he passed, and Elk winked back with great solemnity.

"What is the idea?" asked Dick, his curiosity now thoroughly piqued.

"We're having a smoking concert," said Elk, "to celebrate Balder's promotion. And it will be one of the greatest successes that we've had in the history of the Force. There will be the brothers Mick and Mac, the trick cyclists, in their unrivalled act . . ." He babbled on foolishly.

At Langley the fourth and fifth police cars came past. Dick had long since realized that the slow pace at which his own car was moving was designed to allow these laden machines to overtake them. Beyond Langley, the Windsor road turned abruptly to the left, and, leaning over the driver, Elk gave new instructions. There was no sign of the police cars: they had apparently gone on to Slough. A solitary country policeman stood at the cross-roads and watched them as they disappeared in the dusk with a certain languid interest.

"We'll stop here," said Elk, and the car was pulled from the road on to the green sidewalk.

Elk got down.

"Walk a little up the road while I talk to Captain Gordon," he said to the chauffeur, and then he talked, and Dick listened in amazement and unbelief.

"Now," said Elk, "we've got about five minutes' walk, as far as I can remember. I haven't been to Windsor races for so long that I've almost forgotten where the houses are."

They found the entrance to the Seven Gables between two stiff yew hedges. There was no gateway; a broad, gravelled path ran between a thick belt of pine trees, behind which the house was hidden. Elk went a little ahead. Presently he stopped and raised his hand warningly. Dick came a little nearer, and, looking over the shoulder of the detective, had his first view of Seven Gables.

It was a large house, with timbered walls and high, twisted chimney-stacks.

"Pseudo-Elizabethan," said Dick admiringly.

"1066," murmured Elk, "or was it 1599? That's *some* house!"

It was growing dusk, and lights were showing from a broad window at the farther end of the building. The arched doorway was facing them.

"Let us go back," whispered Elk, and they retraced their steps.

It was not until darkness had fallen that he led the way up the carriage drive to the point they had reached on their earlier excursion. The light still showed in the window, but the cream-coloured blinds were drawn down.

"It is safe up as far as the door," whispered Elk; "but right and left of that, watch out!"

He had pulled a pair of thick stockings over his shoes, and handed another pair to Dick; and then, with an electric torch in his hand, he began to move along the path which ran parallel with the building. Presently he stopped.

"Step over," he whispered.

Dick, looking down, saw the black thread traversing the path, and very cautiously avoided the obstacle.

A few more paces, and again Elk stopped and warned Dick to step high, turning to show his light upon the second of the threads, almost invisible even in the powerful glare of the electric lamp. He did not move from where he stood until he had made a careful examination of the path ahead; and it was well that he did so, for the third trip wire was less than two feet from the second.

They were half-an-hour covering the twenty yards which separated them from the window. The night was warm, and one of the casements was open. Elk crept close under the window-sill, his sensitive fingers feeling for the alarm which he expected to find protecting the broad sill. This he discovered and avoided, and, raising his hand, he gently drew aside the window blind.

He saw a large, oaken-panelled room, luxuriously furnished. The wide, open stone fireplace was banked with flowers, and before it, at a small table, sat two men. The first was Balder—unmistakably Balder, and strangely good-looking. Balder's red nose was no longer red. He was in evening dress and between his teeth was a long amber cigarette-holder.

Dick saw it all, his cheek against Elk's head, heard the quick intake of the detective's breath, and then noticed the second man. It was Mr. Maitland.

Mr. Maitland sat, his face in his hands, and Balder was looking at him with a cynical smile.

They were too far away to hear what the men were saying, but apparently Maitland was being made the object of reproof. He looked up after a while, and got on to his feet and began talking. They heard the rumble of his excited voice, but again no word was intelligible. Then they saw him raise his fist and shake it at the smiling man, who watched him with a calm, detached interest, as though he were some strange insect which had come into his ken. With this parting gesture of defiance, old Maitland shuffled from the room and the door closed behind him. In a few minutes he came out of the house, not through the doorway, as they expected, but apparently through a gateway on the other side of the hedge, for they saw the gleam of the headlights of his car as it passed.

Left alone, Balder poured himself a drink and apparently rang for one of the servants. The man who came in arrested Dick's attention instantly. He wore the conventional uniform of a footman, the dark trousers and the striped waistcoat, but it was easy to see, from the way he moved, that he was not an ordinary type of servant. A big man, powerfully built, his every action was slow and curiously deliberate. Balder said something to him, and the footman nodded, and, taking up the tray, went out with the same leisurely, almost pompous, step that had distinguished his entry.

And then it flashed upon Dick, and he whispered into the detective's ear one word.

"Blind!"

Elk nodded. Again the door opened, and this time three footmen came in, carrying a heavy-looking table with a canvas cover. At first Gordon thought that it was Balder's meal that was being brought, but he was soon to discover the truth. Above the fireplace, hanging on a single wire, was a large electric lamp, which was not alight. Standing on a chair, one of the footmen took out the lamp and inserted a plug from the end of which ran a wire connecting with the table.

"They're all blind," said Elk in a whisper. "And that is Balder's own broadcasting apparatus, and the aerial is attached to the lamp."

The three servants went out, and, rising, Balder walked to the door and locked it.

There were another set of windows in the room, looking out upon the side of the house, and one by one Balder closed and shuttered them. He was busy with the second of the three, when Elk put his foot upon a ledge of brick, and, tearing aside the curtain, leapt into the room.

At the sound, Balder spun round.

"Evening, Balder," said Elk.

The man made no reply. He stood, watching his sometime chief, with eyes that did not waver.

"Thought I'd come along and tell you that you've got your promotion," said Elk, "as Acting-Sergeant from the 1st of May, in recognition of the services you've rendered to the State by poisoning Frog Mills, loosing Frog Hagn, and blowing up my office with a bomb that you planted overnight."

Still the man did not speak, nor did he move; and here he was discreet, for the long-barrelled Browning in Elk's hand covered the lower button of his white piqué waistcoat.

"And now," said Elk—there was a ring of triumph in his voice—"you'll take a little walk with me—I want you, *Number Seven!*"

"Haven't you made a mistake?" drawled Balder, so unlike his usual voice that Elk was for a moment taken aback.

"I never have made a mistake except about the date when Henry the Eighth married," said Elk.

"Who do you imagine I am?" asked this debonair man of the world.

"I've ceased imagining anything about you, Balder—I know!"

Elk walked with a quick movement toward him and thrust the muzzle of the pistol in his prisoner's diaphragm.

"Put up your hands and turn round," he said.

Balder obeyed. Slipping a pair of handcuffs from his pocket, Elk snapped them on to the wrists. Deftly the detective strapped the arms from behind, drawing them tight, so that the manacled hands had no play.

"This is very uncomfortable," said Balder. "Is it usual for you to make mistakes of this character, Mr. Elk? My name is Collett-Banson."

"Your name is Mud," said Elk, "but I'm willing to listen to anything you like to say. I'd rather have your views on cyanide of potassium than anything. You can sit down."

Dick saw a gleam come to the man's eye; it flashed for a second and was gone. Evidently Elk saw it too.

"Don't let your hopes rest upon any monkey tricks that might be played by your attendants," he said, "because fifty C.I.D. men, most of whom are known personally to you, are disposed round this house."

Balder laughed.

"If they were round the house and on top of the house, they wouldn't worry me," he said. "I tell you, inspector, you've made a very grave error, and one which will cost you dear. If a gentleman cannot sit in his own drawing-room"—he glanced at the table—"listening to a wireless concert at The Hague without interfering policemen—then it is about time the police force was disbanded."

He walked across to the fireplace carelessly and stood with his back to it; then, lifting his foot, he kicked back one of the steel fire-dogs which stood on either side of the wide hearth, and the "dog" fell over on its side. It was a nervous act of a man who was greatly worried and was not quite conscious of what he was doing. Even Elk, who was all suspicion, saw nothing to excite his apprehension.

"You think my name is Balder, do you?" the man went on. "Well, all I can say is— —"

Suddenly he flung himself sideways on to the hearthrug, but Elk was quicker. As an oblong slip of the floor gave way beneath the man's weight, Elk gripped him by the collar and together they dragged him back to the room.

In a second the three were struggling on the floor together, and in his desperation Balder's strength was unbelievable. His roaring cry for help was heard. There came a heavy blow on the door, the babble of angry voices without, and then, from the ground outside, a series of sharp explosions, as the army of detectives raced across the lawn, oblivious to the presence of the alarm-guns.

The fight was short and sharp. The six blind men who comprised the household of No. 7 were hustled away, and in the last car travelled Acting-Sergeant Balder, that redoubtable No. 7, who was the right hand and the left hand of the terrible Frog.

CHAPTER XXVII

MR. BROAD IS INTERESTING

DICK GORDON ended his interview with Mr. Ezra Maitland at three o'clock in the morning, and went to Headquarters, to find the charge-room at Cannon Row singularly empty. When he had left, it was impossible to get in or out for the crowd of detectives which filled or surrounded the place.

"On the whole, Pentonville is safest, and I've got him there. I asked the Governor to put him in the condemned cell, but it is not etiquette. Anyway, Pentonville is the safest spot I know, and I think that, unless Frogs eat stones, he'll stay. What has Maitland got to say, Captain?"

"Maitland's story, so far as one can get a story from him, is that he went to see Balder by invitation. 'When you're sent for by the police, what can you do?' he asked, and the question is unanswerable."

"There is no doubt at all," said Elk, "that Maitland knew Balder's character, and it was not in his capacity as policeman that the old man visited him. There is less doubt that this man is hand in glove with the Frog, but it is going to be very difficult to prove."

"Maitland puzzles me," said Dick. "He's such a bully, and yet such a frightened old man. I thought he was going to drop through the floor when I told him who I was, and why I had come. And when I mentioned the fact that Balder had been arrested, he almost collapsed."

"That line has to be followed," said Elk thoughtfully. "I have sent for Johnson. He ought to be here by now. Johnson must know something about the old man's business, and he will be a very valuable witness if we can connect the two."

The philosopher arrived half-an-hour later, having been aroused from his sleep to learn that his presence was required at Headquarters.

"Mr. Elk will tell you something which will be public property in a day or two," said Gordon. "Balder has been arrested in connection with the explosion which occurred in Mr. Elk's office."

It was necessary to explain to Johnson exactly who Balder was, and Dick went on to tell him of the old man's visit to Slough. Johnson shook his head.

"I didn't know that Maitland had a friend of that name," he said. "Balder? What other name had he?"

"He called himself Collett-Banson," said Dick, and a look of understanding came to the face of Johnson.

"I know that name very well. Mr. Banson used frequently to call at the office, generally late in the evenings—Maitland spends three nights a week working after the clerks have gone, as I know to my cost," he said. "A rather tall, good-looking fellow of about forty?"

"Yes, that is the man."

"He has a house near Windsor. I have never been there, but I know because I have posted letters to him."

"What sort of business did Collett-Banson have with Maitland?"

"I've never been able to discover. I always thought of him as a man who had property to sell, for that was the only type of outsider who was ever admitted to Maitland's presence. I remember that he had the child staying with him for about a week——"

"That is, the child in Maitland's house?"

Johnson nodded.

"You don't know what association there is between the child and these two men?"

"No, sir, except that I am certain that Mr. Collett-Banson had the little boy with him, because I sent toys—mechanical engines or something of the sort—by Mr. Maitland's directions. It was the day that Mr. Maitland made his will, about eighteen months ago. I remember the day particularly for a peculiar reason. I had expected Mr. Maitland to ask me to witness the will and was piqued, for no cause, because he brought two clerks up from the office to sign. These little things impress themselves upon one," he added.

"Was the will made in favour of the child?"

Johnson shook his head.

"I haven't the slightest knowledge of how the property goes," he said. "He never discussed the matter with me; he wouldn't even employ a lawyer. In fact, I don't remember his ever employing a lawyer all the time I was with him, except for conveyancing work. He told me he had copied the form of will from a book, but beyond feeling hurt that I, an old and faithful servant of his, hadn't been taken a little into his confidence, I wasn't greatly interested in the matter. But I do remember that that morning I went down to a store and bought a whole lot of toys, had them packed and brought them back to the office. The old man played with them all the afternoon!"

Early in the morning Dick Gordon interviewed the prisoners at Pentonville, and found them in a very obstinate mood.

"I know nothing about babies or children; and if Johnson says he sent toys, he is lying," said Balder defiantly. "I refuse to make any statement about Maitland or my association with Maitland. I am the victim of police persecution, and I defy you to bring any proof that I have committed a single act in my life—unless it is a crime to live like a gentleman—for which you can imprison me."

"Have you any message for your wife and children?" asked Dick sarcastically, and the sullen features of the man relaxed for a second.

"No, Elk will look after them," he said humorously.

The most stringent precautions had been taken to prevent a rescue, and the greatest care was exercised that no communication passed between No. 7 and the outside world. He was charged at Bow Street an hour before the court usually sat. Evidence of arrest was taken, and he was remanded, being removed to Pentonville in a motor-van under armed guard.

On the third night of his imprisonment, romance came into the life of the second chief warder of Pentonville Prison. He was comparatively young and single, not without good looks, and lived, with his widowed mother, at Shepherd's Bush. It was his practice to return home after his day's duty by omnibus, and he was alighting on this day when a lady, who had got off before him, stumbled and fell. Instantly he was by her side, and had lifted her to her feet. She was young and astonishingly pretty and he helped her gain the pavement.

"It was nothing," she said smilingly, but with a grimace of pain. "It was very foolish of me to come by 'bus; I was visiting an old servant of mine who is ill. Will you call me a taxi, please?"

"Certainly, madam," said the gallant chief warder.

The taxi which was passing was beckoned to the kerb. The girl looked round helplessly.

"I wish I could see somebody I know. I don't want to go home alone; I'm so afraid of fainting."

"If you would not object to my escort," said the man, with all the warm-hearted earnestness which the sight of a woman in distress awakens in the bosom of impressionable man, "I will see you home."

She shot a glance at him which was full of gratitude and accepted his escort, murmuring her regret for the trouble she was giving him.

It was a beautiful apartment she occupied. The chief warder thought he had never met so gracious and beautiful a lady before, so appropriately housed, and he was right. He would have attended to her injury, but she felt so much better, and her maid was coming in soon, and would he have a whisky-and-soda, and would he please smoke? She indicated where the cigarettes were to be found, and for an hour the chief warder spoke about himself, and had an enjoyable evening.

"I'm very much obliged to you, Mr. Bron," she said at parting. "I feel I've wasted your evening."

"I can assure you," said Mr. Bron earnestly, "that if this is a waste of time, then time has no use!"

She laughed.

"That is a pretty speech," she said, "and I will let you call to-morrow and see me."

He took a careful note of the address; it was an exclusive maisonette in Bloomsbury Square; and the next evening found him ringing the bell, but this time he was not in uniform.

He left at ten o'clock, an ecstatic man who held his head high and dreamt golden dreams, for the fragrance of her charm (as he wrote her) "permeated his very being." Ten minutes after he had gone, the girl came out, closed the door behind her and went out into the street, and the idler who had been promenading the pavement threw away his cigar.

"Good evening. Miss Bassano," he said.

She drew herself up.

"I am afraid you have made a mistake," she said stiffly.

"Not at all. You're Miss Bassano, and my only excuse for addressing you is that I am a neighbour of yours."

She looked more closely at him.

"Oh, Mr. Broad!" she said in a more gracious tone. "I've been visiting a friend of mine who is rather ill."

"So I'm told, and a nice flat your friend occupies," he said as he fell in by her side. "I was thinking of hiring it a few days ago. These furnished apartments are difficult to find. Maybe it was a week ago—yes, it was a week ago," he said carefully; "it was the day before you had your lamentable accident in Shepherd's Bush."

"I don't quite understand you," she said, on her guard at once.

"The truth is," said Mr. Broad apologetically, "that I've been trying to get at Bron too. I've been making a very careful study of the prison staff for the past two months, and I've a list of the easy boys that has cost me a lot of money to compile. I suppose you didn't reach the stage where you persuaded him to talk about his interesting prisoner? I tried him last week," he went on reminiscently. "He goes to a dance club at Hammersmith, and I got acquainted with him through a girl he's keen about—you're not the only young love of his life, by the way."

She laughed softly.

"What a clever man you are, Mr. Broad!" she said. "No, I'm not very interested in prisoners. By the way, who is this person you were referring to?"

"I was referring to Number Seven, who is in Pentonville Gaol," said Mr. Broad coolly, "and I've got an idea he is a friend of yours."

"Number Seven?" Her perplexity would have convinced a less hardened man than Joshua Broad. "I have an idea that that is something to do with the Frogs."

"That is something to do with the Frogs," agreed the other gravely, "about whom I daresay you have read. Miss Bassano, I'll make you an offer."

"Offer me a taxi, for I'm tired of walking," she said, and when they were seated side by side she asked: "What is your offer?"

"I offer you all that you require to get out of this country and to keep you out for a few years, until this old Frog busts—as he will bust! I've been watching you for a long time, and, if you won't consider it an impertinence, I like you. There's something about you that is very attractive—don't stop me, because I'm not going to get fresh with you, or suggest that you're the only girl that ever made tobacco taste like molasses—I like you in a kind of pitying way, and you needn't get offended at that either. And I don't want to see you hurt."

He was very serious; she recognized his sincerity, and the word of sarcasm that rose to her lips remained unuttered.

"Are you wholly disinterested?" she asked.

"So far as you are concerned, I am," he replied. "There is going to be an almighty smash, and it is more than likely that you'll get in the way of some of the flying pieces."

She did not answer him at once. What he had said merely intensified her own uneasiness.

"I suppose you know I'm married?"

"I guessed that," he answered. "Take your husband with you. What are you going to do with that boy?"

"You mean Ray Bennett?"

It was curious that she made no attempt to disguise either her position or the part that she was playing. She wondered at herself after she was home. But Joshua Broad had a compelling way, and she never dreamt of deceiving him.

"I don't know," she said. "I wish he wasn't in it. He is on my conscience. Are you smiling?"

"At your having a conscience? No, I fancied that was how you stood. And the growing beard?"

She did not laugh.

"I don't know about that. All I know is that we've had—why am I telling you this? Who are you, Mr. Broad?"

He chuckled.

"Some day I'll tell you," he said; "and I promise you that, if you're handy, you shall be the first to know. Go easy with that boy, Lola."

She did not resent the employment of her first name, but rather it warmed her towards this mystery man.

"And write to Mr. Bron, Assistant Chief Warder of Pentonville Gaol, and tell him that you've been called out of town and won't be able to see him again for ten years."

To this she made no rejoinder. He left her at the door of her flat and took her little hand in his.

"If you want money to get away, I'll send you a blank cheque," he said. "There is no one else on the face of the earth that I'd give a blank cheque to, believe me."

She nodded, most unusual tears in her eyes. Lola was breaking under the strain, and nobody knew it better than the hawk-faced man who watched her as she passed into her flat.

CHAPTER XXVIII

MURDER

THE stone which woke Ella Bennett was aimed with such force that the pane cracked. She slipped quickly from bed and pulled aside the curtains. There had been a thunderstorm in the night, and the skies were so grey and heavy, and the light so bad, that she could only distinguish the shape of the man that stood under her window. John Bennett heard her go from her room and came to his door.

"Is it Maitland?" he asked.

"I think so," she said.

He frowned.

"I can't understand these visits," he said. "Do you think he's mad?"

She shook her head. After the precipitate flight of the old man on his last visit, she had not expected that he would come again, and guessed that only some matter of the greatest urgency would bring him. She heard her father moving about his room as she went through the darkened dining-room into the passage which opened directly on to the garden.

"Is that you, miss?" quavered a voice in the darkness.

"Yes, Mr. Maitland."

"Is *he* up?" he asked in an awe-stricken whisper.

"You mean my father? Yes, he's awake."

"I've got to see you," the old man almost wailed. "They've took him."

"Taken whom?" she asked with a catch in her voice.

"That fellow Balder. I knew they would."

She remembered having heard Elk mention Balder.

"The policeman?" she asked. "Mr. Elk's man?"

But he was off on another tack.

"It's you he's after." He came nearer to her and clutched her arm. "I warned you—don't forget I warned you. Tell him that I warned you. He'll make it good for me, won't he?" he almost pleaded, and she began to understand dimly that the "he" to whom the old man was referring was Dick Gordon. "He's been with me most of the night, prying and asking questions. I've had a terrible night, miss, terrible," he almost sobbed. "First Balder and then him. He'll get you—not that police gentleman I don't mean, but Frog. That's why I wrote you the letter, telling you to come up. You didn't get no letter, did you, miss?"

She could not make head or tail of what he was saying or to whom he was referring, as he went on babbling his story of fear, a story interspersed with wild imprecations against "him."

"Tell your father, dearie, what I said to you." He became suddenly calmer. "Matilda said I ought to have told your father, but I'm afraid of him, my dear, I'm afraid of him!"

He took one of her hands in his and fondled it.

"You'll speak a word for me, won't you?" She knew he was weeping, though she could not see his face.

"Of course I'll speak a word for you, Mr. Maitland. Oughtn't you to see a doctor?" she asked anxiously.

"No, no, no doctors for me. But tell him, won't you—not your father, I mean, the other feller—that I did all I could for you. That's what I've come to see you about. They've got Balder——" He stopped short suddenly and craned his head forward. "Is that your father?" he asked in a husky whisper.

She had heard the footsteps of John Bennett on the stairs.

"Yes, I think it is, Mr. Maitland," and at her words he pulled his hand from hers with a jerk and went shuffling down the pathway into the road and out of sight.

"What did he want?"

"I really don't know, father," she said. "I don't think he can be very well."

"Do you mean mad?"

"Yes, and yet he was quite sensible for a little time. He said they've got Balder."

He did not reply to her, and she thought he had not heard her.

"They've taken Balder, Mr. Elk's assistant. I suppose that means he has been arrested?"

"I suppose so," said John Bennett, and then: "My dear, you ought to be in bed. Which way did he go?"

"He went toward Shoreham," said the girl. "Are you going after him, father?" she asked in surprise.

"I'll walk up the road. I'd like to see him," said John Bennett. "You go to bed, my dear."

But she stood waiting by the door, long after his footsteps had ceased to sound on the road. Five minutes, ten minutes passed, a quarter of an hour, and then she heard the whine of a car and the big limousine flew past the gate, spattering mud, and then came John Bennett.

"Aren't you in bed?" he asked almost roughly.

"No, father, I don't feel sleepy. It is late now, so I think I'll do some work. Did you see him?"

"Who, the old man? Yes, I saw him for a minute or two."

"Did you speak to him?"

"Yes, I spoke to him." The man did not seem inclined to pursue the subject, but this time Ella persisted.

"Father, why is he frightened of you?"

"Will you make me some coffee?" said Bennett.

"Why is he frightened of you?"

"How do I know? My dear, don't ask so many questions. You worry me. He knows me, he's seen me—that is all. Balder is held for murder. I think he is a very bad man."

Later in the day she revived the subject of Maitland's visit.

"I wish he would not come," she said. "He frightens me."

"He will not come again," said John Bennett prophetically.

* * * * * *

The house in Berkeley Square which had passed into the possession of Ezra Maitland had been built by a nobleman to whom money had no significance. Loosely described as one of the show places of the Metropolis, very few outsiders had ever marvelled at the beauty of its interior. It was a palace, though none could guess as much from viewing its conventional exterior. In the gorgeous saloon, with its lapis-lazuli columns, its fireplaces of onyx and silver, its delicately panelled walls and silken hangings, Mr. Ezra Maitland sat huddled in a large Louis Quinze chair, a glass of beer before him, a blackened clay pipe between his gums. The muddy marks of his feet showed on the priceless

Persian carpet; his hat half eclipsed a golden Venus of Marrionnet, which stood on a pedestal by his side. His hands clasped across his stomach, he glared from under his white eyebrows at the floor. One shaded lamp relieved the gloom, for the silken curtains were drawn and the light of day did not enter.

Presently, with an effort, he reached out, took the mug of beer, which had gone flat, and drained its contents. This done and the mug replaced, he sank back into his former condition of torpor. There was a gentle knock at the door and a footman came in, a man of powder and calves.

"Three gentlemen to see you, sir. Captain Gordon, Mr. Elk, and Mr. Johnson."

The old man suddenly sat up.

"Johnson?" he said. "What does he want?"

"They are in the little drawing-room, sir."

"Push them in," growled the old man.

He seemed indifferent to the presence of the two police officers, and it was Johnson he addressed.

"What do you want?" he asked violently. "What do you mean by coming here?"

"It was my suggestion that Mr. Johnson should come," said Dick.

"Oh, your suggestion, was it?" said the old man, and his attitude was strangely insolent compared with his dejection of the early morning.

Elk's eyes fell upon the empty beer-mug, and he wondered how often that had been filled since Ezra Maitland had returned to the house. He guessed it had been employed fairly often, for there was a truculence in the ancient man's tone, a defiance in his eye, which suggested something more than spiritual exaltation.

"I'm not going to answer any questions," he said loudly. "I'm not going to tell any truth, and I'm not going to tell any lies."

"Mr. Maitland," said Johnson hesitatingly, "these gentlemen are anxious to know about the child."

The old man closed his eyes.

"I'm not going to tell no truth and I'm not going to tell no lies," he repeated monotonously.

"Now, Mr. Maitland," said the good-humoured Elk, "forget your good resolution and tell us just why you lived in that slum of Eldor Street."

"No truth and no lies," murmured the old man. "You can lock me up but I won't tell you anything. Lock me up. My name's Ezra Maitland; I am a millionaire. I've got millions and millions and millions! I could buy you up and I could buy up mostly anybody! Old Ezra Maitland! I've been in the workhouse and I've been in quod."

Dick and his companion exchanged glances, and Elk shook his head to signify the futility of further questioning the old man. Nevertheless, Dick tried again.

"Why did you go to Horsham this morning?" he asked, and could have bitten his tongue when he realized his blunder.

Instantly the old man was wide awake.

"I never went to Horsham," he roared. "Don't know what you're talking about. I'm not going to tell you anything. Throw 'em out, Johnson."

When they were in the street again, Elk asked a question.

"No, I've never known him to drink before," said Johnson. "He has always been very abstemious so long as I've known him. I never thought I could persuade him to talk."

"Nor did I," said Dick Gordon—a statement which more than a little surprised the detective.

Dick signalled to the other to get rid of Johnson, and when that philosophical gentleman had been thanked and sent away, Dick Gordon spoke urgently.

"We must have two men in this house at once. What excuse can we offer for planting detectives on Maitland?"

Elk pursed his lips.

"I don't know," he confessed. "We shall have to get a warrant before we arrest him; we could easily get another warrant to search the house; but beyond that I fear we can't go, unless he asks for protection."

"Then put him under arrest," said Dick promptly.

"What is the charge?"

"Hold him on suspicion of being associated with the Frogs, and if necessary move him to the nearest police-station. But it has to be done at once."

Elk was perturbed.

"It isn't a small matter to arrest a millionaire, you know, Captain Gordon. I daresay in America it is simple, and I am told you could pinch the President if you found him with a flask in his pocket. But here it is a little different."

How very different it was, Dick discovered when he made application in private for the necessary warrants. At four o'clock they were delivered to him by the clerk of a reluctant magistrate, and, accompanied by police officers, he went back to Maitland's palatial home.

The footman who admitted them said that Mr. Maitland was lying down and that he did not care to disturb him. In proof, he sent for a second footman, who confirmed the statement.

"Which is his room?" said Dick Gordon. "I am a police officer and I want to see him."

"On the second floor, sir."

He showed them to an electric lift, which carried the five to the second floor. Opposite the lift grille was a large double door, heavily burnished and elaborately gilded.

"Looks more like the entrance to a theatre," said Elk in an undertone.

Dick knocked. There was no answer. He knocked louder. Still there was no answer. And then, to Elk's surprise, the young man launched himself at the door with all his strength. There was a sound of splitting wood and the door parted. Dick stood in the entrance, rooted to the ground.

Ezra Maitland lay half on the bed, his legs dragging over the side. At his feet was the prostrate figure of the old woman whom he called Matilda. They were both dead, and the pungent fumes of cordite still hung in a blue cloud beneath the ceiling.

CHAPTER XXIX

THE FOOTMAN

DICK ran to the bedside, and one glance at the still figures told him all he wanted to know.

"Both shot," he said, and looked up at the filmy cloud under the ceiling. "May have happened any time—a quarter of an hour ago. This stuff hangs about for hours."

"Hold every servant in the house," said Elk in an undertone to the men who were with him.

A doorway led to a smaller bedroom, which was evidently that occupied by Maitland's sister.

"The shot was fired from this entrance," said Dick. "Probably a silencer was used, but we shall hear about that later."

He searched the floor and found two spent cartridges of a heavy calibre automatic.

"They killed the woman, of course," he said, speaking his thoughts aloud. "I was afraid of this. If I could only have got our men in!"

"You expected him to be murdered?" said Elk in astonishment.

Dick nodded. He was trying the window of the woman's room. It was unfastened, and led on to a narrow parapet, protected by a low balustrade. From there, access could be had into another room on the same floor, and no attempt had been made by the murderer to conceal the fact that this was the way he had passed. The window was wide open, and there were wet footmarks on the floor. It was a guest room, slightly overcrowded with surplus furniture, which had been put there apparently by the housekeeper instead of in a lumber-room.

The door opened again into the corridor, and faced a narrow flight of stairs leading to the servants' quarters above. Elk went down on his knees and examined the tread of the carpet carefully.

"Up here, I think," he said, and ran ahead of his chief.

The third floor consisted entirely of servants' rooms, and it was some time before Elk could pick up the footprints which led directly to No. 1. He tried the handle: it was locked. Taking a pace backward, he raised his foot and kicked open the door. He found himself in a servant's bedroom, which was empty. An attic window opened on to the sloping roof of another parapet, and without a second's hesitation Dick went out, following the course of that very precarious alleyway. Farther along, iron rails protected the walker, and this was evidently one of the ways of escape in case of fire. He followed the "path" across three roofs until he came to a short flight of iron stairs, which reached down to the flat roof of another house, and a guard fire-escape. Guarded it had been, but now the iron gate which barred progress was open, and Dick ran down the narrow stairs into a concrete yard surrounded on three sides by high walls and on the fourth by the back of a house, which was apparently unoccupied, for the blinds were all drawn.

There was a gate in the third wall, and it was ajar. Passing through, he was in a mews. A man was washing a motor-car a dozen paces from where he stood, and they hurried toward him.

"Yes, sir," said the cleaner, wiping his streaming forehead with the back of his hand, "I saw a man come out of there about five minutes ago. He was a servant—a footman or something—I didn't recognize him, but he seemed in a hurry."

"Did he wear a hat?"

The man considered.

"Yes, sir, I think he did," he said. "He went out that way," and he pointed.

The two men hurried along, turned into Berkeley Street, and as they did so, the car-washer turned to the closed doors of his garage and whistled softly. The door opened slowly and Mr. Joshua Broad came out.

"Thank you," he said, and a piece of crisp and crackling paper went into the washer's hand.

He was out of sight before Dick and the detective came back from their vain quest.

No doubt existed in Dick's mind as to who the murderer was. One of the footmen was missing. The remaining servants were respectable individuals of unimpeachable character. The seventh had come at the same time as Mr. Maitland; and although he wore a footman's livery, he had apparently no previous experience of the duties which he was expected to perform. He was an ill-favoured man, who spoke very little, and "kept himself to himself," as they described it; took part in none of their pleasures or gossip; was never in the servants' hall a second longer than was necessary.

"Obviously a Frog," said Elk, and was overjoyed to learn that there was a photograph of the man in existence.

The photograph had its origin in an elaborate and somewhat pointless joke which had been played on the cook by the youngest of the footmen. The joke consisted of finding in the cook's workbasket a photograph of the ugly footman, and for this purpose the young servant had taken a snap of the man.

"Do you know him?" asked Dick, looking at the picture.

Elk nodded.

"He has been through my hands, and I don't think I shall have any difficulty in placing him, although for the moment his name escapes me."

A search of the records, however, revealed the identity of the missing man, and by the evening an enlargement of the photograph, and his name, aliases and general characteristics, were locked into the form of every newspaper in the metropolis.

One of the servants had heard the shot, but thought it was the door being slammed—a pardonable mistake, because Mr. Maitland was in the habit of banging doors.

"Maitland was a Frog all right," reported Elk after he had seen the body removed to the mortuary. "He's well decorated on the left wrist—yes, slightly askew. That is one of the points that you've never cleared up to me, Captain Gordon. Why they should be tattooed on the left wrist I can understand, but why the frog shouldn't be stamped square I've never understood."

"That is one of the little mysteries that can't be cleared up until we are through with the big ones," said Dick.

A telegram had been received that afternoon by the missing footman. This fact was not remembered until after Elk had returned to headquarters. A 'phone message through to the district post-office brought a copy of the message. It was very simple.

"Finish and clear," were the three words. The message was unsigned. It had been handed in at the Temple Post Office at two o'clock, and the murderer had lost no time in carrying out his instructions.

Maitland's office was in the hands of the police, and a systematic search had already begun of its documents and books. At seven o'clock that night Elk went to Fitzroy Square, and Johnson opened the door to him. Looking past him, Elk saw that the passage was filled with furniture and packing cases, and remembered that early in the morning Johnson had mentioned that he was moving, and had taken two cheaper rooms in South London.

"You've packed?"

Johnson nodded.

"I hate leaving this place," he said, "but it's much too expensive. It seems as though I shall never get another job, and I'd better face that fact sensibly. If I live at Balham, I can live comfortably. I've very few expensive tastes."

"If you have, you can indulge them," said Elk. "We found the old man's will. He has left you everything!"

Johnson's jaw dropped, his eyes opened wide.

"Are you joking?" he said.

"I was never more serious in my life. The old man has left you every penny he had. Here is a copy of the will: I thought you'd like to see it."

He opened his pocket-case, producing a sheet of foolscap, and Johnson read:

"I, Ezra Maitland, of 193, Eldor Road, in the County of Middlesex, declare this to be my last will and testament, and I formally revoke all other wills and codicils to such wills. I bequeath all my property, movable or immovable, all lands, houses, deeds, shares in stock companies whatsoever, and all jewellery, reversions, carriages, motor-cars, and all other possessions absolutely, to Philip Johnson, of 471, Fitzroy Square, in the County of London, clerk. I declare him to be the only honest man I have ever met with in my long and sorrowful life, and I direct him to devote himself with unremitting care to the destruction of that society or organization which is known as the Frogs, and which for four and twenty years has extracted large sums of blackmail from me."

It was signed in a clerkly hand familiar to Johnson, and was witnessed by two men whose names he knew.

He sat down and did not attempt to speak for a long time.

"I read of the murder in the evening paper," he said after a while. "In fact, I've been up to the house, but the policemen referred me to you, and I knew you were too busy to be bothered. How was he killed?"

"Shot," said Elk.

"Have they caught the man?"

"We shall have him by the morning," said Elk with confidence. "Now that we've taken Balder, there'll be nobody to warn the men we want."

"It is very dreadful," said Johnson after a while. "But this"—he looked at the paper—"this has quite knocked me out. I don't know what to say. Where was it found?"

"In one of his deed boxes."

"I wish he hadn't," said Johnson with emphasis. "I mean, left me his money. I hate responsibility. I'm temperamentally unfitted to run a big business . . . I wish he hadn't!"

"How did he take it?" asked Dick when Elk had returned.

"He's absolutely hazed. Poor devil, I felt sorry for him, and I never thought I should feel sorry for any man who came into money. He was just getting ready to move into a cheaper house when I arrived. I suppose he won't go to the Prince of Caux's mansion. The change in Johnson's prospects might make a difference to Ray Bennett: does that strike you, Captain Gordon?"

"I thought of that possibility," said Dick shortly.

He had an interview in the afternoon with the Director of Public Prosecutions in regard to Balder. And that learned gentleman echoed his own fears.

"I can't see how we're going to get a verdict of murder against this man, although it is as plain as daylight that he poisoned Mills and was responsible for the bomb outrage. But you can't hang a man on suspicion, even though the suspicion is not open to doubt. How did he kill Mills, do you think?"

"Mills had a cold," said Dick. "He had been coughing all the way up in the car, and had asked Balder to close the window of the room. Balder obviously closed, or nearly closed the window, and probably slipped a cyanide tablet to the man, telling him it was good for his cold. It was a fairly natural thing for Mills to take and swallow the tablet, and that, I am sure, is what happened. We made a search of Balder's house at Slough, and found a duplicate set of keys, including one to Elk's safe. Balder got there early in the morning and planted the bomb, knowing that Elk and I would be opening the bags that morning."

"And helped Hagn to escape," said the Public Prosecutor.

"That was much more simple," explained Dick. "I gather that the inspector who was seen walking out at half-past-two was Hagn. When Balder went into the cell to keep the man company, he must have been dressed underneath in the police uniform, and have carried the necessary handcuffs and pass-keys with him. He was not searched—a fact for which I am as much responsible as Elk. The chief danger we had to fear from Balder came from his closeness to us, and his ability to communicate immediately to his chief every movement which we made. His name is Kramer, and he is by birth a Lithuanian. He was expelled from Germany at the age of eighteen for his revolutionary activities, and came to this country two years later, where he joined the police. At what time he came into contact with the Frogs I do not know, but it is fairly clear, from evidence we have obtained, that the man has been engaged in various illegal operations for many years past. I'm afraid you are right about Balder: it will be immensely difficult to get a conviction until we have caught Frog himself."

"And will you catch the Frog, do you think?"

Dick Gordon smiled cryptically.

No fresh news had come about the murder of Maitland and his sister, and he seized the opportunity which the lull gave to him. Ella Bennett was in the vegetable garden, engaged in the prosaic task of digging potatoes when he appeared, and she came running toward him, stripping her leather gloves.

"This is a splendid surprise," she said, and flushed at the consciousness of her own enthusiasm. "Poor man, you must be having a terrible time! I saw the newspaper this morning. Isn't it dreadful about poor Mr. Maitland? He was here yesterday morning."

He nodded.

"Is it true that Mr. Johnson has been left the whole of Maitland's money? Isn't that splendid!"

"Do you like Johnson?" he asked.

"Yes, he's a nice man," she nodded. "I don't know a great deal about him; indeed, I've only met him once or twice, but he was very kind to Ray, and saved him from getting into trouble. I am wondering whether, now that he is rich, he will induce Ray to go back to Maitlands."

"I wonder if he will induce you— —" He stopped.

"Induce me to what?" she asked in astonishment.

"Johnson is rather fond of you—he's never made any disguise of the fact, and he's a very rich man. Not that I think that would make any difference to you," he added hastily. "I'm not a very rich man, but I'm comfortably off."

The fingers in his hand stole round his, and pressed them tightly, and then suddenly they relaxed.

"I don't know," she said, and drew herself free.

"Father said— —" She hesitated. "I don't think father would like it. He thinks there is such a difference between our social positions."

"Rats!" said Dick inelegantly.

"And there's something else." She found it an effort to tell him what that something was. "I don't know what father does for a living, but it is . . . work that he never wishes to speak about; something that he looks upon as disgraceful."

The last words were spoken so low that he hardly caught them.

"Suppose I know the worst about your father?" he asked quietly, and she stood back, looking at him from under knit brows.

"Do you mean that? What is it, Dick?"

He shook his head.

"I may know or I may not. It is only a wild guess. And you're not to tell him that I know, or that I'm in any way suspicious. Will you please do that for me?"

"And knowing this, would it make any difference to you?"

"None."

She had plucked a flower, and was pulling it petal from petal in her abstraction.

"Is it very dreadful?" she asked. "Has he committed a crime? No, no, don't tell me."

Once more he was near her, his arm about her trembling shoulders, his hand beneath her chin.

"My dear!" murmured the youthful Public Prosecutor, and forgot there was such a thing as murder in the world.

John Bennett was glad to see him, eager to tell the news of his triumph. He had a drawer full of press cuttings, headed "Wonderful Nature Studies. Remarkable Pictures by an Amateur," and others equally flattering. And there had come to him a cheque which had left him gasping.

"This means—you don't know what it means to me, Mr. Gordon," he said, "or Captain Gordon—I always forget you've got a military title. When that boy of mine recovers his senses and returns home, he's going to have just the good time he wants. He's at the age when most boys are fools—what I call the showing-off age. Sometimes it runs to pimples and introspection, sometimes to the kind of life that a man doesn't like to look back on. Ray has probably taken the less vicious course."

It was a relief to hear the man speak so. Dick always thought of Ray Bennett as one who had committed the unforgiveable sin.

"This time next year I'm going to be an artist of leisure," said John Bennett, who looked ten years younger.

Dick offered to drive him to town, but this he would not hear of. He had to make a call at Dorking. Apparently he had letters addressed to him in that town (Dick learnt of this from the girl) concerning his mysterious errands. Dick left Horsham with a heart lighter than he had brought to that little country town, and was in the mood to rally Inspector Elk for the profound gloom which had settled on him since he had discovered that there was not sufficient evidence to try Balder for his life.

CHAPTER XXX

THE TRAMPS

LEW BRADY sat disconsolately in Lola Bassano's pretty drawing-room, and a more incongruous figure in that delicate setting it was impossible to imagine. A week's growth of beard had transfigured him into the most unsavoury looking ruffian, and the soiled old clothes he wore, the broken and discoloured boots, the grimy shirt, no less than his own personal uncleanliness of appearance made him a revolting object.

So Lola thought, eyeing him anxiously, a foreboding of trouble in her heart.

"I'm finished with the Frog," growled Brady. "He pays—of course he pays! But how long is it going on, Lola? You brought me into this!" He glowered at her.

"I brought you in, when you wanted to be brought into something," she said calmly. "You can't live on my savings all your life, Lew, and it was nearly time you made a little on the side."

He played with a silver seal, twiddling it between his fingers, his eyes gloomily downcast.

"Balder's caught, and the old man's dead," he said. "They're the big people. What chance have I got?"

"What were your instructions, Lew?" she asked for the twentieth time that day.

He shook his head.

"I'm taking no risks, Lola. I don't trust anybody, not even you."

He took a small bottle from his pocket and examined it.

"What is that?" she asked curiously.

"Dope of some kind."

"Is that part of the instructions too?"

He nodded.

"Are you going in your own name?"

"No, I'm not," he snapped. "Don't ask questions. I'm not going to tell you anything, see? This trip's going to last a fortnight, and when it's finished, I'm finished with Frog."

"The boy—is he going with you?"

"How do I know? I'm to meet somebody somewhere, and that's all about it." He looked at the clock and rose with a grunt. "It's the last time I shall sit in a decent parlour for a fortnight." He gave a curt nod and walked to the door.

There was a servants' entrance, a gallery which was reached through the kitchen, and he passed down the stairs unobserved, into the night.

It was dark by the time he reached Barnet; his feet were aching; he was hot and wretched. He had suffered the indignity of being chased off the pavement by a policeman he could have licked with one hand, and he cursed the Frog with every step he took. There was still a long walk ahead of him once he was clear of Barnet; and it was not until a village clock was striking the hour of eleven that he ambled up to a figure that was sitting on the side of the road, just visible in the pale moonlight, but only recognizable when he spoke.

"Is that you?" said a voice.

"Yes, it's me. You're Carter, aren't you?"

"Good Lord!" gasped Ray as he recognized the voice. "It's Lew Brady!"

"It's nothing of the kind!" snarled the other man. "My name's Phenan. Yours is Carter. Sit down for a bit. I'm dead beat."

"What is the idea?" asked the youth as they sat side by side.

"How the devil do I know?" said the other savagely as, with a tender movement, he slipped off his boots and rubbed his bruised feet.

"I had no idea it was you," said Ray.

"I knew it was you, all right," said the other. "And why I should be called upon to take a mug around this country, God knows!"

After a while he was rested sufficiently to continue the tramp.

"There's a barn belonging to a shopkeeper in the next village. He'll let us sleep there for a few pence."

"Why not try to get a room?"

"Don't be a fool," snapped Lew. "Who's going to take in a couple of tramps, do you think? We know we're clean, but they don't. No, we've got to go the way the tramps go."

"Where? To Nottingham?"

"I don't know. If they told you Nottingham, I should say that's the last place in the world we shall go to. I've got a sealed envelope in my pocket. When we reach Baldock I shall open it."

They slept that night in the accommodating barn—a draughty shed, populated, it seemed, by chickens and rats, and Ray had a restless night and thought longingly of his own little bed at Maytree Cottage. Strangely enough, he did not dwell on the more palatial establishment in Knightsbridge.

The next day it rained, and they did not reach Baldock until late in the afternoon, and, sitting down under the cover of a hedge, Brady opened the envelope and read its contents, his companion watching him expectantly.

"You will branch from Baldock and take the nearest G.W. train for Bath. Then by road to Gloucester. At the village of Laverstock you will reveal to Carter the fact that you are married to Lola Bassano. You should take him to the *Red Lion* for this purpose, and tell him as offensively as possible in order to force a quarrel, but in no circumstances are you to allow him to part company from you. Go on to Ibbley Copse. You will find an open space near where three dead trees stand, and there you will stop, take back the statement you made that you are married to Lola, and make an apology. You are carrying with you a whisky flask; you must have the dope and the whisky together at this point. After he is asleep, you will make your way to Gloucester, to 289 Hendry Street, where you will find a complete change of clothing. Here you will shave and return to town by the 2.19."

Every word, every syllable, he read over and over again, until he had mastered the details. Then, striking a match, he set fire to the paper and watched it burn.

"What are the orders?" asked Ray.

"The same as yours, I suppose. What did you do with yours?"

"Burnt them," said Ray. "Did he tell you where we're going?"

"We are going to take the Gloucester Road; I thought we should. That means striking across country till we reach the Bath Road. We can take a train to Bath."

"Thank goodness for that!" said Ray fervently. "I don't feel I can walk another step."

At seven o'clock that night, two tramps turned out of a third-class carriage on Bath station. One, the younger, was limping slightly, and sat down on a station seat.

"Come on, you can't stay here," said the other gruffly. "We'll get a bed in the town. There's a Salvation Army shelter somewhere in Bath."

"Wait a bit," said the other. "I'm so cramped with sitting in that infernal carriage that I can hardly move."

They had joined the London train at Reading, and the passengers were pouring down the steps to the subway. Ray looked at them enviously. They had homes to go to, clean and comfortable beds to sleep in. The thought of it gave him a pain. And then he saw a figure and shrank back. A tall, angular man, who carried a heavy box in one hand and a bag in the other.

It was his father.

John Bennett went down the steps, with a casual glance at the two unsavoury tramps on the seat, never dreaming that one was the son whose future he was at that moment planning.

John Bennett spent an ugly night, and an even more ugly early morning. He collected the camera where he had left it, at a beerhouse on the outskirts of the town, and, fixing the improvised carrier, he slipped the big box on his back, and, with his bag in his hand, took the road. A policeman eyed him disapprovingly as he passed, and seemed in two minds as to whether or not he should stop him, but refrained. The strength and stamina of this grey man were remarkable. He breasted a hill and, without slackening his pace, reached the top, and strode steadily along the white road that was cut in the face of the hill. Below him stretched the meadow lands of Somerset, vast fields speckled with herds, glittering streaks of light where the river wound; above his head a blue sky, flecked white here and there. As he walked, the load on his heart was absorbed. All that was bright and happy in life came to him. His hand strayed to his waistcoat pocket mechanically.

There were the precious press cuttings that he had brought from town and had read and re-read in the sleepless hours of the night.

He thought of Ella, and all that Ella meant to him, and of Dick Gordon—but that made him wince, and he came back to the comfort of his pictures. Somebody had told him that there were badgers to be seen; a man in the train had carefully located a veritable paradise for the lover of Nature; and it was toward this beauty spot that he was making his way with the aid of a survey map which he had bought overnight at a stationer's shop.

Another hour's tramp brought him to a wooden hollow, and, consulting his map, he found he had reached his objective. There was ample evidence of the truth that his chance-found friend had told him. He saw a stoat, flying on the heels of a terrified rabbit; a hawk wheeled ceaselessly on stiff pinions above him; and presently he found the "run" he was looking for, the artfully concealed entrance to a badger's lair.

In the years he had been following his hobby he had overcome many difficulties, learnt much. To-day, failure had taught him something of the art of concealment. It took him time to poise and hide the camera in a bush of wild laurel, and even then it was necessary that he should take a long shot, for the badger is the shyest of its kind. There were young ones in the lair: he saw evidence of that; and a badger who has young is doubly shy.

He had replaced the pneumatic attachment which set the camera moving, by an electrical contrivance, and this enabled him to work with greater surety. He unwound the long flex and laid it to its fullest extent, taking a position on the slope of the hill eighty yards away, making himself comfortable. Taking off his coat, which acted as a pillow on which his arms rested, he put his field-glasses near at hand.

He had been waiting half an hour when he thought he saw a movement at the mouth of the burrow, and slowly focussed his glasses. It was the tip of a black nose he saw, and he took the switch of the starter in his hand, ready to set the camera revolving. Minutes followed minutes; five—ten—fifteen—but there was no further movement in the burrow, and in a dull way John Bennett was glad, because the warmth of the day, combined with his own weariness and his relaxed position, brought to him a rare sensation of bodily comfort and well-being. Deeper and deeper grew the languorous haze of comfort that fell on him like a fog, until it obscured all that was visible and audible. John Bennett slept, and, sleeping, dreamed of success and of peace and of freedom from all that had broken his heart, and had dried up the sweet waters of life within him. In his dream he heard voices and a sharp sound, like a shot. But he knew it was not a shot, and shivered. He knew that "crack," and in his sleep clenched his hands convulsively. The electric starter was still in his hand.

* * * * * *

At nine o'clock that morning there had come into Laverstock two limping tramps, though one limped more than the other. The bigger of the two stopped at the door of the *Red Lion*, and an unfriendly landlord surveyed the men over the top of the curtain which gave the habitués of the bar a semi-privacy.

"Come in," growled Lew Brady.

Ray was glad to follow. The landlord's bulk blocked the entrance to the bar.

"What do you want?" he asked.

"I want a drink."

"There's no free drinks going in this parish," said the landlord, looking at the unpromising customer.

"Where did you get that 'free drink' stuff from?" snarled Lew. "My money's as good as anybody else's, isn't it?"

"If it's honestly come by," said the landlord. "Let us have a look at it."

Lew pulled out a handful of silver, and the master of the *Red Lion* stood back.

"Come in," he said, "but don't make a home of my bar. You can have your drink and go."

Lew growled the order, and the landlord poured out the two portions of whisky.

"Here's yours, Carter," said Lew, and Ray swallowed the fiery dram and choked.

"I'll be glad to get back," said Lew in a low voice. "It's all right for you single men, but this tramping is pretty tough on us fellows who've got wives—even though the wives aren't all they might be."

"I didn't know you were married," said Ray, faintly interested.

"There's a lot you don't know," sneered the other. "Of course I'm married. You were told once, and you hadn't the brains to believe it."

Ray looked at the man open-mouthed.

"Do you mean—what Gordon said?"

The other nodded.

"You mean that Lola is your wife?"

"Why, certainly she's my wife," said Lew coolly. "I don't know how many husbands she's had, but I'm her present one."

"Oh, my God!"

Ray whispered the words.

"What's the matter with you? And take that look off your face," said Lew Brady viciously. "I'm not blaming you for being sweet on her. I like to see people admire my wife, even such kids as you."

"Your wife!" said Ray again. He could not believe the man was speaking the truth. "Is she—is she a Frog?"

"Why shouldn't she be?" said Brady. "And keep your voice down, can't you? That fat old devil behind the counter is trying hard to listen. Of course she's Frog, and she's crook. We're all crooks. You're crook too. That's the way with Lola, she likes the crooks best. Perhaps you'll have a chance, after you've done a job or two——"

"You beast!" hissed Ray, and struck the man full in the face.

Before Lew Brady could come to his feet, the landlord was between them.

"Outside, both of you!" he shouted, and, dashing to the door, roared half a dozen names. He was back in time to see Lew Brady on his feet, glaring at the other.

"You'll know all about that, Mr. Carter, one of these days," he said. "I'll settle with you!"

"And, by God, I'll settle with you!" said Ray furiously, and at that moment a brawny ostler caught him by the arm and flung him into the road outside.

He waited for Brady to come out.

"I've finished with you," he said. His face was white, his voice was quivering. "Finished with the whole rotten shoot of you! I'm going back."

"You're not going back," said Lew. "Oh, listen, boy, what's making you mad? We've got to go on to Gloucester, and we might as well finish our job. And if you don't want to be with me after that—well, you can go ahead just as you like."

"I'm going alone," said Ray.

"Don't be a fool." Lew Brady came after him and seized his arm.

For a second the situation looked ugly to the onlookers, and then, with a shrug, Ray Bennett suffered the arm to remain.

"I don't believe you," he said—the first words he spoke for half an hour after they had left the *Red Lion*. "Why should you have lied?"

"I've got sick of your good temper, that's the whole truth, Ray—just sick to death of it. I had to make you mad, or I'd have gone mad myself."

"But is it true about Lola?"

"Of course it's not true," lied Brady contemptuously. "Do you think she'd have anything to do with a chap like me? Not likely! Lola's a good girl. Forget all I said, Ray."

"I shall ask her myself. She wouldn't lie to me," said the boy.

"Of course she wouldn't lie to you," agreed the other.

They were nearing their rendezvous now—the tree-furred cut in the hills—and his eyes were searching for the three white trunks that the lightning had struck. Presently he saw them.

"Come on in, and I'll tell you all about it," he said. "I'm not going to walk much farther to-day. My feet are so raw you couldn't cook 'em!"

He led the way between the trees, over the age-old carpet of pine needles, and presently he stopped.

"Sit down here, boy," he said, "and let us have a drink and a smoke."

Ray sat with his head on his hands, a figure so supremely miserable that any other man than Lew Brady would have felt sorry for him.

"The whole truth is," began Lew slowly, "that Lola's very strong for you, boy."

"Then why did you tell me the other thing? Who was that?" He looked round.

"What is it?" asked Lew. His own nerves were on edge.

"I thought I heard somebody moving."

"A twig broke. Rabbits, it may be; there are thousands of 'em round here," said Lew. "No, Lola's a good girl." He fished from his pocket a flask, pulled off the cup at the bottom and unscrewed the stopper, holding the flask to the light. "She's a good girl," he repeated, "and may she never be anything else."

He poured out a cupful, looked at the remainder in the bottle.

"I'm going to drink her health. No, you drink first."

Ray shook his head.

"I don't like the stuff," he said.

The other man laughed.

"For a fellow who's been pickled night after night, that's certainly an amusing view to take," he said. "If you can't hold a dram of whisky for the sake of drinking Lola's health, well, you're a poor——"

"Give it to me." Ray snatched the cup, but spilt a portion, and, drinking down the contents at a draught, he threw the metal holder to his companion.

"Ugh! I don't care for that whisky. I don't think I care for any whisky at all. There's nothing harder to pretend you like than drinking, if you don't happen to like it."

"I don't think anybody likes it at first," said Lew. "It's like tomatoes—a cultivated taste."

He was watching his companion keenly.

"Where do we go from Gloucester?" asked Ray.

"We don't go anywhere from Gloucester. We just stop there for a day, and then we change and come back."

"It's a stupid idea," said Ray Bennett, screwing up his eyes and yawning. "Who is this Frog, Lew?" He yawned again, lay back on the grass, his hands under his head.

Lew Brady emptied the remainder of the flask's contents upon the grass, screwed up the stopper and shook the cup before he rose and walked across to the sleeping boy.

228

"Hi, get up!" he said.

There was no answer.

"Get up, you!"

With a groan, Ray turned over, his head on his arms, and did not move again. A sudden misgiving came to Lew Brady. Suppose he was dead? He went livid at the thought. That quarrel, so cleverly engineered by the Frog, would be enough to convict him. He whipped the flask from his pocket and slipped it into the coat pocket of the sleeper. And then he heard a sound, and, turning, saw a man watching him. Lew stared, opened his mouth to speak, and:

"*Plop!*"

He saw the flash of the flame before the bullet struck him. He tried to open his mouth to speak, and:

"*Plop!*"

Lew Brady was dead before he touched the ground.

The man removed the silencer of the pistol, walked leisurely across to where Ray Bennett was sleeping, and put the pistol by his hand. Then he came back and turned over the body of the dead man, looking down into the face. Taking one of three cigars from his waistcoat pocket, he lit it, being careful to put the match in the box whence he had taken it. He liked smoking cigars—especially other men's cigars. Then, without haste, he walked back the way he had come, gained the main road after a careful reconnaissance, and reached the car he had left by the roadside.

Inside the car a youth was sitting in the shelter of the curtained hood, loose-mouthed, glassy-eyed, staring at nothing. He wore an ill-fitting suit and one end of his collar was unfastened.

"You know this place, Bill?"

"Yes, sir." The voice was guttural and hoarse. "Ibbley Copse."

"You have just killed a man: you shot him, just as you said you did in your confession."

The half-witted youth nodded.

"I killed him because I hated him," he said.

The Frog nodded obediently and got into the driver's seat. . . .

John Bennett woke with a start. He looked at the damp bell-push in his hand with a rueful smile, and began winding up the flex. Presently he reached the bush where the camera was concealed, and, to his dismay, found that the indicator showed the loss—for loss it was—of five hundred feet. He looked at the badger hole resentfully, and there, as in mockery, he saw again the tip of a black nose, and shook his fist at it. Beyond, he saw two men lying, both asleep, and both, apparently, tramps.

He carried the camera back to where he had left his coat, put it on, hoisted the box into position and set off for Laverstock village, where, if his watch was right, he could catch the local that would connect him with Bath in time for the London express; and as he walked, he calculated his loss.

CHAPTER XXXI

THE CHEMICAL CORPORATION

ELK had promised to dine at Gordon's club. Dick waited for him until twenty minutes past the hour of appointment, and Elk had neither telephoned nor put in an appearance. At twenty-five minutes past he arrived in a hurry.

"Good Lord!" he gasped, looking at the clock. "I had no idea it was so late, Captain. I must buy a watch."

They went into the dining-hall together, and Elk felt that he was entering a church, there was such solemn dignity about the stately room, with its prim and silent diners.

"It certainly has Heron's beat in the matter of Dicky-Orum."

"I don't know the gentleman," said the puzzled Dick. "Oh, do you mean decorum? Yes, this is a little more sedate. What kept you, Elk? I'm not complaining, but when you're not on time, I worry as to what has happened to you."

"Nothing has happened to me," said Elk, nodding pleasantly to an embarrassed club waiter. "Only we had an inquiry in Gloucester. I thought we'd struck another Frog case, but the two men involved had no Frog marks."

"Who are they?"

"Phenan is one—he's the man that's dead."

"A murder?"

"I think so," said Elk, spearing a sardine. "I think he was thoroughly dead when they found him at Ibbley Copse. They pinched the man who was with him; he was drunk. Apparently they'd been to Laverstock and had quarrelled and fought in the bar of the *Red Lion*. The police were informed later, and telephoned through to the next village, to tell the constable to keep his eye on these two fellows, but they hadn't passed through, so they sent a bicycle patrol to look for them—there's been one or two housebreakings in that neighbourhood."

"And they found them?"

Elk nodded.

"One man dead and the other man bottled. Apparently they'd quarrelled, and the drunken gentleman shot the other. They're both tramps or of that class. Identification marks on them show they've come from Wales. They slept at Bath last night, at Rooney's lodging-house, and that's all that's known of 'em. Carter is the murderer—they've taken him to Gloucester Gaol. It's a very simple case, and the Gloucester police gave a haughty smile at the idea of calling in Headquarters. It is a crime, anyway, that is up to the intellectual level of the country police."

Dick's lips twitched.

"Just now, the country police are passing unpleasant comments on our intelligence," he said.

"Let 'um," scoffed Elk. "Those people are certainly entitled to their simple pleasures, and I'd be the last to deny them the right. I saw John Bennett in town to-night, at Paddington this time. I'm always knocking against him at railway stations. That man is certainly a traveller. He had his old camera with him too. I spoke to him this time, and he's full of trouble: went to sleep, pushed the gadget in his dreams and wasted a fortune in film. But he's pleased with himself, and I don't wonder. I saw a note about his pictures the other day in one of the newspapers. He looks like turning into a first-class success."

"I sincerely hope so," said Dick quietly, and something in his tone made his guest look up.

"Which reminds me," he said, "that I had a note from friend Johnson asking me whether I knew Ray Bennett's address. He said he called up Heron's Club, but Ray hadn't been there for days. He wants to give him a job. Quite a big position, too. There's a lot that's very fine in Johnson."

"Did you give the address?"

Elk nodded.

"I gave him the address, and I called on the boy, but he's out of town—went out a few days ago, and is not likely to be back for a fortnight. It will be too bad if he loses this job. I think Johnson was sore with the side young Bennett put on, but he doesn't seem to bear any malice. Perhaps there's another influence at work," he said significantly.

Dick knew that he meant Ella, but did not accept the opening.

They adjourned to the smoke-room after dinner, and whilst Elk puffed luxuriously at one of his host's best cigars, Dick wrote a brief note to the girl, who had been in his thoughts all that day. It was an unnecessary note, as such epistles are liable to be; but it might have had, as its excuse, the news that he had heard from Elk, only, for some reason, he never thought of that until after the letter was finished and sealed. When he turned to his companion, Elk propounded a theory.

"I sent a man up to look at some chemical works. It's a fake company—less than a dozen hands employed, and those only occasionally. But it has a very powerful electrical installation. It is an old poison gas factory. The present company bought it for a song, and two fellows we are holding were the nominal purchasers."

"Where is it?" asked Dick.

"Between Newbury and Didcot. I found out a great deal about them for a curious reason. It appears there was some arrangement between the factory, when it was under Government control, that it should make an annual contribution to the Newbury Fire Brigade, and, in taking over the property, the company also took over that contract, which they're now trying to get out of, for the charge is a stiff one. They told the Newbury Brigade, in so many words, to disconnect the factory from their alarm service, but the Newbury Brigade, being on a good thing and having lost money by the arrangement during the war, refused to cancel the contract, which has still three years to run."

Dick was not interested in the slightest degree in the quarrel between the chemical factory and the fire brigade. Later, he had cause to be thankful that conversation had drifted into such a prosaic channel; but this he could not foresee.

"Yes, very remarkable," he said absent-mindedly.

* * * * * *

A fortnight after the disappearance from town of Ray Bennett, Elk accepted the invitation of the American to lunch. It was an invitation often given, and only accepted now because there had arisen in Elk's mind a certain doubt about Joshua Broad—a doubt which he wished to mould into assurance.

Broad was waiting for the detective when he arrived, and Elk, to whom time had no particular significance, arrived ten minutes late.

"Ten minutes after one," said Elk. "I can't keep on time anyhow. There's been a lot of trouble at the office over the new safe they've got me. Somethin's wrong with it, and even the lock-maker doesn't know what it is."

"Can't you open it?"

"That's just it, I can't, and I've got to get some papers out to-day that are mighty important," said Elk. "I was wondering, as I came along, whether, having such a wide experience of the criminal classes, you've ever heard any way by which it could be opened—it needs a proper engineer, and, if I remember rightly, you told me you were an engineer once, Mr. Broad?"

"Your memory is at fault," said the other calmly as he unfolded his napkin and regarded the detective with a twinkle in his eye. "Safe-opening is not my profession."

"And I never dreamt it was," said Elk heartily. "But it has always struck me that the Americans are much more clever with their hands than the people in this country, and I thought that you might be able to give me a word of advice."

"Maybe I'll introduce you to my pet burglar," said Broad gravely, and they laughed together. "What do you think of me?" asked the American unexpectedly. "I'm not expecting you to give your view of my character or personal appearance, but what do you think I am doing in London, dodging around, doing nothing but a whole lot of amateur police work?"

"I've never given you much thought," said Elk untruthfully. "Being an American, I expect you to be out of the ordinary——"

"Flatterer," murmured Mr. Broad.

"I wouldn't go so far as to flatter you," protested Elk. "Flattery is repugnant to me anyway."

He unfolded an evening newspaper he had brought.

"Looking for those tailless amphibians?"

"Eh?" Elk looked up puzzled.

"Frogs," explained the other.

"No, I'm not exactly looking for Frogs, though I understand a few of 'em are looking for me. As a matter of fact, there's very little in the newspaper about those interesting animals, but there's going to be!"

"When?"

The question was a challenge.

"When we get Frog Number One."

Mr. Broad crumpled a roll in his hand, and broke it.

"Do you think you'll get Number One before I get him?" he asked quietly, and Elk looked across the table over his spectacles.

"I've been wondering that for a long time," he said, and for a second their eyes met.

"Do you think I shall get him?" asked Broad.

"If all my speculations and surmises are what they ought to be, I think you will," said Elk, and suddenly his attention was focussed upon a paragraph. "Quick work," he said. "We beat you Americans in that respect."

"In what respect is that?" asked Broad. "I'm sufficient of a cosmopolitan to agree that there are many things in England which you do better than we in America."

Elk looked up at the ceiling.

"Fifteen days?" he said. "Of course, he just managed to catch the Assizes."

"Who's that?"

"That man Carter, who shot a tramp near Gloucester," said Elk.

"What has happened to him?" asked the other.

"He was sentenced to death this morning," said the detective.

Joshua Broad frowned.

"Sentenced to death this morning? Carter, you say? I didn't read the story of the murder."

"There was nothing complicated about it," said Elk. "Two tramps had a quarrel—I think they got drinking—and one shot the other and was found lying in a drunken sleep by the dead man's side. There's practically no evidence; the prisoner refused to make any statement, or to instruct a lawyer—it must have been one of the shortest murder trials on record."

"Where did this happen?" asked Broad, arousing himself from the reverie into which he had fallen.

"Near Gloucester. There was little in the paper; it wasn't a really interesting murder. There was no woman in it, so far as the evidence went, and who cared a cent about two tramps?"

He folded the paper and put it down, and for the rest of the meal was engaged in a much more fascinating discussion, the police methods of the United States, on which matter Mr. Broad was, apparently, something of an authority.

The object of the American's invitation was very apparent. Again and again he attempted to turn the conversation to the man under arrest; and as skilfully as he introduced the subject of Balder, did Elk turn the discussion back to the merits of the third degree as a method of crime detection.

"Elk, you're as close as an oyster," said Broad, beckoning a waiter to bring his bill. "And yet I could tell you almost as much about this man Balder as you know."

"Tell me the prison he's in?" demanded Elk.

"He's in Pentonville, Ward Seven, Cell Eighty-four," said the other immediately, and Elk sat bolt upright. "And you needn't trouble to shift him to somewhere else, just because I happen to know his exact location; I should be just as well informed if he was at Brixton, Wandsworth, Holloway, Wormwood Scrubbs, Maidstone, or Chelmsford."

CHAPTER XXXII

IN GLOUCESTER PRISON

THERE is a cell in Gloucester Prison; the end cell in a long corridor of the old building. Next door is another cell, which is never occupied, for an excellent reason. That in which Ray Bennett sat was furnished more expensively than any other in the prison. There was an iron bedstead, a plain deal table, a comfortable Windsor chair and two other chairs, on one of which, night and day, sat a warder.

The walls were distempered pink. One big window, near the ceiling, heavily barred, covered with toughened opaque glass, admitted light, which was augmented all the time by an electric globe in the arched ceiling.

Three doors led from the cell: one into the corridor, the other into a little annexe fitted with a washing-bowl and a bath; the third into the unoccupied cell, which had a wooden floor, and in the centre of the floor a square trap. Ray Bennett did not know then how close he was to the death house, and if he had known he would not have cared. For death was the least of the terrors which oppressed him.

He had awakened from his drugged sleep, to find himself in the cell of a country lock-up, and had heard, bemused, the charge of murder that had been made against him. He had no clear recollection of what had happened. All that he knew was that he had hated Lew Brady and that he had wanted to kill him. After that, he had a recollection of walking with him and of sitting down somewhere.

They told him that Brady was dead, and that the weapon with which the murder was committed had been found in his hand. Ray had racked his brains in an effort to remember whether he had a revolver or not. He must have had. And of course he had been drugged. They had had whisky at the *Red Lion*, and Lew must have said something about Lola and he had shot him. It was strange that he did not think longingly of Lola. His love for her had gone. He thought of her as he thought of Lew Brady, as something unimportant that belonged to the past. All that mattered now was that his father and Ella should not know. At all costs the disgrace must be kept from them. He had waited in a fever of impatience for the trial to end, so that he might get away from the public gaze. Fortunately, the murder was not of sufficient interest even for the ubiquitous press photographers. He wanted to be done with it all, to go out of life unknown. The greatest tragedy that could occur to him was that he should be identified.

He dared not think of Ella or of his father. He was Jim Carter, without parents or friends; and if he died as Jim Carter, he must spend his last days of life as Jim Carter. He was not frightened; he had no fear, his only nightmare was that he should be recognized.

The warder who was with him, and who was not supposed to speak to him, had told him that, by the law, three clear Sundays must elapse between his sentence and execution. The chaplain visited him every day, and the Governor. A tap at the cell door told him it was the Governor's hour, and he rose as the grey-haired official came in.

"Any complaints, Carter?"

"None, sir."

"Is there anything you want?"

"No, sir."

The Governor looked at the table. The writing-pad, which had been placed for the condemned prisoner's use, had not been touched.

"You have no letters to write? I suppose you can write?"

"Yes, sir. I've no letters to write."

"What are you, Carter? You're not an ordinary tramp. You're better educated than that class."

"I'm an ordinary tramp, sir," said Ray quietly.

"Have you all the books you need?"

Ray nodded, and the Governor went out. Every day came these inevitable inquiries. Sometimes the Governor made reference to his friends, but he grew tired of asking questions about the unused blotting-pad.

Ray Bennett had reached the stage of sane understanding where he did not even regret. It was inevitable. He had been caught up in the machinery of circumstance, and must go slowly round to the crashing-place. Every morning and afternoon he paced the square exercise yard, watched by three men in uniform, and jealously screened from the observation of other prisoners; and his serenity amazed all who saw him. He was caught up in the wheel and must go the full round. He could even smile at himself, observe his own vanity with the eye of an outsider. And he could not weep, because there was nothing left to weep about. He was already a dead man. Nobody troubled to organize a reprieve for him; he was too uninteresting a murderer. The newspapers did not flame into headlines, demanding a new trial. Fashionable lawyers would not foregather to discuss an appeal. He had murdered; he must die.

Once, when he was washing, and was about to put his hand in the water, he saw the reflection of his face staring back at him, and he did not recognize himself, for his beard had grown weedily. He laughed, and when the wondering warders looked at him, he said:

"I'm only now beginning to cultivate a sense of humour—I've left it rather late, haven't I?"

He could have had visitors, could have seen anybody he wished, but derived a strange satisfaction from his isolation. He had done with all that was artificial and emotional in life. Lola? He thought of her again and shook his head. She was very pretty. He wondered what she would do now that Lew was dead; what she was doing at that moment. He thought, too, of Dick Gordon, remembered that he liked him that day when Dick had given him a ride in his big Rolls. How queerly far off that seemed! And yet it could have only been a few months ago.

One day the Governor came in a more ceremonial style, and with him was a gentleman whom Ray remembered having seen in the court-house on the day of the trial. It was the Under Sheriff, and there was an important communication to be made. The Governor had to clear his throat twice.

"Carter," he said a little unsteadily, "the Secretary of State has informed me that he sees no reason for interfering with the course of the law. The High Sheriff has fixed next Wednesday morning at eight o'clock as the date and hour of your execution."

Ray inclined his head.

"Thank you, sir," he said.

CHAPTER XXXIII

THE FROG OF THE NIGHT

JOHN BENNETT emerged from the wood-shed, which he had converted into a dark room, bearing a flat square box in either hand.

"Don't talk to me for a minute, Ella," he said as she rose from her knees—she was weeding her own pet garden—"or I shall get these blamed things mixed. This one"—he shook his right hand—"is a picture of trout, and it is a great picture," he said enthusiastically. "The man who runs the trout farm, let me take it through the glass side of the trench, and it was a beautifully sunny day."

"What is the other one, daddy?" she asked, and John Bennett pulled a face.

"That is the dud," he said regretfully. "Five hundred feet of good film gone west! I may have got a picture by accident, but I can't afford to have it developed on the off-chance. I'll keep it by, and one day, when I'm rolling in money, I'll go to the expense of satisfying my curiosity."

He took the boxes into the house, and turned round to his stationery rack to find two adhesive labels, and had finished writing them, when Dick Gordon's cheery voice came through the open window. He rose eagerly and went out to him.

"Well, Captain Gordon, did you get it?" he asked.

"I got it," said Dick solemnly, waving an envelope. "You're the first cinematographer that has been allowed in the Zoological Gardens, and I had to *crawl* to the powers that be to secure the permission!"

The pale face of John Bennett flushed with pleasure.

"It is a tremendous thing," he said. "The Zoo has never been put on the pictures, and Selinski has promised me a fabulous sum for the film if I can take it."

"The fabulous sum is in your pocket, Mr. Bennett," said Dick, "and I am glad that you mentioned it."

"I am under the impression you mentioned it first," said John Bennett. Ella did not remember having seen her father smile before.

"Perhaps I did," said Dick cheerfully. "I knew you were interested in animal photography."

He did not tell John Bennett that it was Ella who had first spoken about the difficulties of securing Zoo photographs and her father's inability to obtain the necessary permission.

John Bennett went back to his labelling with a lighter heart than he had borne for many a day. He wrote the two slips, wetted the gum and hesitated. Then he laid down the papers and went into the garden.

"Ella, do you remember which of those boxes had the trout in?"

"The one in your right hand, daddy," she said.

"I thought so," he said, and went to finish his work.

It was only after the boxes were labelled that he had any misgivings. Where had he stood when he put them down? On which side of the table? Then, with a shrug, he began to wrap the trout picture, and they saw him carrying it under his arm to the village post-office.

"No news of Ray?" asked Dick.

The girl shook her head.

"What does your father think?"

"He doesn't talk about Ray, and I haven't emphasized the fact that it is such a long time since I had a letter."

They were strolling through the garden toward the little summer-house that John Bennett had built in the days when Ray was a schoolboy.

"You have not heard?" she asked. "I credit you with an omniscience which perhaps isn't deserved. You have not found the man who killed Mr. Maitland?"

"No," said Dick. "I don't expect we shall until we catch Frog himself."

"Will you?" she asked quietly.

He nodded.

"Yes, he can't go on for ever. Even Elk is taking a cheerful view. Ella," he asked suddenly, "are you the kind of person who keeps a promise?"

"Yes," she said in surprise.

"In all circumstances, if you make a promise, do you keep it?"

"Why, of course. If I do not think I can keep it, I do not make a promise. Why?"

"Well, I want you to make me a promise—and to keep it," he said.

She looked past him, and then:

"It depends what the promise is."

"I want you to promise to be my wife," said Dick Gordon.

Her hand lay in his, and she did not draw it from him.

"It is . . . very . . . businesslike, isn't it?" she said, biting her unruly underlip.

"Will you promise?"

She looked round at him, tears in her eyes, though her lips were smiling, and he caught her in his arms.

John Bennett waited a long time for his lunch that day. Going out to see where his daughter was, he met Dick, and in a few words Dick Gordon told him all. He saw the pain in the man's face, and dropped his hand upon the broad shoulder.

"Ella has promised me, and she will not go back on her promise. Whatever happens, whatever she learns."

The man raised his eyes to the other's face.

"Will you go back on your promise?" he asked huskily. "Whatever you learn?"

"I know," said Dick simply.

Ella Bennett walked on air that day. A new and splendid colour had come into her life; a tremendous certainty which banished all the fears and doubts she had felt; a light which revealed delightful vistas.

Her father went over to Dorking that afternoon, and came back hurriedly, wearing that strained look which it hurt her to see.

"I shall have to go to town, dearie," he said. "There's been a letter waiting for me for two days. I've been so absorbed in my picture work that I'd forgotten I had any other responsibility."

He did not look for her in the garden to kiss her good-bye, and when she came back to the house he was gone, and in such a hurry that he had not taken his camera with him.

Ella did not mind being alone; in the days when Ray was at home, she had spent many nights in the cottage by herself, and the house was on the main road. She made some tea and sat down to write to Dick, though she told herself reprovingly that he hadn't been gone more than two or three hours. Nevertheless, she wrote, for the spirit of logic avoids the lover.

There was a postal box a hundred yards up the road; it was a bright night and people were standing at their cottage gates, gossipping, as she passed. The letter dropped in the box, she came back to the cottage, went inside, locked and bolted the door, and sat down with a workbasket by her side to fill in the hour which separated her from bedtime.

So working, her mind was completely occupied, to the exclusion of all other thoughts, by Dick Gordon. Once or twice the thought of her father and Ray strayed across her mind, but it was to Dick she returned.

The only illumination in the cosy dining-room was a shaded kerosene lamp which stood on the table by her side and gave her sufficient light for her work. All outside the range of the lamp was shadow. She had finished darning a pair of her father's socks, and had laid down the needle with a happy sigh, when her eyes went to the door leading to the kitchen. It was ajar, and it was opening slowly.

For a moment she sat paralysed with terror, and then leapt to her feet.

"Who's there?" she called.

There came into the shadowy doorway a figure, the very sight of which choked the scream in her throat. It looked tall, by reason of the tightly-fitting black coat it wore. The face and head were hidden behind a hideous mask of rubber and mica. The reflection of the lamp shone on the big goggles and filled them with a baleful fire.

"Don't scream, don't move!" said the masked man, and his voice sounded hollow and far away. "I will not hurt you."

"Who are you?" she managed to gasp.

"I am The Frog," said the stranger.

For an eternity, as it seemed, she stood helpless, incapable of movement, and it was he who spoke.

"How many men love you, Ella Bennett?" he asked. "Gordon and Johnson—and The Frog, who loves you most of all!"

He paused, as though he expected her to speak, but she was incapable of answering him.

"Men work for women, and they murder for women, and behind all that they do, respectably or unrespectably, there is a woman," said the Frog. "And you are that woman for me, Ella."

"Who are you?" she managed to say.

"I am The Frog," he replied again, "and you shall know my name when I have given it to you. I want you! Not now"—he raised his hand as he saw the terror rising in her face. "You shall come to me willingly."

"You're mad!" she cried. "I do not know you. How can I—oh, it's too wicked to suggest . . . please go away."

"I will go presently," said the Frog. "Will you marry me, Ella?"

She shook her head.

"Will you marry me, Ella?" he asked again.

"No." She had recovered her calm and something of her self-possession.

"I will give you——"

"If you gave me all the money there was in the world, I would not many you," she said.

"I will give you something more precious." His voice was softer, scarcely audible. "I will give you a life!"

She thought he was speaking of Dick Gordon.

"I will give you the life of your brother."

For a second the room spun round and she clutched a chair to keep her feet.

"What do you mean?" she asked.

"I will give you the life of your brother, who is lying in Gloucester Gaol under sentence of death!" said the Frog.

With a supreme effort Ella guided herself to a chair and sat down.

"My brother?" she said dully. "Under sentence of death?"

"To-day is Monday," said the Frog. "On Wednesday he dies. Give me your word that when I send for you, you will come, and I will save him."

"How can you save him?" The question came mechanically.

"A man has made a confession—a man named Gill, a half-witted fellow who thinks he killed Lew Brady."

"Brady?" she gasped.

The Frog nodded.

"It isn't true," she breathed. "You're lying! You're telling me this to frighten me."

"Will you marry me?" he asked.

"Never, never!" she cried. "I would rather die. You are lying to me."

"When you want me, send for me," said the Frog. "Put in your window a white card, and I will save your brother."

She half lay on the table, her head upon her folded arms.

"It's not true, it's not true," she muttered.

There was no reply, and, looking up, she saw that the room was empty. Staggering to her feet, she went out into the kitchen. The kitchen door was open; and, peering into the dark garden, she saw no sign of the man. She had strength to bolt the door, and dragged herself up to her room and to her bed, and then she fainted.

Daylight showed in the windows when she sat up. She was painfully weary, her eyes were red with weeping, her head was in a whirl. It had been a night of horror—and it was not true, it could not be true. She had heard of no murder; and if there had been, it could not be Ray. She would have known; Ray would have sent for her father.

She dragged her aching limbs to the bathroom and turned the cold-water tap. Half an hour later she was sane, and looking at her experience dispassionately. Ray was alive. The man had tried to frighten her. Who was he? She shivered.

She saw only one solution to her terrible problem, and after she had made herself a cup of tea, she dressed and walked down into the town, in time to catch an early train. What other thought came to her, she never dreamt for one moment of surrender, never so much as glanced at the window where a white card could be placed, might save the life of her brother. In her heart of hearts, she knew that this man would not have come to her with such a story unless it was well founded. That was not the Frog's way. What advantage would he gain if he had invented this tragedy? Nevertheless, she did not even look for a white card, or think of its possible use.

Dick was at breakfast when she arrived, and a glance at her face told him that she brought bad news.

"Don't go, Mr. Elk," she said as the inspector pushed back his chair. "You must know this."

As briefly as she could, she narrated the events of the night before, and Dick listened with rising wrath until she came to the climax of the story.

"Ray under sentence?" he said incredulously. "Of course it isn't true."

"Where did he say the boy was?" asked Elk.

"In Gloucester Prison."

In their presence her reserve had melted and she was near to tears.

"Gloucester Prison?" repeated Elk slowly. "There *is* a man there under sentence of death, a man named"—he strove to remember—"Carter," he said at last. "That is it—Carter, a tramp. He killed another tramp named Phenan."

"Of course it isn't Ray," said Dick, laying his hand on hers. "This brute tried to frighten you. When did he say the execution had been fixed for?"

"To-morrow." She was weeping; now that the tension had relaxed, it seemed that she had reached the reserve of her strength.

"Ray is probably on the Continent," Dick soothed her, and here Elk thought it expedient and delicate to steal silently forth.

He was not as convinced as Gordon that the Frog had made a bluff. No sooner was he in his office than he rang for his new clerk.

"Records," he said briefly. "I want particulars of a man named Carter, now lying under sentence of death in Gloucester Prison—photograph, finger-prints, and record of the crime."

The man was gone ten minutes, and returned with a small portfolio.

"No photograph has been received yet, sir," he said. "In murder cases we do not get the full records from the County police until after the execution."

Elk cursed the County police fluently, and addressed himself to the examination of the dossier. That told him little or nothing. The height and weight of the man tallied, he guessed, with Ray's. There were no body marks and the description "Slight beard — —"

He sat bolt upright. Slight beard! Ray Bennett had been growing a beard for some reason. He remembered that Broad had told him this.

"Pshaw!" he said, throwing down the finger-print card. "It is impossible!"

It was impossible, and yet — —

He drew a telegraph pad toward him and wrote a wire.

"Governor, H.M. Prison, Gloucester. Very urgent. Send by special messenger prison photograph of James Carter under sentence of death in your prison to Headquarters Records. Messenger must leave by first train. Very urgent."

He took the liberty of signing it with the name of the Chief Commissioner. The telegram despatched, he returned to a scrutiny of the description sheet, and presently he saw a remark which he had overlooked.

"Vaccination marks on right forearm."

That was unusual. People are usually vaccinated on the left arm, a little below the shoulder. He made a note of this fact, and turned to the work that was waiting for him. At noon a wire arrived from Gloucester, saying that the photograph was on its way. That, at least, was satisfactory; though, even if it proved to be Ray, what could be done? In his heart Elk prayed most fervently that the Frog had bluffed.

Just before one, Dick telephoned him and asked him to lunch with them at the Auto Club, an invitation which, in any circumstances, was not to be refused, for Elk had a passion for visiting other people's clubs.

When he arrived—on this occasion strictly on time—he found the girl in a calm, even a cheerful mood, and his quick eye detected upon her finger a ring of surprising brilliance that he had not seen before. Dick Gordon had made very good use of his spare time that morning.

"I feel I'm neglecting my business, Elk," he said after he had led them into the palatial dining-room of the Auto, and had found a cushion for the girl's back, and had placed her chair exactly where it was least comfortable, "but I guess you've got through the morning without feeling my loss."

"I certainly have," said Elk. "A very interesting morning. There is a smallpox scare in the East End," he went on, "and I've heard some talk at Headquarters of having the whole staff vaccinated. If there's one thing that I do not approve of, it is vaccination. At my time of life I ought to be immune from any germ that happens to be going round."

The girl laughed.

"Poor Mr. Elk! I sympathize with you. Ray and I had a dreadful time when we were vaccinated about five years ago during the big epidemic, although I didn't have so bad a time as Ray. And neither of us had such an experience as the majority of victims, because we had an excellent doctor, with unique views on vaccination."

She pulled back the sleeve of her blouse and showed three tiny scars on the underside of the right forearm.

"The doctor said he would put it where it wouldn't show. Isn't that a good idea?"

"Yes," said Elk slowly. "And did he vaccinate your brother the same way?"

She nodded, and then:

"What is the matter, Mr. Elk?"

"I swallowed an olive stone," said Elk. "I wonder somebody doesn't start cultivating olives without stones." He looked out of the window. "You've got a pretty fine day for your visit, Miss Bennett," he said, and launched forth into a rambling condemnation of the English climate.

It seemed hours to Elk before the meal was finished. The girl was going back to Gordon's house to look at catalogues which Dick had ordered to be sent to Harley Terrace by telephone.

"You won't be coming to the office?" asked Elk.

"No: do you think it is necessary?"

"I wanted to see you for ten minutes," drawled the other, "perhaps a quarter of an hour."

"Come back to the house."

"Well, I wasn't thinking of coming back to the house," said Elk. "Perhaps you've got a lady's drawing-room. I remember seeing one as I came through the marble hall, and Miss Bennett would not mind— —"

"Why, of course not," she said. "If I'm in the way, I'll do anything you wish. Show me your lady's drawing-room."

When Dick had come back, the detective was smoking, his elbows on the table, his thin, brown hands clasped under his chin, and he was examining, with the eye of a connoisseur, the beautifully carved ceiling.

"What's the trouble, Elk?" said Gordon as he sat down.

"The man under sentence of death is Ray Bennett," said Elk without preliminary.

CHAPTER XXXIV

THE PHOTO-PLAY

DICK'S face went white.

"How do you know this?"

"Well, there's a photograph coming along; it will be in London this afternoon; but I needn't see that. This man under sentence has three vaccination marks on the right forearm."

There was a dead silence.

"I wondered why you turned the talk to vaccination," said Dick quietly. "I ought to have known there was something in it. What can we do?"

"I'll tell you what you can't do," said Elk. "You can't let that girl know. For good and sufficient reasons, Ray Bennett has decided not to reveal his identity, and he must pass out. You're going to have a rotten afternoon, Captain Gordon," said Elk gently, "and I'd rather be me than you. But you've got to keep up your light-hearted chatter, or that young woman is going to guess that something is wrong."

"My God! How dreadful!" said Dick in a low voice.

"Yes, it is," admitted Elk, "and we can do nothing. We've got to accept it as a fact that he's guilty. If you thought any other way, it would drive you mad. And even if he was as innocent as you or I, what chance have we of getting an inquiry or stopping the sentence being carried into execution?"

"Poor John Bennett!" said Dick in a hushed voice.

"If you're starting to get sentimental," snarled Elk, blinking furiously, "I'm going into a more practical atmosphere. Good afternoon."

"Wait. I can't face this girl for a moment. Come back to the house with me."

Elk hesitated, and then grudgingly agreed.

Ella could not guess, from their demeanour, the horror that was in the minds of these men. Elk fell back upon history and dates—a prolific and a favourite subject.

"Thank heaven those catalogues have arrived!" said Dick, as, with a sigh of relief, he saw the huge pile of literature on his study table.

"Why 'thank heaven'?" she smiled.

"Because his conscience is pricking him, and he wants an excuse for working." Elk came to the rescue.

The strain was one which even he found almost insupportable; and when, after a pleading glance at the other, Dick nodded, he got up with a sense of holiday.

"I'll be going now, Miss Bennett," he said. "I expect you'll be busy all the afternoon furnishing your cottage. I must come down and see it," he went on, wilfully dense. "Though it struck me that there wouldn't be much room for new furniture at Maytree."

So far he got when he heard voices in the hall—the excited voice of a woman, shrill, insistent, hysterical. Before Dick could get to the door, it was flung open, and Lola rushed in.

"Gordon! Gordon! Oh, my God!" she sobbed. "Do you know?"

"Hush!" said Dick, but the girl was beside herself.

"They've got Ray! They're going to hang him! Lew's dead."

The mischief was done. Ella came slowly to her feet, rigid with fear.

"My brother?" she asked, and then Lola saw her for the first time and nodded.

"I found out," she sobbed. "I had a suspicion, and I wrote . . . I've got a photograph of Phenan. I knew it was Lew at once, and I guessed the rest. The Frog did it! He planned it; months in advance he planned it. I'm not sorry about Lew; I swear I'm not sorry about Lew! It's the boy. I sent him to his death, Gordon ——" And then she broke into a fit of hysterical sobbing.

"Put her out," said Gordon, and Elk lifted the helpless girl in his arms and carried her into the dining-room.

"True!" Ella whispered the word, and Dick nodded.

"I'm afraid it's true, Ella."

She sat down slowly.

"I wonder where I can find father," she said, as calmly as though she were discussing some everyday event.

"You can do nothing. He knows nothing. Do you think it is kind to tell him?"

She searched his face wonderingly.

"I think you're right. Of course you're right, Dick. I'm sure you're right. Father mustn't know. Couldn't I see him—Ray, I mean?"

Dick shook his head.

"Ella, if Ray has kept silent to save you from this, all his forbearance, all his courage will be wasted if you go to him."

Again her lips drooped.

"Yes. It is good of you to think for me." She put her hand on his, and he felt no tremor. "I don't know what I can do," she said. "It is so—stunning. What can I do?"

"You can do nothing, my dear." His arm went round her and her tired head fell upon his shoulder.

"No, I can do nothing," she whispered.

Elk came in.

"A telegram for Miss Bennett," he said. "The messenger just arrived with it. Been redirected from Horsham, I expect."

Dick took the wire.

"Open it, please," said the girl. "It may be from father."

He tore open the envelope. The telegram ran:

"Have printed your picture. Cannot understand the murder. Were you trying take photo-play? Come and see me. Silenski House, Wardour Street."

"What does it mean?" she asked.

"It is Greek to me," said Dick. "'Cannot understand murder'—has your father been trying to take photo-plays?"

"No, dear, I'm sure he hasn't; he would have told me."

"What photographs did your father take?"

"It was a picture of trout," she said, gathering her scattered thoughts; "but he took another picture—in his sleep. He was in the country waiting for a badger, and dozed. He must have pressed the starter; he thought that picture was a failure. It can't be the trout; it doesn't mention the trout; it must be the other."

"We will go to Wardour Street."

It was Elk who spoke so definitely, Elk who called a cab and hustled the two people into it. When they arrived at Wardour

Street, Mr. Silenski was out at lunch, and nobody knew anything whatever about the film, or had authority to show it.

For an hour and a half they waited, fuming, in that dingy office, whilst messengers went in search of Silenski. He arrived at last, a polite and pleasant little Hebrew, who was all apologies, though no apology was called for, since he had not expected his visitors.

"Yes, it is a curious picture," he said. "Your father, miss, is a very good amateur; in fact, he's a professional now; and if it is true that he can get these Zoo photographs, he ought to be in the first rank of nature photographers."

They followed him up a flight of stairs into a big room across which were row upon row of chairs. Facing them as they sat was a small white screen, and behind them an iron partition with two square holes.

"This is our theatre," he explained. "You've no idea whether your father is trying to take motion pictures—I mean photo-plays? If he is, then this scene was pretty well acted, but I can't understand why he did it. It's labelled 'Trout in a Pond' or something of the sort, but there are no trout here, and there is no pond either!"

There was a click, and the room went black; and then there was shown on the screen a picture which showed in the foreground a stretch of grey, sandy soil, and the dark opening of a burrow, out of which peeped a queer-looking animal.

"That's a badger," explained Mr. Silenski. "It looked very promising up to there, and then I don't know what he did. You'll see he changed the elevation of the camera."

As he spoke, the picture jerked round a little to the right, as though it had been pulled violently. And they were looking upon two men, obviously tramps. One was sitting with his head on his hands, the other, close by him, was pouring out whisky into a container.

"That's Lew Brady," whispered Elk fiercely, and at that moment the other man looked up, and Ella Bennett uttered a cry.

"It is Ray! Oh, Dick, it is Ray!"

There was no question of it. The light beard he wore melted into the shadows which the strong sunlight cast. They saw Brady offer him a drink, saw him toss it down and throw the cup back to the man; watched him as his arms stretched in a yawn; and then saw him curl up to sleep, lie back, and Lew Brady standing over him. The prostrate figure turned on to its face, and Lew, stooping, put something in his pocket. They caught the reflection of glass.

"The flask," said Elk.

And then the figure standing in the centre of the picture spun round. There walked toward him a man. His face was invisible. Never once during that period did he turn his face to that eager audience.

They saw his arm go up quickly, saw the flash of the two shots, watched breathless, spellbound, horrified, the tragedy that followed.

The man stooped and placed the pistol by the side of the sleeping Ray, and then, as he turned, the screen went white.

"That's the end of the picture," said Mr. Silenski. "And what it means, heaven knows."

"He's innocent! Dick, he's innocent!" the girl cried wildly. "Don't you see, it was not he who fired?"

She was half-mad with grief and terror, and Dick caught her firmly by the shoulders, the dumbfounded Silenski gaping at the scene.

"You are going back to my house and you will read! Do you hear, Ella? You're to do nothing until you hear from me. You are not to go out; you are to sit and *read*! I don't care what you read —the Bible, the Police News, anything you like. But you must not think of this business. Elk and I will do all that is possible."

She mastered her wild terror and tried to smile.

"I know you will," she said between her chattering teeth. "Get me to your house, please."

He left Elk to go to Fleet Street to collect every scrap of information about the murder he could from the newspaper offices, and brought the girl back to Harley Terrace. As he got out of the cab, he saw a man waiting on the steps. It was Joshua Broad. One glance at his face told Dick that he knew of the murder, and he guessed the source.

He waited in the hall until Dick had put the girl in the study, and had collected every illustrated newspaper, every book he could find.

"Lola told me of this business."

"I guessed so," said Dick. "Do you know anything about it?"

"I knew these two men started out in the disguise of tramps," said Broad, "but I understood they were going north. This is Frog work—why?"

"I don't know. Yes, I do," Dick said suddenly. "The Frog came to Miss Bennett last night and asked her to marry him, promising that he would save her brother if she agreed. But it can hardly be that he planned this diabolical trick to that end."

"To no other end," said Broad coolly. "You don't know Frog, Gordon! The man is a strategist—probably the greatest strategist in the world. Can I do anything?"

"I would ask you to stay and keep Miss Bennett amused——" Dick began.

"I think you might do worse," said the American quietly.

Ella looked up with a look of pain as the visitor entered the room. She felt that she could not endure the presence of a stranger at this moment, that she would break under any new strain, and she glanced at Dick imploringly.

"If you don't want me to stay, Miss Bennett," smiled Broad, "well, I'll go just as soon as you tell me. But I've one piece of information to pass to you, and it is this: that your brother will not die."

His eyes met Dick Gordon's, and the Prosecutor bit his lip to restrain the cry that came involuntarily.

"Why?" she asked eagerly, but neither of the men could tell her.

Dick telephoned to the garage for his car, the very machine that Ray Bennett had driven the first day they had met. His first call was at the office of the Public Prosecutor, and to him he stated the facts.

"It is a most remarkable story, and I can do nothing, of course. You'd better see the Secretary of State at once, Gordon."

"Is the House of Commons sitting, sir?"

"No—I've an idea that the Secretary, who is the only man that can do anything for you—is out of town. He may be on the Continent. I'm not sure. There was a conference at San Remo last week, and I've a dim notion that he went there."

Dick's heart almost stood still.

"Is there nobody else at the Home Office who could help?"

"There is the Under Secretary: you'd better see him."

The Public Prosecutor's Department was housed in the Home Office building, and Dick went straight away in search of the responsible official. The permanent secretary, to whom he explained the circumstances, shook his head.

"I'm afraid we can do nothing now, Gordon," he said, "and the Secretary of State is in the country and very ill."

"Where is the Under Secretary?" asked Dick desperately.

"He's at San Remo."

"How far out of town is Mr. Whitby's house?"

The official considered.

"About thirty miles—this side of Tunbridge Wells," and Dick wrote the address on a slip of paper.

Half an hour later, a long yellow Rolls was flying across Westminster Bridge, threading the traffic with a recklessness which brought the hearts of hardened chauffeurs to their mouths; and forty minutes after he had left Whitehall, Dick was speeding up an elm-bordered avenue to the home of the Secretary of State.

The butler who met him could give him no encouragement.

"I'm afraid Mr. Whitby cannot see you, sir. He has a very bad attack of gout, and the doctors have told him that he mustn't touch any kind of business whatever."

"This is a matter of life and death," said Dick, "and I must see him. Or, failing him, I must see the King."

This message, conveyed to the invalid, produced an invitation to walk upstairs.

"What is it, sir?" asked the Minister sharply as Dick came in. "I cannot possibly attend to any business whatever. I'm suffering the tortures of the damned with this infernal foot of mine. Now tell me, what is it?"

Quickly Gordon related his discovery.

"An astounding story," said the Minister, and winced. "Where is the picture?"

"In London, sir."

"I can't come to London: it is humanly impossible. Can't you get somebody at the Home Office to certify this? When is this man to be hanged?"

"To-morrow morning, sir, at eight o'clock."

The Secretary of State considered, rubbing his chin irritably.

"I should be no man if I refused to see this damned picture," he said, and Dick made allowance for his language as he rubbed his suffering limb. "But I can't go to town unless you get me an ambulance. You had better 'phone a garage in London to send a car down, or, better still, get one from the local hospital."

Everything seemed to be conspiring against him, for the local hospital's ambulance was under repair, but at last Dick put through a message to town, with the promise that an ambulance would be on its way in ten minutes.

"An extraordinary story, a perfectly amazing story! And of course, I can grant you a respite. Or, if I'm convinced of the truth of this astounding romance, we could get the King to-night; I could even promise you a reprieve. But my death will lie at your door if I catch cold."

Two hours passed before the ambulance came. The chauffeur had had to change his tyres twice on the journey. Very gingerly, accompanied by furious imprecations from the Cabinet Minister, his stretcher was lifted into the ambulance.

To Dick the journey seemed interminable. He had telephoned through to Silenski, asking him to keep his office open until his arrival. It was eight o'clock by the time the Minister was assisted up to the theatre, and the picture was thrown upon the screen.

Mr. Whitby watched the drama with the keenest interest, and when it was finished he drew a long breath.

"That's all right so far as it goes," he said, "but how do I know this hasn't been play-acted in order to get this man a reprieve? And how am I to be sure that this wretched tramp *is* your man?"

"I can assure you of that, sir," said Elk. "I got the photograph up from Gloucester this afternoon."

He produced from his pocket-book two photographs, one in profile and one full-face, and put them on the table before the Minister.

"Show the picture again," he ordered, and again they watched the presentation of the tragedy. "But how on earth did the man manage to take this picture?"

"I've since discovered, sir, that he was in the neighbourhood on that very day. He went out to get a photograph of a badger—I know this, sir, because Mr. Silenski has given me all the information in his power."

Mr. Whitby looked up at Dick.

"You're in the Public Prosecutor's Department? I remember you very well, Captain Gordon. I must take your word. This is not a matter for respite, but for reprieve, until the whole of the circumstances are investigated."

"Thank you, sir," said Dick, wiping his streaming forehead.

"You'd better take me along to the Home Office," grumbled the great man. "To-morrow I shall be cursing your name and memory, though I must confess that I'm feeling better for the drive. I want that picture."

They had to wait until the picture was replaced in its box, and then Dick Gordon and Elk assisted the Secretary of State to the waiting ambulance.

At a quarter-past eight, a reprieve, ready for the Royal counter-signature, was in Dick's hand, and the miracle, which Mr. Whitby had not dared expect, had happened. He was able, with the aid of a stick, to hobble to a car. Before the great Palace, streams of carriages and motor-cars were passing. It was the night of the first ball of the season, and the hall of the Palace was a brilliant sight. The glitter of women's jewels, the scarlet, blue and green of diplomatic uniforms, the flash of innumerable Orders, no less than the organization of this gorgeous gathering, interested Dick as he stood, a strangely contrasting figure, watching the pageant pass him.

The Minister had disappeared into an ante-room and presently came back and crooked his finger; Dick followed him down a red-carpeted passage past white-haired footmen in scarlet and gold, until they came to a door, before which another footman stood. A whispered word, the footman knocked, and a voice bade them enter. The servant opened the door and they went in.

The man who was sitting at the table rose. He wore the scarlet uniform of a general; across his breast was the blue ribbon of the Garter. There was in his eyes a kindliness and humanity which Dick had not imagined he would find.

"Will you be seated? Now please tell me the story as quickly as you can, because I have an appointment elsewhere, and punctuality is the politeness of princes," he smiled.

He listened attentively, stopping Gordon now and again to ask a question. When Dick had finished, he took up a pen and wrote a word in a bold, boyish hand, blotted it punctiliously and handed it to the Secretary of State.

"There is your reprieve. I am very glad," he said, and Dick, bowing over the extended hand, felt the music of triumph in his soul, forgot for the moment the terrible danger in which this boy had stood; and forgot, too, the most important factor of all—the Frog, still vigilant, still vengeful, still powerful!

When he got back to the Home Office and had taken farewell, with a very earnest expression of gratitude, of the irascible, but kindly Minister, Dick flew up the stairs to his own office and seized the telephone.

"Put me through to Gloucester 8585 Official," he said, and waited for the long-distance signal.

It came after a few minutes.

"Sorry, sir, no call through to Gloucester. Line out of order. Trunk wires cut."

Dick put down the 'phone slowly. Then it was that he remembered that the Frog still lived.

CHAPTER XXXV

GETTING THROUGH

WHEN Elk came up to the Prosecutor's room, Dick was sitting at the table, writing telegrams. They were each addressed to the Governor of Gloucester Prison, and contained a brief intimation that a reprieve for James Carter was on its way. Each was marked viâ a different route.

"What's the idea?" said Elk.

"The 'phone to Gloucester is out of order," said Dick, and Elk bit his lip thoughtfully.

"Is that so?" he drawled. "Then if the 'phone's out of order — —"

"I don't want to think that," said Dick.

Elk took up the instrument.

"Give me the Central Telegraph Office, miss," he said. "I want to speak to the Chief Clerk. . . . Yes, Inspector Elk, C.I.D."

After a pause, he announced himself again.

"We're putting some wires through to Gloucester. I suppose the lines are all right?"

His face did not move a muscle while he listened, then:

"I see," he said. "Any roundabout route we can get? What's the nearest town open?" A wait. "Is that so? Thank you."

He put down the instrument.

"All wires to Gloucester are cut. The trunk wire has been cut in three places; the connection with Birmingham, which runs in an earthenware pipe underground, has been blown up, also in three places." Dick's eyes narrowed.

"Try the Radio Company," he said. "They've got a station at Devizes, and another one somewhere near Cheltenham, and they could send on a message."

Again Elk applied himself to the telephone.

"Is that the Radio Station? Inspector Elk, Headquarters Police, speaking. I want to get a message through to Gloucester, to Gloucester Prison, viâ—eh? . . . But I thought you'd overcome that difficulty. How long has it been jammed? . . . Thank you," he said, and put down the telephone for the second time.

"There's a jam," he said. "No messages are getting through. The radio people say that somebody in this country has got a secret apparatus which was used by the Germans during the war, and that when the jam is on, it is impossible to get anything through."

Dick looked at his watch. It was now half-past nine.

"You can catch the ten-five for Gloucester, Elk, but somehow I don't think it will get through."

"As a telephone expert," said Elk, as he patiently applied himself to the instrument, "I have many of the qualities that make, so to speak, for greatness. Hullo! Get me Great Western, please. Great Western Stationmaster. . . . I have a perfect voice, a tremendous amount of patience, and a faith in my fellow-man, and—Hullo! Is that you, Stationmaster? . . . Inspector Elk. I told you that before—no, it was somebody else. Inspector Elk, C.I.D. Is there any trouble on your road to-night?" . . . A longer pause this time. "Glory be!" said Elk unemotionally. "Any chance of getting through? . . . None whatever? What time will you have trains running? . . . Thank you."

He turned to Dick.

"Three culverts and a bridge down at Swindon, blown at seven o'clock; two men in custody; one man dead, shot by rail guard. Two culverts down at Reading; the metals blown up at Slough. I won't trouble to call up the other roads, because—well, the Frog's thorough."

Dick Gordon opened a cupboard and took out a leather coat and a soft leather helmet. In his drawer he found two ugly-looking Browning pistols and examined their magazines before he slipped them into his pocket. Then he selected half-a-dozen cigars, and packed them carefully in the breast pocket of the coat.

"You're not going alone, Gordon?" asked Elk sternly. Dick nodded.

"I'm going alone," he said. "If I don't get through, you follow. Send a police car after me and tell them to drive carefully. I don't think they'll stop me this side of Newbury," he said. "I can make that before the light goes. Tell Miss Bennett that the reprieve is signed, and that I am on my way."

Elk said nothing, but followed his chief into the street, and stood by him with the policeman who had been left in charge of the car, while Dick made a careful scrutiny of the tyres and petrol tank.

So Dick Gordon took the Bath road; and the party of gunmen that waited at the two aerodromes of London to shoot him down if he attempted to leave by the aerial route, waited in vain. He avoided the direct road to Reading, and was taking the longer way round. He came into Newbury at eleven o'clock, and learnt of more dynamited culverts. The town was full of it. Two laden trains were held up on the down line, and their passengers thronged the old-fashioned streets of the town. Outside *The Chequers* he spoke to the local inspector of police. Beyond the outrages they had heard nothing, and apparently the road was in good order, for a car had come through from Swindon only ten minutes before Dick arrived.

"You're safe as far as Swindon, anyway," said the inspector. "The countryside has been swarming with tramps lately, but my mounted patrols, that have just come in, have seen none on the roads."

A thought struck Dick, and he drove the inspector round to the police-station and went inside with him.

"I want an envelope and some official paper," he said, and, sitting down at the desk, he made a rough copy of the reprieve with its quaint terminology, sealed the envelope with wax and put it into his pocket. Then he took the real reprieve, and, taking off his shoe and sock, put it between his bare foot and his sock. Replacing his shoe, he jumped on to the car and started his cautious way toward Didcot. Both his glare lamps were on, and the road before him was as light as day. Nevertheless, he went at half speed, one of his Brownings on the cushion beside him.

Against the afterglow of the sunset, a faint, pale light which is the glory of late summer, he saw three inverted V's and knew they were the ends of a building, possibly an aerodrome. And then he remembered that Elk had told him of the chemical factory. Probably this was the place, and he drove with greater caution. He had turned the bend, when, ahead of him, he saw three red lights stretched across the road, and in the light of the head-lamps stood a policeman. He slowed the machine and stopped within a few yards of the officer.

"You can't go this way, sir. The road's up."

"How long has it been up?" asked Dick.

"It's been blown up, sir, about twenty minutes ago," was the reply. "There's a side road a mile back, which will bring you to the other side of the railway lines. You can back in here." He indicated a gateway evidently leading to the factory. Dick pulled back his lever to the reverse, and sent the Rolls spinning backward into the opening. His hand was reaching to change the direction, when the policeman, who had walked to the side of the car, struck at him.

Gordon's head was bent. He was incapable of resistance. Only the helmet he wore saved him from death. He saw nothing, only suddenly the world went black. Scarcely had the blow been struck when half-a-dozen men came from the shadows. Somebody jumped into the driver's seat, and, flinging out the limp figure of its owner, brought the car still further backward, and switched off the lights. Another of the party removed the red lamps. The policeman bent over the prostrate figure of Dick Gordon.

"I thought I'd settled him," he said, disappointed.

"Well, settle him now," said somebody in the darkness, but evidently the assailant changed his mind.

"Hagn will want him," he said. "Lift him up."

They carried the inanimate figure over the rough ground, through a sliding door, into a big, ill-lit factory hall, bare of machinery. At the far end was a brick partition forming an office, and into this he was carried and flung on the floor.

"Here's your man, Hagn," growled the policeman. "I think he's through."

Hagn got up from his table and walked across to where Dick Gordon lay.

"I don't think there's much wrong with him," he said. "You couldn't kill a man through that helmet, anyway. Take it off."

They took the leather helmet from the head of the unconscious man, and Hagn made a brief inspection.

"No, he's all right," he said. "Throw some water over him. Wait; you'd better search him first. Those cigars," he said, pointing to the brown cylinders that protruded from his breast pocket, "I want."

The first thing found was the blue envelope, and this Hagn tore open and read.

"It seems all right," he said, and locked it away in the roll-top desk at which he was sitting when Dick had been brought in. "Now give him the water!"

Dick came to his senses with a throbbing head and a feeling of resentment against the consciousness which was being forced upon him. He sat up, rubbing his face like a man roused from a heavy sleep, screwed up his eyes in the face of the bright light, and unsteadily stumbled to his feet, looking around from one to the other of the grinning faces.

"Oh!" he said at last. "I seem to have struck it. Who hit me?"

"We'll give you his card presently," sneered Hagn. "Where are you off to at this time of night?"

"I'm going to Gloucester," said Dick.

"Like hell you are!" scoffed Hagn. "Put him upstairs, boys."

Leading up from the office was a flight of unpainted pine stairs, and up this he was partly pushed and partly dragged. The room above had been used in war time as an additional supervisor's office. It had a large window, commanding a view of the whole of the floor space. The window was now thick with grime, and the floor littered with rubbish which the present occupants had not thought it worth while to move.

"Search him again, and make sure he hasn't any gun on him. And take away his boots," said Hagn.

A small carbon filament lamp cast a sickly yellow light upon the sinister group that surrounded Dick Gordon. He had time to take his bearings. The window he had seen, and escape that way was impossible; the ceiling was covered with matchboards that had once been varnished. There was no other way out, save down the steps.

"You've got to stay here for a day or two, Gordon, but perhaps, if the Government will give us Balder, you'll get away with your life. If they don't, then it'll be a case of 'good-night, nurse!'"

CHAPTER XXXVI

THE POWER CABLE

DICK GORDON knew that any discussion with his captors was a waste of breath, and that repartee was profitless. His head was aching, but no sooner was he left alone than he gave himself a treatment which an osteopath had taught him. He put his chin on his breast, and his two open hands behind his neck, the finger-tips pressing hard, then he slowly raised his head (it was an agony to do so), bringing his fingers down over the jugular. Three times repeated, his head was comparatively clear.

The door was of thin wood and could easily be forced, but the room below was filled with men. Presently the light below went out, and the place was in darkness. He guessed that it was because Hagn did not wish the light to be seen from the road; though it was unlikely that there would come any inquiries, he had taken effective steps to deal with the police car which he knew would follow.

They had not taken his matches away, and Dick struck one and looked round. Standing before a fireplace filled with an indescribable litter of half-burnt papers and dust, was a steel plate, with holes for rivets, evidently part of a tank which had not been assembled. There was a heavy switch on the wall, and Dick turned it, hoping that it controlled the light; but apparently that was on the same circuit as the light below. He struck another match and followed the casing of the switch. By and by he saw a thick black cable running in the angle of the wall and the ceiling. It terminated abruptly on the right of the fireplace; and from the marks on the floor, Dick guessed that at some time or other there had been an experimental welding plant housed there. He turned the switch again and sat down to consider what would be the best thing to do. He could hear the murmur of voices below, and, lying on the floor, put his ear to the trap, which he cleared with a piece of wire he found in the fireplace. Hagn seemed to do most of the talking.

"If we blow up the road between here and Newbury, they'll smell a rat," he said.

"It's a stupid idea you put forward, Hagn. What are you going to do with the chap upstairs?"

"I don't know. I'm waiting to hear from Frog. Perhaps the Frog will want him killed."

"He'd be a good man to hold for Balder, though, if Frog thought it was worth while."

Towards five o'clock, Hagn, who had been out of the office, came back.

"Frog says he's got to die," he said in a low voice.

* * * * * *

Two people sat in Dick Gordon's study. The hour was four o'clock in the morning. Elk had gone, for the twentieth time, to Headquarters, and for the twentieth time was on his way back. Ella Bennett had tried desperately hard to carry out Dick's instructions, and turned page after page determinedly, but had read and yet had seen nothing. With a deep sigh she put down the book and clasped her hands, her eyes fixed upon the clock.

"Do you think he will get to Gloucester?" she asked.

"I certainly do," said Broad confidently. "That young man will get anywhere. He is the right kind and the right type, and nothing is going to hold him."

She picked up the book but did not look at its printed page.

"What happened to the police cars? Mr. Elk was telling me a lot about them last night," she said. "I haven't heard since."

Joshua Broad licked his dry lips.

"Oh, they got through all right," he said vaguely.

He did not tell her that two police cars had been ditched between Newbury and Reading, the cars smashed and three men injured by a mine which had been sprung under them. Nor did he give her the news, that had arrived by motor-cyclist from Swindon, that Dick's car had not been seen.

"They are dreadful people, dreadful!" She shivered. "How did they come into existence, Mr. Broad?"

Broad was smoking (at her request) a long, thin cigar, and he puffed for a long time before he spoke.

"I guess I'm the father of the Frogs," he said to her amazement.

"You!"

He nodded.

"I didn't know I was producing this outfit, but there it is." How, he did not seem disposed to explain at that moment.

Soon he heard the whirr of the bell, and thinking that Elk had perhaps forgotten the key, he rose, and, going along the passage, opened the door. It was not Elk.

"Forgive me for calling. Is that Mr. Broad?" The visitor peered forward in the darkness.

"I'm Broad all right. You're Mr. Johnson, aren't you? Come right in, Mr. Johnson."

He closed the door behind him and turned on the light. The stout man was in a state of pitiable agitation.

"I was up late last night," he said, "and my servant brought me an early copy of the *Post Herald*."

"So you know, eh?"

"It's terrible, terrible! I can't believe it!"

He took a crumpled paper from his pocket and looked at the stop-press space as though to reassure himself.

"I didn't know it was in the paper."

Johnson handed the newspaper to the American.

"Yes, they've got it. I suppose old man Whitby must have given away the story."

"I think it came from the picture man, Silenski. Is it true that Ray is under sentence of death?"

Broad nodded.

"How dreadful!" said Johnson in a hushed voice. "Thank God they've found it out in time! Mr. Broad," he said earnestly, "I hope you will tell Ella Bennett that she can rely on me for every penny I possess to establish her brother's innocence. I suppose there will be a respite and a new trial? If there is, the very best lawyers must be employed."

"She's here. Won't you come in and see her?"

"Here?" Johnson's jaw dropped. "I had no idea," he stammered.

"Come in."

Broad returned to the girl.

"Here is a friend of yours who has turned up—Mr. Johnson."

The philosopher crossed the room with quick, nervous strides, and held out both his hands to the girl.

"I'm so sorry, Miss Bennett," he said, "so very, very sorry! It must be dreadful for you, dreadful! Can I do anything?"

She shook her head, tears of gratitude in her eyes.

"It is very sweet of you, Mr. Johnson. You've done so much for Ray, and Inspector Elk was telling me that you had offered him a position in your office."

Johnson shook his head.

"It is nothing. I'm very fond of Ray, and he really has splendid capabilities. Once we get him out of this mess, I'll put him on his feet again. Your father doesn't know? Thank God for that!"

"I wish this news hadn't got into the papers," she said, when he told her how he had learnt of the happening.

"Silenski, of course," said Broad. "A motion picture publicity man would use his own funeral to get a free par. How are you feeling in your new position, Johnson?" he asked, to distract the girl's mind from the tragic thoughts which were oppressing her.

Johnson smiled.

"I'm bewildered. I can't understand why poor Mr. Maitland did this. But I had my first Frog warning to-day; I feel almost important," he said.

From a worn pocket-case he extracted a sheet of paper. It contained only three words;

"You are next!"

and bore the familiar sign manual of the Frog.

"I don't know what harm I have done to these people, but I presume that it is something fairly bad, for within ten minutes of getting this note, the porter brought me my afternoon tea. I took one sip and it tasted so bitter that I washed my mouth out with a disinfectant."

"When was this?"

"Yesterday," said Johnson. "This morning I had the analysis—I had the tea bottled and sent off at once to an analytical chemist. It contained enough hydrocyanic acid to kill a hundred people.

The chemist cannot understand how I could have taken the sip I did without very serious consequences. I am going to put the matter in the hands of the police to-day."

The front door opened, and Elk came in.

"What is the news?" asked the girl eagerly, rising to meet him.

"Fine!" said Elk. "You needn't worry at all, Miss Bennett. That Gordon man can certainly move. I guess he's in Gloucester by now, sleeping in the best bed in the city."

"But do you *know* he's in Gloucester?" she asked stubbornly.

"I've had no exact news, but I can tell you this, that we've had no bad news," said Elk; "and when there's no news, you can bet that things are going according to schedule."

"How did you hear about it, Johnson?"

The new millionaire explained.

"I ought to have pulled in Silenski and his operator," said Elk thoughtfully. "These motion picture men lack reticence. And how does it feel to be rich, Johnson?" he asked.

"Mr. Johnson doesn't think it feels too good," said Broad. "He has attracted the attention of old man Frog."

Elk examined the warning carefully.

"When did this come?"

"I found it on my desk yesterday morning," said Johnson, and told him of the tea incident. "Do you think, Mr. Elk, you will ever put your hand on the Frog?"

"I'm as certain as that I'm standing here, that Frog will go the way— —" Elk checked himself, and fortunately the girl was not listening.

It was getting light when Johnson left, and Elk walked with him to the door and watched him passing down the deserted street.

"There's a lot about that boy I like," he said; "and he's certainly fortunate. Why the old man didn't leave his money to that baby of his— —"

"Did you ever find the baby?" interrupted Broad.

"No, sir, there was no sign of that innocent child in the house. That's another Frog mystery to be cleared up."

Johnson had reached the corner, and they saw him crossing the road, when a man came out of the shadow to meet him. There was a brief parley, and then Elk saw the flash of a pistol, and heard a shot. Johnson staggered back, and his opponent, turning, fled. In a second Elk was flying along the street. Apparently the philosopher was not hurt, though he seemed shaken.

The inspector ran round the corner, but the assassin had disappeared. He returned to the philosopher, to find him sitting on the edge of the pavement, and at first he thought he had been wounded.

"No, I think I just had a shock," gasped Johnson. "I was quite unprepared for that method of attack."

"What happened?" asked Elk.

"I can hardly realize," said the other, who appeared dazed. "I was crossing the road when a man came up and asked me if my name was Johnson; then, before I knew what had happened, he had fired."

His coat was singed by the flame of the shot, but the bullet must have gone wide. Later in the day, Elk found it embedded in the brickwork of a house.

"No, no, I won't come back," said Johnson. "I don't suppose they'll repeat the attempt."

By this time one of the two detectives who had been guarding Harley Terrace had come up, and under his escort Johnson was sent home.

"They're certainly the busiest little fellows," said Elk, shaking his head. "You'd think they'd be satisfied with the work they were doing at Gloucester, without running sidelines."

Joshua Broad was silent until they were going up the steps of the house.

"When you know as much about the Frog as I know, you'll be surprised at nothing," he said, and did not add to this cryptic remark.

Six o'clock came, and there was no further news from the west. Seven o'clock, and the girl's condition became pitiable. She had borne herself throughout the night with a courage that excited the admiration of the men; but now, as the hour was drawing close, she seemed on the verge of collapse. At half-past seven the telephone bell rang, and Elk answered.

It was the Chief of Police at Newbury speaking.

"Captain Gordon left Didcot an hour ago," was the message.

"Didcot!" gasped Elk in consternation. He looked at the clock. "An hour ago—and he had to make Gloucester in sixty minutes!"

The girl, who had been in the dining-room trying to take coffee which Gordon's servant had prepared, came into the study, and Elk dared not continue the conversation.

"All right," he said loudly, and smashed down the receiver.

"What is the news, Mr. Elk?" The girl's voice was a wail.

"The news," said Elk, twisting his face into a smile, "is fine!"

"What do they say?" she persisted.

"Oh, them?" said Elk, looking at the telephone. "That was a friend of mine, asking me if I'd dine with him to-night."

She went back to the dining-room, only half-satisfied, and Elk called the American to him.

"Go and get a doctor," he said in a low voice, "and tell him to bring something that'll put this young lady to sleep for twelve hours."

"Why?" asked Broad. "Is the news bad?"

Elk nodded.

"There isn't a chance of saving this boy—not the ghost of a chance!" he said.

CHAPTER XXXVII

THE GET-AWAY

DICK, with his ear to the floor, heard the words "Frog says he's got to die," and his cracked lips parted in a grin.

"Have you heard him moving about?" asked Hagn.

"No, he's asleep, I expect," said another voice. "We shall have to wait for light. We can't do it in the dark. We shall be killing one another."

This view commended itself to most of the men present. Dick counted six voices. He struck a match for another survey, and again his eye fell upon the cable. And then an inspiration came to him. Moving stealthily across the floor, he reached up, and, gripping the cable, pulled on it steadily. Under his weight, the supporting insulator broke loose. By great good luck it fell upon the heap of rubbish in the fireplace and made no sound. For the next half-hour he worked feverishly, unwrapping the rubber insulation from the wires of the cable, pulling the copper strands free. His hands were bleeding, his nails broken; but after half-an-hour's hard work, he had the end of the cable frayed. The door opened outward, he remembered with satisfaction, and, lifting the steel plate, he laid it tight against the door, so that whoever entered must step upon it. Then he began to fasten the frayed copper wires of the cable to the rivet holes; and he had hardly finished his work before he heard a stealthy sound on the stairs.

Day had come now, and light was streaming through the glass roof of the factory. He heard a faint whisper, and even as faint a click, as the bolts of the door were pulled; and, creeping to the switch, he turned it down.

The door was jerked open, and a man stepped upon the plate. Before his scream could warn him who followed the second of the party had been flung senseless to the floor.

"What the devil's wrong?" It was Hagn's voice. He came running up the stairs, put one foot on the electric plate, and stood for the space of a second motionless. Then, with a gasping sob, he fell backward, and Dick heard the crash as he struck the stairs.

He did not wait any longer. Jumping over the plate, he leapt down the stairs, treading underfoot the senseless figure of Hagn. The little office was empty. On the table lay one of his pistols. He gripped it, and fled along the bare factory hall, through a door into the open. He heard a shout, and, looking round, saw two of the party coming at him, and, raising his pistol, he pressed the trigger. There was a click—Hagn had emptied the magazine.

A Browning is an excellent weapon even if it is not loaded, and Dick Gordon brought the barrel down with smashing force upon the head of the man who tried to grapple with him. Then he turned and ran.

He had made a mistake when he thought there were only six men in the building; there must have been twenty, and most of them were in full cry.

He tried to reach the road, and was separated only by a line of bushes. But here he blundered. The bushes concealed a barbed wire fence, and he had to run along uneven ground, and in his stockinged feet the effort was painful. His slow progress enabled his pursuers to get ahead. Doubling back, Dick flew for the second of the three buildings, and as he ran, he took out the magazine of his pistol. As he feared, it was empty.

Now they were on him. He could hear the leading man's breath, and he himself was nearly spent. And then, before him, he saw a round fire-alarm, fixed to the wall, and in a flash the memory of an almost forgotten conversation came back to him. With his bare hands he smashed the glass and tugged at the alarm, and at that minute they were on him. He fought desperately, but against their numbers resistance was almost useless. He must gain time.

"Get up, you fellows!" he shouted. "Hagn's dead."

It was an unfortunate statement, for Hagn came out of the next building at that moment, very shaken but very alive. He was livid with rage, and babbled in some language which Dick did not know, but which he guessed was Swedish.

"I'll fix you for that. You shall try electric shock yourself, you dog!"

He drove his fist at the prisoner's face, but Dick twisted his head and the blow struck the brickwork of the building against which he stood. With a scream, the man leapt at him, clawing and tearing with open hands, and this was Dick's salvation. For the men who were gripping his arms released their hold, that their chief might have freer play. Dick struck out, hitting scientifically for the body, and with a yell Hagn collapsed. Before they could stop him, Gordon was away like the wind, this time making for the gate.

He had reached it when the hand of the nearest man fell on him. He flung him aside and staggered into the roadway, and then, from down the straight road, came the clang of bells, a glitter of brass and a touch of crimson. A motor fire-engine was coming at full speed.

For a moment the men grouped about the gate stared at this intervention. Then, without taking any further notice of their quarry, they turned and ran. A word to the fire chief explained the situation. Another engine was coming, at breakneck speed, and firemen were men for whom Frogs had no terror.

Whilst Hagn was being carried to one of the waiting wagons, Dick looked at his watch; it was six o'clock. He went in search of his car, fearing the worst. Hagn, however, had made no attempt to put the car out of gear; probably he had some plan for using it himself. Three minutes later, Dick, dishevelled, grimy, bearing the marks of Hagn's talons upon his face, swung out into the road and set the bonnet of the car for Gloucester. He could not have gone faster even had he known that his watch was stopped.

Through Swindon at breakneck speed, and he was on the Gloucester Road. He looked at his watch again. The hands still pointed to six, and he gave a gasp. He was going all out now, but the road was bad, full of windings, and once he was nearly thrown out of the car when he struck a ridge on the road.

A tyre burst, and he almost swerved into the hedge, but he got her nose straight again and continued on a flat tyre. It brought his speed down appreciably, and he grew hot and cold, as mile after mile of the road flashed past without a sign of the town.

And then, with Gloucester Cathedral showing its spires above the hill, a second tyre exploded. He could not stop: he must go on, if he had to run in to Gloucester on the rims. And now the pace was painfully slow in comparison with that frantic rush which had carried him through Berkshire and Wiltshire to the edge of Somerset.

He was entering the straggling suburbs of the town. The roads were terrible; he was held up by a street car, but, disregarding a policeman's warning, flew past almost under the wheels of a great traction engine. And now he saw the time—two minutes to eight, and the gaol was half a mile farther on. He set his teeth and prayed.

As he turned into the main street, with the gaol gates before him, the clocks of the cathedral struck eight, and to Dick Gordon they were the notes of doom.

They would delay the carrying out of the death penalty for nothing short of the reprieve he carried. Punctually to the second, Ray Bennett would die. The agony of that moment was a memory that turned him grey. He brought the bumping car to a halt before the prison gates and staggered to the bell. Twice he pulled, but the gates remained closed. Dick pulled off his sock and found the soddened reprieve, streaky with blood, for his feet were bleeding. Again he rang with the fury of despair. Then a little wicket opened and the dark face of a warder appeared.

"You're not allowed in," he said curtly. "You know what is happening here."

"Home Office," said Dick thickly, "Home Office messenger. I have a reprieve!"

The wicket closed, and, after an eternity, the lock turned and the heavy door opened.

"I'm Captain Gordon," gasped Dick, "from the Public Prosecutor's office, and I carry a reprieve for James Carter."

The warder shook his head.

"The execution took place five minutes ago, sir," he said.

"But the Cathedral clock!" gasped Dick.

"The Cathedral clock is four minutes slow," said the warder. "I am afraid Carter is dead."

CHAPTER XXXVIII

THE MYSTERY MAN

RAY BENNETT woke from a refreshing sleep and sat up in bed. One of the warders, who had watched him all night, got up and came over.

"Do you want your clothes. Carter?" he said. "The Governor thought you wouldn't care to wear those old things of yours."

"And he was right," said the grateful Ray. "This looks a good suit," he said as he pulled on the trousers.

The warder coughed.

"Yes, it's a good suit," he agreed.

He did not say more, but something in his demeanour betrayed the truth. These were the clothes in which some man had been hanged, and yet Ray's hands did not shake as he fixed the webbed braces which held them. Poor clothes, to do duty on two such dismal occasions! He hoped they would be spared the indignity of a third experience.

They brought him his breakfast at six o'clock. Yet once more his eyes strayed toward the writing-pad, and then, with breakfast over, came the chaplain, a quiet man in minister's garb, strength in every line of his mobile face. They talked awhile, and then the warder suggested that Ray should go to take exercise in the paved yard outside. He was glad of the privilege. He wanted once more to look upon the blue sky, to draw into his lungs the balm of God's air.

Yet he knew that it was not a disinterested kindness, and well guessed why this privilege had been afforded to him, as he walked slowly round the exercise yard, arm in arm with the clergyman. He knew now what lay behind the third door. They were going to try the trap in the death house, and they wished to spare his feelings.

In half an hour he was back in the cell.

"Do you want to make any confession. Carter? Is that your name?"

"No, it is not my name, sir," said Ray quietly, "but that doesn't matter."

"Did you kill this man?"

"I don't know," said Ray. "I wanted to kill him, and therefore it is likely that I did."

At ten minutes to eight came the Governor to shake hands, and with him the Sheriff. The clock in the prison hall moved slowly, inexorably forward. Through the open door of the cell Ray could see it, and, knowing this, the Governor closed the door, for it was one minute to eight, and it would soon open again. Ray saw the door move. For a second his self-possession deserted him, and he turned his back to the man who came with a quick step, and, gripping his hands, strapped them.

"God forgive me! God forgive me!" murmured somebody behind him, and at the sound of that voice Ray spun round and faced the executioner.

The hangman was John Bennett!

Father and son, executioner and convicted murderer soon to be launched to death, they faced one another, and then, in a voice that was almost inaudible, John Bennett breathed the word:

"Ray!"

Ray nodded. It was strange that, in that moment, his mind was going back over the mysterious errands of his father, his hatred of the job into which circumstances had forced him.

"Ray!" breathed the man again.

"Do you know this man?" It was the Governor, and his voice was shaking with emotion.

John Bennett turned.

"He is my son," he said, and with a quick pull loosed the strap.

"You must go on with this, Bennett." The Governor's voice was stern and terrible.

"Go on with it?" repeated John Bennett mechanically. "Go on with this? Kill my own son? Are you mad? Do you think I am mad?" He took the boy in his arms, his cheek against the hairy face. "My boy! Oh, my boy!" he said, and smoothed his hair as he had done in the days when Ray was a child. Then, recovering himself instantly, he thrust the boy through the open door into the death chamber, followed him and slammed the door, bolting it.

There was no other doorway except that, to which he had the key, and this he thrust into the lock that it might not be opened from the other side. Ray looked at the bare chamber, the dangling yellow rope, the marks of the trap, and fell back against the wall, his eyes shut, shivering. Then, standing in the middle of the trap, John Bennett hacked the rope until it was severed, hacked it in pieces as it lay on the floor. Then:

Crack, crash!

The two traps dropped, and into the yawning gap he flung the cut rope.

"Father!"

Ray was staring at him; oblivious to the thunderous blows which were being rained on the door, the old man came towards him, took the boy's face between his hands and kissed him.

"Will you forgive me, Ray?" he asked brokenly. "I had to do this. I was forced to do it. I starved before I did it. I came once . . . out of curiosity to help the executioner—a broken-down doctor, who had taken on the work. And he was ill . . . I hanged the murderer. I had just come from the medical school. It didn't seem so dreadful to me then. I tried to find some other way of making money, and lived in dread all my life that somebody would point his finger at me, and say: 'There goes Benn, the executioner.'"

"Benn, the executioner!" said Ray wonderingly. "Are you Benn?"

The old man nodded.

"Benn, come out! I give you my word of honour that I will postpone the execution until to-morrow. You can't stay there."

John Bennett looked round at the grating, then up to the cut rope. The execution could not proceed. Such was the routine of death that the rope must be expressly issued from the headquarter gaol. No other rope would serve. All the paraphernalia of execution, down to the piece of chalk that marks the "T" on the trap where a man must put his feet, must be punctiliously forwarded from prison headquarters, and as punctiliously returned.

John shot back the bolts, opened the door and stepped out.

The faces of the men in the condemned cell were ghastly. The Governor's was white and drawn, the prison doctor seemed to have shrunk, and the Sheriff sat on the bed, his face hidden in his hands.

"I will telegraph to London and tell them the circumstances," said the Governor. "I'm not condemning you for what you're doing, Benn. It would be monstrous to expect you to have done— this thing."

A warder came along the corridor and through the door of the cell. And behind him, entering the prison by virtue of his authority, a dishevelled, dust-stained, limping figure, his face scratched, streaks of dried blood on his face, his eyes red with weariness. For a second John Bennett did not recognize him, and then:

"A reprieve, by the King's own hand," said Dick Gordon unsteadily, and handed the stained envelope to the Governor.

CHAPTER XXXIX

THE AWAKENING

THROUGHOUT the night Ella Bennett lay, half waking, half sleeping. She remembered the doctor coming; she remembered Elk's urgent request that she should drink the draught he had prepared; and though she had suspected its nature and at first had fought against drinking that milky-white potion, she had at last succumbed, and had lain down on the sofa, determined that she would not sleep until she knew the worst or the best. She was exhausted with the mental fight she had put up to preserve her sanity, and then she had dozed.

She was dimly conscious, as she came back to understanding, that she was lying on a bed, and that somebody had taken off her shoes and loosened her hair. With a tremendous effort she opened her eyes and saw a woman, sitting by a window, reading. The room was intensely masculine; it smelt faintly of smoke.

"Dick's bed," she muttered, and the woman put down her book and got up.

Ella looked at her, puzzled. Why did she wear those white bands about her hair, and that butcher-blue wrapper and the white cuffs? She was a nurse, of course. Satisfied with having solved that problem, Ella closed her eyes and went back again into the land of dreams.

She woke again. The woman was still there, but this time the girl's mind was in order.

"What time is it?" she asked.

The nurse came over with a glass of water, and Ella drank greedily.

"It is seven o'clock," she said.

"Seven!" The girl shivered, and then, with a cry, tried to rise. "It is evening!" she gasped. "Oh, what happened?"

"Your father is downstairs, miss," said the nurse. "I'll call him."

"Father—here?" She frowned. "Is there any other news?"

"Mr. Gordon is downstairs too, miss, and Mr. Johnson."

The woman was faithfully carrying out the instructions which had been given to her.

"Nobody—else?" asked Ella in a whisper.

"No, miss, the other gentleman is coming to-morrow or the next day—your brother, I mean."

With a sob the girl buried her face in the pillow.

"You are not telling the truth!"

"Oh yes, I am," said the woman, and there was something in her laugh which made Ella look up.

The nurse went out of the room and was gone a little while. Presently the door opened, and John Bennett came in. Instantly she was in his arms, sobbing her joy.

"It is true, it is true, daddy?"

"Yes, my love, it is true," said Bennett. "Ray will be here to-morrow. There are some formalities to be gone through; they can't secure a release immediately, as they do in story-books. We are discussing his future. Oh, my girl, my poor girl!"

"When did you know, daddy?"

"I knew this morning," said her father quietly.

"Were you—were you dreadfully hurt?" she asked.

He nodded.

"Johnson wants to give Ray the management of Maitlands Consolidated," he said. "It would be a splendid thing for Ray. Ella, our boy has changed."

"Have you seen him?" she asked in surprise.

"Yes, I saw him this morning."

She thought it was natural that her father should have seen him, and did not question him as to how he managed to get behind the jealously guarded doors of the prison.

"I don't think Ray will accept Johnson's offer," he said. "If I know him as he is now, I am sure he will not accept. He will not take any ready-made position; he wants to work for himself. He is coming back to us, Ella."

She wanted to ask him something, but feared to hurt him.

"Daddy, when Ray comes back," she said after a long silence, "will it be possible for you to leave this—this work you hate so much?"

"I have left it, dear," he replied quietly. "Never again—never again—never again, thank God!"

She did not see his face, but she felt the tremor that passed through the frame of the man who held her.

Downstairs, the study was blue with smoke. Dick Gordon, conspicuously bandaged about the head, something of his good looks spoiled by three latitudinal scratches which ran down his face, sat in his dressing-gown and slippers, a big pipe clenched between his teeth, the picture of battered contentment.

"Very good of you, Johnson," he said. "I wonder whether Bennett will take your offer. Honestly, do you think he's competent to act as the manager of this enormous business?"

Johnson looked dubious.

"He was a clerk at Maitlands. You can have no knowledge of his administrative qualities. Aren't you being just a little too generous?"

"I don't know. Perhaps I am," said Johnson quietly. "I naturally want to help. There may be other positions less important, and perhaps, as you say, Ray might not care to take any quite as responsible."

"I'm sure he won't," said Dick decidedly.

"It seems to me," said Elk, "that the biggest job of all is to get young Bennett out of the clutches of the Frogs. Once a Frog, always a Frog, and this old man is not going to sit down and take his beating like a little gentleman. We had a proof of that yesterday morning. They shot at Johnson in this very street."

Dick took out his pipe, sent a cloud of blue smoke toward the haze that lay on the room.

"The Frog is finished," he said. "The only question now is, what is the best and most effective way to make an end? Balder is caught; Hagn is in gaol; Lew Brady, who was one of their most helpful agents, though he did not hold any executive position— Lew is dead; Lola——"

"Lola is through." It was the American who spoke. "She left this morning for the United States, and I took the liberty of facilitating her passage—there remains Frog himself, and the organization which Frog controls. Catch him, and you've finished with the gang."

John Bennett came back at that moment, and the conversation took another turn; soon after, Joshua Broad and Johnson went away together.

"You have not told Ella anything, Mr. Bennett?"

"About myself? — no. Is it necessary?"

"I hope you will not think so," said Dick quietly. "Let that remain your own secret, and Ray's secret. It has been known to me for a very long time. The day Elk told me he had seen you coming from King's Cross station, and that a burglary had been committed, I saw in the newspapers that a man had been executed in York Prison. And then I took the trouble to look up the files of the newspapers, and I found that your absences had certainly coincided with burglaries — and there are so many burglaries in England in the course of a year that it would have been remarkable if they had not coincided — there were also other coincidences. On the day the murder was committed at Ibbley Copse, you were in Gloucester, and on that day Waldsen, the Hereford murderer, was executed."

John Bennett hung his head.

"You knew, and yet . . ." he hesitated.

Dick nodded.

"I knew none of the circumstances which drove you to this dreadful business, Mr. Bennett," he said gently. "To me you are an officer of the law — no more and no less terrible than I, who have helped send many men to the scaffold. No more unclean than the judge who sentences them and signs the warrant for their death. We are instruments of Order."

Ella and her father stayed that night at Harley Terrace, and in the morning drove down to Paddington Station to meet the boy. Neither Dick nor Elk accompanied them.

"There are two things which strike me as remarkable," said Elk. "One is, that neither you nor I recognized Bennett."

"Why should we?" asked Dick. "Neither you nor I attend executions, and the identity of the hangman has always been more or less unknown except to a very few people. If he cares to advertise himself, he is known. Bennett shrank from publicity, avoided even the stations of the towns where the executions took place, and usually alighted at some wayside village and tramped into the town on foot. The chief warder at Gloucester told me that he never arrived at the gaol until midnight before an execution. Nobody saw him come or go."

"Old man Maitland must have recognized him."

"He did," nodded Dick. "At some period Maitland was in gaol, and it is possible for prisoners, especially privileged prisoners, to catch a glimpse of the hangman. By 'privileged prisoners' I mean men who, by reason of their good conduct, were allowed to move about the gaol freely. Maitland told Miss Bennett that he had been in 'quod,' and I am certain that that is the true explanation. All Bennett's official letters came to him at Dorking, where he rented a room for years. His mysterious journeys to town were not mysterious to the people of Dorking, who did not know him by sight or name."

To Elk's surprise, when he came back to Harley Terrace, Dick was not there. His servant said that his master had had a short sleep, had dressed and gone out, and had left no message as to where he was going. Dick did not, as a rule, go out on these solitary expeditions, and Elk's first thought was that he had gone to Horsham. He ate his dinner, and thought longingly of his comfortable bed. He did not wish to retire for the night until he had seen his chief.

He made himself comfortable in the study, and was fast asleep, when somebody shook him gently by the shoulder. He looked up and saw Dick.

"Hullo!" he said sleepily. "Are you staying up all night?"

"I've got the car at the door," said Dick. "Get your top-coat. We're going to Horsham."

Elk yawned at the clock.

"She'll be thinking of bed," he protested.

"I hope so," said Dick, "but I have my fears. Frog was seen on the Horsham Road at nine o'clock to-night."

"How do you know?" asked Elk, now wide awake.

"I've been shadowing him all the evening," said Dick, "but he slipped me."

"You've been watching Frog?" repeated Elk slowly. "Do you know him?"

"I've known him for the greater part of a month," said Dick Gordon. "Get your gun!"

CHAPTER XL

FROG

THERE is a happiness which has no parallel in life—the happiness which comes when a dear one is restored. Ray Bennett sat by his father's chair, and was content to absorb the love and tenderness which made the room radiant. It seemed like a dream to be back in this cosy sitting-room with its cretonnes, its faint odour of lavender, the wide chimney-place, the leaded windows, and Ella, most glorious vision of all. The rainstorm that lashed the window-panes gave the comfort and peace of his home a new and a more beautiful value. From time to time he fingered his shaven face absently. It was the only sure evidence to him that he was awake and that this experience belonged to the world of reality.

"Pull up your chair, boy," said John Bennett, as Ella carried in a steaming teapot and put it on the table.

Ray rose obediently and placed the big Windsor chair where it had always been when he lived at home, on his father's right hand.

John Bennett sat at the table, his head bent forward. It was the old grace that his father had said for years and years, and which secretly amused him in other days, but which now was invested with a beautiful significance that made him choke.

"For all the blessings we have received this day, may the Lord make us truly thankful!"

It was a wonderful meal, more wonderful than any he had eaten at Heron's or at those expensive restaurants which he had favoured. Home-cured tongue, home-made bread, and a great jar of home-made preserves, tea that was fragrant with the bouquet of the East. He laid down his knife and fork and leant back with a happy smile.

"Home," he said simply, and his father gripped his hand under cover of the table-cloth, gripped and held it so tightly that the boy winced.

"Ray, they want you to take over the management of Maitlands—Johnson does. What do you think of that, son?"

Ray shook his head.

"I'm no more fit to manage Maitlands than I am to be President of the Bank of England," he said with a little laugh. "No, dad, my views are less exalted than they were. I think I might earn a respectable living hoeing potatoes—and I should be happy to do so!"

The older man was looking thoughtfully at the table.

"I—I shall want an assistant if these pictures of mine are the success that Silenski says they will be. Perhaps you can hoe potatoes between whiles—when Ella is married."

The girl went red.

"Is Ella going to be married? Are you, Ella?" Ray jumped up and, going to the girl, kissed her. "Ella, it won't make a difference, will it—about me, I mean?"

"I don't think so, dear. I've promised."

"What is the matter?" asked John Bennett, as he saw the cloud that came to the girl's face.

"I was thinking of something unpleasant, daddy," she said, and for the first time told of the hideous visitation.

"The Frog wanted to marry you?" said Ray with a frown. "It is incredible! Did you see his face?"

She shook her head.

"He was masked," she said. "Don't let us talk about it."

She got up quickly and began to clear away the meal, and, for the first time for many years, Ray helped her.

"A terrible night," she said, coming back from the kitchen. "The wind burst open the window and blew out the lamp, and the rain is coming down in torrents!"

"All nights are good nights to me," said Ray, and in his chuckle she detected a little sob.

No word had been spoken since they met of his terrible ordeal; it was tacitly agreed that that nightmare should remain in the region of bad dreams, and only now and again did he betray the horror of those three weeks of waiting.

"Bolt the back door, darling," said John Bennett, looking up as she went out.

The two men sat smoking, each busy with his own thoughts. Then Ray spoke of Lola.

"I do not think she was bad, father," he said. "She could not have known what was going to happen. The thing was so diabolically planned that even to the very last, until I learnt from Gordon the true story, I was under the impression that I had killed Brady. This man must have the brain of a general."

Bennett nodded.

"I always used to think," Ray went on, "that Maitland had something to do with the Frogs. I suppose he had, really. I first guessed that much after he turned up at Heron's Club—what is the matter?"

"Ella!" called the old man.

There was no answer from the kitchen.

"I don't want her to stay out there, washing up. Ray, boy, call her in."

Ray got up and opened the door of the kitchen. It was in darkness.

"Bring the lamp, father," he called, and John Bennett came hurrying after him.

The door of the kitchen was closed but not bolted. Something white lay on the floor, and Ray stooped to pick it up. It was a torn portion of the apron which Ella had been wearing.

The two men looked at one another, and Ray, running up to his room, came down with a storm lantern, which he lit.

"She may be in the garden," he said in a strained voice, and, throwing open the door, went out into the storm.

The rain beat down unmercifully; the men were wet through before they had gone a dozen yards. Ray held the light down to the ground. There were tracks of many feet in the soft mud, and presently he found one of Ella's. The tracks disappeared on to the edge of the lawn, but they were making straight for the side gate which opened into a narrow lane. This passage-way connected the road with a meadow behind Maytree Cottage, and the roadway gate was usually kept chained and padlocked. Ray was the first to see the car tracks, and then he found that the gate was open and the broken chain lay in the muddy roadway. Running out into the road, he saw that the tracks turned to the right.

"We had better search the garden first to make absolutely sure, father," he said. "I will arouse some of the cottagers and get them to help."

By the time he came back to the house, John Bennett had made a thorough search of the garden and the house, but the girl had disappeared.

"Go down to the town and telephone to Gordon," he said, and his voice was strangely calm.

In a quarter of an hour Ray Bennett jumped off his old bicycle at the door of Maytree Cottage, to tell his grave news.

"The 'phone line has been cut," he said tersely. "I've ordered a car to be sent up from the garage. We will try to follow the tracks."

The machine had arrived when the blazing head-lamps of Dick's car came into view. Gordon knew the worst before he had sprung to the ground. There was a brief, unemotional consultation. Dick went rapidly through the kitchen and followed the tracks until they came back to the road, to find Elk going slowly along the opposite side, examining the ground with an electric lamp.

"There's a small wheel track over here," he said. "Too heavy for a bicycle, too light for a car; looks to me like a motor-cycle."

"It was a car," said Dick briefly, "and a very big one."

He sent Ray and his father to the house to change; insisted on this being done before they moved a step. They came out, wrapped in mackintoshes, and leapt into the car as it was moving.

For five miles the tracks were visible, and then they came to a village. A policeman had seen a car come through "a little time ago"—and a motor-cyclist.

"Where was the cyclist?" asked Elk.

"He was behind, about a hundred yards," said the policeman. "I tried to pull him up because his lamp was out, but he took no notice."

They went on for another mile, and then struck the hard surface of a newly tarred road, and here all trace of the tracks was lost. Going on for a mile farther, they reached a point where the road broke into three. Two of these were macadamized and showed no wheel tracks; nor did the third, although it had a soft surface, offer any encouragement to follow.

"It is one of these two," said Dick. "We had better try the right-hand road first."

The macadam lasted until they reached another village. The road was undergoing repair in the village itself, but the night watchman shook his head when Dick asked him.

"No, sir, no car has passed here for two hours."

"We must drive back," said Dick, despair in his heart, and the car spun round and flew at top speed to the juncture of the roads.

Down this they went, and they had not gone far before Dick half leapt at the sight of the red tail-lamp of the machine ahead. His hopes, however, were fated to be dashed. A car had broken down on the side of the road, but the disgruntled driver was able to give them valuable information. A car had passed him three-quarters of an hour before; he described it minutely, had even been able to distinguish its make. The cyclist was driving a Red Indian.

Again the cyclist!

"How far was he behind the car?"

"A good hundred yards, I should say," was the reply.

From now on they received frequent news of the car, but at the second village, the motor-cyclist had not been seen, nor at subsequent places where the machine had been identified, was there any reference to a motor-cyclist.

It was past midnight when they came up with the machine they were chasing. It stood outside a garage on the Shoreham Road, and Elk was the first to reach it. It was empty and unattended. Inside the garage, the owner of that establishment was busy making room for the last comer.

"Yes, sir, a quarter of an hour ago," he said, when Elk had produced his authority. "The chauffeur said he was going to find lodgings in the town."

With the aid of a powerful electric lamp they made an examination of the car's interior. There was no doubt whatever that Ella had been an inmate. A little ivory pin which John Bennett had given her on her birthday, was found, broken, in a corner of the floor.

"It is not worth while looking for the chauffeur," said Elk. "Our only chance is that he'll come back to the garage."

The local police were called into consultation.

"Shoreham is a very big place," said the police chief. "If you had luck, you might find your man immediately. If he's with a gang of crooks, it is more likely that you'll not find him at all, or that he'll never come back for the machine."

One matter puzzled Elk more than any other. It was the disappearance of the motor-cyclist. If the story was true, that he had been riding a hundred yards behind and that he had fallen out between two villages, they must have passed him. There were a few cottages on the road, into which he might have turned, but Elk dismissed this possibility.

"We had better go back," he said. "It is fairly certain that Miss Bennett has been taken out somewhere on the road. The motor-cyclist is now the best clue, because she evidently went with him. This cyclist was either the Frog, or one of his men."

"They disappeared somewhere between Shoreham and Morby," said Dick. "You know the country about here, Mr. Bennett. Is there any place where they'd be likely to go near Morby?"

"I know the country," agreed Bennett, "and I've been trying to think. There is nothing but a very few houses outside of Morby. Of course, there is Morby Fields, but I can't imagine Ella being taken there."

"What are Morby Fields?" asked Dick, as the car went slowly back the way it had come.

"Morby Fields is a disused quarry. The company went into liquidation some years ago," replied Bennett.

They passed through Morby at snail pace, stopping at the local policeman's house for any further news which might have been gleaned in their absence. There was, however, nothing fresh.

"You are perfectly certain that you did not see the motor-cyclist?"

"I am quite certain, sir," said the man. "The car was as close to me as I am to you. In fact, I had to step to the pavement to prevent myself being splashed with mud; and there was no motor-cyclist. In fact, the impression I had was that the car was empty."

"Why did you think that?" asked Elk quickly.

"It was riding light, for one thing, and the chauffeur was smoking for another. I always associate a smoking chauffeur with an empty car."

"Son," said the admiring Elk, "there are possibilities about you," and a recruit to Headquarters was noted.

"I'm inclined to agree with that village policeman," said Dick when they walked back to their machine. "The car was empty when it came through here, and that accounts for the absence of the motor-cyclist. It is between Morby and Wellan that we've got to look."

And now they moved at a walking pace. The brackets that held the head-lamps were wrenched round to throw a light upon the ditch and hedge on either side of the road. They had not gone five hundred yards when Elk roared:

"Stop!" and jumped into the roadway.

He was gone a few minutes, and then he called Dick, and the three men went back to where the detective was standing, looking at a big red motor-cycle that stood under the shelter of a crumbling stone wall. They had passed it without observation, for its owner had chosen the other side of the wall, and it was only the gleam of the light on a handlebar which showed just above its screen, that had led to its detection.

Dick ran to the car and backed it so that the wall and machine were visible. The cycle was almost new; it was splattered with mud, and its acetylene head-lamps were cold to the touch. Elk had an inspiration. At the back of the seat was a heavy tool-wallet, attached by a firm strap, and this he began to unfasten.

"If this is a new machine, the maker will have put the name and address of the owner in his wallet," he said.

Presently the tool-bag was detached, and Elk unstrapped the last fastening and turned back the flap.

"Great Moses!" said Elk.

Neatly painted on the undressed leather was:

"Joshua Broad, 6, Caverley House, Cavendish Square!"

CHAPTER XLI

IN QUARRY HOUSE

THE first impression that Ella Bennett had when she returned to the kitchen to fasten the door that shut off the sitting-room, was that the tea-cloth, which she had hung up to dry on the line near the lofty ceiling, had fallen. With startling suddenness she was enveloped in the folds of a heavy, musty cloth. And then an arm was flung round her, a hand covered her mouth and drew back her head. She tried to scream, but no sound came. She kicked out toward the door and an arm clutched at her dress and pulled back her foot. She heard the sound of something tearing, and then a strap was put round her ankles. She felt the rush of the cold air as the door was opened, and in another second she was in the garden.

"Walk," hissed a voice, and she discovered her feet were loosened.

She could see nothing, only she could feel the rain beating down upon the cloth that covered her head, and the strength of the wind against her face. It blew the cloth so tightly over her mouth and nose that she could hardly breathe. Where they were taking her she could only guess. It was not until she felt her feet squelch in liquid mud that she knew she was in the lane by the side of the house. She had hardly identified the place before she was lifted bodily into the waiting car; she heard somebody scrambling in by her side, and the car jerked forward. Then with dexterous hand, one of the men sitting at her side whisked the cloth from her head. Ahead, in one of the two bucket seats, the only one occupied, was a dark figure, the face of which she could not see.

"What are you doing? Who are you?" she asked, and no sooner did the voice of the man before her come to her ears than she knew she was in the power of the Frog.

"I'm going to give you your last chance," he said. "After to-night that chance is gone."

She composed the tremor in her voice with an effort, and then:

"What do you mean by my last chance?" she asked.

"You will undertake to marry me, and to leave the country with me in the morning. I've such faith in you that I will take your word," he said.

She shook her head, until she realized that, in the darkness, he could not see her.

"I will never do that," she answered quietly, and no other word was spoken through the journey. Once, at a whispered word from the man in the mask—she saw the reflection of his mica eye-pieces even though the blinds were drawn, as the car went through some village street—one of the men looked back through the glass in the hood.

"Nothing," he said.

No violence was offered to her; she was not bound, or restricted in any way, though she knew it was perfectly hopeless for her to dream of escape.

They were running along a dark country road when the car slowed and stopped. The passengers turned out quickly; she was the last. A man caught her arm as she descended and led her, through an opening of the hedge, into what seemed to her to be a ploughed field.

The other came after her, bringing her an oilskin coat and helping her into it.

The rain flogged across the waste, rattling against the oil-coat; she heard the man holding her arm mutter something under his breath. The Frog walked ahead, only looking back once. She slipped and stumbled, and would have often fallen but for the hand which held her up.

"Where are you taking me?" she asked at last.

There was no reply. She wondered if she could wrench herself free, and trust to the cover of darkness to hide her, but even as the thought occurred, she saw a gleam of water to the right—a round, ghostly patch.

"These are Morby Fields," she said suddenly, recognizing the place. "You're taking me to the quarry."

Again no answer. They tramped on doggedly, until she knew they were within measurable distance of the quarry itself. She wondered what would be her fate when she finally refused, as she would refuse. Did this terrible man intend to kill her?

"Wait," said the Frog suddenly, and disappeared into the gloom.

Then she saw a light, which came from a small wooden house; two patches of light, one long, one square—a window and a door. The window disappeared as he closed the shutter. Then his figure stood silhouetted in the doorway.

"Come," he said, and she went forward.

At the door of the hut she drew back, but the hand on her arm tightened. She was pushed into the interior, and the door was slammed and bolted.

She was alone with Frog!

Curiosity overcame her fear. She looked round the little room. It was about ten feet long by six feet broad. The furnishings were simple: a bed, a table, two chairs and a fireplace. The wooden floor was covered by an old and grimy rug. Against one of the walls were piled two shallow wooden boxes, and the wood was new. The mask followed the direction of her eyes and she heard his slow chuckle.

"Money," he said tersely, "your money and my money. There is a million there."

She looked, fascinated. Near the boxes were four long glass cylinders, containing an opaque substance or liquid—she could not tell from where she stood. The nature of this the Frog did not then trouble to explain.

"Sit down," he said.

His manner was brisk and businesslike. She expected him to take off his mask as he seated himself opposite her, but in this she was disappointed. He sat, and through the mica pieces she saw his hard eyes watching her.

"Well, Ella Bennett, what do you say? Will you marry me, or will you go into a welcome oblivion? You leave this hut either as my wife, or we leave together—dead."

He got up and went to where the glass cylinders lay and touched one.

"I will smash one of these with my foot and take off my mask, and you shall have at least the satisfaction that you know who I am before you die—but only just before you die!"

She looked at him steadily.

"I will never marry you," she said, "never! If for no other reason, for your villainous plot against my brother."

"Your brother is a fool," said the hollow voice. "He need never have gone through that agony, if you had only promised to marry me. I had a man ready to confess, I myself would have taken the risk of supporting his confession."

"Why do you want to marry me?" she asked.

It sounded banal, stupid. Yet so grotesque was the suggestion, that she could talk of the matter in cold blood and almost without emotion.

"Because I love you," was the reply. "Whether I love you as Dick Gordon loves you, I do not know. It may well be that you are something which I cannot possess, and therefore are all the more precious to me—I have never been thwarted in any desire."

"I would welcome death," she said quickly, and she heard the muffled chuckle.

"There are worse things than death to a sensitive woman," he said significantly, "and you shall not die until the end."

He did not attempt to speak again, but, pulling a pack of cards from his pocket, played solitaire. After an hour's play, he swept the cards into the fireplace and rose.

He looked at her and there was something in his eyes that froze her blood.

"Perhaps you will never see my face," he said, and reached out his hand to the oil lamp which stood on the table.

Lower and lower sank the flame, and then came a gentle tap at the door.

Tap . . . tap . . . tappity . . . tap!

The Frog stood still, his hand upon the lamp.

Tap . . . tap . . . tappity . . . tap!

It came again. He turned up the light a little and went to the door.

"Who's that?" he asked.

"Hagn," said a deep voice, and the Frog took a startled step backward. "Quick! Open!'"

The mask turned the heavy bar, and, taking a key from his pocket, he drew back the lock.

"Hagn, how did you get away?"

The door was pushed open with such violence that he was flung back against the wall, and Ella uttered a scream of joy.

Standing in the doorway was a bareheaded man, in a shining trench-coat.

It was Joshua Broad.

"Keep back!"

He did not look round, but she knew the words were addressed to her and stood stock-still. Both Broad's hands were in the deep pockets of his coat; his eyes did not leave the mask.

"Harry," he said softly, "you know what I want."

"Take yours!" screeched the Frog. His hand moved so quickly that the girl could not follow it.

Two shots rang out together and the Frog staggered back against the wall. His foot was within a few inches of the glass cylinders, and he raised it. Again Broad fired, and the Frog fell backward, his head in the fireplace. He came struggling to his feet, and then, with a little choking sob, fell backward, his arms outstretched.

There was a sound of voices outside, a scraping of feet on the muddy path, and John Bennett came into the hut. In a moment the girl was in his arms. Broad looked round. Elk and Dick Gordon were standing in the doorway, taking in the scene.

"Gentlemen," said Joshua Broad, "I call you to witness that I killed this man in self-defence."

"Who is it?" said Dick.

"It is the Frog," said Joshua Broad calmly. "His other name is Harry Lyme. He is an English convict."

"I knew it was Harry Lyme." It was Elk who spoke. "Is he dead?"

Broad stooped and thrust his hand under the man's waistcoat.

"Yes, he is dead," he announced simply. "I'm sorry that I have robbed you of your prey, Mr. Elk, but it was vitally necessary that he should be killed before I was, and one of us had to die this night!"

Elk knelt by the still figure and began to unfasten the hideous rubber mask.

"It was here that Genter was killed," said Dick Gordon in a low voice. "Do you see the gas?"

Elk looked at the glass cylinders and nodded. Then his eyes came back to the bareheaded American.

"Saul Morris, I believe?" he said, and "Joshua Broad" nodded.

Elk pursed his lips thoughtfully, and his eyes went back to the still figure at his feet.

"Now, Frog, let me see you," he said, and tore away the mask.

He looked down into the face of Philosopher Johnson!

CHAPTER XLII

JOSHUA BROAD EXPLAINS

THE sunlight was pouring through the windows of Maytree Cottage; the breakfast things still stood upon the table, when the American began his story.

"My name, as you rightly surmised, Mr. Elk, is Saul Morris. I am, by all moral standards, a criminal, though I have not been guilty of any criminal practice for the past ten years. I was born at Hertford in Connecticut.

"I am not going to offer you an apology, conventional or unconventional, for my ultimate choice; nor will I insult your intelligence by inviting sympathy for my first fall. I guess I was born with light fingers and a desire for money that I had not earned. I was not corrupted, I was not tempted, I had no evil companions; in fact, the beginnings of my career were singularly unlike any of the careers of criminals which I have ever read.

"I studied bank robberies as a doctor might take up the study of anatomy. I understand perfectly every system of banking—and there are only two, one of which succeeds, the other produces a plentiful crop of fraudulent directors—and I have added to this a knowledge of lockcraft. A burglar who starts business without understanding the difficulties and obstacles he has to overcome is —to use the parallel I have already employed—like the doctor who starts off to operate without knowing what arteries, tissues and nerves he will be severing. The difference between a surgeon and a butcher is that one doesn't know the name of the tissues he is cutting!

"When I decided upon my career, I served for five years in the factory of the greatest English safe-maker in Wolverhampton. I studied locks, safes, the tensile qualities of steel, until I was proficient, and my spare time I gave up to as important a study— the transportation of negotiable currency. That in itself is a study which might well occupy a man's full time.

"I returned to America at the age of twenty-five, and accumulated a kit of tools, which cost me several thousand dollars, and with these, and alone, I smashed the Ninth National Bank, getting away, on my first attempt, with three hundred thousand dollars. I will not give you a long list of my many crimes; some of them I have conveniently forgotten. Others are too unimportant, and contain too many disappointments to tell you in detail. It is sufficient to say that there is no proof, other than my word, that I was responsible for any of these depredations. My name has only been associated with one — the robbery of the strong-room on the *Mantania*.

"In 1898 I learnt that the *Mantania* was carrying to France fifty-five million francs in paper currency. The money was packed in two stout wooden cases, and before being packed, was submitted to hydraulic pressure in order to reduce the bulk. In one case were thirty-five packets, each containing a thousand mille notes, and in the second case twenty packets. I particularly want you to remember that there were two cases, because you will understand a little better what happened subsequently.

"It was intended that the ship should call at a French port; I think it was Havre, because the trans-Atlantic boats in those days did not call at Cherbourg. I had made all my plans for getting away with the stuff, and the robbery had actually been committed and the boxes were in my cabin trunk, substitute boxes of an exact shape having been left in the strong-room of the *Mantania*, when to my dismay we lost a propeller blade whilst off the coast of Ireland, and the captain of the *Mantania* decided to put in to Southampton without making the French port.

"A change of plans, to a man of my profession, is almost as embarrassing as a change of plan in the middle of a battle. I had on this occasion an assistant — a man who afterwards died in *delirium tremens*. It was absolutely impossible to work alone; the job was too big, and my assistant was a man I had every reason to trust."

"Harry Lyme?" suggested Elk.

"Joshua Broad" shook his head.

"No, you're wrong. I will not tell you his name — the man is dead, and he was a very faithful and loyal fellow, though inclined to booze, a weakness which I never shared. However, the reason we were so embarrassed was that, had we gone ashore at the French port, the robbery in the strong-room would not have been discovered, because it was unlikely that the purser would go to the strong-room until the ship was in Southampton Water. I had fixed everything, the passing of my bags through the Customs being the most important. This change meant that we must improvise a method to get ashore at Southampton before the hue and cry was raised, and, if possible, before the robbery was discovered, though it did not seem possible that we should succeed.

"Fortunately, there was a fog in the Solent, and we had to go dead slow; and, if you remember the circumstances, as the *Mantania* came up the Solent, she collided with a steam dredger that was going into Portsmouth. The dredger's foremast became entangled in the bowsprit of the *Mantania* and it was some time before they were extricated. It was then that I seized my opportunity. From an open port-way on my deck, where we were waiting with our baggage, ready to land, we were level with the side of the dredger as she swung round under the impact. I flung the two grips that held the boxes on to the dredger's deck, and I and my friend jumped together.

"As I say, a fog lay on the water, and we were not seen, and not discovered by the crew of the dredger until we had parted company with the *Mantania*, and although the story we told to the dredger's captain was the thinnest imaginable—namely, that we thought it was a tender that had come off to collect us—he very readily accepted it, and the twenty-dollar bill which I gave him.

"We made Portsmouth after a great deal of difficulty late in the evening. There was no Customs inspection and we got our bags safely on land. I intended staying the night at Portsmouth, but after we had taken our lodgings, my friend and I went round to a little bar to get a drink, and there we heard something which sent us back to our rooms at full pelt. What we heard was that the robbery had been discovered, and that the police were looking for two men who had made their escape on the dredger. As it was the dredger's captain who had recommended our lodgings, I had little expectation of getting into the room and out again without capture.

"However, we did, and as we passed out of the street at one end, the police came in at the other. I carried one bag, my friend the lighter, and we started on foot across country, and before the morning we had reached a place called Eastleigh. It was to Eastleigh, you will remember, Mr. Elk, that I came when I left the cattle-boat during the war and suddenly changed my character from a hard-up cattle-puncher to a wealthy gambler at Monte Carlo.

"That matter I will explain later. When we reached Eastleigh, I had a talk with my companion, and it was a pretty straight talk, because he'd got a load of liquor on board and was becoming more and more unreliable. It ended by his going into the town to buy some food and not returning. When I went in search of him, I found him lying in the street, incapably drunk. There was nothing to do but to leave him; and getting a little food, I took the two bags and struck the road. The bags, however, were much too heavy for me, and I had to consider my position.

"Standing by the road was an old cottage, and on a board was an announcement that it was to be sold. I took the address; it was the name of a Winchester lawyer; and then I got over the fence and made an inspection of the ground, to find that, at the lower end of the rank garden, was an old, disused well, boarded over by rotten planks. I could in safety drop the lighter of my burdens down the well and cover it up with the rubble, of which there was plenty around. I might have buried both; in many ways a lot of trouble would have been saved if I had. But I was loth to leave all that I had striven for with such care and pains, and I took the second box on with me, reached Winchester, bought a change of clothing, and spent a comfortable day there, interviewing the lawyer, who owned the cottage.

"I had some English money with me, and the purchase was effected. I gave strict instructions that the place was not to be let in any circumstances, and that it was to remain as it was until I came back from Australia—I posed as a wealthy Australian who was repurchasing the house in which he was born.

"From Winchester I reached London, never dreaming that I was in any danger. My companion had given me the name of an English crook, an acquaintance of his, who, he said, was the finest safe-man in Europe—a man who was called 'Lyme' and who, I discovered many years after, was the same Harry Lyme. He told me Lyme would help me in any emergency.

"And that emergency soon arose. The first man I saw when I put my foot on the platform at Waterloo was the purser of the *Mantania*, and with him was the ship's detective. I dodged back, and, fortunately for me, there was a suburban train leaving from the opposite platform, and I went on to Surbiton, reaching London by another route. Afterwards, I learnt that my companion had been arrested, and in his half-drunken state had told all he knew. The thing to do now was to cache the remainder of the money—thirty-five million francs. I immediately thought of Harry Lyme. I have never suffered from the illusion that there is honour amongst thieves. My own experience is that that is one of the most stupid of proverbs. But I thought that at least I might make it worth Lyme's while to help me out of a mess.

"I learnt from the newspapers that there was a special force of police looking for me, and that they were watching the houses of well-known criminals, to whom, they thought, I might gravitate. At first I thought this was a bluff, but I was to discover that this was not the case. I reached Lyme's house, in a disreputable thoroughfare in Camden Town. The fog was thick and yellow, and I had some difficulty in finding my way. It was a small house in a mean, squalid street, and at first I could get no reply to my knocking. Then the door was opened cautiously.

"'Is that Lyme?' I asked. 'He's not at home,' said a man, and he would have shut the door, but my instinct told me this was the fellow I was seeking, and I put my foot in the way of the closing door. 'Come in,' he said at last, and led the way into a small room, the only light of which was a lantern which stood on the table. The room was thick with fog, for the window was open, as I learnt afterwards, to allow Lyme to make his escape.

"'Are you the American?' he asked. 'You're mad to come here. The police have been watching this place ever since this afternoon.' I told him briefly what my difficulty was. 'I have here thirty-five million francs—that's a million, three hundred thousand pounds,' said I, 'and there's enough for both of us. Can you plant this whilst I make a get-away?' 'Yes, I will,' he said. 'What do I get out of it?' 'I'll give you half,' I promised, and he seemed to be satisfied with that.

"I was surprised that he spoke in the voice and tone of an educated man, and I learnt afterwards that he also had been intended for some profession, and, like myself, had chosen the easier way. Now, you'll not believe me when I tell you that I did not see his face, and that I carried no very vivid impression away with me. This is due to the fact that I concentrated my attention upon the frog which was tattooed on his wrist, and which afterwards, at great expense, he succeeded in having removed by a Spanish doctor at Valladolid, who specialized in that kind of work. That frog was tattooed a little askew, and I knew, and he knew too, that, whether I remembered his face or not, he had a mark which was certain to guide me back to him.

"The arrangement I made was that, when I got back to America, I should send a cable to him, at an address we agreed upon, and that he was then to send me, by registered post to the Grand Hotel, Montreal, a half of the money he had in the box. To cut a long story short, I made my escape, and eventually reached the Continent by way of Hook of Holland. Encumbered with any baggage, that would have been impossible. In due course I left for the United States from Bremen, Germany, and immediately on my arrival sent the cable to Lyme, and went up to Montreal to await the arrival of the money. It did not come. I cabled again; still it did not come.

"It was months after that I learnt what had happened. It came from a cutting of a newspaper, saying that Lyme had been drowned on his way to Guernsey. How he sent that, I don't know and never have inquired. Lyme was, in fact, very much alive. He had some six million dollars' worth of French notes, and his job was to negotiate them. His first step was to move to a Midland town, where for six months he posed as a man of business, in the meantime changing his whole appearance, shaving off his moustache and producing an artificial baldness by the application of some chemical.

"Whilst he was doing this, and determined that every penny he had taken from me he would hold, he decided to make assurance doubly sure, and started in a small way the Fellowship of the Frog. The object of this was to spread the mark of identification by which I should know him, as far and wide as possible. He may have had no other idea in his mind, and probably had not, but to broadcast this mark of the frog, a little askew, the exact replica of his. Obviously, no class would be willing to suffer the tortures of tattooing for nothing. So began this curious Benefit Fund of his. From this little beginning grew the great Frog organization. Almost one of the first men he came into contact with was an old criminal named Maitland, a man who could neither read nor write."

There was a gasp.

"Why, of course!" said Elk, and smacked his knee impatiently. "That is the explanation of the baby!"

"There never was a baby," smiled "Broad." "The baby was Maitland himself, learning to write. The clothes of the baby, which were planted for your special benefit in the Elder Street house, were put there by Johnson. The toys for the baby were inventions to keep you guessing. There never was a baby. Once he had Maitland properly coached, he came to London, and Maitlands Consolidated was formed. Maitland had nothing to do except to sit around and look picturesque. His alleged clerk, one of the cleverest actors I have ever met, was the real head of the business, and remained Maitland's clerk just as long as it suited him. When he thought suspicion was veering toward him, he had himself dismissed; just as, when he thought you had identified him with the Frog, he made one of his men shoot at him with a blank cartridge in Harley Terrace. He was the real Maitland.

"In the meantime the Frog organization was growing, and he sat down to consider how best he could use the society for his advantage. Money was going out, and he naturally hated to see it go. New recruits were appearing every day, and they all cost money. But what he did get from this rabble were one or two brilliant minds. Balder was one, Hagn was one, and there were others, who perhaps will now never be known.

"As the controlling force of Maitlands Consolidated, he had not the slightest difficulty in disposing of his francs. And then he set Maitlands speculating in other directions, and when his speculations were failing, he found ways of cutting his loss. He was once caught short in a wool transaction—the Frog maimed the only man who could have ruined him. Whenever he found it expedient for the benefit of himself to club a man, whether he was a military attaché or a very plain City merchant speculating in his own stocks, Johnson never hesitated. People who were bothering him were put beyond the opportunities of mischief. He made one great mistake. He allowed Maitland to live like a hog in a house he had bought. That was folly. When he found that the old man had been trailed, he shifted him to Berkeley Square, got him tailored, and eventually murdered him for daring to go to Horsham. I saw the murderer escape, for I was on the roof when the shots were fired. Incidentally, I had a narrow escape myself.

"But to return to my own narrative. Five years ago I was broke, and I decided to have another attempt to get my money; and there was also the fact that a very large sum of money waited reclaiming at Eastleigh, always providing that I had not been identified as the man who bought the house. It took me a long time before I made absolutely certain that I was unknown, and then, with the title deeds in my pocket, I sailed on a cattle-boat and landed, as you have said, Mr. Elk, with a few dollars in my pocket, at Southampton. I went straight to the house, which was now in a shocking state of repair, and there I made myself as comfortable as I possibly could whilst, night after night, I toiled in the well to recover the small box of money, amounting to a very considerable sum. When this was recovered, I left for Paris, and the rest, so far as my public history is concerned, you know.

"I then began my search for Frog, and I very soon saw that, if I depended upon the identification of the tattoo marks, my search was hopeless. Naturally, when I discovered, as I soon did, that Maitland was a Frog, I narrowed my search to that office. I discovered that Maitland was an illiterate by the simple expedient of stopping him in the street one day near his house, and showing him an envelope on which I had written 'You are a fake,' and asking him if he knew the address. He pointed to a house farther along the street, and hurried in."

"I knew that Maitland could neither read nor write when I learnt that the children's clothes had been left at Eldor Street," said Dick, "and from that moment I knew that Johnson was the Frog."

"Joshua Broad" nodded.

"That, I think, is about all I have to say. Johnson was a genius. The way he handled that huge organization, which he ran practically in his spare time when he was away from the office, was a revelation. He drew everybody into his net, and yet nobody knew him. Balder was a godsend; he was perhaps the highest paid agent of the lot. You will find that his income ran into six figures!"

* * * * * *

When "Joshua Broad" had gone back to London, Dick walked with Elk to the garden gate.

"I shan't be coming up for a little while," he said.

"I never expected you would," said Elk. "Say, Captain Gordon, what happened to those two wooden boxes that were in the quarry hut last night?"

"I didn't see the boxes."

"I saw them," said Elk, nodding. "They were there when we took Miss Bennett away, and when I came back with the police they were gone, and 'Joshua Broad' was there all the time," he added.

They looked at one another.

"I don't think I should inquire too closely into that matter," said Dick. "I owe 'Broad' something."

"I owe him a bit too," said Elk with a hint of enthusiasm. "Do you know, he taught me a rhyme last night? There are about a hundred and fifty verses, but I only know four. It starts:
William the Conqueror started his tricks,
Battle of Hastings, ten sixty-six.
That's a grand rhyme, Captain Gordon. If I'd only known that ten years ago I might have been a Chief Commissioner by now!"

He walked down the road towards the station, for he was returning by tram. The sun glittered upon the rain-fringed banners of the hollyhocks that filled the cottagers' gardens. Then from the hedge a tiny green figure hopped, and Elk stood still and watched it. The little reptile looked round and eyed the detective with black, staring eyes.

"Frog," Elk raised a reproachful finger, "have a heart and go home—this is not your Day!"

And, as if he understood what the man had said, the frog leaped back to the shelter of the long grass.

THE END

Printed in Great Britain
by Amazon